WHERE THE BODIES ARE BURIED

By Janet Dawson

Kindred Crimes
Till the Old Men Die
Take a Number
Don't Turn Your Back on the Ocean
Nobody's Child
A Credible Threat
Witness to Evil
Where the Bodies Are Buried

WHERE THE BODIES ARE BURIED

JANET DAWSON

Fawcett Columbine
The Ballantine Publishing Group • New York

A Fawcett Columbine Book
Published by The Ballantine Publishing Group

Copyright © 1998 by Janet Dawson

http://www.randomhouse.com

Library of Congress Cataloging-in-Publication Data
Dawson, Janet.
    Where the bodies are buried / Janet Dawson.—1st ed.
        p.   cm.
    "A Fawcett Columbine book."
    ISBN 0-449-00198-9 (alk. paper)
    I. Title.
  PS3554.A949W43 1998
  813'.54—dc21   98-15756
                                                                      CIP

Manufactured in the United States of America

First Edition: November 1998
10 9 8 7 6 5 4 3 2 1

This one's for Sam. It's also for everyone who's ever been laid off, downsized, restructured, reengineered, or shoehorned into cubicles.

ACKNOWLEDGMENTS

I would like to thank the following people for sharing their time and expertise: Susan M. Lowe, attorney extraordinaire and good friend, for her command of food law, her sharp eyes, and her counsel; and Chuck Stoffers, for his knowledge of bacteria and food safety. *Muchas gracias* to my Carlsbad, New Mexico, connections, Diane Metcalf Dominguez and Tony Dominguez.

WHERE THE BODIES ARE BURIED

THE PHONE RANG AT ONE IN THE MORNING. AT LEAST that's what the faintly glowing red digits on my clock radio said.

As the phone jangled, I struggled from the tangled embrace of sheets, dislodging my cat Abigail, who was curled up at the hollow of my back. As I groped for the switch on the bedside lamp, my other cat, Black Bart, jumped to the floor, as though to escape the hullabaloo. I picked up the telephone receiver, mercifully cutting the racket in midpeal.

Before I had time to croak out a greeting, I heard my ex-husband's voice. "You got a client named Rob Lawter?"

"And good morning to you, too." I squinted at the clock readout and said what generally comes to mind in a situation such as this. "Do you know what time it is?"

"Never mind what time it is," Sid growled. "Rob Lawter, male Caucasian, twenty-nine, brown hair, brown eyes. He lived in a fifth-floor apartment in a building on Alice Street."

I picked up on the past tense right away. You notice words like that, particularly when they're used by a homicide detective.

"Yeah, he's a client," I said slowly. "What's going on, Sid?"

"*Was* a client. He's dead. He took a header out his living room window a couple of hours ago. Your business card was in his wallet."

I'D ALREADY CASHED THE RETAINER CHECK ROB LAWTER had given me. But I hadn't yet started my investigation. I hadn't started because I wasn't quite sure just what he wanted me to do.

He'd asked me to hold off, during our initial meeting in my office. Wait, he'd said. I'll give you the details soon. Now I had a dead client and minimal information to go on.

On my way to work that warm Friday morning the second week in September, I drove by the building where Rob had lived—and died. It was on Alice Street near Seventeenth, an older L-shaped structure, with its long end pointing toward the street. Built of rosy brown brick, it had an air of faded elegance, unlike the more modern stucco buildings that lined both sides of the street.

I found a parking spot farther down Alice and walked back for a closer look at the building. As I went up the sidewalk, aware of the apartment windows and double-door entrance on my left, my attention was focused on the yellow crime scene tape still in place, directly in front of me. It stretched across the entrance to a square concrete patio, where a round table and several plastic chairs had been shoved out of the way, making it easy for me to see the irregular dark stains on the pale gray cement.

I stared at the bloodstains for a moment, then raised my eyes from the patio to the building, following a vertical line of windows upward to the top floor, the fifth. The windows, tall and wide, had wooden sills and no screens. That was common in older buildings around here. The one on the fifth floor, Rob's, was still open.

Did he jump? Fall? Or was he pushed?

As I stood next to the crime scene tape, trying to sort it all out, one of the double doors opened. A woman in a business suit came out, wearing running shoes. She carried a briefcase in one hand and a couple of envelopes in the other. She didn't say anything, but she eyed me suspiciously, as though I were some kind of sick voyeur who got off looking at places where people died. Then she hurried toward the street, moving at quite a clip. I followed her out to the street and saw her drop the envelopes into a blue mail collection box. She set off again toward Seventeenth Street. I headed for my car.

Fifteen minutes later, in my office on Franklin Street in downtown Oakland, I opened the window at the back of the long narrow room and started a pot of coffee. While the water dripped through the grounds I unlocked the filing cabinet and pulled the almost empty folder marked "Lawter, Rob" from the drawer that held active cases. As soon as the coffee was ready, I poured myself a cup and sat at my desk, pondering the man's death and the case I hadn't even started.

I didn't know much about either. The incident had occurred after this morning's edition of the Oakland *Tribune* had gone to press, so all I had was the sketchy information Sid had given me during his brief early morning phone call. Rob had fallen out the window of his apartment and landed on the patio below. Sid hadn't elaborated, but I figured Rob died instantly. I'd have to wait for the autopsy results to know for certain.

I looked up from the file, at the empty chair opposite my desk, the one clients sat in. Then I mentally placed Rob Lawter in the chair he'd occupied two days earlier and animated him beyond the terse "brown hair, brown eyes" description Sid had recited on the phone.

Rob's eyes had indeed been brown, but they sparkled with wit and intelligence. The hair was an ashy brown, like a fallen leaf, worn long and curling around the ears. He was lean, about six feet tall, comfortable in blue slacks and a pale yellow shirt. He loosened his tie as he sat back in the chair and crossed one leg over the other.

That was early Wednesday afternoon, during Rob's lunch hour. My good friend Cassie Taylor had brought him to my office a few minutes earlier, on her way to a hearing at the Alameda County Courthouse. Cassie and I used to be legal secretaries together before Cassie went to law school and I got into the investigating business.

Now she's a partner in the firm of Alwin, Taylor and Chao, just down the hall from my third-floor office.

"Be nice to Rob," Cassie said after she'd made the introductions. "He's a paralegal, like you used to be, before you became a private investigator. Rob and I have known each other for years. We met when I was a baby lawyer, over at that big firm in San Francisco."

I smiled at Cassie's words. When she and I had worked together at another law firm in Oakland, we called the first-year associates "baby lawyers," meaning we knew more about the legal biz than they did.

"Rob's thinking of hiring you," Cassie continued. "I'll let him tell you about it."

After Cassie had breezed out the door, I toyed with the lined pad and pencil in the center of my desk and examined Rob Lawter. "So why does a paralegal need a private investigator?"

"I'm not a hundred percent convinced that I do," Rob said, with a warm smile. "Need an investigator, I mean. But Cassie was concerned. She said I should talk with you."

He leaned forward and reached into the back pocket of his slacks, pulling out a brown letter-sized envelope that had been folded in half. "I found this on my desk this morning when I got to work." He handed it to me. On the front, someone had typed, "ROB LAWTER, PERSONAL. TO BE OPENED BY ADDRESSEE ONLY." I opened the flap and removed a single sheet of white paper.

The message was hand printed in black marker and big capital letters. "BACK OFF IF YOU KNOW WHAT'S GOOD FOR YOU."

"That's straightforward and to the point," I said. "What are you supposed to back away from?"

"Have you heard of Bates Inc.?" Rob asked.

"Sure. I have a few cans of Bates Best beans in my cupboard at home. It's a local company, family owned."

"Not family owned, not since the early days," Rob said. "It was publicly held, even before the company went through a leveraged buyout a year ago. Now it's owned by a couple of corporate money men. Anyway, it's a food processing company, canned goods, cereal, dairy products—stuff like that. Not only the Bates Best label, but they do a lot of private label work for grocery chains, things that show up at your neighborhood store as house brands. Bates also sells products to school districts and military commissaries. You're right about the company being local. Headquarters is right here in Oakland, down by the waterfront." He pointed in the general direction of the estuary that separates Oakland from Alameda. "They've got several plants here in the East Bay. I've worked in the legal department at Bates since I left that law firm Cassie told you about, four years ago."

"Why did you come to see Cassie?" I asked. "Was it this note?"

Rob smiled. "The note is only the latest part of it. Something's going on at the company that shouldn't be happening. And I'm about to blow the whistle. I figure I need to get some legal advice before I stick my neck out, in case my employer retaliates by firing me." He gestured at the note. "I didn't anticipate this kind of retaliation. It may be that someone's aware of my plan to expose the . . ." He paused, then went on. "The scam, for want of a better word."

"What sort of scam?" I asked. "I need more details. Just what is it you're going to expose?"

He shook his head. "I didn't tell Cassie, either. I'd rather play this hand close to my chest, at least for now. The fewer people who know, the better. I don't have all my facts lined up yet, but I will soon, in the next couple of days. Maybe my coming to see Cassie, and you, is premature. But I should have someone watching my back while I blow the whistle."

"Then what do you want me to do?" I asked, feeling intrigued and frustrated. "It's difficult for me to watch your back if you don't tell me why someone is threatening you."

"I know. But I think I would like to have you in place." He glanced at the clock on my wall. "I hate to cut this short, but my lunch hour's almost up. I've got to get back to work. I'll give you a retainer now, and we'll talk details in a day or so."

Turns out a day or so was all the time Rob Lawter had left.

CHAPTER 3

MEMORIES OF WEDNESDAY DISAPPEARED, AND I CAME back to Friday morning. My coffee was cold. I set the mug aside and opened Rob Lawter's file, staring down at the photocopy of his retainer check that I'd deposited Wednesday afternoon. The only other contents were a copy of the anonymous note and a single page from my yellow lined notepad. On this were written Rob's address and phone number, and the words "paralegal" and "Bates Inc." The answers, or some of them, must be at the company where Rob had worked.

I got up to get another cup of coffee. My office door opened and Cassie walked in, so I poured her some coffee, too. She wore her usual cheery smile and a copper-colored linen dress that set off her warm brown skin. Her feet were shod in running shoes and thick white socks. She used to wear high heels all the time, but an ankle injury a few months back had changed that.

I handed her the coffee mug and she took a sip. "Mmmm . . . thanks. You want to walk down to the Farmers' Market at noon? I need a few things. We can have lunch at Ratto's."

She didn't know about Rob. She couldn't have known, since news of his death wasn't in this morning's newspaper. And I knew she wasn't in the habit of listening to the radio in the morning.

"Sit down, Cassie." I sounded as somber as I felt.

She frowned. "Why?"

"I have something to tell you. Sit down, okay?" Playing along with me, she perched on the chair. "Rob Lawter's dead."

I watched Cassie's lips move from a smile to a stunned O. "What? When? How did it happen?"

"Early this morning." I told her what little I knew of Rob's death. "What can you tell me about him?"

"Not much." Cassie shook her head and sipped the coffee. "I wouldn't even call him a friend. An acquaintance, a person I knew from work. And when I didn't work there anymore . . . well, you know how people drift away. I hadn't seen him in years."

"You pick up a few things, even if you only know a person at work."

"True," Cassie said thoughtfully. "Let's see . . . We met about six years ago, at Berkshire and Gentry, that big law firm I worked at right after I got out of law school and passed the bar. I only stayed there a year. I knew right away a huge firm like that wasn't for me. I wanted my own shop, though it took me a few years to get it. I did run into Rob now and then, because he lived here in Oakland. Rode his bike everywhere, and commuted to the city on BART or on the ferry."

"Did he ever say anything about family?"

"Grew up in the Bay Area, I think, and his parents died some time ago. He had a sister. But I don't know her name."

"Would someone at that law firm know, or have access to the information? I know it's been four years since he worked there, but maybe his next of kin's name would still be on file."

Cassie set the mug on my desk and stood. "I still know plenty of people who work at Berkshire and Gentry. Let me call in a few markers."

"Lunch and the Farmers' Market," I said. "Noon?"

Cassie nodded and left me to my thoughts and the Lawter file. I reached for the phone and punched in the number, that of the Oakland Police Department's Homicide Section, asking for Sergeant Vernon. Sid picked up his extension, with a terse "Sergeant Vernon."

"It's Jeri. What have you got on Rob Lawter's death?"

"Nothing I can tell you," he growled, sounding much as he had earlier that morning.

"Hey, you're the one who called me at one A.M. I'm assuming you wanted me to know. You could have just let me find out when it hits the *Trib*. Have you notified his sister?" I sent Sid a vibe through the telephone wires, willing him to tell me the sister's name.

He didn't cooperate. "We're trying to locate the next of kin right now. Until that's done, I'm not going to tell you anything."

"Don't you want to know why he hired me?" I asked, glancing at the photocopy of the note Rob had received, the one warning him to back off.

"You mean you'll tell me?"

"It might have some bearing on his death. But I won't know until you tell me the autopsy results."

Share and share alike, I thought. Sid's silence told me he was considering it. Then I heard several loud voices shouting in the background, as though all hell was breaking loose in Homicide. "Jeri, it's a bad time for me to talk. I'll call you later."

He hung up and I was right back where I started, with three pieces of paper in Rob Lawter's file. I closed the folder, tucked it into the filing cabinet, and turned my attention to other business.

By the time Cassie and I returned from the Farmers' Market, she'd received a phone message from the friend of a friend at Berkshire and Gentry. Rob Lawter's sister was named Carol Hartzell. Four years ago she'd lived on Estabrook Street in San Leandro. She didn't live there now. When I checked the listings in the phone book and the crisscross directory, one that gives the address for a particular phone number, I found that Carol Hartzell had moved to an address on Clarke Street, a couple of blocks from the San Leandro BART station. There was also a Leon Gomes living at that address. Gomes is Portuguese, a common name in the East Bay, where lots of Portuguese immigrants settled in San Leandro and San Lorenzo.

I left my office at a quarter to five Friday afternoon. I carried my Farmers' Market purchases down to my car and drove over to Alice Street, parking in the shade several doors down from Rob Lawter's building. I was hoping to catch some of his neighbors as they returned from work. The first few people I approached ignored me, or said they knew nothing about Rob Lawter or last night's incident.

At five-thirty I saw the woman I'd seen this morning round the corner from Seventeenth Street, briefcase swinging at her side as she walked briskly in her running shoes. She was in her late twenties, I guessed. Her dark hair was chin length, and she'd tried to subdue her curls with a big plastic barrette, the same shade of blue as her lightweight suit. She saw me standing in front of the building and her pace quickened.

"May I talk with you?" I asked as she stepped past me and headed up the sidewalk.

She turned and glared at me, her mouth tightening. "I don't know who you are, but I saw you hanging around here this morning. Go away. What happened last night has nothing to do with you."

"Actually it does." I pulled my license from my shoulder bag and held out the leather case so she could see it. "My name is Jeri Howard. I'm a private investigator. Rob Lawter was my client."

She narrowed her eyes, stared at the license, then at me. "Why would he hire a private investigator?"

"I can't tell you that. It's confidential. However, it was a legal matter and his attorney can vouch for me. Her name's Cassie Taylor, law firm of Alwin, Taylor and Chao. They're in the book." I stuck my license back into my bag. "If you'd like to call Ms. Taylor . . ."

"I believe you," the woman said with a frown. "You know, I think I've even seen your name someplace, in the newspaper, maybe. But I've already talked with the police."

"Sergeant Vernon called me earlier this morning to let me know Rob was dead," I said. "But I haven't been able to get any details on what happened. I was hoping one of Rob's neighbors could fill me in. I haven't had much luck so far."

She snorted derisively. "Most of these people wouldn't see an earthquake if the ground opened under their feet."

"Did you see or hear something? Ms.? . . ."

She hesitated, gripping the handle of her briefcase. Then she relented, glancing first at the building, as though she wanted to make certain we weren't being observed. "My name's Sally Morgan. As to what I saw or heard, I'd rather not talk standing out here on the street. Let's go inside."

She had her key in her hand by the time we reached the building's double doors. I followed her into the lobby, where a faded umber area rug covered most of the brown tile. Directly in front of us was a staircase and, to the left of this, an elevator. She stepped up to a bank of mailboxes to the right of the stairway and unlocked the one labeled "Morgan, 5-B." It was right next to the one labeled "Lawter, 5-C."

"You lived next door to Rob?"

She confirmed this with a nod as she pulled a couple of flyers and several envelopes from her mailbox. Then she motioned me to the elevator. Neither of us spoke as the car moved upward. As we stepped out onto the fifth floor I glanced to my left and saw yellow crime scene tape stretched across the door leading to Rob's apartment.

I heard the cat even before Sally Morgan unlocked her own front door. It was singing a variation on that old familiar theme, the empty food bowl blues. As we walked into the apartment, a large gray and white cat wearing a red collar floated up to the back of a wing chair and let out a plaintive meow. Despite the creature's complaints, it didn't look as though it had missed any meals.

"I've heard that song from my two cats," I said. "The food bowl's empty. To hear that one tell it, anyway."

"Our afternoon ritual." Sally Morgan smiled as she set her briefcase on the floor, kicked off her shoes, and crossed the living room. The cat leapt from the chair to the beige carpet and beat her to the kitchen. "Hah. You've got food in your bowl, Queenie."

Queenie made an indignant cry that I translated as "but it's not fresh!" Her protestations had an effect. I soon heard the rattle of cat crunchies being poured into the bowl.

I took the opportunity for a look around. Sally Morgan's apartment had charm, with its high ceilings and big living room window that looked down on the sidewalk. Arrayed in front of the window, to take advantage of the afternoon sun, I saw brightly colored ceramic pots containing a ficus benjamina, Swedish ivy, and African violets. There were two doors on the wall to my left, one leading to a bathroom, and the other to a spacious bedroom where a platform bed was covered with a yellow and blue flowered quilt. In the living room, the wing chair and a cream-colored sofa faced an entertainment center complete with TV, VCR, and CD player. An alcove near the kitchen had been turned into an office, with a computer, monitor, and printer on a wheeled cart.

I glanced into the kitchen, which was small and utilitarian. Queenie had her face in her cat food bowl and was crunching happily on kibble. Sally Morgan had opened her refrigerator door and was leaning over, reaching for some cans of soda on one of the lower shelves. "You want something to drink?" she asked, glancing up at me.

"Thank you, yes."

She grabbed two cans and handed one to me. We returned to the living room, where she waved me toward the sofa. She sat in the wing chair and tucked her nylon-clad legs under her, popping the top on the soda.

"Does Rob's apartment have the same layout?" I asked.

"Same but reversed," she told me. "We shared a bedroom wall."

"How well did you know him?"

She took a sip from the can and shrugged. "Not all that well. I mean, we weren't really close friends. Just . . . neighborly. He was living here when I moved in four years ago. We saw each other in the hallways, the laundry room, that sort of thing. I know he worked at Bates, you know, the food company. And he had a sister living in San Leandro."

I nodded and thought about how well I knew—or didn't know—my own neighbors at my building over on Adams Street. "Girlfriends?" I asked. "Or boyfriends?"

"Girlfriends," Sally Morgan said. "I saw him with a few over the years. There was one I saw more frequently than any of the others. Really striking, a blonde."

"Do you recall a name?"

She thought for a moment before shaking her head. "Sorry, no. And I haven't seen her in awhile. I think they broke up."

"Did he ever talk about work?" I asked. "Such as projects he was working on, or what was going on at the office?"

She shrugged and sipped at her can of soda. "Not much. I remember once that we talked about the fact that we both worked here in Oakland. I walk to work. My office is at the Kaiser Center, near the lake. Bates headquarters is about twenty minutes from here, on the waterfront, so Rob rode his bike most of the time."

"Did you ever meet his sister?"

Now Sally Morgan shook her head. "Not formally. I saw her here once or twice, with her two teenagers, a boy and a girl. Those kids visited Rob more often. The sister's divorced, and he was the father figure. I believe she has a live-in boyfriend. I got the impression Rob wasn't all that enthusiastic about the guy."

I swallowed a mouthful of soda before moving on to the main event. "Let's talk about last night, and what you saw or heard."

CHAPTER 4

"**I** HEARD VOICES," SALLY MORGAN SAID. SHE'D HESITATED before speaking, and when she did, the words came slowly, as though she wasn't sure of the veracity of what she was telling me. "I'm sure I heard voices. It could have been the TV, but I don't think so."

"What makes you say that?"

"Rob didn't watch much TV," she said. "Unless it was *Star Trek*."

"Back up a little," I said. "When did you hear the voices?"

Queenie strolled out of the kitchen, licking her whiskers in that self-satisfied way cats have. She jumped into Sally's lap, circled twice, and settled down for a good wash.

"I went to bed around eleven," Sally said, stroking the cat's back. "I heard the voices about half past."

"Were you asleep? Did the voices wake you?" From what Sid had told me earlier on the phone, Rob went out his window around eleven-thirty.

She nodded. "Asleep or just drifting off. But it wasn't the voices that woke me. There was this loud bang. For a minute I thought Queenie had knocked something off the dresser. She does that all the time." Sally looked down affectionately at the big gray and white cat in her lap. "But Queenie was right there in bed with me."

"The dresser is on which wall?" I asked.

"The wall I share with Rob's apartment," she said, understanding where I was headed. "Yes, the bang came from that direction. Then I heard the voices."

"How many voices?"

"More than one. But I can't say if there were two or three or even more. All I know is one voice sounded like it belonged to a woman. At least it was higher in pitch."

"Could you make out what anyone was saying?"

Sally shook her head again. "Nothing. Just a lot of words all garbled together. Maybe 'no' and 'stop,' but I can't be sure. I've been thinking about it all day, but I come up with the same thing. Voices, talking, and I'm not sure what they were saying. That's why I'm not even certain I heard people talking. It could have been the TV."

"Do you believe Rob jumped out the window?"

"Not suicide." She shook her head vigorously. "I can't imagine him killing himself. Granted, I didn't know him that well, but he just didn't seem the type to take that way out. I suppose he could have fallen, but . . . if it weren't for my hearing those voices."

"How long did you hear the voices?"

"Not long. At least it didn't seem long. Maybe a couple of minutes. I was just about to drift back to sleep. Then I heard someone scream." She shuddered at the memory. "I got up and went to the window. Don't ask me how I knew, but there was something about that scream. . . ."

The sound of a human voice falling away, I thought, as Rob fell to his death on that concrete square below.

"I looked out," Sally said, words coming with difficulty now. She looked shaken as she remembered. "I saw someone lying on the patio, all crumpled, like a broken doll. I grabbed the phone off my nightstand and called the police."

We sat in silence for a moment. "May I see your bedroom?" I asked. She nodded.

I got up and walked into the bedroom, noting the queen-sized bed with its headboard against the wall the room shared with the bathroom, and the dresser on the far wall. The bedroom window, covered with half-closed blinds, was open a couple of inches, just enough to let in some air and keep Queenie from exploring the sill outside. I moved close to the glass and peered out. I couldn't actually see Rob's bedroom window, though I knew it was there, just a few feet to my left. I looked down at the patio below, imagining the trajectory of Rob's body, the impact, the sprawling limbs, the blood splashing onto the concrete. . . .

I raised my eyes, trying to erase that image, but it stayed with me. I focused on the other windows, those that were placed at intervals in the short rear L of the building that paralleled the street. I stepped back from my vantage point and returned to the living room.

"What about the other neighbors?" I asked Sally, who still stroked her cat, as though the motion and the softness of Queenie's fur would block out what she'd seen last night.

She frowned. "I'm not sure what you mean."

"Did you see any other neighbors looking out their windows? If someone at the back of the building had been looking, Rob's windows would have been visible."

"I don't recall. I'm sure the police talked to everyone on this floor."

Knowing Sid and his partner, Wayne Hobart, I was sure they'd talked to everyone in the building. Question was whether Sid would share any of that information with me. I tried a different tack. "Let's go back to what you heard. Anything after the scream?"

She thought about it, then shook her head. "I just remember calling the police and talking to the 911 operator. Only thing I heard after that was the siren."

"Who lives in the apartment on the other side of Rob's place?" I asked. "That unit, 5-D, would share a living room wall with his."

"Oh, that's Charlie Kellerman," she said. "He wouldn't be any help. He's a drunk."

"How so?" I asked.

"I don't mean he's a skid row bum," she said hurriedly. "I guess he's only one step up, though. He used to have a job, I don't know where. But he got fired because he wouldn't go into treatment. Now his brother pays his rent and gives him an allowance. He's not loud or obnoxious. I hardly ever see him. He holes up in his apartment with piles of magazines and newspapers. I've heard the place is a real fire hazard. He comes in with sacks full of frozen entrees and whiskey bottles. He drinks the cheap stuff. I know, because I've seen the bottles. Most of the time he just stays in his apartment and drinks himself into a stupor."

"How do you know so much about him?"

"Rob told me. Rob felt sorry for him."

Charlie Kellerman, the guy in 5-D, may have been pickled in booze, but I still wanted to talk with him. After I thanked Sally Morgan for her time and left the door open for further questions, I walked down the fifth-floor hall, past Rob's door, to Charlie's apartment, the last one on the right before the hallway made its right turn, forming the bottom of the L.

I knocked but I didn't get any response. Perhaps he wasn't home. Or if he was, and Sally was right about his drinking, Charlie might be well on his way to oblivion. It was now almost six-thirty. I continued knocking on fifth-floor doors, interrupting several people at their Friday evening dinners and several more who were preparing to go out. A couple of residents whose windows overlooked the patio hadn't seen Rob Lawter fall, but they'd heard him scream and had looked out to see the body below. Others whose apartments were on the opposite side of the building had heard some sort of commotion and opened their doors onto the central hallway, trying to determine the source of the disturbance. None of the people I spoke with had seen anything that would give me a clue as to what happened before Rob went out that window.

I gave Charlie Kellerman's door another try before I left the fifth floor. Still no answer. I leaned forward, listening, to see if I could discern any sounds inside.

"Don't waste your time," said a voice behind me. I jumped, startled, then turned. It was a young man I'd talked with fifteen minutes earlier. "Charlie spends all his time in a bottle. He couldn't have seen anything. He was probably passed out by then. Hell, he's probably passed out now."

I looked at my watch. Past seven on a Friday evening, and my stomach was growling so loudly as to be audible. I left the building and retrieved my car from its parking spot on Alice Street, and headed home.

My one-bedroom apartment is located in an Oakland neighborhood known as Adams Point. I've lived there since my divorce from Sid, with my cats Abigail and Black Bart. I'd had Abigail for eleven years, ever since she was a tiny tabby kitten just out of the litter. Since she was an enthusiastic eater, the days when she could fit into the palm of my hand were long gone. Black Bart came to live with us last Christmas, a no-longer-feral kitten who'd gotten friendlier and larger as the months rolled by.

Lately the apartment seemed cramped, though, awakening an urge for a home of my own that would provide more space, as well as a tax deduction. The Stefano case last spring and summer earned me enough money for a down payment on a house or condo, so I'd contacted a real estate agent. However, the house hunt had been sporadic. The nature of the private investigative business is such that I was not always available to look at the listings trotted out for my inspection by Eva, my real estate agent. In fact, in July and August I had had to leave town for a week or so at a time on two different cases.

Now that Labor Day had passed, I was still looking, but so far I'd seen a lot of places that left me cold. In the neighborhoods I liked, the houses were priced out of my range of affordability. The houses I could afford were located in neighborhoods where I didn't want to live. I was getting frustrated, wondering if buying a place of my own was in the cards this year.

Abigail and Black Bart met me at the door, tails up, with their own riff on the empty bowl blues. I did my duty as resident human and provided crunchies before opening the refrigerator and reaching for the remains of a casserole I'd fixed earlier in the week. I nuked it in the microwave and sat at my dining room table to eat, mopping up the last bit with a hunk of bread torn from a loaf of sourdough.

As I put away my Farmers' Market purchases, I listened to my messages. One was from Kaz Pelligrino, the doctor I was involved with, saying he wasn't sure he could keep our date Saturday night. He worked with AIDS and HIV-positive kids over at Oakland's Children's Hospital. His schedule kept him busy and was sometimes erratic. There was also a message from Eva, who sounded extremely enthusiastic about a house she wanted me to see. But then, she was always enthusiastic. I was the picky one. Hey, I might as well be. I was the one who'd have to pay the mortgage and live there.

I didn't return either message, at least not then. Instead I went back out to my car and headed for Interstate 580 and San Leandro. I drove southeast along the Oakland hills, which were covered with vegetation dun-colored after a summer without rain. I wondered if I'd delayed my trip to San Leandro long enough. I didn't want to show up on Carol Hartzell's doorstep and be the one to tell her that her brother was dead. But surely by now the Oakland Police Department had located and notified Rob's next of kin.

I took the Dutton Avenue exit off the freeway and headed west, toward the bay. Clarke Street was close to downtown San Leandro, just past the main drag, East Fourteenth Street, and below Davis. The address I was looking for was near the corner of Clarke and Parrott streets, a one-story stucco painted an unappetizing gray, with a small lawn covered in patchy brown grass. A four-door Buick sedan, mostly green with rust spots here and there on its dinged finish, was parked in the driveway.

The front door was open on this September evening. Loud music with lots of twanging guitars and thumping drums reverberated out the screen door and onto the street. I rang the bell. The music didn't abate, but a teenage boy appeared. He was about fourteen, wearing the currently popular uniform of baggy pants and T-shirt. His scraggly brown hair drooped onto his forehead and he had an earring in his left lobe.

"Yeah?" he said.

"Is this the Hartzell residence?"

"Yeah," he said again, only there wasn't a question mark behind it.

"I'm looking for Carol Hartzell. Do I have the right place?"

"Yeah."

This was getting tiresome. "May I speak with her?"

"She's not here."

"When will she be back?" I felt as though I were pulling teeth. Was there someone more articulate in residence?

In answer to my unspoken prayer, another face loomed over the boy's shoulder. The girl was a couple of years older, perhaps sixteen or seventeen, but her face was older still, as though she'd had too much to deal with in this life. Short brown hair framed a round face punctuated with a pair of wary brown eyes. She wore shorts, a T-shirt, and a frown.

"Doug, for God's sake, turn that down," she barked at the boy, raising her voice over the music. He glared at her, then shuffled away, evidently toward the stereo. The decibel level dropped several notches, making normal conversation possible. The girl looked me up and down. "Are you looking for my mother?"

"If your mother is Carol Hartzell."

"What is this about?" Neither her voice nor her face answered my query.

"It's about your uncle. Rob Lawter."

"My uncle's dead," the girl said abruptly. "He fell—or jumped— out a window last night. Or so they say."

"Who told you that?" I asked.

Neither Sid Vernon nor his partner, Wayne Hobart, would have described the incident as a suicide, unless they had evidence to back up that scenario. Besides, the girl sounded as though she didn't believe in either theory.

The boy, Doug, shuffled back to the door and added his two cents. "The cops said he fell, when they came to tell Mom. They wanted her to go identify the body. She didn't want to go by herself, so she called Leon at work. He said Rob must've jumped."

"Is Leon your stepfather?" I asked.

This question was met by a derisive snort from Doug. The girl tightened her mouth. "He's her boyfriend."

Why would Leon Gomes assume that Rob jumped? Did he know something the police didn't? "Were you here when the police came?"

Doug shook his head. "Nah, it was during the day. We were at school. Mom stayed home from work today 'cause she wasn't feeling well. When we got home this afternoon Mom and Leon were just leaving to go to Oakland. That's where it happened."

The girl shot him a sideways look, then turned her attention back to me. "You haven't said why you're here."

"I met your uncle a couple of days ago," I said. "He wanted me to do something for him. I was really surprised to find out he was dead. My name's Jeri, by the way. What's yours?"

"Robin," she said, sounding reluctant to tell me even that. "What did my uncle want you to do for him?"

"I'd rather discuss that with your mother."

The girl didn't say anything. Then she shrugged. Her mouth twisted as she looked over my shoulder, out toward the street. "Looks like you'll get your chance. There she is now."

CHAPTER 5

ROBIN HARTZELL DIDN'T LIKE HER MOTHER'S BOYFRIEND.
She wasn't crazy about her mother, either.

Her feelings were clear on her face for a moment as she watched the two adults climb out of the silver van that had just pulled up to the curb, its shiny finish gleaming despite the fading light of evening. I left the van in the periphery of my vision and watched as Robin masked those feelings with smooth blankness. She reached to her right and flicked on the exterior light, creating a circle of harsh yellow glare. Then she opened the screen door and stepped out onto the little square of concrete that served as a front porch.

I moved my eyes away from the teenage girl, waiting in watchful silence, and looked down the sidewalk. The woman walked slowly toward the house. The man was at her side, his arm draped protectively around her shoulder. As they came closer I took a good look at both of them.

Carol Hartzell was a few years older than my thirty-four years. Beyond her coloring, I didn't see much resemblance to her brother. She had his slender frame, but it was dwarfed by the slacks and blouse she wore, a nondescript blue and white seersucker that looked several sizes too big for her. Where Rob's brown hair had been curly, hers was lank, falling to her shoulders. His eyes had been lively and animated, Carol's were dull. She looked like a woman defeated by life, over and over, until she didn't have strength for one more return engagement.

She leaned into the man's embrace, as though he were her lifeline.

Leon Gomes was fortyish and thickset, his bulky torso clad in dark brown slacks and a short-sleeved shirt of lighter brown, with something embroidered just above the left pocket flap. He had a beeper attached to his belt. A well-trimmed mustache bisected his square face. His black hair was cropped short, but this didn't disguise the fact that it was thinning.

He seemed very protective of Carol, yet there was something possessive in his manner as he led her up onto the porch. She stumbled as the edge of one sandal caught on the concrete step. He caught her and half carried her into the house. Robin's eyes were still carefully blank, but Doug looked worried, his face suddenly young and unprotected as he stared at his mother.

I seized the moment and followed them inside the house, into a rectangular living room with green shag carpet that had seen better days. A hallway to my left led to the bedrooms and bathroom. A counter directly in front of me separated the living room from a big kitchen furnished with harvest-gold appliances and an oval dining table. I saw a sliding glass door leading to the backyard. On the wall to the right of this was another door. From its placement, I guessed it led to the garage at the side of the house.

The sofa on the wall immediately to my left was brown and gold plaid, as was the chair near the front window. A low rectangular coffee table made of some dark wood stood in front of the sofa, which faced a large-screen TV on the opposite wall. A shelf next to this held the CD player, which was still blaring out cacophonous music.

Leon Gomes settled Carol onto the sofa, then straightened. At this distance I could see the embroidery above his pocket, two words in dark blue. I'd seen the words before. Bates Best, the brand name for foods processed by Bates Inc. So Leon worked for the same company Rob had.

Call it a hunch, but suddenly I didn't want Leon to know why I was here.

He didn't seem to notice me, at least not at first. Instead a frown furrowed his face as his eyes swept over both teenagers. He barked orders at them.

"Robin, get your mother something to drink. Doug, turn off that crap. Can't you see your mother's upset?"

Robin's mouth tightened rebelliously and her brown eyes flashed, but she didn't say anything. She sidestepped Leon and moved toward the kitchen. Doug scurried over to the CD player and hit a button. The music stopped in midcrash and was replaced by the fainter background noise of traffic a few blocks away, and the sound of a BART train moving along the nearby track.

Leon noticed I was there. "Who the hell are you?"

"I heard about Rob," I said. "I came to see Carol."

"How'd you hear about it?" He eyed me suspiciously. "Hasn't been in the paper yet."

"Maybe she heard about it on the radio. After all, it happened last night." Robin had returned from the kitchen, carrying a plastic tumbler full of water. She thrust it at her mother. When Carol didn't reach for it, Robin set the glass down on a square cork coaster and moved away, standing near the counter with her arms folded across her chest.

Leon glared at her and picked up the glass. He sat down next to Carol and held the glass out to her. "Here, babe, drink some of this," he said, his tone coaxing her.

She'd been staring at the TV but not really seeing anything. Now she raised her eyes to Leon's face. The skin around them was red, as though she'd been crying. She took the glass obediently, sipped some water, then held the glass cradled in her lap. She sighed, a despairing gust of air, then spoke, her voice thin and tremulous. "Oh, God, I can't believe he's gone. Why would he do such a thing?"

She thought her brother had committed suicide.

This reaction didn't surprise me, when I recalled what the Hartzell kids had said earlier, reporting Leon's theory that Rob jumped out that window. Why did Carol Hartzell think her brother killed himself? Had the idea been planted in her head by her boyfriend? Why did he believe Rob's death was suicide?

"You think Rob jumped?" I asked, keeping my voice neutral.

"What the hell else could have happened?" Leon growled at me.

"The cops said he fell," Doug offered. "Maybe it was an accident."

"Maybe he was pushed." Robin's voice was dry and toneless.

"That's nonsense." Leon turned argumentative, as though he wasn't used to tolerating any other opinion but his own. "That's crazy."

"It's no more crazy than the idea of Uncle Rob killing himself," Robin declared stubbornly. "Why would he do something like that?"

"I don't know why. Who knows why people do things like that?" Leon glared at her as though that settled it, but I got the distinct feeling Leon had his own theory as to why Rob would commit suicide.

I stared back mildly, unimpressed with his macho act. Even though he lived here, I found myself wishing he'd leave so I could talk with Carol. Unfortunately he looked like he was settling in for the evening, determined to give his lady all the moral support she could stand, and more.

But luck was a lady tonight. Leon's beeper went off.

"Damn," he said, reaching for it. He squinted at the readout and got to his feet. "That's the plant. It's one damn thing after another." He strode toward the kitchen counter and grabbed a cordless phone, punching in some numbers. After a one-sided conversation in low growls flavored by the occasional expletive, he punched the button that terminated the connection and slammed the phone down on the counter. He crossed the room to the sofa, placing a hand on Carol's shoulder.

"I'm sorry, babe, I've gotta go. Crisis at the plant. I'll be back as soon as I can." He leaned over and kissed her on the forehead, then banged out the screen door. A moment later I heard the squeal of his engine as the van peeled away from the curb.

"Don't hurry back." Robin's words were tart, her eyes narrowed in contempt as she stared out at the departing van.

"Robin," her mother admonished, "is that any way to talk about Leon?"

"It's the only way." Robin now turned her gaze on her mother. Her brother backed away, then slumped into the chair near the window, preferring to remain on the sidelines of this particular battle.

"Leon works at Bates, like Rob did?" I asked.

Carol sighed deeply, then set the glass on the coaster. She looked at me, registering my presence for the first time. "Yes, he's manager of the dairy plant in Oakland. I'm sorry, I don't think we've met."

"My name is Jeri Howard," I said. "I was . . . acquainted with your brother. I'm sorry for your loss."

Tears welled up in Carol's eyes. "I don't know what I'll do without him. Our parents died about ten years ago, and all we had left was each other. I can't believe he's gone. When those detectives came to the door this afternoon, I just lost it."

I sat down next to her on the sofa. "Do you really think Rob killed himself?" She winced at the words. "You said just now that you couldn't think of any reason why he would do such a thing. Rob seemed so well-adjusted, normal, as though there wasn't anything bad going on in his life. I suppose if the police had found a note . . ."

Carol's mouth turned down in a frown. "They didn't. I mean, that detective who was here this afternoon didn't say anything about a note. I called Leon as soon as I found out, and he came right over from the plant. Leon said he must have jumped."

"Why would Leon think that?" I asked.

Carol avoided my question. "Rob could have fallen." She looked at me eagerly, as though grasping for some other solution besides suicide. "He was on the fifth floor, and the windows in that building are awfully big, and they don't have screens. It was warm last night. Maybe he had the window wide open and he stumbled and . . ." She nodded. "He could have fallen."

Or maybe he was pushed.

I glanced over at Robin, still standing by the counter, and read the same thought in her eyes. That kid knows something, I thought, moving her to the top of the list of people I wanted to interview. I had a feeling she knew—and saw—more than her mother did.

"Had something happened recently, that might have upset Rob?" I asked.

"He broke up with a girl, a couple of months ago. What was her name, Robin?"

"Diana Palmer," Robin said tersely.

"Yes, Diana. But he didn't seem upset. I mean, they weren't serious. Were they?"

"They were going to get married." Robin's voice took on a withering scorn.

"What?" Carol said. "That's the first I've heard of it. How did you know that?"

"He told me."

"Oh, dear—" Carol stopped. "Maybe that's why—" She stopped again, then looked at me and changed the subject. "Were you a friend of Rob's, from work?"

I shook my head. I didn't want to tell her I was a private investigator. Whatever I told her would go straight into Leon's ears. And for some reason I hadn't yet determined, I didn't trust the guy.

Robin threw me an out. "Are you hungry, Mom?"

"Why, yes, just a little bit." Carol looked past me at Doug, still slumped in the chair near the window. "Did you kids have dinner?"

Doug reverted to his earlier scintillating conversation. "Yeah."

"We ordered pizza," Robin said, becoming a bit more solicitous of her mother. "There's still some left. Do you want me to heat up a piece for you?"

"I'll do it." Carol got to her feet. So did I. She looked at me, still confused about why I was there.

I edged toward the door. "I'll check with you about funeral services."

"I'll walk you to your car," Robin told me, crossing the living room.

CHAPTER 6

ROBIN HARTZELL FOLLOWED ME OUT THE FRONT DOOR. By now it was after eight, the darkness pierced by lights from the houses across the street. She didn't say anything until we'd reached my Toyota, parked near the corner, at the edge of a pool of light spilling from a nearby streetlamp. I pulled my key from my purse, but I took my time, in no hurry to unlock the driver's side door. Robin circled my car, then slouched against the hood.

"Who are you, really?" she asked.

"A private investigator." I took one of my business cards from my purse and handed it to her.

She drifted into the light and glanced at the card. Then she stuck it into the pocket of her shorts and moved into the shadow. "So what are you investigating? Does this have something to do with my uncle?"

"He came to see me Wednesday. He wanted me to look into something. But we hadn't gotten to the details by the time he died."

"You think he was murdered?" she asked.

I thought about the threatening note, and those voices his neighbor heard last night, just before Rob Lawter went out the window.

"It's possible." It was more than possible.

Evidently Robin felt that way, too, since she'd challenged the assumptions that Rob had fallen or committed suicide. She straightened, moved close enough so that I could see her face, and folded her arms across her chest, with a determined set to her jaw. "Okay, I want you to find out who killed him. I have some money put away for college. I can pay you with that."

I waved away the suggestion. "Thanks, Robin. But save your money for school. Your uncle already paid me."

It would take more than words to convince her. Her mouth tightened. "But I have to do something. I can't just leave it there and have jerks like Leon running around saying my uncle killed himself. He's even got Mom believing it."

"Why does Leon think Rob killed himself?"

Robin snorted derisively. I was about to get an earful of how the girl felt about her mother's boyfriend. "Leon thinks Rob was gay. He's spouting some bullshit scenario that Rob killed himself because of that, like maybe he had AIDS, or maybe Diana found out Rob was gay and broke up with him."

"But Rob wasn't gay?"

"I doubt it. Not that I would have cared one way or another. He only dated women, as far as I know. Leon just thinks anyone who isn't a macho dickwad like him is homosexual. He's always calling my kid brother sissy or pansy. And of course, since I don't roll over every time he barks at me, there must be something wrong with me, too. I mean, gee, I could be a dyke."

The more I heard about Leon, the less I liked him, and I'd barely met the guy.

"I know Rob didn't commit suicide," Robin said. "He wouldn't do that to us. Somebody must have killed him. You gotta find out who. You gotta let me help. Tell me how."

"I need information. That's something you can give me. I didn't know Rob at all. He was in my office for only half an hour. Tell me about him."

"He was great. I loved him." The tough look on the girl's face gave way to vulnerability. "I was named for him. His name was Robin, too. Damn," she said, scrubbing away the tears that sprang into her eyes. "I hate to think of him being dead." She fought for control, her mouth working. "He was like a father . . . No, Rob was better than a father."

I looked back at the house and wondered about her real father and the substitute her mother had provided. "Your parents are . . ."

"Useless," Robin finished, her voice full of acid. I hated to see such disillusionment in one so young. "My old man left when I was in the fourth grade. He sends a birthday card once a year, if he remembers to, and some money now and then, if he hasn't got something better he wants to do with his cash. And Mom . . ." She shook her head. "She tries, but if it wasn't for me, nothing would get done. Sometimes I get so tired of being the grownup."

"How old are you, Robin?"

"Seventeen. I just started my senior year in high school. Doug's fourteen."

"How long have your mother and Leon been together?"

She grimaced. "She's been dating him for about a year. He moved in last spring."

"You don't like Leon." It was a statement rather than a question.

"Don't get me started," Robin said, but of course, that's exactly what I had in mind. "I hate him. He's such an arrogant slob, thinks he's a big shot, 'cause he's a plant manager. He met Mom when Rob took us all to a Bates company picnic a year ago. Mom started going out with him, and then he moves in. He figures just because he sleeps with my mother, he can order us around. Everything I do, I get the third degree. Like who am I hanging out with, where did I go. We were doing just fine, the three of us, without him."

It didn't sound as though the Hartzells were doing fine at all, but sometimes teenagers aren't known for their logic.

"How did Rob feel about Leon?"

"Rob didn't like him much, either," she said. "He and Leon were always arguing about something. He didn't butt in, though. Not about Mom and Leon. But he did have an argument with Leon recently."

I frowned. "An argument? When? What about?"

"I think it was a couple of weeks ago," Robin said. "I don't know what it was about. I'll try to find out, though. Could have been politics, or about the environment. Rob and Leon didn't agree on a lot of things, and Leon thinks no one's entitled to an opinion but him."

"You saw a lot of Rob?"

"Yeah. Once a week, sometimes twice. We talked on the phone all the time. He always had time for us. We did all kinds of things." Her mouth moved, curving into a ghost of a smile. "He was a real Trekker. Last year he took Doug and me to a *Star Trek* convention in

San Francisco. We didn't dress up like space aliens, but we had a fabulous time."

The picture of my client was starting to emerge as his niece talked. He sounded like a nice guy. I wished I'd had the chance to know him better.

"What else did he like to do?" I prompted. "Did he like a particular kind of music? Was he into art? Did he take you to movies? On picnics?"

"Oh, yeah. All of those," Robin said. "He liked rock 'n' roll, not that heavy metal stuff Doug listens to. He liked to go to the Museum of Modern Art in San Francisco. I don't much care for that kind of art, but to each his own. That's what Rob used to say. He'd take us to all those slam-bang action adventure things Doug likes, but his favorites were foreign movies. You know, the ones with subtitles, that only play in Berkeley. Sometimes he'd take me with him."

Robin smiled, once again transforming her face. "He'd take us to Point Reyes and Muir Woods, and down to Half Moon Bay and Pescadero. Sometimes we'd go up in the Napa Valley and picnic on the grounds of one of the wineries. Or we'd have dinner at an Italian restaurant. Rob was crazy about Italian food. Once he took us up to Calistoga for mud baths, and we wound up having dinner at this fabulous restaurant in St. Helena, called Tra Vigne. It was great. He said it was his favorite."

"It's one of mine, too. Tell me about Diana Palmer, the woman he was engaged to marry. I'd like to talk with her. Do you know where she lives?"

Robin thought for a moment. "Oakland or Berkeley. I'm not sure. But I know where she works. At the Oakland Museum. Something to do with history. Does that help?"

I nodded. "I'll find her. When did they break up? And was it his idea, or hers?"

"July. I'm not sure why."

"Was Rob involved with anyone else since then?"

"I don't think so," Robin said. "At least, I don't remember him talking about anyone special. Not like Diana."

"Did your uncle talk about his job at all, when he was with you?"

Robin shook her head. "Not much. Mom, she always bitches

about work. She's never had a job she liked. But Rob left it at the office, if you know what I mean."

"Where does your mother work?"

"She's a receptionist at some place over in San Francisco, at the Embarcadero Center. I think the name of the place is R&W. I'll find out more about it, if that'll help."

"It might, thanks." I never knew when some scrap of information might be important. "When was the last time you saw Rob?"

"Labor Day weekend. Mom and Leon—" She said the man's name as though it left a bad taste in her mouth. "—they went to Santa Cruz on Saturday and came back Monday. Rob came Sunday morning and took us to brunch."

Her face looked happy as she remembered. Then she scowled as a vehicle rounded the corner, its wheels squealing. It was Leon's van. She shrank back into the darkness as the van parked in front of the house, as though she didn't want him to see her. She needn't have worried. Leon got out of the van and walked quickly toward the house, without a glance in our direction.

Something else had been niggling at me. "You said your mother stayed home from work today."

Robin nodded. "Yeah. She was still in bed when Doug and I went to school."

"And when you came home from school, Leon was here, and your mother told you about Rob."

"Right. The police had just left."

"What time was that?"

"I got home from school about four-thirty," she said, "and I guess Doug got here around then, too. I think the police were here about four, from what Mom said."

"Was your mother's phone number and address in Rob's apartment?"

"Sure. He had one of those little Rolodexes, right on his desk."

It shouldn't have taken the Oakland Police Department all day to locate Rob's next of kin. I remembered my conversation with Sid Friday morning. He'd said they were trying to locate Rob's sister. If she wasn't here, where was she?

Easy, Jeri, I told myself. You're jumping to conclusions. The woman stayed home from work because she was ill. Maybe she'd gone to the doctor.

If I was curious about Carol Hartzell's whereabouts today, I also needed to ask the next logical question. "Were your mother and Leon home last night?"

Robin shook her head. "No. They went out. And they didn't get home till after midnight. I know because they woke me up when they came in. It sounded like they were arguing."

How long after midnight? And where had they been when Rob went out that window?

I didn't get the chance to voice my questions. A figure appeared at the door of the house, opened the screen door, and stepped onto the porch. I heard Carol Hartzell's thin voice calling out to Robin.

"I better go," she said. "But I've got your card. I can call you, right? If I remember anything important, or to see how you're do-ing? I'll call you, instead of you calling here. You never know who's gonna answer the phone."

"You can call me at the office. If I'm not there, leave a message. Just don't say anything to anyone else, at least not right now."

"Don't worry," Robin said, glancing toward the house. "I can keep a secret. I've had lots of practice."

WHEN I GOT BACK TO MY APARTMENT, MY ANSWERING machine held yet another phone call from my real estate agent, asking me to call her at home. I sat down on one of the kitchen chairs, propped up my feet, and grabbed the cordless phone, punching in her number.

"Hi, Eva," I said when she picked up the phone. "It's Jeri Howard, returning your call."

She got right down to business, in her usual staccato tones. "There's this place in lower Rockridge you've got to see. It isn't even listed yet, so we've got to move fast."

"Condo or house?"

"House. It's small, it's a fixer. But you'll like it. It has lots of possibilities."

I really did want a house, a freestanding structure with a bit of ground, so I could have a garden, as well. But in the Bay Area's over-heated real estate market, most houses were out of my price range. That meant I'd have to settle for a condo. I didn't like the idea of set-tling instead of buying what I wanted. Lately all Eva had been show-ing me were condos, and none of them had done anything for me but make me depressed. Since I'd started looking for a place to buy, several people had assured me that I'd know the right place as soon as I saw it. I hadn't seen it yet.

I mulled for a moment, translating real estate talk. "Small" could mean "tiny." I was already feeling cramped in this one-bedroom apartment, and I didn't want even less square footage. "Fixer-upper" often euphemizes "serious structural problems," both inside and out. I know my way around a hammer and a paintbrush, but when it comes to electrical work and plumbing problems, I'm at the mercy of the highly paid professional.

"Has lots of possibilities" usually means "requires lots of money," which I didn't have. Down payment and closing costs would probably clean out the housing budget.

"Okay," I said. "My schedule's clear. Where is it, and what time should I meet you?"

She gave me the address. "Eight o'clock tomorrow morning."

"On a Saturday?" I protested. There went my hopes of sleeping in.

"Believe me, Jeri, this place will go fast. And I really think it's what you've been looking for. We've got to strike while the iron's hot, and all that."

"Eight-thirty," I bargained, and she agreed.

I disconnected the call, then glanced at the clock on the wall above the sideboard. It was nine-thirty. I took the chance that Sid might be home. I called his house in North Oakland, and he answered on the third ring.

"It's late, and I've had a long day," he grumbled when I identified myself.

"Not as late—or early—as it was when you called me this morning. Just give me something on this Rob Lawter thing. I talked with his sister, Carol Hartzell, and got the impression she thinks he jumped."

"I didn't tell her anything of the sort."

"I didn't think you had. What time did you notify her, by the way?"

"Late afternoon. I don't know exactly what time. Couldn't locate her till then."

Interesting, I thought, Carol Hartzell had supposedly been at home today, having called her employer to say she was sick. The fact that she and Leon hadn't been home at the time of Rob's death only added to my list of questions.

"So there wasn't a suicide note?" I asked. Sid growled a terse confirmation. "Did he fall? Or was he pushed?" When Sid didn't reply, I pushed him. "Come on, Sid, the guy was my client. I already cashed his retainer check, so I owe him. Did Rob Lawter have some help going out that window?"

"He looked like somebody hit him a few times," Sid said. "I'll know more when I get the autopsy results. It's possible he interrupted a burglary."

"As a rule burglars don't kill people."

"I know a few smash-and-grab guys who'd kill you for a sawbuck," he said.

"On the street," I argued. "An apartment takes a little more planning. Particularly one on the fifth floor of a security building. Got any witnesses, other than the next-door neighbor who heard voices?"

"You've talked with the sister and the neighbor, too. You have been busy. No, we haven't interviewed anyone who saw anything before Lawter went out the window."

"What about the neighbor on the other side?" I asked, referring to Charlie, the one everyone said was a drunk.

"Haven't been able to locate him." He yawned in my ear. "I'm going to bed."

"Why do you think it's a burglary? Is something missing from the apartment?"

"The usual signs. Drawers rifled, jewelry box contents tossed onto the bed and picked over. The neighbor said he had a computer. That's gone. So's the CD player. Easy to grab, easy to get rid of."

"What about the computer monitor and the printer?"

"Still there."

"Doesn't that strike you as odd?"

"At the moment I'm so tired it doesn't strike me at all."

"Did his sister tell you she and her boyfriend were out late? Didn't get home till after midnight, I understand."

Sid didn't say anything right away, and when he did he sounded more awake than he had been earlier. "She didn't volunteer that information. Anything else you want to tell me?"

"When Rob Lawter was in my office on Wednesday, he gave me a copy of a threatening note he received at work."

"I want a copy of that note," he said.

"Done. In exchange for a copy of the autopsy report."

He laughed. "I saw that coming. Okay, it's a deal. Good night, Jeri."

Sid hung up. I sat back in my chair, the phone still in my hand,

and thought about one of my recent cases, in which the objective of a break-in had been the information contained on computer disks and on the device's hard drive. It seemed clear that the voices Sally Morgan had heard in the apartment next door were real, and whoever they belonged to had some part in Rob Lawter's death. If I wanted to steal a computer and a CD player, just to sell it for money, there were easier ways to do it. First-floor apartments, for example.

No, this crime was individual, aimed at Rob. I recalled the words in that note he'd received. *Back off if you know what's good for you.* I doubted that Rob had backed away from whatever illegality he was planning to expose. He seemed to think that blowing the whistle was very important, certainly worth risking whatever consequences came with the whistle.

Now he was dead. I didn't think he'd anticipated that.

Abigail raced through the dining room, faster than I'd seen the overweight and aging cat move in a long time. Black Bart was at her heels. Both cats thumped past me into the kitchen and went sliding across the linoleum on the woven throw rug that was usually positioned in front of the sink. I heard a thunk as they skidded into the cabinet doors on the far side of the kitchen.

Black Bart righted himself, wiggled his rear end, and brought forth a meowing sound that must have translated as "you're it." He turned and raced out of the kitchen with Abigail in hot pursuit. She was good in short spurts only, however. By the time they got to the living room, she stopped chasing him and plopped onto her side on the carpet, panting. Black Bart continued running until he'd streaked up the back of the sofa, where he sat looking smug and twitching his tail back and forth.

"You're a pair," I told them. "Of what, I'm not sure."

Rockridge is the section of Oakland near the Berkeley border, and it's a desirable neighborhood with housing prices to match. Upper Rockridge usually meant the hilly terrain above Broadway, while lower Rockridge encompassed that section along College Avenue between Broadway and Claremont Avenue. Midway down College, which was lined with shops and restaurants, both Highway 24 and the Rockridge BART crossed overhead.

I liked this part of town, but didn't think I could afford to buy a house here. As I drove to my rendezvous with Eva Saturday morning, I wondered if there was any chance at all. The address she had given me was on Chabot Road, three blocks north of the BART station. Eva had instructed me to turn right off College, heading east on Chabot, toward the hills.

I located the house and parked my Toyota at the curb. As I walked toward the place, I cataloged its exterior faults. It was a small wood frame structure with peeling brown paint and a one-car garage on the right side, tucked under a set of windows. The garage had those old-fashioned doors that opened to the sides, and the driveway was gravel, not concrete. A path to the right led around to a gate and the backyard. There was hardly any front yard, and what there was featured more weeds than grass. On either side of the house, the fence, the part that wasn't covered with ivy, looked as though it was falling down.

"This doesn't look promising," I told Eva, who had been waiting impatiently on a small front porch that had a definite list to starboard. "I mean, aside from the condition of the outside, it's close to both the fire zone and the Hayward fault."

"The fire didn't get down this far," she told me blithely, unlocking the big multiple listing holder that contained the key. We were both referring to the 1991 fire that destroyed lives and property in the East Bay Hills. "You're close to the Hayward fault almost anywhere on this side of the Bay. Besides, wood frame structures do very well in earthquakes. And this house is bolted to the foundation." I must not have looked convinced. She smiled and laid a hand on my arm. "I know it looks a little down at heels. But structurally, it's quite sound. Just reserve judgment till you see the inside."

Eva unlocked the door, and we stepped into a small entry hall. Directly in front of me I saw stairs leading to the house's lower level. A doorway to my left led to the living room, and beyond that, the kitchen. The living room had a sooty-looking fireplace opposite the doorway. That was a plus. A fireplace was on my list of things I'd like to have but was willing to live without. So were the scuffed hardwood floors.

The living room ran the entire depth of the house. I walked toward the French doors at the back of the living room and opened them, stepping out onto a deck. I felt a small flutter of pleasure as I looked down on a large sloping backyard, overgrown with weeds but sunlit. An uneven row of pine trees ranged along the disreputable fences on three sides that separated the yard from its neighbors. The uneven boards of the fences were covered with a profusion of abutilon, otherwise known as flowering maple, a climber with bell-shaped blossoms in red, yellow, pink, and orange.

Morning sun, I thought, looking at the yard. I could grow tomatoes over there. To my left, a flash of green caught my eye. I squinted and saw a hummingbird, its tiny wings beating rapidly as it hovered in front of a red abutilon flower, sipping the nectar with its beak. I heard the warbling of other birds, coming from the nearest pine tree.

I saw a twinkle in Eva's eyes as I turned and went back into the living room, but she didn't say anything. Instead she let me explore. There was a dining room in the front corner of the house. Between this and the kitchen, two doors led to a good-sized closet and a half bath with toilet and sink. The kitchen was square and seemed larger than the one in my apartment. It had windows on two sides, one looking down on the backyard, and there was a walk-in pantry, with plenty of built-in drawers and shelves. The refrigerator looked elderly, and the stove was a gas range that was even more ancient.

"Bedroom?" I asked Eva.

"Downstairs," she said, crooking a finger.

She led me down the stairs I'd seen when we first entered the house. At the bottom we turned to the left and I saw that the bedroom took up most of the lower level, with another set of French doors leading out to the backyard. There was a full bath down here, along with a walk-in closet, a narrow room with a washer and dryer hookup, and a good-sized alcove that could be turned into a home office. I took it all in, then moved toward the French doors. I opened them and stepped onto a small patio made of uneven brick, then walked farther out into that backyard that had so enticed me from the deck. I soaked in the birdsong and gazed at the abutilon, hoping for another glimpse of the hummingbird. Then I turned to Eva, who was grinning at me like the Cheshire Cat.

"This is it," I told her. "I don't care if it's in the fire zone. I don't care if it's on top of the earthquake fault. This is my house."

CHAPTER 8

"Y OU STILL HAVEN'T SEEN IT ALL," EVA ADVISED ME, chuckling over my declaration of love. "There's a studio apartment above the garage."

I remembered the windows I'd seen above the garage as I'd approached the house earlier. "Can't be a very big one."

"It's bigger than you'd think. One closet, a small kitchen, and bathroom. You could turn it into an office, if you don't want to rent it."

I had no desire for a tenant, and my office arrangements in the building on Franklin Street suited me. Still, the garage apartment would make a fine guest room, I decided, after taking a look at the space. It had a separate entrance near the gate that led to the backyard, a set of wooden steps leading up the side of the garage, and it was well lit, with plenty of windows. The kitchen was really more of a counter at one end of the space, with a two-burner stove and a half-size refrigerator in addition to a small sink and about three feet of counter space. The bathroom was barely big enough for the toilet, sink, and shower stall.

I was full of questions as Eva and I returned to the backyard I was already thinking of as mine. "How much is it? Who was the previous owner? What do we do next?"

"It's a probate sale, which means you take it as is, rough edges, peeling paint, and all. I know it's going to need some work, but I really think it's a great buy. The previous owner was an artist, a woman who'd lived here for several years. She died a few months ago, and the heirs want to get rid of the place. As for the asking price, it's higher than you had in mind. We might be able to get that down a bit when we make the offer."

She quoted a figure that was more than a bit higher than I had in mind. I had taken steps to get preapproved for a loan, despite some difficulties because I was self-employed. More important, I had my nest egg stashed in the bank, at the ready. Just in case that wasn't enough, my father had offered to help sweeten the down payment pot if I found the right place. And this was the right place.

"I want this house," I told her. "Let's do it."

We went back to her office to set the paperwork in motion. By the time I left, it was almost noon, and I drove back to my apartment with my thoughts whirling around, thinking of appraisers, and termite inspections, and all the things that had to happen before closing the deal.

Whoa, Jeri, I told myself. Take a deep breath. There are all sorts of things that could go wrong. Someone else might make a better offer. The loan could fall through. But my cautionary thoughts had little effect. In my head I was already selecting paint samples, polishing those hardwood floors, and deciding where to put my furniture. And landscaping my garden.

I was wired all weekend, sharing my news about the house with everyone from my father, who was ready to write me a check to assist with the down payment, to Cassie and Eric, who were themselves looking for a place to buy. Kaz was able to make our Saturday night date, so we had a celebratory dinner at Nan Yang, my favorite Burmese restaurant, which had closed its Oakland Chinatown location in favor of a College Avenue address, not far from the house I was already calling my own. After dinner, I showed him where it was.

The Lawter case hadn't fled my mind, however. When I left Eva's office that Saturday morning, I went to my own office to see if I could locate an address and phone number for Diana Palmer. A search of the phone directory and an Internet database provided me with an address on Blair Avenue in Piedmont, a small town within the confines of Oakland. My phone call to that address netted me an answering machine recording of a crisp female voice advising me that Diana wasn't available to take a call. After the usual beep I left my name and phone number, asking that she call me.

Then I called the Oakland Museum. I was bounced around to several offices before I confirmed that Diana Palmer worked there. But she wasn't working this weekend. In fact, she was out of town, attending a conference, and wasn't due back at the museum until Wednesday.

I went back to Rob's apartment building on Alice Street Saturday and again on Sunday, trying to locate Charlie Kellerman, Rob's other neighbor, the one Sally Morgan had described as a drunk. Kellerman may have been in the apartment, but he didn't answer my knock either day. I ran into Sally on Sunday afternoon as I was leaving the building. She said she hadn't seen Kellerman at all during the weekend.

"He's probably in there," she said, looking up at the fifth-floor windows. "Drinking, or passed out."

Even drunks have to replenish their supplies. That was how I finally caught up with Kellerman, Monday morning. I stopped at the apartment building after leaving Eva's real estate office. She had called first thing that morning, just as I arrived at my Franklin Street office, to let me know my offer on the Chabot Road house had been accepted. Now the wheels really were in motion. I was going to be a homeowner.

I was still basking in the glow and thinking about all I had to do before the deal closed as I walked up the sidewalk of the Alice Street apartment building and slipped in through the security door with an elderly woman towing a wheeled shopping cart. She stopped to wait for the elevator, which we'd just missed, according to the indicator. I hiked up the stairs instead. As I stepped from the stairwell I heard the elevator bell ping. The doors opened with a slow metallic squeak. A man got off and walked quickly toward the rear of the building, passing what had been Rob Lawter's front door. Then he stopped in front of the next door, 5-D.

"Mr. Kellerman?" I caught up with the man as he fumbled in his pocket for his key.

He glanced up, startled, and shrank into his rumpled brown pants and stained shirt. I'm five feet eight inches, and Kellerman was shorter, about five six. As I loomed closer, the man looked frightened. I stopped a few paces from him, smiled my best nonthreatening smile, and examined him.

Charlie Kellerman was a drunk, all right. His pale blue eyes were watery, and the whites were bloodshot. Broken capillaries reddened the rough skin on his nose and cheeks. He was unshaven, his chin covered with the graying stubble of several days' beard. He hadn't bathed, either. From where I stood I could smell stale perspiration that stank of booze and lack of personal hygiene. His thinning hair was brownish gray, shaggy as though it had been awhile since he'd remembered to get a haircut. He was in his late forties, I guessed, although the effects of his alcohol addiction may have made him look older than he was.

Kellerman stared at me, turning the key over and over in his right hand. He carried a large brown paper bag cradled in the elbow of his left arm, and when he turned toward me I heard the unmistakable sound of glass connecting with glass. The light in the hallway glinted dully on metal caps. Bottles, I thought. Lots of them. I peered into the sack and read a Chivas Regal label.

"Mr. Kellerman, my name is Jeri Howard. I'd like to talk with you about what happened Thursday night."

"Wha? . . ." Kellerman said, his voice rusty with disuse. He looked confused.

"Your neighbor," I explained. "Rob Lawter, in 5-C. He fell from the window in the apartment next door. Late Thursday night. Were you home then?"

He hugged the paper sack closer to his chest, frowning. He furrowed his brow with an effort, then I saw comprehension dawn slowly on his ravaged face. "Thursday night? What about Thursday night?" His watery blue eyes blinked once, then narrowed, at once curious and avid. "Did they send you?"

Now I was curious, too. "Did who send me? Who are 'they'?"

He stared at me, and then his expression turned sly. Kellerman shook his head and puffed a reeking breath in my face. "Don't know nothing. Go away."

He turned toward his front door and, after two tries, stuck his key into the lock. The door opened and I caught a glimpse of a dark, cluttered room, with magazines and newspapers piled everywhere. There was an empty bottle of Chivas Regal on the soiled carpet near the door. I glanced down at the paper sack he held again. More Chivas and, if I wasn't mistaken, a bottle of pricey brandy.

Kellerman had expensive taste, at least today. When I'd talked with Sally Morgan on Friday, she'd said the man had been fired from his job because of his drinking, and he lived on a bare-bones allowance provided by a brother. She'd also said he drank cheap whiskey. Which made sense, if you were an alcoholic who didn't want to run dry.

But today Kellerman was drinking the good stuff. Where did he get the money to buy high-priced liquor? Had he just gotten a check from his brother?

Before I could ask him, he scurried into his lair, the bottles rattling in his paper sack, and shut the door in my face. I heard a click as the deadbolt shot into place. I knocked, twice, but he didn't respond. Unless you counted the cackling laughter coming from behind the door.

I had obtained some information, though. Charlie Kellerman had been expecting someone. Perhaps two someones, whose voices Sally Morgan heard the night Rob died.

"IT ALL COMES BACK TO BATES," I TOLD CASSIE MONDAY afternoon. "When he was here last week, Rob said something was going on at the company that wasn't supposed to be happening."

"And he was going to blow the whistle," Cassie finished. She crossed her elegant legs and took a sip from the mug of coffee I'd handed her when she showed up in my office a few minutes earlier. "I just wish Rob hadn't been so stingy with details."

I looked down at the open manila folder on my desk, at the photocopy of the threatening note Rob had received. "Whatever is going on at Bates is hot enough to make someone send him this note."

"Or he was getting too close," Cassie said. "What did Sid say about the autopsy?"

"It's scheduled for this afternoon. We'll know more when I see the report. But when I talked with Sid Friday night, he told me it looked like Rob had been struck several times. He wasn't specific."

Cassie frowned. "Sounds like we can definitely rule out accident or suicide, no matter what the sister and her boyfriend think. Not that I ever believed he killed himself. The Rob Lawter I knew wouldn't do such a thing."

"Carol and Leon weren't home at the time of Rob's death," I said. "I'd certainly like to know where they were. And the sister called in sick Friday morning, but she wasn't home when the police came to notify her about her brother."

"That could be as simple as a doctor's appointment," Cassie pointed out.

"Agreed."

"I detect the boyfriend's hand in the suicide theory," she continued. "Question is, why is he so sure Rob committed suicide? Does he have a reason for wanting Rob's death to be suicide?"

"Robin said Leon and her uncle had an argument a couple of weeks ago, but she didn't know why. I've asked her to see if she can find out. That's one discussion I'd like to know more about. Leon's a plant manager for Bates. Did he know what Rob was planning to do? Did he send the note?"

I didn't have any answers, but I certainly wanted some. "It all comes back to Bates," I said again. "The answers are there."

"But if you go sniffing around Bates headquarters, how do you know what to do?"

"I have to get in there. So I can figure out which questions to ask."

"How are you going to do that?" Cassie asked.

I took a sip of coffee, then grinned. "Remember what I told you, a long time ago when we were both working as secretaries?"

She laughed, then raised her mug to salute me. "They always need someone who can type."

My typing might be a little rusty, but operating a keyboard is somewhat like riding a bicycle. You never forget how.

After Cassie returned to her own office, I left mine and walked toward the rear of the third floor, where Ruby Woods rented a suite. Woods Temporaries had been here a long time, providing general office and administrative workers, as well as legal secretaries and paralegals, to firms all over the East Bay. Ruby was a self-made woman who'd started the firm twenty years ago and managed to compete successfully with the larger, better-known temp agencies.

Once through the entry door, I nodded at the receptionist, who knew me, and walked back to Ruby's office. She was on the phone, but she waved me to a chair while she finished the call. When she hung up the phone, she grinned at me and leaned back in her chair.

"Well, I haven't seen you in awhile. Private investigator business keeping you busy?"

"As always." I paused. "Ruby, I need a favor. It's a big one."

"You know I owe you. You kept my baby brother out of jail. He

has cleaned up his act, by the way. Has a good job and he's getting married in the spring. Now, what can I do for you?"

I told her. The smile left her face as she contemplated what I was saying. She didn't say anything for a moment.

"Oh, Jeri, that is a big one," she said finally. "The only reason a small temp agency like mine provides office workers to a large company like Bates is because old Clyde Bates made a point of using Oakland firms whenever possible. That, and because they trust that I'll provide them with the best workers I can. I can't jeopardize my business relationship with the company. If anything should happen . . ."

"I understand," I said. She looked distressed. "I really do, Ruby. If they found out I was a ringer, it would reflect badly on you. I don't want that to happen. It's hard enough these days to make a living. It's just an idea I had."

It was a good idea, too. Too bad it wasn't going to pan out. Ruby's reluctance to put me into Bates Inc. as a temp left me, for the moment, back at square one. I could, of course, offer my warm body and my rusty typing skills to one of the many other temp agencies in the Bay Area. But there was no guarantee any of those would place me in the company where I needed to be. I needed to get in there quickly, and I needed to be able to take care of the other investigations I had on my caseload as well.

I shook my head and thought about alternatives. Cleaning crew? That would get me in, but working as an office cleaner would put me at Bates in the evening, and I had the feeling I needed to be there during regular working hours. A messenger, or a delivery person? That might get me into the building, but only for a short time, and I'd only be able to get as far as a front office receptionist or the guy in the mail room.

There had to be another way. I'd just have to give it more thought.

The phone rang, jarring me out of my funk. I sat up straighter, as I heard Robin Hartzell's voice. In the background I heard the same cacophonous music her brother had been playing when I'd visited the San Leandro house on Friday night. From this, I guessed Robin was home, and her mother and Leon weren't.

"I called to tell you about Rob's funeral," she said. "It's at the

Santos-Robinson Mortuary on Estudillo, near East Fourteenth. Eleven o'clock Saturday morning."

"I should be able to make it," I told her. "But I want to be as unobtrusive as possible. It would be better if you didn't act as though you know me."

"Not a problem. I'll have my hands full with Mom. She's still being awfully weepy, even though she did go back to work. About that place she works, I got some more information for you. It's Rittlestone and Weper, Embarcadero Four, San Francisco." She gave me the floor and suite numbers and spelled the names. "She makes good money, and I guess she likes the place okay. She's complained about it less than the last job she had. She said one of the bigwigs has a real bad temper, though. Shouting, slamming his fist against the wall, that kinda thing."

I knew the type, a pain to work with. "Thanks. Did anyone from Bates contact your mother about returning Rob's personal items from his office there?"

"Yeah," Robin said. "One of the secretaries he worked with called Mom last night. She said she's planning to bring some stuff by the house later in the week."

"I'd like to look at it, if we can figure out how to get me into the house without your mother or Leon finding out."

Robin thought for a moment. "I'm home from school by four-thirty, so I could let you in. Doug's here, too, though, unless he's off somewhere with one of his friends. Mom gets off work at five and takes BART, so she's usually home by six. The big problem is Leon. Since the plant's in East Oakland, close to where we live, he's in and out of the house a lot. I can't predict when."

"We'll figure out a time. What about Rob's apartment? Same reason. I want a look at his things."

"His rent was paid till the end of September," Robin said. "But I guess the sooner we get the stuff out of there, the better. I'll let you know for sure."

"Did you find out anything about that argument Rob and Leon had?"

"I can't remember. I must have just tuned it out. But my kid brother was there, too. He says he thinks it was about work."

Robin told me she'd check in later in the week. Once she'd hung up, I finished the report I'd been working on, printed it out, and addressed an envelope to my client, an attorney in Concord. I was just about to lock up my office when Sid opened the door.

My ex-husband is a tall man with broad shoulders, blond hair that's going gray at the temples, a neatly trimmed mustache, and a pair of unsettling yellow cat's eyes. He looked as handsome as ever in his gray suit, so I sat back in my chair to admire the view. Sid and I have been divorced for awhile. As far as I was concerned, I liked the guy but we weren't meant to live together. I loved him once. I must have, or I wouldn't have married him. Well, there was a lot of water under that particular bridge.

"To what do I owe the honor, Sergeant Vernon?"

He smiled and removed a letter-sized envelope from the inner pocket of his suit coat. "A copy of the autopsy report on Rob Lawter. I believe you have something for me, Ms. Howard."

"I do indeed." I stood up and crossed to my filing cabinet, unlocking it and removing the copy I'd made of the note Rob had received. I handed it to Sid, then sat down again and motioned him to the chair in front of my desk. I gave him an overview of my conversation with Rob last week.

"It's not much," Sid said. "You don't have any idea why he was going to blow the whistle?"

I shook my head. "Bates is a good-sized company. It could be anything. Since Rob worked in the legal department, I'm guessing whatever it is, it's illegal."

Sid nodded, staring at the note as though hoping for inspiration. I opened the envelope he'd given me and glanced through the autopsy report. "He was struck more than a few times," I said. "From the looks of this, he was badly beaten before he was shoved out that window." Sid gave me a look. "Oh, come on. You and I both know he was murdered."

"A good homicide cop keeps all his options open," he told me, getting to his feet.

"Did you ask his sister and her boyfriend where they were Thursday night?"

He nodded. "Playing cards with some friends, he says. She didn't have much to say."

"No, she doesn't. And you believe them?"

"Look, Jeri, I don't have any reason not to believe them. Leon Gomes says they played cards with a buddy of his from work and his wife. They were there until about a quarter to eleven and got home around a quarter after eleven."

"Robin says they got home after midnight."

"Maybe Robin's timepiece isn't as accurate as it could be," Sid said, his hand on the doorknob. "Gomes says the host and hostess will back them up."

"The buddy lives where?"

"Oakland, off Seminary Avenue."

"Rob went out that window sometime around eleven-thirty. Between eleven and eleven-thirty, he had visitors, at least two of them, possibly a man and a woman. It takes about fifteen to twenty minutes to drive from Seminary Avenue to Alice Street, if you take the MacArthur Freeway."

"That's a real stretch, Jeri. The neighbor's not clear on what she heard. Besides," Sid added, "give me a reason why Carol Hartzell and Leon Gomes would want to kill her brother."

I couldn't. At least, not at the moment.

I spent Tuesday morning out in Contra Costa County, first delivering the report to the Concord attorney. Then I headed for the courthouse in Martinez to look up some information on the plaintiff in a personal injury lawsuit. From there I headed east on Highway 4 to take photos of the accident scene. I dropped the roll of film off at one of those quick-developing places, had lunch at a nearby deli, then picked up the photos.

I headed back to my office, somewhat frazzled because of all that traffic trying to get through the maze where Highway 24 and Interstate 680 connect in Walnut Creek. The California Department of Transportation, better known to the state's drivers as Caltrans, had been working on the interchange for what seemed like decades, and I didn't anticipate completion until I was old and gray. I swear, each time I drove through there, they'd moved the road.

There were several messages on my answering machine, including one from Eva, my real estate agent, with a list of things we needed to do in order to acquire my dream house. I returned calls, then I booted up the computer and wrote a report on the background check on the plaintiff in the personal injury case.

I had just sent the document to the printer when Ruby Woods came barreling through my office door. Her eyes blazed with fury.

"I'll do it," she declared.

CHAPTER 10

"WHAT BROUGHT THIS ON?" I ASKED. "YESTERDAY IT was no go."

Ruby settled into the chair in front of my desk, her face a study in indignation. "I'll tell you what brought this on. My contact at Bates is somebody I went to high school with at McClymonds. Her name's Laverne Carson. Worked for that company damn near thirty years. Well, she called me this morning to tell me that a week from Friday is her last day. She's being forced to retire. And she's being replaced by some sweet young thing who probably doesn't have half the knowledge and skills Laverne does."

"It happens a lot these days. Am I sensing a possible age discrimination lawsuit?"

"I wouldn't doubt it. They picked the wrong person when they decided to mess with Laverne. There's already a class action wrongful termination case against Bates as a result of that first round of layoffs they had after their buyout last year."

"Something tells me it's not just your friend Laverne's fate that brought you here," I said. "You're giving off sparks, Ruby."

"You better believe I am. Laverne told me after she's gone not to expect any more work requests from Bates. They're not going to use the services of Woods Temporaries anymore. As of the end of the month, in favor of some big outfit over in the city. According to Laverne, that temp agency is owned by a subsidiary of the outfit that took over Bates in that buyout. And that's where her replacement is coming from, too."

That sounded like dirty pool to me. So did the forced retirement of Laverne Carson. I was just glad that both had made Ruby Woods so angry she was going to do what I'd asked.

"So you're going to send me in there as a temp, the sooner the better."

"It'll have to be before the end of the month," Ruby told me with a frown. "I haven't had any requests from Bates this week. But when I do, where is it you need to be?"

"The legal department. Or something on the floor where the legal department is located. And I don't have any idea where that is."

Ruby frowned. "I don't think I've ever had a request for a temp from the legal department. Not that I can remember, anyway."

"I happen to know they are short one paralegal," I said grimly.

"I'll figure something out. I don't want to tell Laverne what I'm doing. She's got enough on her plate, training her replacement." Ruby snorted.

"I agree with you there. The fewer people who know about this, the better."

"Well, we've got work to do in the meantime. We have to update your résumé and pretend you haven't been a private investigator for the past few years. Maybe you've been on sabbatical or going to school or something." She looked at me, her head tilted to one side. "And we've got to do something about your clothes."

I looked down at the brown slacks and green checked shirt I wore. Okay, there was a mustard stain on my collar, from the pastrami sandwich I'd eaten for lunch. "What's wrong with my clothes?" I asked. But I knew what Ruby was driving at.

When you're self-employed, you can dress the way you want. I like comfortable slacks and shoes. And in my line of work, I don't want to stick out too much. So I hadn't worn pantyhose in months. Suits? Forget it. My wardrobe was definitely on the casual side.

"I suppose Cassie might let me borrow some suits," I said, wrinkling my nose at the prospect. "I can buy some pantyhose. But I draw the line at high heels."

Ruby looked at me critically. "You're a few pounds heavier than Cassie, and lighter than me. I probably have some things in my closet you can wear. Now, Laverne dresses to the nines. But hell, she gets gussied up to do the laundry. Bates may be more casual than those high-powered law firms over in San Francisco. I just don't think your usual slacks and shirts will be appropriate."

I followed Ruby back to her office, where we embellished my résumé. That evening, I reported to her house in North Oakland, and we embellished my wardrobe. It wasn't easy. Ruby, perhaps because of her name, favored red, not a color I wear much because of my auburn hair. She was also shorter than my five feet eight inches, and wider through the hips. When I left her place, it was late, but I had three outfits in neutral shades that would look good in any office.

Okay, I thought, as I hung the clothes in my closet. I'm ready. Just as long as I don't have to wear high heels.

There was a message from Diana Palmer on my answering machine when I arrived at my office Wednesday morning. After I returned the call, I left my office and walked over to the Oakland Museum, on Oak Street between Tenth and Twelfth, near the Alameda County Courthouse. The multileveled museum is surrounded by terraces, courts, and gardens, a pleasant island in the urban landscape.

The museum is the only one in California dedicated to the state's art, history, and ecology. As I reached the upper level, where the Great Hall featured changing exhibits, I passed a group of elementary school children whose teachers were trying to herd them down to the first level, for a walk through the exhibit that covered the state's diverse ecology. I stopped at the information booth, where Diana Palmer and I had agreed to meet. While I waited, I glanced at a brochure that gave me information on the exhibits at the Gallery of California Art and the Cowell Hall of California History.

On the phone, Diana Palmer told me she worked in an office somewhere in the bowels of the building, but that morning she was putting together a display in Cowell Hall. The history exhibits were on the second level. Five minutes after I arrived, I saw a slender woman in crisp blue linen slacks and a matching jacket moving briskly up the stairs toward me. Under the jacket she wore a white silk blouse with a scooped neckline that showed off the gold chain around her neck. She had straight blond hair, cut asymmetrically, showing more gold, this time in her earlobes. Her face was oval, with a pale complexion that wouldn't take much sun. Her eyes were blue, quick, and intelligent. I guessed her age as late twenties, same as Rob's. An employee identification badge was clipped to the lapel of her jacket.

"Diana Palmer?" I asked, glancing at the badge.

"Yes. You're Jeri Howard?" Her voice was as brisk as her stride.

"Yes. Thank you for meeting with me."

"Well, I can't talk long. I have a meeting to go to. You said you wanted to talk about Rob Lawter." She seemed subdued under her businesslike manner. "I was sorry to hear he was dead."

For someone who had been engaged to the deceased, she showed very little grief. But then, she and Rob had ended their relationship in July, according to Robin Hartzell. Maybe Diana Palmer was one of those people who didn't show emotions readily. She looked me over, waiting for me to say something else. I let the silence grow, hoping she'd fill it.

"You said you're a private investigator," she asked finally.

"Yes. He hired me because of something that was happening at work. But he died before he could give me any details. I thought you might know what was going on."

Her mouth curved down. "Sorry, I don't think I can help you there. I hadn't seen Rob in . . ." She thought for a moment. "Nearly two months."

"His sister thinks he killed himself. So does his sister's boyfriend."

"That's ridiculous. Rob would never have committed suicide." Now Diana Palmer grimaced. Contempt colored her voice as she spoke of Carol Hartzell. "That's typical of Carol, and that oaf she's living with. I'll never understand that relationship. They met at a Bates picnic last year. He's an idiot, and she acts as though she can't function without him. I couldn't carry on a simple conversation with the woman."

"Maybe she hasn't got your independent spirit." Diana Palmer wasn't the easiest person to converse with, either, so I let some sarcasm show in my words.

She picked up on it, her mouth curving into the barest of smiles. "Obviously not. What do the police think about Rob's death?"

"They haven't shared any theories with me. Personally, I think he was murdered."

She regarded me thoughtfully. "So the question is, why would anyone want to kill Rob? I don't know the answer to that. He was a perfectly nice human being."

Which, I thought, was a rather tepid way to describe someone she'd been planning to marry. "I need background information about Rob."

"You could talk with his sister." Then Diana Palmer shook her head vehemently. "But why am I even suggesting that? She didn't know him at all."

"I need to talk with someone who did know him. I guess that's you."

"I guess it is." For a moment she looked sad, as though the news of Rob's death had hit her harder than I thought.

Another school group clattered by, this time made up of loud and boisterous teenagers whose voices echoed through the courtyard where we stood, near the entrance to the history exhibit. "Is there somewhere we can talk that's quieter?" I asked, now that she seemed to have thawed a little. "Your office, maybe."

"I've been here such a short time that I share an office," she said. "And my office mate is there, working diligently at the computer. Let's go to the café and get some coffee."

We went back up the steps to the upper level, where the museum café was located near the entrance to the Great Hall. The café was empty except for the workers behind the counter. With coffee mugs in hand, we took a table near the window that looked down on one of the museum gardens.

"Tell me about the last time you saw Rob."

Diana Palmer cupped both hands around the coffee mug on the table in front of her and glanced sideways at the greenery in the garden. "It was early July when we stopped seeing one another. I think he would have liked to get back together. I'm the one who broke it off and I'm not . . . I wasn't interested in regrouping."

"Why'd you break up?"

She slewed her eyes back toward me. "I decided I didn't want to get married. And that's all I intend to say on the subject."

My, she was the prickly one. "What did Rob say to you, before you broke up? Did he talk about work, about whatever else was going on in his life?"

"He was planning a bicycle trip to Point Reyes," she said, tracing an abstract design on the tabletop. "A long weekend. He'd had to delay it once, because he couldn't get time off from the office. Work was hectic, but it always was. The legal department at Bates needs two paralegals, not one, and the workload was getting him down. Supposedly, with all the cutbacks, there was never any money in the budget to hire someone. At least, that's what the bean counters always say in situations like that."

I noticed the emphasis she'd placed on the word "supposedly," as well as a note of contempt in her voice as she discussed the Bates legal department. It reminded me of something Robin had said Friday night when I was at the Hartzell place.

"You met Rob at work. That's what his niece told me. Did you work at Bates before coming to the Oakland Museum? You sound as though you're familiar with the company."

Diana Palmer's smile didn't extend to her eyes. "I was there. Not as an employee, though. But I have more than a passing familiarity with the inner workings of the place. You see, my mother is Bette Bates. She and her brother Jeff inherited the whole damn company from their father, Clyde Bates. Mother's not involved in the company anymore, but she was on the board for quite a few years. Uncle Jeff is still the chief executive officer. Not that he has any power left since the buyout last year."

My ears pricked with interest. I needed information about the company. It looked as though Diana could provide it. "What were you doing at Bates? How did you meet Rob?"

"I was working on my master's in history at Cal State, about two years ago," Diana said. "I took a course in public history, and for a research project I decided to do a corporate genealogy of Bates."

"History? You must know my father, then. Timothy Howard."

"Dr. Howard's your father? You're kidding. He was my advisor." Diana laughed. "God, it's a small world. So small you keep tripping over people." When she looked at me now, I could see that a thaw was underway. "Last fall I spent two or three days a week at Bates, over a period of about two months, in the legal department primarily. They have all the old minute books of Bates and its subsidiaries and all the companies it bought over the years. My hours on the project varied. I met Rob, of course, since he worked in the legal department. We started eating lunch together. We'd pick up something at a deli and walk along the estuary there at Jack London Square. After awhile he asked me out."

"Do you know anyone else in the legal department?" I asked.

She shrugged. "Just Alexander Campbell, the general counsel. My father was an attorney, and he was general counsel before he died. That's when Alex took over. Mother's known him for years. And of course, with Uncle Jeff giving the thumbs-up, all doors were open. Anyway, Rob and I got more involved after I finished the project and moved on to work on my thesis. Rob was a little more serious than I was. He asked me to marry him on Valentine's Day. I said yes, but I began having second thoughts. When I broke it off, Rob was disappointed, but hopeful that I'd change my mind."

"But you didn't."

She shook her head again, and I thought I saw a faint hint of regret in her eyes. "No, I didn't. So now he's dead."

"Do you know anyone at Bates who might want to kill him?"

Her eyebrows went up. "Now that's an interesting question. What prompted it?"

I leaned back in my chair. "Rob came to see me a week ago. All he said was that something was going on at Bates that shouldn't be happening and he was planning to blow the whistle."

"Something illegal?" Diana asked, eyes widening.

"Unfortunately, he didn't give me any additional information. He'd also received an anonymous note, warning him to back off from whatever he was doing. Evidently he didn't." I shook my head. "That's all I have to go on. So I'm back to my original question. Do you know anyone at Bates who might want to kill Rob Lawter?"

Diana Palmer had been staring at me over the rim of her coffee cup. Now she set it down with a resolute thump.

"No, I don't. But if anyone can give you the lowdown on Bates, it's my mother."

CHAPTER 11

"I'M NOT SURE HOW I CAN HELP," BETTE BATES PALMER told me later as I sat on her patio, watching the midday sun turn San Francisco Bay into a pool of glittering silver and gold.

She was a big handsome woman in her late fifties, with shoulder-length salt-and-pepper hair. Her athletic body looked comfortable in khaki slacks and a sleeveless yellow shirt, and the tanned skin of her arms and face told me she spent a lot of time outdoors.

She lived on Euclid Avenue in North Berkeley, just past Codornices Park and the Rose Garden. Her big square stucco house was painted white and had a red-tiled roof and lots of curlicues near the eaves. The front of the house was smack up against the street, with a half-circle drive and not much in the way of a front yard. From the rear, however, there was a spectacular view framed by the Monterey pines that grew along the property line. Between the tall green trees, I could see the fog moving through the Golden Gate Bridge, and Mount Tamalpais looming over Marin County.

I wasn't sure she could help, either, but it was worth finding out what she might be able to tell me. Diana had made the phone call from the Oakland Museum, to see if her mother was home. I had driven from there straight to Berkeley, after extracting a promise from Diana for a copy of the Bates corporate genealogy she'd put together.

Now we sat in Adirondack chairs on the flagstone patio, enjoying the warm September sun and the spectacular view, surrounded by weathered redwood planters full of red and pink geraniums, yellow daylilies, and orange marigolds. Mrs. Palmer, who insisted I call her Bette, had opened a bottle of merlot to go with the pungent Stilton we were spreading on crackers. I sipped the red wine, then set the glass on a nearby table.

"I haven't had much to do with the company for more than a year," Bette continued. "Certainly not since Rattlesnake and Viper took over."

"Rattlesnake and Viper?" I repeated, not sure I'd heard her correctly.

Bette flashed a sardonic smile and lifted her wineglass in a mock salute. "Better known to the fawning minions of Wall Street as Rittlestone and Weper."

While she swallowed a mouthful of merlot, I digested the tidbit she'd just handed me. Carol Hartzell, Rob's sister, worked for the same company that had taken over the firm that had employed her brother. Was this a coincidence, or a piece of the puzzle?

"Those scumbags," Bette continued, fueled by anger and wine, "took a perfectly good company and raped it. They'll discard the carcass once they've sucked all the life out of it. That's what those people do."

"Diana tells me you were on the board for a number of years."

"Yes, I was. Almost fifteen years. And I warned my fellow board members what would happen. They didn't listen. I was outnumbered. So I resigned. I couldn't stand to see what they were doing. My brother Jeff thought he could work with those bastards. He was wrong. They've cut off his balls."

I took a bite of Stilton and washed it down with some wine. "Tell me about the company. As I understand it, your father, Clyde Bates, was born in West Oakland."

Bette nodded. "They had a house on Adeline Street. It's still there, cut up into apartments. Dad's father—my grandfather—was a longshoreman at the port. Grandma took in laundry and did whatever else she could to make a buck. They had five kids, three boys and two girls. Dad started the company in the thirties, right there in the Produce District, canning fruits and vegetables in that building down on Webster Street, near the Embarcadero."

"The building that's still corporate headquarters."

"Yes." Bette poured more merlot into her glass. "The plant and the warehouse were on the lower floors, and the offices were on the top floor. Dad made a decent living for the first few years. Then the war came along, and he got a contract to supply food to the army. Business boomed. He built a cannery in Oakland and converted the original building into office space. It's been that way ever since. Of course, the biggest growth came after the war. Dad expanded the operation. He built plants in Oakland, San Leandro, and Hayward. Not only does Bates can fruits and vegetables, but it makes and packages cereals, breads, cookies and crackers, dairy products."

"Peanut butter and jelly," I said, recalling the array of products with the Bates Best label I'd seen in my local supermarket. "Spaghetti sauce, ice cream, and yogurt."

"You bet," she declared. "If it's in a can, a box, a jar, or a carton, Bates puts it there. They do a damn good job of it, too. Bates products consistently get high ratings in taste tests. And in consumer confidence. Bates means quality. Or at least it did before the buyout. Who know what corners Rattlesnake and Viper have cut in their quest to bleed every dollar from the company." She raised her glass and drank.

"So . . . back to the family saga. Dad married Mom. Her name was Emma Hamlin, and her family grew rice out in the Delta. Mom and Dad only had the two of us, Jeff and me. Jeff's the oldest. I'm four years younger."

"Was Jeff groomed to take over the company?"

"Of course. There was no doubt that he was going to be CEO eventually. He's got an MBA. But he started at the bottom. Dad insisted on that. Jeff worked in the plants during the summers all through college. Then he managed a plant for awhile, before moving up to corporate."

"What about you?" I asked.

"Me?" She grinned. "I got married. That's what girls in my day did. Steve was one of my brother's classmates, when he was an undergraduate at Cal." She gestured in the general direction of the sprawling campus of the University of California.

"Jeff brought Steve home for dinner one weekend. I was smitten, and so was Steve. We didn't get married right away, though. I had just graduated from high school, and Mom insisted that I go to college, so off I went to Mills, right there in Oakland. Steve wanted to go to Boalt Hall. Once he'd gotten his law degree and passed the bar, Dad put him to work as a junior lawyer in the legal department. He was general counsel when he died. It'll be six years in November. Just up and had a heart attack one morning, while he was putting on his tie."

She sighed and got a faraway look in her eyes, but only for a moment. "So, Alex Campbell took over as general counsel. Dad died eight years ago. That's when Jeff became CEO. Then last year, everything went to hell."

"The leveraged buyout," I said.

The term was a familiar corporate buzzword in the recent decades, known by its initials, LBO. An LBO occurred when a purchaser acquired the assets or stock of a company, accomplishing the transaction with a lot of debt and little or no capital. Such buyouts were usually achieved by issuing risky and speculative junk bonds.

"The leveraged buyout," she repeated, mouth twisting as though the words were poison. "What a perfectly bland description for the murder of a perfectly good business."

She fortified herself with a swallow of wine, then continued. "You see, when Dad started the company, it was privately held. But in the fifties, Bates went public. The stock had its ups and downs, mostly ups. So that made it a good solid value. Not one of these flashy, gonna-make-a-million-overnight companies, just the kind of steady performer a lot of people like to have in their stock portfolios."

"But there were takeover bids."

Bette nodded. "Several, over the past fifteen years. All of them hostile, because Dad and Jeff had no intention of relinquishing control. Then, about eighteen months ago, this company called TZI, Inc. mounted a hostile takeover bid that looked as though it was going to succeed. So the board, over my objections, went looking for someone to save them from TZI. What they call a 'white knight.' You know what that is?"

"I'm familiar with the term." Finding the "white knight" usually led to a takeover, friendly rather than hostile, though I supposed friendly and hostile were matters of degree. To my mind, a takeover was a takeover.

"Well, in this case, the knight was riding a Trojan horse. The whole idea was that the rescuers would raise the cash to buy out

Bates stock, at a higher rate than the TZI tender offer, by selling junk bonds. After the transaction was complete, current management would continue to run the company. Unfortunately the money men my brother and the board found were Rattlesnake and Viper."

"Why do you call them that?" I asked, even though I was reasonably sure of the answer.

"Because they're a couple of snakes," Bette said. "Their names are actually Yale Rittlestone and Frank Weper."

"I've never heard of them," I said. At least, not until a couple of days ago.

"No one had, until they took over Bates." Bette made a sour face, and her next words were full of scorn. "Since the LBO, their pictures are on the covers of those business magazines that like to kiss the feet of corporate raiders. What a mismatched pair they are."

I reached for the knife and spread some Stilton on a cracker. "How so?"

"Weper's older, mid-sixties, I'd say. Gray, quiet, totally unremarkable. Looks like a college professor with a good tailor. He prefers to be in the background. I've heard he was forced out of, or retired from, a larger firm in New York City. Rittlestone signed him on because he needed a name with a track record, to give him legitimacy. Weper's from Chicago and that's where he lives. R&W has an office there, on the Loop." Bette paused, then went on to describe the second partner.

"As for Rittlestone, he runs the San Francisco office, which is located at Embarcadero Four. He lives in the city. He claims to be a New England blue blood, supposedly Newport, Rhode Island. But he doesn't have the accent those people usually have. Either he's lost it, or he's lying about his past. They say he went to Harvard, not Yale. Probably out of pure perversity, if it's true. He's blond, tall, and thin. Attractive, if you like that sort. I don't. Fancies himself a playboy and likes to get mentioned in the society columns. I wouldn't turn my back on the son of a bitch, let alone break bread with him. He's got a nasty edge. Something tells me he'd be bad news in a street fight."

"I guess they both are, if the fight's on Wall Street."

"You better believe it. Bates was R&W's first takeover after joining forces, and it made quite a splash. That hostile takeover bid from TZI sent Bates Inc. stock spiraling upward, at prices we'd never seen before. There was an absolute feeding frenzy, lots of speculation buying in the weeks before the deal was done. The price of the takeover offer was high enough to tempt a majority of Bates shareholders."

"Enter the white knights," I said.

"The old pro and the young Turk. That's how the press described them. They seduced the board with promises that upper management would remain in place. To hell with the peons below, of course. Merely cannon fodder to be jettisoned in the first round of layoffs. Not that they kept their promises, of course. As soon as the deal was done, they started making changes. A lot of the people who were interested in saving their own jobs suddenly found themselves clinging to their golden parachutes."

She shook her head, her mouth twisting with bitterness. "So that's how Rattlesnake and Viper wound up in charge of the company it took my father years to build. It's been a disaster. Employee morale is in the toilet, after two big layoffs in less than a year. My brother Jeff is still the CEO. But it's only a matter of time before they boot him out the door. Rumor has it he'll be replaced by a Rattlesnake and Viper minion. They've brought in plenty of their own people to replace long-term Bates employees, not only executives, but even people at midlevel."

"It's an interesting story. One I've heard all too often these days." I set my glass on a nearby table. "But I'm not sure it helps me answer the question I asked your daughter earlier today. Is there anyone at Bates who might want to kill Rob Lawter? And why?"

"I wouldn't put murder past either of those sharks," Bette said, taking another sip of her wine. "But Rob? Who'd want to kill him? He was a nice guy. I kept hoping my daughter would come to her senses and marry him."

"Rob was a paralegal who worked in the legal department for four years." I toyed with the stem of my wineglass. "He was there during the leveraged buyout, but did he have any contact with either Rittlestone or Weper? I think it unlikely, even in the scope of his employment."

"I doubt it," Bette agreed. "I can check with Alex Campbell, the general counsel. Perhaps he could help. I'm sure he'd talk with you, if I suggested it."

"I'd rather you said nothing about this to anyone," I told her. "At least for right now. But if you think of anything that's been going on in the company over the past year that might help . . ."

"I've heard they're going public again," she said. "Between now and the end of the year. Maybe that's it. Maybe those bastards have done something the Securities and Exchange Commission might not like. You can really get your tit in a wringer if you cross the SEC."

I drove back to Oakland and left my Toyota at a parking meter outside the main library. I spent a couple of hours reading everything I could find on Bates Inc., getting the story of the leveraged buyout without Bette's bias, which was considerable, however justified.

Then I turned my attention to the two men Bette had called scumbags. Her physical descriptions had been dead-on, I decided, looking at the color photograph on the cover of a year-old issue of *Forbes*. Frank Weper did indeed look like a college professor with a good tailor. His sixtyish bespectacled face wouldn't have been out of place at any of the Cal State faculty gatherings I'd attended with my father.

Posed next to Weper, the well-dressed and well-barbered Yale Rittlestone stood with arms crossed over his chest, smiling at the camera. He was good-looking in a patrician sort of way, pale blue eyes in a thin face topped with a shock of straight blond hair. I searched for some evidence of the coldhearted businessman Bette had described, but the Rittlestone in the cover picture looked affable enough. Perhaps he was showing his public face for public consumption. Most people do, when you get right down to it. It's only when you start looking under rocks that you find that private face that some people would like to keep hidden.

Was I letting Bette's contempt for the men she'd dubbed Rattlesnake and Viper influence me? I told myself firmly that I'd have to make my own assessment of them. Since Weper was in the firm's Chicago office, Rittlestone was a more likely target for my scrutiny.

The articles I read all had some variation on the theme of Frank Weper as the old pro and Yale Rittlestone as the young Turk. They were presented as capitalist heroes making their mark in the rough-and-tumble business world, bringing fresh blood into an old stale enterprise, so it would make more money and its stock would rise in value.

But based on what I'd read, it looked to me as though Bates had been doing just fine before the takeover. Slow and steady, I thought, like the tortoise instead of the hare. Was there any room these days for tortoises?

Sometimes it seems that nothing is valued in our society, unless it makes a profit. And the bigger the profit, the better.

I worked my way through a pile of change making photocopies of the articles, enough so that I had quite a file on Bates Inc. and Rittlestone and Weper when I returned to my office. The red light on my answering machine was blinking furiously, indicating several messages. Before I could even check to see who had called, Ruby Woods came through my front door. She was grinning from ear to ear.

"A secretary in the legal department at Bates quit this afternoon, without giving notice. I told 'em you could start tomorrow morning."

CHAPTER *12*

"THIS IS YOUR WORKSTATION," NANCY FONG TOLD ME IN
a businesslike voice.

She was a short, slender woman in her mid-forties, her straight
black hair streaked with gray and cut into a no-nonsense ear-length
bob. She had a tiny mole just to the left of her mouth. Her navy blue
dress and her manner were equally crisp. I hadn't seen her smile
since I'd stepped off the elevator.

Back to the world of time cards and regular paychecks, I told myself Thursday morning as I dressed in one of Ruby's borrowed suits,
a gray linen number that was a little too big in the hips. But my
workday wouldn't be limited to those hours I would spend working
as a temporary employee. I'd had to reschedule a number of appointments for early morning or late afternoon. Working this undercover job meant fitting the rest of my active cases in around the
edges.

The corporate headquarters of Bates Inc. was a rectangular four-
story building on Webster Street between Second and Third, in the
middle of what Oakland old-timers called the Produce District.
More recently, people referred to this area as the Jack London
Square district, since the square itself was nearby, where Broadway dead-ended at the Embarcadero. But I always associated it with
the produce warehouses clustered along the streets in this part of
town. From early morning to midday it was difficult driving through
this part of town, what with having to dodge forklifts hauling crates
of tomatoes. The air smelled of squashed onions and oranges, and

the litter at the curbs often contained bruised and discarded fruit and vegetables, easy pickings for the street people who frequented the area.

The other reason it was sometimes difficult to navigate this area was because of the trains. Tracks ran down the middle of the Embarcadero and, until recently, Third Street. Sometimes freights loaded with containers would inexplicably stop, leaving impatient vehicles and walkers stranded until the train rumbled and, with stiff metallic protests, began moving again. To mitigate the problem, two pedestrian bridges had been built over the Embarcadero.

A train pulled into the new Oakland Amtrak terminal as I walked toward the Bates building. There was a parking garage underneath, Ruby had told me, but it was for the executives only. The rest of the employees had to make do with a crowded lot across Third Street, or parked on the streets themselves. I'd wedged my Toyota into a narrow spot next to one of those oversized vans that always seemed to take more than its share of space.

As I crossed the street, heading toward the wide front steps and the wheelchair ramp at the front of the building, I thought that Clyde Bates had chosen his location well. It might not be the most glamorous place for a business, but it had access to both the produce warehouses and the tracks. It was a plain, solid, utilitarian building, its stucco exterior painted pale blue, streaked with soot due to the proximity of the Nimitz Freeway barely two blocks away. On the lower floors, I could see where the loading docks had once been. But this was office space now. It looked like the windows opened, which was a nice change from the sealed glass of the modern skyscraper.

I went up the steps, through the double glass doors, and presented myself to the receptionist. She was a well-dressed woman in her fifties who presided over a counter and a console, an earphone affixed to her right ear. She told me to have a seat on one of the low gray chairs ranged in a semicircle in front of her counter. She phoned the legal department, then directed me to the elevator, visible behind her, and told me to go up to the fourth floor.

Nancy Fong met me at the elevator, introduced herself, and escorted me down the hallway on the south, on the Webster Street side. We rounded the corner into another corridor and stepped into a windowless rectangular room on the interior of the building. It was divided into three identical square cubicles, separated by gray metal partitions about five feet high. Where there weren't shelves, the cubicle walls were covered with gray cloth. Each had a telephone with lots of buttons, a transcriber with earphones, and a computer with a monitor resting on top of it and a pullout keyboard drawer.

The workstation Nancy Fong had indicated as mine was in the middle, and it didn't offer much in the way of privacy. It also looked as though its former occupant had left it without a backward glance. Pens and paper clips were scattered across its gray surface. A bright pink message pad and some yellow Post-its provided notes of color. A precarious pile of papers was stacked in a black plastic in box, waiting for someone to file them away. That someone would be me.

To the right of the door was a long table. On one end sat three plastic letter trays, in red, yellow, and white, each containing several documents. An oversized wire basket at the other end was overflowing with papers. Next to the table was a bookcase, its shelves piled with reams of paper and other supplies. In the corner I saw a stand holding a laser printer and a fax machine.

"We have three attorneys," Nancy Fong said briskly as I surveyed my new surroundings. "Alexander Campbell is the general counsel. He also handles labor and employment matters. Hank Irvin handles corporate and antitrust matters. Patricia Mayhew's specialty is regulatory, federal, local, and state. Food law is of major importance in our business, of course. Both Hank and Patricia write and review various contracts and agreements." She looked at me as I digested all of this. "I understand you used to work in a law office."

"Yes. I imagine this will be different."

She nodded. "We don't usually handle litigation directly. We have outside counsel for that. Our attorneys act as advisors. There's a lot of variety here you won't find in a law firm."

"Not as much pressure?" If memory served from my days as a legal secretary, the pressure in high-powered law firms was the primary reason for the burnout rate in legal secretaries.

"I can't promise that," she said with a slight frown. "Things can get hectic around here. We're backed up right now. The secretary who left didn't give us any notice." Her mouth tightened with disapproval at this breach of employee protocol. "We have . . . had a paralegal. That position is vacant, too, but we'll be filling it soon, I'm sure."

It was a rather bloodless way to describe Rob's death, but I guessed Nancy Fong was a woman who kept information to herself most of the time. She wasn't going to tell a temp fresh off the street just why the paralegal position was open.

She pointed to the three letter trays on the table. "The attorneys prioritize their work requests. If something's in the red tray, that means it should be done right away. Yellow means it's needed in a day or so. White means it can wait. I'm the general counsel's secretary, but when there's work to be done, we all pitch in. That includes the filing, which needs catching up." She indicated the overflowing wire basket. "The attorneys have some files in their offices, but most everything else is in our file room near the freight elevator. I'll give you the tour."

She stopped as a woman about my own age entered the room, carrying a coffee mug and an attitude. "This is Gladys Olivette, our other secretary. Gladys, this is Jeri. She's our temp, for the time being."

Gladys Olivette was tall, thin, and elegantly dressed in a teal blue suit with a yellow blouse. She tilted her head back, gold earrings visible on the lobes beneath her short black curls. She gave me the once-over, then her bright red lips curved into a smile. Evidently I'd been deemed acceptable.

"Glad to have you, Jeri," Gladys said. "Otherwise known as, thank God you're here. Welcome to the funny farm. Martha just up and quit yesterday, without so much as a by-your-leave or a two-week notice."

"Why would she do that?" I asked, returning her smile.

"Rats deserting a sinking ship," Gladys said. On my right I saw Nancy Fong narrow her eyes and frown. "Actually, Martha got a better job and she starts Monday. Of course, that left us overworked and shorthanded. Especially since our paralegal took a dive out a window last week."

"No kidding," I said, wide-eyed.

Nancy's frown got deeper. She was plainly unhappy that Gladys had mentioned Rob's death. "Alex is looking for the Ralston file,

Gladys. It's on my desk. Would you take it to him, please? While I show Jeri around."

Gladys rolled her eyes. She set the coffee mug she was carrying on the table, picked up the thick folder Nancy had indicated, and left the room.

Nancy continued with my orientation. "Working hours are eight to four-thirty. You get an hour for lunch. People usually go around noon or twelve-thirty. The employee cafeteria is on the first floor, and it's open for lunch from eleven-thirty to one. The food's okay, but not great. And of course, there are all sorts of restaurants in the Jack London Square area. Now, let me show you where a few things are. Then I'll introduce you to the attorneys."

I followed her out of the room. We were on the Third Street side of the building, so that made this the east hall. Nancy turned left. All the doors along this corridor had square opaque glass panes that showed the light from the offices they led to. We passed the door of a darkened office and turned left again, into the north hallway. Midway along this passage were the restrooms. Just this side of the entrance to the women's room an open doorway led to a short hall, its carpet of lesser quality. The first room on the right held the copy machine.

Nancy walked past this to the open area in front of the freight elevator. On the wall next to this I saw a time clock and a metal tray full of time cards. I wouldn't have to worry about punching in and out. As a temp, I would note the hours I worked on a Woods Temporaries time card, which Nancy, as my supervisor, would sign.

"This is our file room," she said, opening a door beyond the freight elevator. I peered in at a square room, its walls lined with beige metal cabinets. Then Nancy turned, and we retraced our steps to the copy room.

The huge copy machine looked as though it required one to be a NASA engineer to operate it. Pale green buttons were spread across its white exterior, and at the moment it issued forth a variety of hums and thumps as it went about its business, shuffling paper into the collator at the side.

The woman who was waiting for her copies stood with her hands folded across her chest, staring as though mesmerized at a large green posterboard affixed to the wall above the copier. In block letters, the sign warned copier users on pain of equipment jams not to let a single staple, paper clip, or Post-it drift anywhere near this expensive and delicate machine.

"What is that?" I asked Nancy, pointing at a keypad with an electronic readout. It protruded from the top of the copier like a brown rectangular mushroom.

"It's a pain in the ass," said the woman who was making copies. She was short, with gray hair and a disgruntled expression.

The machine stopped its sorting serenade after emitting a series of whines and clicks as it stapled her copies. She stacked the papers on top of the copier, then gathered them to the bosom of her green seersucker dress and departed. I looked inquiringly at Nancy.

"It's something that's just been added, like the time clock," she explained, compressing her lips into a thin line that told me just what she thought of both innovations. "This device is on all our copiers now, to keep track of supply usage. Before you can use the machine, you have to punch in your user code, then the department ID number. You have to do the same thing when you send a fax or make a long-distance telephone call. It takes some getting used to."

"I'll bet." In fact, I thought, it's damned cumbersome. I could see why the woman in the green dress called it a pain in the ass.

Another woman hurried into the room bearing a single sheet of paper, placed it into the sheet feeder, and doggedly punched in a series of numbers. The keypad beeped at her, evidently refusing her access to the machine. She swore at it, and punched in some more numbers. This time the keypad deigned to let her make a copy.

All those numbers, I thought, were going to put a crimp in my investigation. What if I found some documents that could shed some light on Rob's death? This made unauthorized copying a bit difficult. I'd have to figure out a way around it.

Nancy was already moving back out to the north hallway. I followed her. "These offices along here are human resources and public affairs," she said, waving at the doors, again with opaque glass insets, lining either side of the corridor. "The offices of the chief executive officer and the chief financial officer are on the west side of the building."

We headed back the way we'd come. When we turned the corner, Nancy stopped abruptly. The office that had been dark now showed light through the pebbled glass. Nancy opened the door. I saw a small windowless room, about eight feet square, with a desk facing the door. The walls were crowded with filing cabinets and bookcases, and it looked as though every surface was covered with documents and files. Gladys sat behind the desk, rummaging through some files that had been piled there.

"What are you doing in here?" Nancy asked, her voice sharp.

Gladys looked up. Her expression told me that she was surprised at Nancy's tone. When she replied, her voice was tart. "Hank wants the Barelo Industries file. I know Rob had been working on it before . . . Well, Rob was the last person to have it."

"This was the paralegal's office?" I asked, stepping into the doorway so I could get a better look. I itched to get in there and dig around, the way Gladys was doing right now.

"Yes, it was," Nancy said. "I haven't had time to sort through things. It's only been a week since he died."

"You packed up all his personal stuff, didn't you?" Gladys asked.

"Yes, earlier in the week," Nancy said. "I delivered it to his sister last night after work. But now I need to sort through all these files, to see what he was working on."

"Well, I'm positive he had that Barelo Industries file." Gladys rooted through some more files, then cried, "Aha!" in triumph. She unearthed a folder from the middle of the pile and held it aloft. "I knew it." She stepped between Nancy and me and headed down the hall with the folder tucked under her arm.

Nancy turned off the overhead light and firmly shut the door to the room that had been Rob's. "I'll deal with that later," she said, more to herself than to me.

I would have liked to deal with it there and then. But Nancy was already beckoning me to follow her.

CHAPTER **13**

"THIS CORNER OFFICE IS ALEX CAMPBELL'S," NANCY SAID, continuing with her commentary as we walked along the east hallway. "He's in a meeting, so I'll introduce you to him later. Hank Irvin has the office next to Alex."

She tapped on the door she'd indicated, then opened it. I stepped from the perfectly adequate carpeting of the hallway onto the thick plush. The carpet was a deep rich brown, setting off the furniture, which looked like mahogany. At one end of the room stood two filing cabinets, wooden with lateral drawers. Next to this was a small round conference table with three chairs. The wide desk had a few files neatly arrayed on its surface. At a right angle from the desk I saw a matching computer stand with the usual equipment— computer, monitor, keyboard.

Behind the desk, leaning back in a brown leather chair, was an athletic-looking man with short blond hair. He wore a well-cut gray pinstriped suit complete with snowy white shirt and red power tie. He was talking on the telephone, hands moving as he spoke. He gestured, indicating we should wait. Nancy pulled out one of the chairs at the conference table, and I did the same, glancing briefly out the window at the water glinting in the estuary. A moment later, the man ended his conversation and hung up the phone. He stood and moved around the desk, smiling.

"Jeri, this is Hank Irvin," Nancy said. "Hank, this is Jeri Howard. She'll be working with us temporarily."

"Hi." Hank Irvin stuck out his right hand and flashed a friendly smile. His eyes were blue, and I saw a dusting of freckles across the fair skin of his face. Mid-thirties, I guessed, about the same age as I was, with a firm handshake. As I shook his hand, I noticed that the knuckles were skinned. He looked as though he worked out. Perhaps he'd had an encounter with some exercise equipment.

"Welcome aboard," he said. "Glad you were able to get someone in at such short notice, Nancy. I've got quite a few projects coming up, some of the things that Rob was supposed to be handling." Nancy tightened her mouth and nodded. Hank Irvin turned to me. "Have you ever worked for a corporate lawyer, Jeri?"

"I've worked for many different kinds of lawyers." It was true. Not only had I worked for several law firms as a legal secretary and paralegal, but some of my regular clients as a private investigator were attorneys.

"I think you'll find things are different around here than in a law firm," he said. His phone rang again, and Nancy took that as our exit line. "Nice meeting you, Jeri."

I'd noticed that everyone seemed to be on a first-name basis around here. That was different from the law offices where I'd worked years ago. Things were considerably more formal then. But perhaps that had changed, as well.

Out in the hall, Nancy repeated her knock-and-enter routine at the next door. The office it opened onto was decorated differently from the one we'd just left. The carpet was cranberry, the miniblinds on the window pink. A clear vase that looked like expensive crystal sat on the credenza behind the desk, full of lush red roses dropping petals onto the oak surface. Bright red slashed through the abstract painting on the wall above the credenza.

The woman wore red, as well, her suit the shade of an excellent cabernet. She was a sleek brunette whose curly hair had been resolutely tamed. It was wound into a tight knot at the nape of her neck. She herself looked as though she was wound too tightly. She was on the phone, standing between the oak desk and the credenza that held the flowers and her computer setup. As she listened to whoever was talking on the other end of the line, her posture was rigid and she clutched the receiver with slender fingers that ended in bright red fingernails. Tension marred her oval face, as did the dark rings under her brown eyes.

Before I had a chance to speculate at the meaning of her body language and the shadow of unease emanating from her, she wiped the expression from her face and spoke into the telephone receiver. "I'll have to call you back." She hung up the phone and took a deep breath, composing herself.

"Sorry, Patricia, I didn't mean to interrupt." Nancy's face was unreadable, but something in her voice made me look at her sharply, then at the woman in red who stood at the other side of the desk.

"What is it, Nancy?" Patricia Mayhew smiled as she spoke, but her voice held a bit more acid than was necessary.

There was definitely hostility between the two women. Enough so that it was worth looking into. In any office, there's always someone who is difficult to work with. Was Mayhew the one? I guessed I was about to find out.

Nancy introduced me to Patricia Mayhew, who greeted me coolly, without any of Hank's questions about my experience. "I would appreciate your getting caught up on the filing," she said, waving her hand at the papers and folders in her out box. "Martha was somewhat lacking in that quarter."

"We'll take care of it," Nancy said tersely, as she stacked the pile in the crook of her arm. The phone rang, and Patricia Mayhew reached for the receiver with her bloodred talons, a bit too eagerly. We were dismissed.

"What's her problem?" I asked, as Nancy and I walked back down the hall. Either she didn't hear me or she wasn't disposed to answer.

When we'd returned to the room with its row of cubicles, Nancy added the pile she was carrying to the already overflowing wire basket. "Let me show you how to log onto the computer system," she said, walking to the middle cubicle. "You've been given a temporary password that will get you onto the network."

I sat down at the computer, while Nancy stood to my right, walking me through what I needed to know. The word processing program was one I was familiar with, and it looked as though the legal department had standard templates for letters, memos, and other documents. She explained that all the computers in the legal department were wired to the one laser printer in this room. That was a lot of strain to put on one machine, but Nancy added that she was trying to get authorization to purchase another printer. Budget constraints, of course.

After giving me the user code and department code for the high-tech copy machine, Nancy showed me how to work the phone and voice mail system. Then she glanced at the wire basket full of things to be filed and the letter trays with projects that needed to be completed.

"All of us need to get caught up on the filing," she said, her voice subdued. "Martha did have a tendency to let it go, and it's really backed up. But it looks as though there are several things in the priority stack, as well."

The phone at my workstation began to ring, an insistent electronic whine. "That's Patricia's line," Nancy said. "If the attorneys don't answer their phones, their lines roll over to yours. If you don't answer, it goes into their voice mail."

"Got it." I picked up the phone in the middle of the third ring and said, "Patricia Mayhew's office," in my best secretarial tone. As I tucked the receiver between chin and shoulder and reached for the message pad and the nearest pen, it felt as though I'd never left the legal-secretary world I'd worked in so many years ago. The person on the other end of the line was male, and asked if he could leave a message in Patricia's voice mail. I had a second of panic, trying to recall Nancy's quick lesson in how to transfer such a call. Then I saw that my predecessor, the recently departed Martha Bronson, had a crib sheet pinned to the wall of the cubicle, right above the phone. I punched the appropriate series of buttons, then hung up, feeling as though I'd jumped over the first hurdle without clipping the crossbar.

While I was on the phone, Nancy had returned to her own cubicle. I was on my own. I felt as though I'd been at Bates for eight hours, but a glance at my watch told me it was only ten o'clock in the morning. A long time till lunch, and even longer until the end of the day.

I got up and walked to the table, glancing at the filing that had to be done. I hate filing. When I worked as a secretary, I often declared that I'd rather scrub the kitchen floor than file. My attitude hadn't changed. The piles of paper generated by the average law firm or corporation made me doubt the prospect of the paperless society computers were supposed to give us.

I glanced in the red letter tray and saw a dictation tape and a work request from Hank Irvin labeled "Rush." I picked it up and headed back toward my cubicle.

Gladys bustled into the room and to her cubicle, humming as she raised her mug to her lips. I looked at it longingly. "Where can I get some coffee?" I asked her, already missing the pot I usually kept going in the back of my office.

"They've got it all the time in the cafeteria," she told me with a grin. "The only reason I drink it is because I'm a caffeine junkie. So keep in mind, it ain't Peet's."

Crankcase oil was more like it, I thought with a grimace, after I found my way to the first-floor cafeteria and took a sip of what was available. If I didn't need caffeine so badly . . .

I carried the disposable cup back up the stairs to the place I was already calling Cube City. Martha hadn't been much of a cubicle housekeeper, either, I decided, as I shoved the clutter to one side and set the container down. I reached for Hank Irvin's rush job and plugged the cassette into the transcriber. I fit the earpieces into my ears and punched the rewind button. The machine beeped loudly as it finished rewinding. I winced at the noise. Then I depressed the foot pedal.

I hoped Hank wasn't a mumbler. Fortunately he enunciated clearly when he dictated, but he was forever going back and changing the previous sentence. It took me more than an hour to transcribe the document, which was a supply agreement. In this case, Bates was supplying canned fruit to a well-known grocery chain, to be marketed under that company's house label. The resulting contract wasn't that long when I printed it out, but while I was typing it, I had to deal with the constant interruption of the ringing phone, not only the one at my workstation, but those of Gladys and Nancy.

By the time I was finished typing, my stomach was growling. No wonder I was hungry. It was almost noon, a long time since I'd downed some granola in my own kitchen.

I stood up and stretched, surprised at the ache in my lower back and the tightness in my arms and shoulders from sitting and typing.

I'd had to adjust the height of the chair as well as the angle of the keyboard drawer, but I still hurt.

Don't let anyone tell you being a secretary isn't hard work. You feel it at the end of the day, in your back and shoulders.

I carried the completed document around to Hank Irvin's office and left it in his in basket. When I got back to my work space, Gladys looked as though she was just leaving.

"So how's the cafeteria?" I asked her.

"Abysmal, just like the coffee," Gladys told me as she looped the strap of a leather bag over her shoulder. "You're better off going out, or bringing your own, like Nancy."

"Like Nancy what?" Nancy said as she stepped through the door.

"I was just telling Jeri you bring your lunch most of the time. You eat at your desk, even."

"Not all the time." Nancy shook her head, with the first hint of a smile I'd seen on her face all day. "Sometimes I go home."

"You're close enough to go home for lunch?" I asked.

"Sure. I live in Chinatown. It's a ten-minute walk from here."

"Talk about a great commute," Gladys said. She glanced down at her watch. "Bye, all. I've got a lunch date, and I don't like to keep him waiting."

When Gladys had gone, I turned to Nancy. "Well, I guess I'll get something to eat in the cafeteria."

"Stick with the salad bar," Nancy said, with the sage voice of someone who'd been eating in the employee cafeteria for years. "It's safer."

I retrieved my handbag from the drawer where I'd stashed it and headed downstairs to the cafeteria, a square room at the rear of the first floor. When I'd come in search of coffee earlier, I hadn't paid much attention to my surroundings. Now I surveyed the brown and gold linoleum flooring and bright yellow wallpaper, someone's idea of a way to cheer up the windowless room. Rows of tables, some rectangular and others round and all with brown Formica tops, crowded the room. The chairs were metal framed with brown and yellow vinyl backs and seats, and most were crowded with Bates employees, talking in a hundred conversations as they ate lunch.

The salad bar was set up in the corner to the left of the food line.

When I looked it over, I wasn't sure I agreed with Nancy that it was the safest way to go. I examined the metal tray full of colorless iceberg lettuce and did not feel inspired by that, or the accompanying bins of chopped-up vegetables, shredded cheese, and greasy-looking dressings. I stood for a moment, poised in my indecision, then turned away, holding my empty plastic tray under my arm. The hot entree was meatloaf, never one of my favorites, with mashed potatoes and brown gravy. The green beans that accompanied it looked overcooked. I held the dessert offering, coconut cream pie, in less esteem than the meatloaf.

There was another choice, an assortment of premade sandwiches lined up next to containers of flavored yogurt in a cooler near the beverage dispenser. I opted for peanut butter and jelly, theorizing that it was hard to do anything bad to that combination.

I was wrong. The peanut butter tasted rancid, the jelly was too damn sweet, and the bread was stale. How long had the damn thing been in there? After a couple of bites, I covered the remains with a white paper napkin shroud and conceded that Nancy was probably right about the salad bar.

I went back to the food line and got a container of yogurt, which was Bates Best, of course. As I spooned it out, I examined the people around me. They varied in age, ethnicity, and dress. From what I could see, there wasn't much variation in the business plumage of the American male. He limited himself to a very narrow section of the color palette. Suits were in dark shades of blue, gray, or brown, with the occasional foray into black, tan, or green. These were usually worn with a white shirt. Sometimes the wearer was so daring as to opt for light blue or even pale yellow. How boring, I thought.

The tie was the only place creativity reigned, and then infrequently. I'd never seen so many dull solid colors and subdued understated stripes. Here and there I saw a bold red or a bright multicolored floral. And I wondered about that guy one table over, with iridescent yellow Tweety Birds marching across an emerald background.

I was so glad I'd never had to wear ties. Hell, I didn't even like blouses with bows.

I noticed something else about the people around me. Many of them looked unhappy. "Employee morale is in the toilet," Bette Bates Palmer had told me the previous day. All I had to do to see the evidence was look around me.

I saw Patricia Mayhew walk into the cafeteria, alone, looking preoccupied, almost sad. She carried a ceramic mug bearing the Bates Best logo, which she filled with coffee at the dispenser. Then she turned to leave. Near the cafeteria door, she was intercepted by Hank Irvin. I watched them, itching to know what they were talking about. Business? Or something else? She shook her head, as though responding to a question, then suddenly she smiled. It transformed her face. She was quite pretty, but I hadn't noticed it until now. Each time I'd seen her that morning, she looked as though she labored under a great strain.

Someone loomed in my field of vision, a tall, skinny man with curly gray hair. His body was thin, all angles, and so was his face. He had a hawk nose and the look of a predator. The expensively tailored black suit fit him perfectly, and the big gold watch on his left wrist had to be a Rolex. He was the first person I'd seen eating lunch here in the cafeteria who looked like one of the executives from the top floor rather than a midlevel manager or an hourly wage slave like me. He regarded me briefly with a pair of chilly gray eyes, then sat down at a chair on the other side of the rectangular table. He'd stuck with the salad bar. Now he poked a fork into his lunch.

I was interested when Hank Irvin sat down beside him. With his blond hair and freckles he had a certain California boy charm that the older man lacked. I would have loved to eavesdrop on their conversation, but that would have been too obvious. Besides, I needed to get out of the building, if only for a few minutes.

I tossed my yogurt container and plastic spoon in a nearby trash basket and headed for the exit. A walk around the block not only cleared my head, it stretched the muscles that had been sitting at the desk most of the morning.

I found a coffeehouse on the Embarcadero near Franklin. Real coffee, I exulted. Espresso, even. Hot damn! I returned to Bates with the biggest latte I could carry.

CHAPTER *14*

"YOU WERE RIGHT ABOUT THE CAFETERIA BEING AWFUL," I told Gladys Olivette on Friday morning, as we stood at the state-of-the-art copy machine waiting to make copies.

She laughed. "I warned you. But you didn't listen. You had to try it yourself."

The woman who was using the copier swore under her breath as the machine jammed. "Why did they put this thing in?" she asked plaintively, rolling her eyes toward the fluorescent light fixture overhead. "I hate this thing. The other machine was better."

"Paper clip?" Gladys waggled her pearl pink fingernails at the warning sign.

"Not me," the woman declared as she opened the front of the machine gingerly, leaning forward to read the numbered instructions on how to clear the paper jam. "I remove all staples and paper clips in my office before ever coming near this piece of junk. I don't want Ken Pacheco breathing down my neck." She reached out and, with some hesitation, pulled a lever.

By now Gladys, too, had leaned over to peer at the copier instructions. "You break this thing, and Ken Pacheco will have you whipped down the center of the Embarcadero."

"Who's he?" I directed my question to the air between the two women.

"Head of office services. A little tin god made out of paper clips and staples. I think he's got something on the side with whoever convinced him to buy this copy machine." Gladys pulled another lever, and both women peered into the innards of the copy machine. "There it is. Grab that sucker and press the clear button."

The woman tugged the crinkled paper from wherever it had been stuck, and tossed it into a blue recycling bin. Then she shut the front panel and pressed one of the green buttons strewn across the surface.

"Don't you dare make me punch in my user ID and department code again," she threatened the copier. "Or I'll give you a swift kick."

Fortunately the machine heeded her warning, and all she had to do was press the START button. It rumbled, wheezed, and spewed forth the required copies.

On the way back to our row of cubicles, Gladys turned to me and smiled. "Listen, there's a great little deli over in Jack London Village. That's where I'm headed for lunch. You're welcome to join me if you like."

"Thanks, I'd love to."

I would welcome some company and some decent food during the upcoming lunch hour, but that wasn't the only reason I was happy about the invitation. Based on yesterday's observation of my new coworkers, Nancy Fong played her hand close to the chest. Gladys Olivette was a talker, with an up-to-date knowledge of all the Bates corporate gossip. And the office scuttlebutt was what I wanted to hear. I needed to find out what was going on here that had Rob Lawter ready to blow the whistle.

The sooner I nailed down a lead, the better. I didn't want to have to spend an indefinite time pretending to be a temp. After leaving Bates last night, I'd spent another three hours in my own office on Franklin Street, doing things I normally would have done during the working day. I was tired already, and it was only my second day on this undercover job.

I had wisely stopped at the coffeehouse on Fourth on my way to work this morning. Life's too short to drink bad coffee, and I was an admitted coffee addict. Now the latte was gone. I tossed the empty cup into the trash. Nancy was at the fax machine, sending a document through. My ears pricked as I heard her ask Gladys if she was going to Rob's funeral.

"Of course I am," Gladys said. "Martha will be there, too. Who else is going?"

I saw Nancy frown as she turned, and I wondered if it was the mention of the faithless Martha that caused her mouth to turn down. "I am, of course. Alex and Hank are going, too. Patricia said she'll be out of town this weekend."

Hearing Martha's name spurred me to do something about the mess she'd left behind. I headed for the women's bathroom, returning to my cubicle with some dampened paper towels. I transferred everything on the surface of the desk to one of the empty paper boxes near the printer, then I wiped down the whole surface and started arranging things. Martha had left a three-ring binder that contained a company directory. Another binder held a list of officers with information such as addresses, social security numbers, and dates of birth. She also had left me a folder containing information on office procedures.

As I was organizing my work space, I noticed how spare and utilitarian it was. I needed to bring in something to make it look less like a padded cell. Nancy and Gladys had decorated their cubicles with personal items, such as family photos. One wall of Nancy's workstation was decorated with snapshots of her three children, two girls and a boy who looked as though they were in their teens. There was also a more formal framed photo showing all the Fongs, including Nancy, the kids, and an attractive man of about fifty. Her calendar was a desk type, spiral bound, one page showing the week, and the opposite page, a photograph of flowers.

Gladys, on the other hand, was a bit more cluttered than Nancy. She had two photos, each showing her and her daughter, a girl of about eight. She was a single mother, I guessed, since I saw no photos of a man. Her pens and pencils were stuck into an oversized mug shaped like a pink pig with wings. On her cubicle wall was a *Dilbert* calendar and a laminated sign that read, in big block letters, "LACK OF PLANNING ON YOUR PART DOES NOT JUSTIFY A CRISIS ON MINE."

Here in Cube City, the phones rang constantly. Sometimes the attorneys picked up the calls, other times I took messages or transferred callers to voice mail. This meant I was constantly walking back and forth from my cubicle to their offices to deliver message slips and pick up whatever was in their out boxes. This gave me a better feel for the building's layout, as well as my first crack at the correspondence and other documents that passed through their hands.

Much as I hated filing, doing it would give me the opportunity to prowl around the file room, to give me a clearer picture of Bates Inc. I didn't see any priority items in the red letter tray, so I picked up an armful of papers from the wire basket and began separating them into subject categories. I was just getting into the rhythm of it when Hank Irvin walked in, flashing his easy ingratiating smile as he handed me a cassette to transcribe.

"Can you do this right away?" he asked. "I have to go to San Francisco, and I'd like to take it with me."

"Of course," I said. Was there any other answer?

I transcribed the document, which related to the upcoming initial public offering, or IPO, in which Bates Inc. would go public again, its stock to be listed on the New York Stock Exchange. As Bette Bates Palmer had indicated in our conversation earlier in the week, if Bates stock was to be publicly traded, that meant the company had to comply with a number of Securities and Exchange Commission requirements and regulations. Had Rob discovered something amiss in the upcoming IPO?

The prose Hank dictated was so dry, dense, and full of corporate buzzwords I wasn't able to discern any hidden meanings, even though I read through it again after I'd printed it out. I was straightening the pages when Hank poked his head through the door of Cube City. He wore his suit coat and carried a slim leather briefcase. "Is that done?" he asked.

"Just finished," I said, handing it over.

He glanced through the document, then opened the briefcase and tossed it inside. "I'll be back in the middle of the afternoon."

He hadn't said exactly where he was going, I thought as he disappeared. Just to San Francisco. But that gave me a chance to have a look around his office, under the guise of filing.

I finished sorting papers, then made my first foray into the file room back by the freight elevator. The documents in my arms, and the labels on the folders in the file drawers, gave me an idea of the kind of law practiced here in the Bates legal department.

There were all sorts of agreements, many concerning manufacturing, warehousing, and distribution of Bates Best products. I saw joint venture agreements, trademark license agreements, and copies of the type of contract known in corporate legalese as an indemnification and hold harmless agreement. Alex Campbell's files leaned toward labor union bargaining contracts and employee benefits matters, such as the Employee Retirement Income Security Act of 1974, otherwise known as ERISA. He also had files on things like compensatory time and at-will employment.

Patricia's files were the regulatory side of the house, antitrust, environmental rules, Food and Drug Administration regulations, the Uniform Commercial Code, and California weights and measures laws. She kept most of the FDA and food-safety files in her office rather than the file room, I discovered. And she didn't like to have secretaries filing while she was there. When I showed up with a handful of things to be filed, she asked me to come back that afternoon, since she was planning to leave early.

I shrugged, backed out of her office, and went to Hank's. He handled trademarks, copyrights, and patents, as well as financial matters, such as letters of credit and promissory notes. In the two lateral filing cabinets in his office, I found files related to the corporation, such as bylaws and articles of incorporation, directors and officers obligations, D&O insurance, and conflicts of interest. In the credenza behind Hank's desk, I found a file containing personal information on Bates corporate officers. I read through it, then I examined the papers on the desk surface. Nothing leapt out and told me it was a clue.

There was a file drawer on the lower left side of Hank's desk. It was locked, however. I was just about to jimmy the lock with a paper clip when the door to Hank's office opened. I straightened and reached for the papers in the out box, smoothing all expression from my face. I hoped I didn't look too much like a person who'd been caught in the act.

I raised my eyes and found myself staring into the raptor's eyes of the angular hawk-nosed man I'd seen yesterday in the cafeteria.

Ichabod Crane in a designer suit, I thought, flashing that Rolex on his wrist.

Today he wore another elegant suit, this time a gray that matched his eyes, and a silk tie decorated with tiny red horses. There was something about him, something I couldn't quite put my finger on, that seemed out of place. As I looked at the gray eyes and the curly gray hair I noticed a scar on his left earlobe. It looked for all the world as though this particular businessman had once pierced his ear.

"Hank around?" His voice was a low rasp. His eyes swept around the room, noticing the open file drawer and the stack of folders I'd piled on the conference table. I had a feeling this guy didn't miss much. Did he guess I was snooping, not filing?

"He went to the city for a meeting," I said politely. "I don't know when he'll be back."

"Berkshire and Gentry? Or Rittlestone and Weper?"

"Sorry, he didn't say." I closed the folder and quickly crossed to Hank's desk, glancing down at his calendar. "Rittlestone and Weper."

I looked at the man and smiled. He gave me a tight little smile in return, one that wouldn't have looked out of place on an Old West gunslinger facing down a challenger on a dusty Main Street. "Tell him David Vanitzky dropped by."

When he'd gone, I opened the folder I'd found containing personal information on corporate officers. David R. Vanitzky was Bates's executive vice president and chief financial officer. He was forty-eight years old, born in Chicago. He now lived in San Francisco, at a Russian Hill address. There was no wife's name listed, as there had been with all the other officers. I guessed he'd never married or, more likely at his age, was widowed or divorced.

Chief financial officer? I glanced at the door through which Vanitzky had disappeared. I wasn't sure I'd trust him with my meager financial assets. I'd seen eyes like that across a poker table.

CHAPTER 15

"I'M STARVED," GLADYS SAID WHEN I RETURNED TO CUBE City. "Let's go to lunch."

"I'm ready." I grabbed my purse and followed her around to the freight elevator, where she punched out. Then we headed for the stairs.

Once outside, we walked to the end of Webster Street and crossed the Embarcadero and cut through a large parking lot. Jack London Village was a shopping area located along the waterfront, a two-story collection of stores and restaurants constructed of wood and arrayed around a small landscaped square, with the estuary visible between two buildings. The deli was on the second floor, with tables inside as well as outside, along the railing.

"The sandwiches are good," Gladys said, as we scanned the bill of fare chalked on a board behind the counter. "Of course, what this area really needs is a good burrito joint. There are a lot of restaurants now that the Port of Oakland has put some money into development."

I nodded. "I can remember when it was almost deserted down here." Now the waterfront district along this three- or four-block stretch of the Embarcadero bustled, especially since the Jack London Cinema, a multiplex, had been built just the other side of Broadway.

Gladys ordered a turkey sandwich and I stuck to my old favorite, pastrami on rye. The guy behind the counter said he'd bring the sandwiches to us, so Gladys and I carried our soft drinks outside and snagged a recently vacated table with a view of the estuary.

"How long have you worked at Bates?" I asked, sipping root beer through a straw.

"Eleven years, as of last April. I used to work for a law firm over in San Francisco. Bates is much more low-key. It's not the way it was, though." She sighed. "There have certainly been a lot of changes in the last year. Not all of them good."

"I gathered that. I mean, what you said yesterday about Martha, leaving the sinking ship and all."

"I don't know if the ship's sinking for sure," Gladys said with a wry smile. "But it's taking on water, as my ex-husband the sailor used to say." The deli clerk arrived and placed our sandwiches on the table. When he'd gone, she said, "It must be easier if you're a temp. You can just pick up and leave. You always know the assignment is going to be over."

"They don't pay me as well," I pointed out. "And I don't have medical or retirement benefits."

"True." Gladys picked up half her sandwich and examined the turkey and lettuce leaves. "Now that I'm vested in the retirement plan, I'm not inclined to leave. Unless they decide to boot me out the door. A single mother like me depends on things like medical benefits and the pension plan."

"So what was it with Martha?" I nibbled my pastrami. "Didn't she like being stuck in those dull gray cubicles?"

Gladys rolled her eyes. "You are closer to the mark than you think. Those goddamned cubicles. I hate them. You can hear everything that goes on. That room we're in used to be the legal department conference room. Once upon a time, all the secretaries had their own offices, like that one you saw me in."

"The paralegal's office."

"Right. Nancy was next to Alex, where Hank is now. She's been Alex's secretary for more than fifteen years, since before he was general counsel. Of course, they remodeled the office when they put him in there. Same story with me and Martha. We each had offices next to the attorney we worked for." She regarded her turkey sandwich, looking nostalgic for better days. "Our offices had windows. Even if I did have a view of the freeway, it was sure nice to have a

window, especially one that opened. You know, those modern buildings with sealed windows make me feel trapped. Just like those damn
cubicles. At least when I had my own office, I felt like a human being
instead of furniture."

"What happened?" I asked, raising my pastrami on rye to my
mouth.

"We had this leveraged buyout about a year ago," Gladys said.
"Since the LBO, there have been two layoffs. And this summer, the
big wheels over on the executive side decided to shut down our production office down in San Leandro, where several of our plants are
located."

She took a bite of her sandwich and chewed while I leaned
forward, waiting for the rest of the story. "They brought all those
buyers, merchandisers, manufacturing and marketing people to
Oakland. Of course, they all have to have offices. They took over the
third floor, where human resources used to be, and HR moved up to
our floor. They had to have offices, too. So all the support staff—the
secretaries—got shochorned into these cubicles they threw up.
Three, four, sometimes five or six people in an office, where there
used to be one. At least there's only three of us in legal. They're even
more crowded in other departments. The secretaries just hate it.
Then they added the time clock."

"I saw it, back by the freight elevator."

"All these years I've been filling out a time card by hand, and now
I have to punch a clock. I suppose that's the modern, efficient way.
But to me, it feels like they don't trust me." Gladys frowned. "Bates
used to be a good place to work. I've heard so many people say that
over the past twelve months."

"So Martha decided to bail out."

"She's been looking for another job since the last layoff. Y'know,
layoff used to mean you were temporarily out of work, until they
called you back. Now it just means your ass is fired."

I nodded in agreement, reflecting on the state of the corporate
worker now that "downsizing," "restructuring," and "reengineering"
were popular buzzwords. The people who got downsized never
seemed to be those whose offices were on the top floor, and whose
salaries were continually restructured upward.

Gladys told me that Martha had found a high-paying job with a law firm in Palo Alto. "It means a hellacious commute," she added. "She lives in San Lorenzo. Now she's got to make that drive over to the Peninsula every day. No thanks. I know I could make more money if I worked in one of those big law offices over in San Francisco. But there's a lot of pressure in an outfit like that, and I really don't want to commute to the city. I live right here in Oakland, so it only takes me twenty minutes to drive to work. And you heard Nancy say it's just a ten-minute walk to where she lives in Chinatown."

"Tell me about Nancy. She seems a little prickly." I polished off the rest of my pastrami and reached for my root beer.

"Oh, she's like that till you get to know her." Gladys picked at the remains of her turkey sandwich. "Nancy's worked for Bates more than twenty years. Started as a clerk down in accounting." She took a sip of her drink. "Now, if you want prickly, you got Patricia Mayhew."

I nodded. "I notice she seems a little moody."

That was putting it mildly, I thought, recalling the attorney's abrupt manner when we'd been introduced yesterday. But she'd been more pleasant this morning, when she asked me to delay filing until she was out of the office this afternoon. Hank Irvin, on the other hand, seemed relaxed and easygoing all the time. I'd finally met Alex Campbell this morning, and the distinguished, gray-haired general counsel seemed equally friendly.

"I used to work for her, back before all the changes," Gladys said. "Now we all function like a typing pool. Nancy hates that. She likes to think she runs the legal department. Anyway, about Patricia, I never know whether she's going to be Miss Sweetness and Light, or bite my head off. She's been on the down side all week. Must be something bothering her."

"What could that be? Business, or personal?"

"Not sure." Gladys shot me a knowing look. "But I can guess. She's getting a divorce, and the Bates rumor mill says it's a nasty one. Maybe she's fighting with her soon-to-be ex. He's a litigator in some big law firm over in the city. You know how litigators are."

"Sure do." I laughed. "They take no prisoners. How long has Patricia been with Bates?"

"About eight years. It was really different back then. We used to have four attorneys and four secretaries, now we have three of each. We really need two paralegals, and now we don't have one. I know Alex is insisting on replacing Rob."

"Why wouldn't he?"

"The damned bean counters." Her face grew serious. "When Martha quit Wednesday morning, the powers that be over in human resources weren't going to authorize the department to hire a temp for her job. Cost-cutting measures and all that. In fact, Tonya Russell, the new HR director, told Alex Campbell that HR was planning to eliminate the position. That's how they reduce head count, as they call it these days. Easy, just don't hire anyone to replace the person who quit."

Tonya Russell was a familiar name, I thought. She was taking over the job of Laverne Carson, Ruby's friend.

Gladys continued with her story. "Well, Alex said, absolutely not, there are three attorneys and we need three secretaries. So Russell said, okay, we'll advertise the position and hire someone. But you can't have a temp. Now, that's ridiculous. It could take weeks to interview and hire someone. By that time Nancy was just furious. After lunch, she went in to talk with Alex, and next thing I know, HR gave in on hiring a temp. I have a feeling Nancy threatened to quit if they didn't."

"So here I am, for the duration." I leaned back in my chair. "Thanks for telling me. It's always nice to know what's going on when you work temp jobs. Office politics and all that. What do you know about Tonya Russell?"

"She came from Rittlestone and Weper's Chicago office, I hear. She'll keep Ed Decker on his toes. He's the vice president in charge of human resources. Laverne's retiring, not by choice, according to the grapevine. Which also says she's not too happy about it."

I gathered up the remains of my lunch. "Like you, I'd always heard Bates was a good place to work. But what you're telling me seems to say otherwise."

"It was, until that LBO," Gladys said, frowning as she finished her drink. "Then everything changed. Things got meaner. Everyone's looking out for number one, if you know what I mean." A train whistle blew, sounding as though it was close. "Uh-oh, a train. We'd better go."

We hurried down the steps and spotted the train as we hit the parking lot. It was a slow-moving freight, headed toward the Port of Oakland piers to the northwest. Slow or not, I wasn't going to play chicken with a train just so I could get back to work on time.

"We'd better take the pedestrian bridge," I said, pointing at the structure that loomed at the corner of Alice and the Embarcadero.

"Thank God they built this thing." Gladys changed direction, and we headed across the parking lot toward the pedestrian overpass. "Once I got stuck on this side for thirty minutes. I have seen people climb through the trains when they're stopped, but that's foolhardy. That engine could start moving again, and you could fall on the tracks. Besides," she added with a laugh, "being caught by a train down here is a time-honored excuse for being late back from lunch. Or it used to be. Until they installed that damn time clock."

We climbed the stairs of the overpass and crossed the walkway, looking down at the freight train, stacked double high with containers. On the other side was the Amtrak station, a couple of blocks from the Bates building.

"What about this paralegal who died?" I asked as we walked through the railroad station parking lot. "Any idea what happened?"

Gladys shook her head. "His name was Rob Lawter. He'd worked here four years, a really nice guy. He lived in an apartment on Alice Street, near Lake Merritt, and rode his bike to work. I don't know much about it. I guess he fell out the window of his apartment. I found out about it Friday morning. Some policeman came to the office and told Alex Campbell. Alex called everyone into his office and broke the news. It was a really weird scene."

Her choice of words was curious. "Weird? How so?"

Gladys looked troubled. "Well, we'd just found out Rob was dead. Nancy, Martha, and I were really upset. So was Alex. But it seemed to me that Patricia and Hank were just going through the motions. Not really sorry Rob was dead, y'know. Only worried about whether we were getting another paralegal to replace him, since the work is piled up. Of course, it's always piled up."

"That's pretty damn cold," I said.

"Yeah, you know it." Gladys gave me a sardonic smile. "These days, I feel like just one interchangeable cog in the machine. Welcome to corporate America."

CHAPTER *16*

WHEN GLADYS AND I STEPPED OFF THE ELEVATOR ON
the fourth floor of the Bates building, we turned left and
walked along the south hallway toward Cube City. As we reached the
corner, the door to the general counsel's office opened and three men
walked out. One of them I recognized as Alex Campbell. The second
man I'd never seen before. He had a look that shouted "retired military," from the way he carried himself to the iron-gray buzz cut.

The third man was my ex-husband, Sergeant Sid Vernon of the
Oakland Police Department's Homicide Section.

Uh-oh, I told myself. I was going to get a phone call from him, bet
on it.

I managed to keep my poker face as Gladys and I walked past
them. Sid's mouth tightened. His tawny gold eyes flicked over me, in
my unaccustomed business attire. But he didn't say anything. I felt
the gray-haired man's eyes on me as Sid turned his attention back to
the two men in the doorway.

I followed Gladys into Cube City. Nancy wasn't at her workstation. "Who were those men with Alex Campbell?" I asked.

"Don't know that tall one with the sandy hair, but hmm . . . I
wouldn't kick him out of bed."

I repressed a grin at Gladys's assessment of my ex. Sid was a
good-looking man, with his tall, broad-shouldered frame and the
gold cat's eyes that went with his gold hair, threaded now with a lot
of silver. He moved like a tiger cat, and he was pretty good in bed, as
I recalled. "What about the other guy, with the short gray hair?"

"Buck Tarcher. He's the head of corporate security. Used to be in the Marines."

"I thought so," I said. "I know a retired admiral. They've all got that look, like they're still in uniform."

If Sid was here talking with Campbell and Tarcher, it had to be about Rob's death and that threatening note he'd received. Sid was doing the same thing I was, checking out possible leads at Rob's workplace, but his was the more official visit. As for me, I was wondering when and how I could get into Rob's office for a look at the place.

Patricia Mayhew had eaten lunch at her desk. When I took her the afternoon mail, she was just sweeping the remains of a sandwich into her wastebasket. She'd been blowing hot and cold in the two days I'd been working at Bates, mostly cold. But this afternoon her manner had moved toward the warm end of the spectrum. Must have something to do with the fact that it was Friday and the weekend loomed on the horizon. When I saw the small overnight bag on the floor next to the credenza, I recalled what Nancy had said this morning. Patricia planned to be out of town this weekend, so she couldn't attend Rob's funeral.

"There's a long document on this tape," she told me, handing me a cassette and a work request. "I'd like you to do that right away. I'm leaving early, and I want to see a draft before I go."

"Sure thing," I told her, as I scooped papers and files from her out basket. "Going away for the weekend?"

"Yes." Her mouth curved into a smile. "Mendocino. We want to get on the road before the traffic gets too bad."

I noticed her use of the plural pronoun. According to Gladys, Patricia was going through a divorce. I didn't think her ex was the reason for the smile, so there must be a significant other in the picture.

I headed for Hank Irvin's office and placed his opened mail on the top of an already overflowing in box. There wasn't anything in the out box, since he was still gone. As I turned to leave, the office door opened. Hank had returned from San Francisco. He smiled as he shed his suit coat and hung it on a nearby coatrack. "Hold down the fort while I was gone?" he asked.

"It's been fairly quiet. Oh, David Vanitzky dropped by this morning, looking for you."

"Ah." Something in the way Hank said that made me look up at him. My private investigator antennae went up and started vibrating. "Did you tell him where I was?" he asked, his voice casual, as though it didn't really matter.

"Yes. Rittlestone and Weper. It was on your calendar."

A flicker passed over Hank's face. Curious. Didn't he want Vanitzky to know where he'd gone? If that was the case, why?

Come to think of it, Vanitzky had specifically asked whether Hank had gone to Rittlestone and Weper or Berkshire and Gentry. The name of the big law firm was doubly familiar. Rob Lawter had been employed there, as a paralegal, before coming to work at Bates.

"Berkshire and Gentry," I said. "That's a big law firm over in the city. I saw their letterhead on a lot of the correspondence I filed this morning. They must handle a lot of work for Bates."

"Oh, yeah." Hank glanced down, his right hand sifting through some papers on the top of his in box. "I used to work there myself."

"Really? What made you leave the fast track and come to work at Bates?"

Hank's head came up, and his look was guarded, as though he thought he'd said something he shouldn't have. "Oh, a lot of things. Listen, I have a priority project for you." He pulled open the top drawer of one of the filing cabinets and removed a folder, opening it. He jotted a document number on a small notepad and tore off the sheet, handing it to me. "Print out a copy of this agreement for me. I'll make the changes in red ink, then you'll input the revisions. It's a draft, highly confidential, and it'll have to go out this afternoon, FedEx, Saturday delivery."

I glanced at the piece of paper he'd just handed me, and thought of the long document Patricia wanted before she left early. Looked like this would be a typical Friday afternoon reminiscent of my law firm days, when everyone was scrambling to get work completed before the weekend. I turned to go and nearly bumped into David Vanitzky, who'd just opened the door.

"Sorry," I said, practically nose to nose with the chief financial officer. Yes, his left earlobe had been pierced at one time. As I glanced away I saw amusement glinting in his gray eyes and a smile playing on the thin lips beneath his bony nose. He stepped aside, holding the door open for me so I could carry my armload of work out to the hall. I felt his gaze on my back, and it wasn't businesslike. I was definitely being checked out.

"Joe had to cancel," I heard Vanitzky tell Hank as the door shut. "So the poker game's at my place. Tonight, eight o'clock."

I was right, I thought. Vanitzky's a cardsharp. And I'd bet playing poker with that guy meant bring money and be prepared to leave it.

I sped across the hall to my cubicle, dumped my load of mail, and looked through the computer files for the document Hank wanted me to print. I located it, opened the file, and skimmed through the words that appeared on my screen. It was a separation agreement, outlining the terms of departure and the severance package given to someone whose name I didn't recognize. He'd been a vice president down in accounting, and it was a good bet he hadn't left Bates by his own choice. I recalled Nancy telling me that Alex Campbell handled employment matters. I would have thought he'd draft this kind of agreement.

I sent the document to the printer. When it was done, I picked it up and headed back across the hall to Hank's office, wondering if Vanitzky was still there.

I leaned close to the door, listening. I heard Hank's tenor, saying something I couldn't quite make out. Were they still talking about poker?

"A million dollars," Vanitzky said, his low raspy voice carrying through the door. "Give or take a few thousand." Then he laughed, as though it didn't matter.

If they were talking about poker, the game was way out of my price range. It sounded as though Vanitzky thought it was small change. When you're a corporate CFO, however, I suppose a million bucks doesn't sound like much. From the standpoint of Jeri Howard, self-employed private investigator, it's more than I'll ever see in my lifetime.

Hank was talking now. "First I've heard of it. What about Morris and Ed?"

Vanitzky laughed again, the sound both cynical and derisive. "Morris couldn't find his ass with both hands. Now Ed, he's a different matter. When it comes to asses, he's only concerned about covering his own."

"We may not need to worry about Ed. Who else knows about this?" I heard the buzz of an intercom, but Hank evidently ignored it.

"Besides Morris and Ed? You, me, Tonya, Jeff, Alex."

"You haven't told Yale? Or Frank?"

"Not yet."

There was a pause, then Hank muttered, ". . . damage control."

When Vanitzky spoke again, his tone had turned serious. "Damage control? There's blood all over the floor. Mopping it up ain't gonna be pretty. In fact, you and I are gonna get blood all over our hands."

I tried to make sense of what I'd just heard. It was clear Vanitzky didn't have a high opinion of Morris and Ed. And he hadn't told Yale Rittlestone or Frank Weper that something was going on, something that involved money and required damage control. But what? Some sort of financial discrepancy, to the tune of a million dollars? Where was the money supposed to be, and where had it gone? I leaned closer, hoping to hear more.

"What about Yale and Frank?" Hank asked.

"I'll handle them," Vanitzky said. "Jeff is . . ."

At that moment, Nancy Fong exited Alex Campbell's office. I raised my hand and rapped sharply on the door, then opened it. Hank was standing behind his desk, mouth open as though he'd been about to say something. Vanitzky sat in one of the chairs in front of the desk, one long leg crossed over the other. He was slumped down on his backbone, shoulders and head back. Though the posture was relaxed, he wasn't. He watched me as I walked over to Hank and handed him the document he'd requested.

Nancy had followed me into Hank's office. She glanced at me sharply, making me wonder if she'd seen me with my ear to Hank's door. "Hank," she said, "Alex would like to see you in his office." As she turned to leave, she nodded at Vanitzky. "Hello, David."

"Hello, Nancy." Vanitzky unfolded himself from the chair and stood up. "I'll talk with you later," he said, glancing at Hank. Then his eyes rested on me. "I don't believe we've been formally introduced."

"Jeri Howard," I said.

"David Vanitzky." He held out his right hand, and I took it. He had a strong handshake, and his fingers seemed to linger as they touched mine.

"Jeri's taking Martha's place," Hank said, stepping from behind his desk. "She just started yesterday. Jeri, as soon as I talk with Alex, I'll mark up that document, and you can make the changes."

Vanitzky relinquished my hand, then headed for the door, followed by Hank.

I returned to my cubicle and got started on the tape Patricia wanted me to transcribe. It was a long internal memorandum addressed to Alex Campbell and Nolan Ward, the senior vice president in charge of production. It concerned the Food and Drug Administration's latest proposals concerning food safety.

By the time I was finished, my ears were hurting from the earpieces of the transcriber, and both my back and shoulders ached. I printed out a draft and carried it back to her office. "Good," she said, a bit impatiently. "I'll read it over, and then I want you to fax it to outside counsel over at Berkshire and Gentry."

When I got back to my cubicle, Gladys was muttering to herself as she typed an address on a label. "If it's Friday, it's the FedEx Follies," she groused. "Everything's got to be done Friday afternoon so it can go overnight."

"I hear that," I said.

Hank came in carrying several pages marked liberally in red ink, with "Draft" and "Confidential" printed in block letters at the top of the first page. When I glanced through the separation agreement, noting the changes Hank had made, I saw that he'd inserted the name of the person who was getting separated from his job.

Ed Decker, the executive Gladys had mentioned at lunch. Was this the same Ed that Hank and Vanitzky had been talking about earlier? I recalled Hank's words. "We may not need to worry about Ed." I guessed they didn't, not if Ed was on his way out the door.

I hauled out the three-ring binder I'd found on my desk, the one that contained the company directory. Sure enough, Ed Decker was a senior vice president, the head of the Bates Inc. human resources department. As HR director, Ruby's friend Laverne Carson reported to him. But only for another week. Laverne had been replaced by Tonya Russell, from Rittlestone and Weper's Chicago office.

So why was Ed Decker being fired? Was it because of that million dollars, give or take a few thousand, that Vanitzky spoke of so casually?

I checked the listing of corporate officers in the front of the directory. Morris, the guy who was supposed to be doing damage control, was Morris Upton, senior vice president for public affairs. Then I got busy, making the changes that Hank wanted in the document. Ed Decker might be looking at unemployment, but he'd be doing so with a severance package that would cushion the blow. It included a sizable check as well as lots of stock options he could use when Bates went public again.

I finished making the changes, ran the spell checker, and sent the document to the printer. Then I took it to Hank, who asked me to wait while he read it over. I watched his eyes flick quickly over the pages.

"Looks good," he said. "Now, after you make a copy, put the original in a plain envelope marked 'Confidential,' then FedEx it to Eric Nybaken over at Rittlestone and Weper in San Francisco. His address should be in Martha's Rolodex. Make sure that's for Saturday delivery."

I followed Hank's instructions, then flipped through the Rolodex to find the address of Rittlestone and Weper at Four Embarcadero Center in San Francisco. As it turned out, Eric Nybaken was Yale Rittlestone's personal assistant. Too bad he had to work Saturday.

I carried the completed FedEx package downstairs to the first-floor mail room, where it would be picked up later that afternoon. When I returned, both Gladys and Nancy were away from their desks.

I looked through the Rolodex again, hoping Martha Bronson had left behind some indication of how I could get in touch with her. She hadn't.

With one eye on the door, I moved around the end of my cubicle, toward Gladys's desk. I flipped through the B section of her Rolodex for Martha. Pay dirt. Martha Bronson's address and phone number were written on one of the cards. I quickly scribbled the information I needed on a slip of paper and stuck the paper into the pocket of the skirt I wore. I heard Gladys's voice out in the hall. By the time she came through the door, I was back at my own desk, phone in hand as though I were just finishing a call.

Martha presented something of a problem. I wanted to talk with her about Rob Lawter, to see what she knew about him and what he was working on when he died. But I didn't want Martha to know I was a private investigator. I had a feeling she and Gladys were friends, and I didn't want to risk her mentioning my name to Gladys.

"Long day," I said as I hung up the phone. Then I stretched my arms above my head. I didn't have to fake my yawn. It was nearly four. Patricia had long since departed. As for me, I was tired and remembering why most workers thanked God it was Friday. "Say, who is this Vanitzky guy? I ran into him in Hank's office."

"Oh, ho." Gladys had a wicked twinkle in her brown eyes. There was a can of soda on her desk, and she took a sip before saying anything else. "He's a Rattlesnake and Viper man."

"Rattlesnake and Viper?" I repeated, looking confused, just the way I had when Bette Bates Palmer had used the term.

"That's what everyone calls Rittlestone and Weper. The LBO, remember?"

"So Vanitzky used to work for them?"

"Yeah. He was Frank Weper's right-hand man, back in Chicago. The old chief financial officer was Len Turley. He'd been here since Moses was an altar boy. After the LBO he retired, except I think he was helped out the door, if you know what I mean. Same situation as Laverne Carson over in HR."

The way Ed Decker, Laverne's boss, was about to be helped out the door. I wondered how many others of Bates's old guard, the officers who'd run the company before the takeover, had been replaced by Rattlesnake and Viper men.

"So Vanitzky took over Turley's job," I said. "He looks like a corporate raider."

"A walk-the-plank pirate, that's what he reminds me of. He's always making eyes at the ladies. His own secretary is Esther Roades. She's a battle-ax who's been with the company for a hundred years. I guess they stuck him with an older woman so he won't make a pass at her and land us all with a sexual harassment charge." Gladys made a face. "I hear he's a gambler, too, at the racetrack all the time. Just the kind of guy you want handling the company's money."

And he played poker on Friday nights with Hank Irvin. From what I'd heard, it sounded like a regular game that rotated around the homes of the participants. Was Hank a gambler, too?

"He seems to be friends with Hank."

"Oh, yeah," Gladys told me. "Hank's a Rattlesnake and Viper man, too. He used to be a partner at Berkshire and Gentry, which is Rittlestone and Weper's pet law firm. First chance they got, R&W got rid of Lauren Musso, the lawyer who used to handle corporate, and brought in their fair-haired boy Hank."

I mulled this over. Hank had told me he used to work for Berkshire and Gentry, but when I'd asked him why he made the change from a law firm to a corporate legal department, he'd been vague. With her next words, Gladys provided the answer that Hank hadn't.

"You mark my words, they're gonna do it to Alex Campbell, too. And after they boot him out the door, Hank Irvin will be the next general counsel."

CHAPTER *17*

FRIDAY AFTERNOON SID LEFT A MESSAGE ON MY OFFICE AN-
swering machine and another on the machine at home. Both
messages demanded an answer to essentially the same question.
What was I doing over at Bates?

I didn't call Sid back. I managed to avoid speaking with him until
Saturday morning. I was standing in front of my open closet, in my
underwear, trying to decide what to wear to Rob's funeral. When the
phone rang, I picked up the receiver, expecting Cassie.

"What the hell do you think you're doing?" Sid growled at me.

"A little investigating. Thank you for not blowing my cover."

"Yet." He underscored the word ominously. "If I should happen
to mention it to that security guy, Tarcher, he'd bounce you out of
there so fast—"

"Just trying to find out who killed my client."

"That's my job. I'm the homicide detective, remember. You're the
pushy PI who's got no business getting involved in this investigation."

"I'm the PI whose client got pushed out a fifth-floor window, remember. So I'm already involved." The best defense is an offense, I
figured, so I turned the question back at him. "Why were you at
Bates yesterday, Sid?"

"I'm not telling you squat, Jeri."

"Is that fair?" I wheedled. With the phone tucked under my chin,
I took a gray linen dress, then a navy blue cotton, from the closet
and held them up, examining each for wrinkles, fallen hems, or missing buttons. "I gave you a copy of that threatening note Rob re-

ceived, just like a good citizen. That's what you were doing, admit it. You were following up my lead. And all I get in the way of thanks is the rough side of your tongue."

He sighed. "You wear me out, damn it. I don't like it when you get in the middle of a murder investigation. You run into any leads over at Bates?"

I hung both dresses back in the closet and sat down on my bed. "Not yet. I've only worked there two days. Give me some time."

"You'll pass along any information you get." The way he said it, that was an order, not a request. "And get out of there at the first sign of trouble, or if you're made. Buck Tarcher's no fool. You get out of line with your snooping, he'll spot you for sure."

"I promise. And I'll be careful." He groused at me some more, but I could tell it was just part of the routine. "So, did Campbell or Tarcher have anything to say about the note?"

"Nothing," Sid told me. "Neither of them had any theories as to why someone would send Lawter a note like that."

But now that Alex Campbell and Buck Tarcher knew about it, they'd start investigating internally, which meant they'd be looking for the same information I was. It increased my chances of being found out. On the other hand, if I kept an eye on what Campbell was doing, maybe I'd find out what had prompted Rob to blow the whistle.

I leaned back against the pillows on my bed and switched the phone from one ear to the other. "Hey, Sid. I'm buying a house."

"No kidding? Where?"

"Chabot Road in Rockridge, near the Berkeley border. We'll be neighbors, sort of." Sid lived on Manila Avenue in the Temescal section of Oakland, southwest of the house I was already thinking of as mine. "It's really a terrific house, even if it does need some work. I knew it was perfect the minute I saw it. Which was just last week, but the sellers have accepted the offer. We've got the termite inspection scheduled for next week, and then the appraiser."

"That's great news, Jeri." His voice changed, and he was no longer the gruff cop, but the man I still liked, even though our brief marriage hadn't worked out. "Congratulations. I'm glad you were able to swing it."

"Thanks. I'll call you when it comes time to move. Maybe you can help me carry boxes."

"You buy the pizza and beer," he said with a laugh, "and I could be persuaded."

I hung up the phone and went back to the closet, deciding I would wear the gray linen. Once I'd dressed, I left Abigail and Black Bart catnapping together on the sofa and headed out to my car. Cassie and Eric lived in the condo Cassie had bought several years ago, on Lakeshore Avenue. They were looking for a house to buy, as well, but so far hadn't found anything they liked. I was familiar with that song and dance.

Cassie wore a forest green dress, with a tiny hat to match. She also carried another hat, black straw with a wide brim and a veil. This was for me. Since I'd heard Nancy Fong and Gladys Olivette talking about the funeral yesterday, I knew that they, Alex Campbell, and Hank Irvin would be there. It was also possible that others from Bates would attend. If any of them saw me, they'd wonder why I was there, hence the disguise. Besides paying my respects to my client, I wasn't sure what else I hoped to discover at Rob's funeral. An unguarded look on someone's face, an overheard conversation, a curious interaction between some of the people attending—any of these might provide a lead, an avenue of inquiry.

Cassie set the hat on the back seat. Once she was belted into the passenger seat of my Toyota, I headed for the MacArthur Freeway. We drove southeast along the hills, dry in the Indian summer heat of September.

"When you were at Berkshire and Gentry, did you know an attorney named Hank Irvin?" I asked Cassie. "He was a partner until he left to go to work for Bates."

"It's been six years since I left. Berkshire's a big firm with lots of attorneys. Irvin . . ." She shook her head. "The name doesn't sound familiar."

"If he's at the funeral, I'll point him out to you. Maybe he'll look familiar. Next question. He took over as corporate attorney from a woman named Lauren Musso, who was evidently fired to make room for Irvin. How do I find her, short of ransacking someone's desk for a forwarding address?"

"There I can help you," Cassie said. "Surely she's a member of the California State Bar Association. If she is, I can locate her with a couple of calls."

"You have your assignment," I told her, as I took the exit off the freeway.

There was a parking lot across the street from the Santos-Robinson Mortuary on Estudillo Avenue, but I parked on the street a block away, near the San Leandro Public Library. Cassie arranged the hat and veil so that it obscured most of my face, then we walked toward the building. We stayed on the periphery of the small group of people who had gathered on the sidewalk outside.

In a black dress with white collar and cuffs, Robin Hartzell stood next to her brother, Doug, who'd cleaned up and put on a suit. She spotted me with Cassie, but other than a tiny nod in my direction, she ignored my presence.

Carol Hartzell was getting plenty of support as she leaned on the arm of her boyfriend, Leon Gomes. She greeted people and dabbed her eyes with a white handkerchief. Gomes, on the other hand, seemed distracted. He was talking with another man, a frown on his dark face, gesturing with his thick-fingered hands. As Cassie and I approached, I heard Leon say, "There isn't going to be any strike. Take it from me, the union's just bluffing."

A strike threat at Bates? That was interesting, though I wasn't sure whether it had anything to do with my current dilemma, who killed Rob Lawter and why. I'd have to put out some feelers on Monday when I went back to work in the legal department.

I glanced around. Diana Palmer, Rob's former fiancée, was here, and so was Sally Morgan, Rob's next-door neighbor. But I kept my head tilted down and hoped they saw only the hat and veil. It seemed to be working. Their eyes moved past me without recognition.

Then I saw a knot of people crossing the street from the parking lot. It looked like the contingent from Bates Inc. Alex Campbell and Nancy Fong were in the lead followed by Gladys Olivette and Hank Irvin. Several other people, mostly women, brought up the rear. A couple of faces I recognized, although I couldn't put names to them. Perhaps I'd seen them in the hallways at Bates.

"That's Irvin," I said. "The good-looking guy in the blue suit."

Cassie peered at him. "He does look vaguely familiar. But that's all. Guess we were at Berkshire the same time."

As the Bates people approached the steps leading to the mortuary, a large blond woman in a blue dress left the shady spot where she'd been standing and walked up to greet Gladys and the others, who all seemed to know her. I could tell from Nancy Fong's body language that she didn't much care for the woman. Martha Bronson, I told myself. This must be the woman who had quit without notice, thus complicating Nancy's life and providing me with the opportunity to fill her job.

Cassie and I waited until everyone had filed into the mortuary before we entered and took a seat on the back row of chairs. The assembled mourners numbered about fifty. The service itself was brief and perfunctory, performed by someone I took to be a minister. I guessed from the way he read his lines, he hadn't known Rob.

When it was over, Cassie and I skipped the line of people who were filing past Rob's sister and her children. We were the first ones out of the building, and we stood near the hedge that bordered the mortuary property. The Bates people headed across the street, but the blond woman in the blue dress walked past us and headed down the sidewalk, in the direction of the library, where I'd parked my car. I nodded at Cassie, indicating that we should follow.

"You ask the questions," I told her.

"What am I asking?" she whispered, her sidelong glance full of consternation.

"Find out who she is and how she knew Rob. You're a trial lawyer, for God's sake. You can do that."

"I do it better in a courtroom."

We quickened our pace to catch up with the woman. As we did so, Cassie glanced toward her and sighed. "I just hate funerals, don't you? Especially for someone like Rob."

The blond woman turned her head and gave us a once-over. She was in her forties, with a round tanned face and crinkly lines at the corners of her eyes and mouth. When she spoke, her voice was pleasant and noncommittal. "Yes, he was a nice guy. I hate to see anyone go that way. Or that young."

"I really got to know him when we worked at Berkshire, over in the city," Cassie continued. "Such a wonderful sense of humor, and he always had good things to say about people, no matter how frantic the job got. That's hard to do, what with the pressure of a big law firm like that."

The woman laughed. "I guess that would be a good way to describe Rob. Grace under pressure."

"You worked with him, too?" Cassie asked.

She glanced at me, then at Cassie, as though considering her response. "Yes, I did. At Bates, the food processing company, in the legal department. We had a lot of pressure there, too, even if it wasn't a law firm. I got so frustrated with the place I quit. But Rob, he'd just smile and say, Martha, don't let it get to you."

"Hi, Martha. I'm Cassie."

Martha Bronson looked at me, as though waiting for me to introduce myself. I slumped a bit, and tilted my head so the veil obscured my face. "Jeri," I said, so quietly I hoped it sounded like Mary or Terry. "Bates? Isn't that the place that had the leveraged buyout last year?"

"Leveraged buyout." Martha spat out the words as though they tasted bad. "Just another term for firing all the peons so the bigwigs on the top floor can make money."

"There's sure a lot of that merger mania stuff going on," I said. "And you're right, it always seems like the workers lose out when that happens. Is that why you left Bates?"

Martha stopped next to a brown Ford and pulled a key ring from her handbag. "I managed to survive both layoffs. But still, that's small comfort. Even if I didn't lose my job, I'd wonder if my name would be on the list for the next one. So I started looking for a new job. Found one in Palo Alto. It wasn't my first choice and it's a longer commute, but it's more money than I was getting at Bates."

"Last time I talked with Rob, he was uncertain about his future with Bates," Cassie said, which was fairly close to the truth. If he'd blown the whistle on some illegal activity, his job would have been in jeopardy, so he'd consulted Cassie about his rights. By mentioning it now, Cassie was fishing. We both waited to see if Martha took the bait.

"Rob liked Bates." Martha shrugged as she unlocked the car. "He told me once it was the kind of homegrown company that inspired loyalty. People used to work for Bates for their whole adult life. I knew a guy out in one of the plants who'd been with the company nearly fifty years. But all that's changed now. That kind of relationship is long gone. Why should employees be loyal to a company when it doesn't give a damn about them? When I think about what they did to one of the lawyers I used to work with . . ."

Cassie and I traded looks. Martha had to be referring to the woman Hank Irvin had replaced. "I think I know who you mean," Cassie said, without missing a beat. "I met her at a party a few months ago. Her name was Lauren . . ."

"Musso," Martha said obligingly. "She'd been with Bates a long time. Right after the LBO, they dumped her to make room for another attorney. They being those fat-cat executives. If Alex Campbell had any starch in his backbone, he wouldn't have let it happen. But he's too busy watching his own back, from what I hear. Poor Lauren. It took her months to find another job. But she really likes where she's working now. In fact, I interviewed with that company. That job was my first choice, but I didn't get it. I must say, the Financial District would have been a shorter commute."

I HADN'T FORGOTTEN ABOUT CHARLIE KELLERMAN.
I was sure Rob Lawter's other next-door neighbor had seen something, perhaps the two people Sally Morgan heard in Rob's apartment before my client took his fatal plunge out the window. All I had to back up that theory was what Charlie said Monday morning at the Alice Street apartment building.

"Did they send you?" he'd asked, before he clammed up and scooted into his messy apartment, carrying his sack full of expensive booze.

Who were "they"? I asked myself Sunday afternoon, as I sat in my car across the street from the apartment building. I hadn't seen Charlie Kellerman in the hour I'd been there. Then I spotted Leon Gomes at the wheel of a rented truck, jockeying the vehicle into a space in front. With him were half a dozen guys I'd never seen before. After Leon parked the truck, they opened the back of the truck and hoisted out two dollies, some furniture pads, and several stacks of flattened cardboard that I identified as moving boxes that hadn't been put together yet. They hauled all of this down the sidewalk, stood waiting while Leon fiddled with some keys, then went into the building.

I didn't have to have a printed scorecard to know what they were doing. I was just curious as to why Carol Hartzell and her children weren't part of this packing party. About twenty minutes after the men went into the building, they started carrying Rob's furniture out and loading it into the truck. This was followed by a procession of boxes and odd-sized things that wouldn't fit into cartons. The last things to be loaded into the truck were Rob's bicycle and four potted plants of varying sizes.

Someone must have done some preliminary packing during the week, because the whole process took them less than two hours. All that was left of Rob's presence in this building was an empty apartment.

I watched Leon get into the truck and pilot it away from the curb, wondering where Rob's things were going and whether I could get close enough to take a look at them. I still hadn't seen Charlie Kellerman, but fifteen minutes after Leon left, my quarry came through the front door of the building. He stopped for a moment, as though surveying the street, then slowly and carefully came down the shallow steps. He walked toward Alice Street with the same deliberation, then turned right, moving toward Seventeenth. I got out of my car and followed him. At the corner, he turned right, then right again on Jackson Street. I kept my distance as he strolled past the first building. Then he turned and entered a market on the ground floor of the second apartment building.

I followed him inside. The store was larger than it looked from the outside, and it had plentiful supplies of things a city dweller might want to have conveniently near, primarily food and drink. I suspected it was drink Charlie was after, the kind with an alcohol content.

He picked up a red plastic basket from a stack near the door and made his way down one of the aisles, ignoring the cans and boxes. He was more interested in bottles, especially the hard stuff. I watched as he loaded his basket with Scotch, jamming in as many bottles as the basket would hold. When he turned to carry his supplies to the market's only cash register, he found me blocking his way.

"Hello, Charlie," I said. "Remember me?"

He squinted as though he wasn't sure. Then his eyes turned wary and he licked his lips. "Yeah."

"Good so far. Who did you see a week ago Thursday night, when Rob died?"

He raised a hand and scratched at the gray stubble on his chin. "Wha' makes you think I saw anything?"

"The last time I saw you, Charlie, you asked if 'they' sent me. That makes me think you saw something. Who are 'they'?"

His eyes moved quickly from left to right, as though he was looking for an escape route. But he was stymied in either direction. On his right was a tall wire rack, its shelves full of bread from several East Bay bakeries. On his left, a middle-aged woman set her over-flowing basket on the floor near Charlie's feet, then straightened as she peered at bottles of wine. Then there was me, standing in front of him.

"Do you know who 'they' are?" I asked.

"I might," he said, after a moment. He looked longingly at the Scotch in his basket and then at the cash register.

"Come on, Charlie. I need something more specific than that. Two men? Two women?" I watched for body language, some give-away in his bloodshot blue eyes. He didn't react to either suggestion. "Or one of each?"

Now Kellerman's eyes flickered, and he stared at me for a moment. He raised his hand to his chin again. Then he looked away. Okay, I thought. Progress. It was a man and a woman. "You'd seen one of them, or both, before. Where?"

He licked his lips again as the woman next to him made her selection, picked up her basket, and moved off. He took a step in that direction, the Scotch bottles in his basket clinking together as he moved. One of them tipped precariously near the edge, and I reached out to straighten it. He gazed at the amber liquid in the bottle as though he hated the thought of losing a drop. His voice was a whispery rasp. "What's it worth to you?"

I'd figured someone had slipped him some cash, when I'd seen the pricey liquor in his grocery sack last Monday. From the looks of his basket, he was still drinking the good stuff. I wondered if he'd gotten another infusion of capital from whoever wanted to keep him quiet. A recent payoff, I thought, mindful of the fact that Leon Gomes had just been at the Alice Street building.

"Is there an asking price?" I countered.

Charlie narrowed his eyes as though he were deciding how much to charge me for the information I wanted. Then someone bumped into me, an elderly woman with one of those small wheeled shopping

carts. Charlie took advantage of the distraction to make a break for
the cash register. I followed, keeping some space between us, noting
the large denominations of the bills he used to pay for his liquor. For
someone who didn't have a job and supposedly relied on the kind-
ness of his brother for spending money, Charlie had quite a bankroll.
I didn't know if the twenty bucks I'd been prepared to slip him
would buy me much more than the information I'd already pried
out of him.

"Are we going to talk?" I asked him when we were outside the
market.

Charlie ignored me and walked quickly back in the direction he'd
come. I kept up with him. He didn't speak until we were back on Alice Street, in front of his building. "Maybe I'll call you," he said.

I dropped one of my business cards into the sack of Scotch bottles. "You do that. And soon." I watched him scurry up the sidewalk
and into the building.

I drove over to my office on Franklin Street and started a background search on Charlie Kellerman. He must know one or both of
the people who were in Rob's apartment before he died. They knew
it, too. I was betting that's how Charlie got the thick wad of bills I'd
seen in his wallet at the market.

A man and a woman, I thought, leaning back in my chair. Could
it be Leon Gomes and Carol Hartzell?

Charlie might know who they were, if he'd seen them in the hall
during a visit to Rob. I couldn't picture Carol being involved in
Rob's death, though. Both times I'd seen her, she behaved like a
woman who was genuinely grieving the loss of her brother. Unless
she was a better actress than I gave her credit for. That was certainly
a possibility.

Leon had been at the apartment building earlier this afternoon,
with the men who'd helped him clear out Rob's apartment. He
could have given Charlie some of those greenbacks. And it was Leon
who'd been telling everyone that Rob had killed himself. Were his
words a ruse to direct attention away from the fact that Leon knew
Rob's death wasn't a suicide?

Why would Leon want to kill Rob? It must have something to
do with that argument they'd had more than a week before Rob's
death. Something to do with work, Robin Hartzell had told me the

last time we'd talked. I wondered if she'd been able to find out anything more.

The phone rang. Somehow I wasn't surprised to hear Robin's voice, as though she knew I'd been thinking about her. "I saw Leon this afternoon," I told her. "At Rob's building."

"Yeah, he and a bunch of guys from the plant went over there to clear out Rob's apartment. He even arranged for a cleaning service to come in afterward. He didn't even tell us he was going to do it, until right before he left. I offered to help, so did Doug. But Leon said he wanted to spare us all the trouble, Mom included. Spare us." Her voice was edged with scorn. "Can you believe that?"

"Sounds like you don't. Why?" I wasn't sure I did, either. Leon's gesture would feel more altruistic if I hadn't just been auditioning him for the role of Rob's killer.

"I dunno," Robin said. "He's just such a control freak. And we're Rob's family. I think he should have consulted us before he jumped right in with his usual take-charge trip. Besides, I can't help feeling he wants to pry into Rob's stuff."

"So do I. Where did he take it?"

"They were unloading all of Rob's things into the garage when I left. I'm calling from the library, where I'm supposed to be studying. Mom says she's gonna keep all that stuff there until she decides what to do with it. We might use some of the furniture, and she's already said Doug could have Rob's bike. I'm pretty sure she wants to go through the papers and books and pictures and all that. I don't know when she's going to start, though. She's still pretty weepy, especially after the funeral. You want to come over some time this week?"

"Yes, I do. Soon. I need to get a look at Rob's things before your mother does. But I'll have to see how the week plays out. Any luck in remembering what Leon and Rob were arguing about?"

"Not so far," Robin told me. "But I'm sure it had something to do with Bates. I could just come right out and ask Leon about it."

"Not yet. I don't want Leon to know anyone's interested."

"Okay," she said reluctantly. "But if I find him prowling around in Rob's stuff, I'm sure as hell gonna ask him why."

CHAPTER 19

IT SEEMED AS THOUGH EVERYONE WAS INTERESTED IN ROB Lawter's things. On Monday morning I caught Hank Irvin rummaging through the drawers in Rob's desk. He was only the first of many.

I had just left Cube City, heading for the copy room off the north hallway. As I walked toward the corner, I saw light through the clouded glass door of Rob's office. I stopped, listening to the sound of drawers being pulled open, then slammed shut.

When I opened the door, Hank was sitting at the desk, his hands rifling impatiently through the files on the surface, a frown on his face. Then his eyes came up to meet mine. There was a startled expression on his face that he quickly smoothed over.

"Looking for something?" I asked, pasting on a cheerful smile.

"Rob was working on something for me, before he died. I can't seem to find it."

"Can I help? Where would it normally be filed?"

"It's a corporate matter," he said, looking distracted. "I thought maybe it got stuck in the wrong file folder by mistake."

"I'll help you look." I stepped through the doorway toward the desk. Hank pushed back from the desk and stood up, shaking his head.

"No, it'll turn up. It's not time critical, and I've got other stuff for you to do that is. I've got to go to Texas this afternoon, and I won't be back till Wednesday. Before I go, that document you did Friday afternoon has to be revised as soon as possible. It's in my out basket."

"Why are you going to Texas?"

"Oh, business."

I'd assumed that, but I wanted details. He wasn't giving me any.

I followed Hank back to his office and picked up the separation agreement concerning Ed Decker from the out basket. I pulled off the large paper clip that held the pages together and sifted through them, assessing the extent of the additional revisions, which Hank had scribbled in red ink. Behind this was a fax copy, one sent, according to the date and time information on the upper margin, on Saturday afternoon. It was from Eric Nybaken at Rittlestone and Weper, and it, too, contained a lot of handwritten comments. It looked as though Hank had incorporated Nybaken's changes and added a few of his own.

As I left Hank's office I saw that Patricia's light was off. Just to be sure, I opened the door. There was no sign that she'd arrived at work yet. Must have been a terrific weekend in Mendocino. I crossed the hall to Cube City.

So Hank was looking for something that might have been mis-filed. Why then was he looking in Rob's desk drawers, and only belatedly at the files on Rob's desk? I was sure I'd heard him opening and shutting drawers.

Gladys and Nancy were both in their cubicles. Nancy had been transcribing a dictation tape. Now she stood up and walked over to the printer, waiting for the document to appear in the tray.

Gladys was sorting some filing. On her way to work, she had stopped at the same place I had, the coffeehouse on the Embarcadero. I recognized the logo on the disposable cup. Now she leaned back in her chair and took the lid off what looked like a mocha.

"Did you have a nice weekend?" I asked her, taking a sip from my own latte.

"Went to a funeral," she said, wrinkling her face.

I nodded. "Rob, that paralegal who died?"

"Yes. I just hate funerals, especially for people who are younger than me. That reminds me." She looked in Nancy's direction. "I guess one of us needs to go over to Rob's office and clean it up. There's a lot of filing piled up on that desk."

"Leave it," Nancy said, her back to us as she stood at the printer.

Gladys looked exasperated. "But you know there are files in there people will be looking for. Both Hank and Patricia were in there last week. We need to get that stuff back to the file room, the sooner the better. So why shouldn't we?"

Nancy took her time answering. I'd noticed she was stingy with information. She operated on a need-to-know system, and she usually figured that Gladys and I didn't need to know. I could understand her attitude in terms of letting me in on the company secrets, since I was a temporary worker. But Gladys was a long-term employee. It was plain that Nancy's reticence irritated her.

Nancy frowned and ran one hand through her straight black hair. "Buck Tarcher and the police want to look at the office."

"Tarcher?" Gladys wrinkled her nose. "And the cops? Whatever for? Do they think Rob was selling the secret formula for Bates Best ice cream?"

"Just routine, I guess." Nancy's tone was deprecating, and she shrugged her shoulders. "Rob did die in unusual circumstances."

"Yeah, I guess taking a flyer out a window is unusual," Gladys snapped back, shaking her head. "But I don't see what it has to do with work." She took another swig of her coffee and went back to her cubicle.

Had Alex Campbell told his secretary the reason Tarcher wanted a crack at the office? Looking at her now, I had the feeling he had. Nancy knew something, and she didn't want to share it. If I was correct in assuming that threatening note Rob had received was the reason Tarcher and Sid had visited the Bates general counsel on Friday, Tarcher must be trying to find a reason someone would tell Rob to back off.

Over the weekend I'd driven over to Alameda to visit an acquaintance, a retired Navy admiral named Joe Franklin. I wanted to find out if he knew Tarcher, who was an ex-Marine. Joe knew him, but not well. Tarcher, he told me, was an uncompromising, by-the-book officer, and likely to have the same mind-set now that he was head of security at Bates.

I'd first encountered Joe about a year and a half earlier, while working on a case. I hadn't liked him at the time. Then, about a year ago, his daughter Ruth had been the prime suspect in the murder of her estranged husband, and Joe had worked with me to clear her. In the process, he'd become interested in helping the Bay Area's burgeoning homeless population. Now he ran a food bank staffed by other military retirees. Earlier this year, he'd rented a storefront on Santa Clara Avenue in Alameda, where the Franklins lived, and Ruth managed his office, with an occasional assist from Joe's wife, Lenore.

"Do you get much in the way of donations from Bates?" I asked Joe. We were drinking beer on the patio of the Franklin house on Gibbons Drive. "I mean, it is a food processing company, so I'd guess they donate food."

"Yes, canned goods, pasta, nonperishables." He squinted, gazing out at the lawn where Ruth was playing croquet with her young daughter, Wendy. Lenore was on her hands and knees in a flower bed, separating iris rhizomes. "But their donations are way down this year. And people I've talked with say Bates's monetary contributions to local charities have dropped drastically since that leveraged buyout." He sighed and shook his head. "That happens with a lot of corporations, I'm finding out. In the midst of plenty . . ."

"Some of the plenty seems to be in the executives' salaries," I said, thinking of the well-padded severance package Ed Decker was getting.

"They say corporate executives nowadays make more than two hundred times what most of their employees make." He downed some beer. "Even as an admiral, my salary didn't attain such heights. We're living in strange times, Jeri. With people getting laid off all over the place, requests for food are going up, and donations are going down. Some people just don't have enough to share. But there are a lot of others who don't seem to care."

My recollection of the conversation with Joe was interrupted by a buzzing sound from Nancy's intercom. She picked up the receiver, then said, "I'll be right there."

When she'd left the office, I stood up and peered at Gladys over the partition. "Do you know why Hank's going to Texas this afternoon?"

"Beats me," she said, sounding huffy. "That must be why the legal staff meeting's been moved to ten o'clock. It's usually at two. Nancy makes all the travel arrangements, for everyone. As you can see, she likes to keep me out of the loop."

"No idea what it's about? Not even a guess?"

She shook her head. "Must be one of those hush-hush projects. The attorneys do it all the time. Cloak-and-dagger stuff, like they were buying nuclear weapons instead of some bakery in Oakland. They label the file folders 'Project Umbrella' or some such nonsense and keep them locked in their offices. I think it's kinda silly." She stopped and took a swig of her mocha. "If I had to guess, I'd say Bates must be planning to build a new plant. Or buy one."

Acquisitions and divestitures, I thought. I'd seen several folders on the subject in the file room. But now my nose was twitching at the prospect of some top-secret project Hank might be working on. Maybe while he was gone I could pick the lock on the file drawer in his desk.

"I thought all the Bates plants were here in the Bay Area," I said. "Has there been any talk of expanding to other states?"

"Come to think of it, there was. Right before the LBO, there was some talk of expanding our sales area, selling Bates products in other states. I'll bet that's what it's about. Maybe we'll pick up some information in the staff meeting."

"If the company's broadening its market, maybe that's a good sign."

"Hold that thought," Gladys said, saluting me with her coffee container.

I wasn't sure what to expect from the staff meeting, but I hoped Gladys was correct in her assumption that we might be able to find out what was going on at Bates, at least in the legal department. I finished making the revisions Hank wanted in the settlement agreement and took the new printout to him. After he'd skimmed through it, he told me to send the original back to Nybaken, by messenger. By the time I'd returned from the mail room, where the messenger service would pick up the envelope, it was nearly ten o'clock.

Nancy, Gladys, and I filed out of Cube City and trooped across the hall to Alex Campbell's corner office. Hank and Patricia were already there, Patricia looking windblown and not quite put together, as though she'd just driven down to the Bay Area from her weekend getaway in Mendocino.

We took seats around the circular conference table in front of Alex's desk. The general counsel told us that he'd gotten approval from human resources to fill Rob Lawter's job and that an ad would start running in the Bay Area legal newspapers, *The Recorder* and *The Daily Journal*, the following week.

"That's good news," Hank said. "What about a secretary to replace Martha?" He nodded at me. "Not that we're dissatisfied with Jeri's work. Very pleased, as a matter of fact."

"Perhaps you'll consider applying," Alex said to me, seconding the compliment with a pleasant smile. "An internal memo has gone around, as is customary, giving secretaries within the company the chance to apply first. But if you'd like to stay here with us, we'll put in a good word with human resources."

Gladys flashed me a grin. She thought it was a good idea. Nancy, however, gave me a look, as though she wasn't thrilled with the prospect of having me around on a permanent basis.

Neither was I. I fervently hoped I could get some leads, wrap up this case, and get back to my own life. I returned Alex's smile, even as I hedged. "I hadn't really considered a permanent position right now. Let me think about it."

Personnel matters out of the way, Alex launched into the next phase of the meeting, which turned out to be reports from the attorneys on their various projects. Alex was working on a company-wide survey regarding compliance with the Americans with Disabilities Act. He also said the company was making progress in the labor negotiations. Could this be the source of the possible strike I'd heard Leon Gomes mention at Rob's funeral? If there was a problem between Bates and the union, I wouldn't have guessed from Alex's brief, bland description.

When it was her turn, Patricia looked preoccupied, and not by work. "The FDA food-safety proposals," she said quickly. "I've been analyzing them, with the help of Nolan Ward in production. In fact, I've got a meeting with him at one. We should have a report ready in a week to ten days."

Alex nodded, then glanced at Hank, who reported on the status of Bates's plans to go public again. It sounded like the timetable for this was the end of October.

"What about that trademark infringement lawsuit?" Alex asked him.

"We're in settlement negotiations," Hank said. "I expect some action when I get back from Texas."

Alex nodded. "Ah, yes. Project Rio."

Hank compressed his lips. Was I the only one who caught the slight downturn of his lips? It was as though he didn't want to mention the name of the project, let alone talk about it.

All the more reason I needed to find out just what Project Rio was.

CHAPTER 20

"HOW ARE THINGS WORKING OUT?" NANCY ASKED WHEN we returned to Cube City. Despite the look I'd caught on her face at the staff meeting, her words were friendly, as though she was genuinely interested. "Are you feeling overwhelmed?"

"No, I think I'm getting up to speed." I smiled at her. Now it was Nancy's turn to get some office gossip, courtesy of what I'd heard this weekend from Leon Gomes. "Say, hearing Alex talk about the contract negotiations reminds me of something I heard this weekend. Someone told me there's a possibility of a strike at the Bates plants. But Alex seemed confident there wasn't a problem."

"Oh, I don't think there is," Nancy said, her voice cooling a bit. "The union always threatens a strike when they're negotiating."

"Sounds like you've been through a few cycles."

"I've worked here a long time." She stepped over to the fax machine, where a couple of sheets of paper rested in the paper tray. She picked it up, glanced at it, and then stapled the pages together. "This one's for Hank." She handed it to me.

"What's the sticking point in the negotiations this time?"

"Health and retirement benefits." Nancy returned to her workstation, pulled out her chair, and sat down, reaching for the earpieces of her transcriber. "That's always a bone of contention lately. The company pays into one of those multiemployer pension funds for the union, which is different from the retirement plan the rest of us have. I've heard the company wants to cut back on the number of medical plans the union members can choose from, and have them pay more of the premium costs. I wouldn't be surprised if they did something like that here, with the nonunion personnel. If they do, of course, we don't have the option to strike, like the union."

She stopped suddenly, looking as though she thought she'd said too much. The expression on her face made me wonder if Nancy was just as discontented as Gladys seemed to be, and as Martha had been.

She fitted the rubber-tipped earpieces into her ears and started another transcription job. Gladys had detoured to the women's room after the staff meeting, and now returned to her cubicle, humming tunelessly.

I glanced through the just-arrived fax in my hand, the one addressed to Hank. On the cover sheet I saw the name Berkshire and Gentry, and the firm's address at Embarcadero West, a high-rise on Battery near Sacramento Street in San Francisco. The sender was an attorney named Stephen Cookson. The fax itself was a one-page letter with a subject line that read "Project Rio." The only information the letter contained was that someone named Art Walton would pick Hank up at the El Paso airport this evening.

I read through the words again, trying to read between the maddeningly uninformative lines. Okay, Hank was going to El Paso. Texas was a very large state, and I was glad to have his destination narrowed to a specific city. Project Rio and El Paso together brought the Rio Grande immediately to mind. If Art Walton was an attorney, Cassie could look him up in her Martindale-Hubbell directory and find out where he worked and what sort of law his firm practiced. I was betting on real estate. If Bates was acquiring land or an existing plant in Texas, that could mean that the guess Gladys and I made earlier about company expansion was correct. But why that look on Hank's face at the staff meeting?

I carried the fax across the hall to Hank's office. He wasn't there, but the lower file drawer in his desk, the one that had been locked, was open. I moved toward it, hoping for a glimpse of the contents. I'd just spotted an accordion folder labeled "Project Rio" when I heard the door open behind me.

I turned and saw Hank. "This fax came for you."

"Thanks," he said. He took it and glanced through it. Then he took some papers from the accordion file and put them into his briefcase. Then he closed and locked the file drawer.

As I stepped out of Hank's office, I saw Buck Tarcher, the corporate security chief, open the door to Rob's office. He acted as though he hadn't seen me. I walked to the door, where the interior light was visible through the pebbly opaque glass. The sound was unmistakable, just like what I'd heard this morning when Hank had been inside. Tarcher was going through the drawers in Rob's desk.

I opened the door. "Hi," I said brightly. "Are you looking for something? Maybe I can help you find it."

The corporate security chief looked up, startled, then he gave me a penetrating gaze, as if to ask why I was standing here rather than going about my business. The way he'd examined me made me wonder if he'd noticed the brief look that passed between Sid and me on Friday.

"No, thank you. I can find it myself." His voice was clipped, full of dismissal, and the look in his eyes left no doubt that I was supposed to disappear. So I did.

It was nearly one when I went to lunch, just as Patricia was heading downstairs to production for her meeting with Nolan Ward. I walked over to Jack London Village and bought a chicken salad sandwich and a root beer at the deli where Gladys and I had eaten Friday. Then I walked along the waterfront until I reached the Franklin Delano Roosevelt Pier at the foot of Clay Street. I sat on one of the benches near the estuary, enjoying the September sunshine and the slight breeze coming off the water, and fending off cheeky seagulls and pigeons who wanted to share my sandwich.

It would be so easy, I thought, to stretch out on this bench and take a nap. I wasn't used to this regularly scheduled office worker stuff anymore. One of the joys of being self-employed is that if I oversleep or take a long lunch, the only boss I have to deal with is me. And I can go home early anytime I feel like it.

A glance at my watch told me my lunch hour was nearly over. I finished my root beer, balled up my sandwich wrappings, and deposited both in a nearby trash receptacle. I was crossing the Embarcadero at Broadway when I heard a voice call my name. I turned. A slender young woman with shoulder-length brown hair ran toward me, bouncing across the Embarcadero tracks on a pair of thick-soled white athletic shoes. She wore powder blue leggings and an over-sized T-shirt in the same color. A pair of sunglasses with glittery frames obscured half her face. It wasn't until she hopped up onto the sidewalk that I recognized her.

"Darcy?"

Darcy Stefano flung her arms around me, giving me a big hug. I hadn't seen her since the close of a particularly difficult case that be-gan in April with my following Darcy to Paris and wound up in July in Bakersfield.

"Jeri, what are you doing down here?" She released me, removed the sunglasses, and hooked one of the earpieces over the neck of her T-shirt as she looked me up and down. "What is it with that suit? It's way big for you, and it makes you look like an office drone."

"It is a tad roomy," I admitted. The brown suit was one I'd bor-rowed from Ruby, and let's face it, she had a bigger butt than I did. "And I am an office drone, sometimes."

"First time I've seen you looking like one." Darcy's brown eyes sparkled and her voice dropped. "Are you, like, undercover?"

"Keep your voice down," I told her. I'd just spotted two people I recognized. After reading through Ed Decker's separation agree-ment, I had made a point of putting a face to the name. The large bulky man in the blue suit who was walking toward us was indeed the senior vice president of human resources, at least until some Bates higher-up dropped that agreement on him. The woman with him was the new HR director, Tonya Russell, a tall big-boned blonde in a lilac-colored suit. I'd made sure I knew what she looked like, too, after I'd heard she came from Rittlestone and Weper's Chicago office.

Neither Decker nor Russell paid any attention to Darcy and me. Instead, they jaywalked across the Embarcadero, heading toward the complex of restaurants and shops that bordered the estuary.

"You are undercover," Darcy said, delight in her voice.

"Try to keep your exuberance under control, and don't say any-thing. To anyone."

"Hey, your secret's safe with me." She raised her hand as though taking an oath. "Zipped lips and all that. Which way are you going? I'll walk with you."

I resumed my original course in the direction of Bates. Darcy told me she'd finished her interrupted senior year of high school by taking an accelerated program in Berkeley. But she'd decided to wait awhile before going to college.

"What are you going to do?"

"I'm doing it," she crowed. "I've got a job. I just started last week. It doesn't pay very much, but I really enjoy it."

The job, she told me, was computer related. Not surprising. Darcy's father was an entrepreneur whose firm designed and produced computer games, and her younger brother Darren had his own eclectic Web site. Some of the Stefano family Silicon Valley fairy dust had evidently rubbed off on Darcy, as well. She was working for an on-line magazine, much like one I'd encountered in cyberspace and Los Angeles while working on the previous case. It was called *CyberMag*, Darcy told me, and the office she worked in was located in one of the Produce District warehouses that had been converted into live-work lofts, on Third Street a few blocks from the Bates building.

"I'm just a gofer right now, but I do get to play with HTML and put in some Net time. I'm having fun. And I'm hoping to save up enough money to get my own place. And a car. I take the bus and BART to work."

"Both of those will be hard to do if you're not making much money," I said. "Rents just keep going up."

"I know. But living at home is just not making it. As you can imagine, Mom and I are like oil and water. We just don't mix."

"I hoped you and your mother might be getting along better."

"It is better than it was before," Darcy said as we rounded the corner and headed toward the Bates building. "But I don't think we'll ever be friends."

"Give it a few years," I said, thinking of my own rocky relationship with my mother. I glanced at my watch. "I've got to go."

"This is where you're working?" She wrinkled her nose and glanced at the Bates building.

"Yes. And remember—"

"I know, I know. My lips are sealed." She looked over my shoulder and whistled softly. "Who's the hunk?"

I turned and glanced at two men who'd just come out the door and were standing on the steps, talking. One of them was David Vanitzky. While he was interesting to look at, I'd never call him a hunk. She must be referring to the other man. Not that he wasn't physically attractive, but he didn't ring my chimes, either. I felt a jolt as I recognized him from the photograph on the cover of *Forbes*. It was Yale Rittlestone.

"They're both too old for you," I told Darcy.

"Why are you so interested in them?" she asked, in a stage whisper accompanied by a wicked smile. "Do they have something to do with your latest case?"

Leave it to Darcy to pick up on my curiosity about both men.

She giggled. "It's the blond guy, right?" I shook my head and raised a cautionary finger to my lips. "He looks like he could be an industrial spy."

Robber baron was more like it. "Now, I've got to get back to work, and so do you."

She laughed again, then walked briskly across Webster and headed down Third Street. I moved up the steps of the Bates building, glancing to my left as I passed Rittlestone and Vanitzky. Rittlestone's back was to me, but I had a clear view of Vanitzky's face. He met my eyes and smiled briefly, then turned his attention back to whatever Rittlestone was saying.

Just as I passed them, Yale Rittlestone turned abruptly and started to move away from Vanitzky. He bumped hard into my left side. I stumbled on the steps, and Vanitzky's hand grabbed my arm, steadying me. "Are you all right?" he asked.

"Yes," I said.

My eyes moved from him to Rittlestone, who inclined his head politely and said, "Sorry." But he looked annoyed, as though he thought our encounter had been my fault. I guessed I was just one of those inconvenient little people, always underfoot.

"It's Jeri, isn't it." Vanitzky's hand was still on my arm. He smiled. I had the disconcerting feeling he knew exactly what was going through my mind. "Jeri works in the legal department, with Hank Irvin. This is Yale Rittlestone, one of our board members."

Rittlestone's face segued from polite to bored. I was quite sure that secretaries were a small blip on his radar screen. "I'll call you later," he told Vanitzky. Then he headed down the steps, toward a big gold Mercedes that had just pulled up to the curb.

"Not long on personality, is he?" I probably shouldn't have said it, but the words were out of my mouth before that tempering thought entered my head.

Vanitzky chuckled and let go of my arm. "No, he isn't."

As I walked up the steps toward the front door, I could have sworn he winked at me. Or maybe it was a trick of the eye.

I hadn't missed my workstation in Cube City. In fact, I was already weary of the place. I checked my voice mail and found a terse message from Cassie, telling me to call her as soon as possible. My adrenaline surged immediately as I picked up the phone and punched in Cassie's number.

"I've located Lauren Musso," Cassie told me. "She works in San Francisco, in one of those high-rises on Market Street. She can meet you after work tonight. Look for her at five-thirty, at Java City in Embarcadero Four."

CHAPTER 21

I CONSULTED THE POCKET-SIZED FERRY SCHEDULE I CARRIED in my purse. If I left Bates at exactly 4:30 P.M., I could make the 4:45 P.M. ferry from Oakland to San Francisco.

The rest of the afternoon dragged. Hank had gone to catch his plane to El Paso, and I didn't see Patricia again. Her meeting with Nolan Ward in production must have gone into extra innings. Instead I concentrated on filing, my least favorite activity.

I managed to leave a few minutes early. Once out the front door of the Bates building, I hurried across the Embarcadero and cut across Jack London Square to the foot of Broadway and followed the shoreline path around the Waterfront Plaza Hotel, formerly the old Boatel.

I arrived at the dock at the end of Clay Street just in time to board the Blue and Gold Fleet catamaran called the *Bay Breeze*. At the lower level bar, I bought a round-trip ticket and went upstairs to sit on one of the outside benches.

Once the boat cast off its mooring, it chugged up the estuary, the narrow channel that separates Oakland and Alameda. On my left was the now-closed Alameda Naval Air Station. To my right was the Port of Oakland, where huge metal cranes towered hundreds of feet over massive container ships that dwarfed the ferry. Containers, each the size of a boxcar, were stacked high along the shore, waiting to be loaded onto the ships.

A sailboat glided past the ferry, heading in the opposite direction. Then a couple of jet skis, piloted by figures in black wet suits, played tag in the ferry's wake. Now the *Bay Breeze* moved out of the estuary and onto San Francisco Bay, where the breeze blew my hair off my forehead. The afternoon sun glinted off the water as the boat moved steadily toward its destination. Here and there the bay was dotted with other vessels, a container ship riding low in the water, a sturdy tugboat, sailboats, and another ferry heading into San Francisco from Marin County. The *Bay Breeze* crossed under the Bay Bridge, clogged with rush-hour traffic high over our heads.

At a quarter after five the ferry docked at the commuter terminal just north of the Ferry Building. The boat rocked in the waves that greeted the shore. I rocked a little, too, as I stepped off the gang-way of the boat and onto the motionless wooden pier that jutted out into the bay. I walked toward the city, passing a line of commuters waiting to board the ferry for its return journey to Alameda and Oakland.

I crossed the Embarcadero to Justin Herman Plaza, past the boxy concrete abstraction that was the Vaillancourt Fountain. At lunch-time the plaza was crowded with office workers enjoying meals purchased at the numerous quick lunch establishments on the lower levels of the four tall buildings that made up Embarcadero Center. There was also a food court in the walkway separating Embarcadero Four from the nearby Hyatt Regency. But it was past five now, and the walk-up and take-away joints were closed, the plaza nearly de-serted. The office buildings around me were emptying of their work-ers, some heading for the ferry terminals, some for BART, and some for the San Francisco Municipal Railway, known as Muni.

Some were stopping at Java City, on the ground level of Embar-cadero Four, to get an espresso to fuel their homeward journey. This is where I was supposed to meet Lauren Musso. I stepped up to the counter and ordered an iced latte, glancing around the shop as the young man behind the counter filled my order. I didn't see anyone matching the description Cassie had given me. Then a dark-haired woman in a dark blue suit and sneakers strode quickly into the shop. She looked around as though espresso wasn't her first objective.

I examined her. She was shorter than me, maybe five three, thin and vibrating with energy. About my age, I guessed, middle thirties, with just a strand of gray here and there in her short black curls. "Are you Lauren Musso?" I asked.

She appraised me with a pair of eyes so dark they looked like black olives in her tanned face. "You're Jeri Howard?"

I stuck out my hand. "The same. Thanks for taking the time to talk with me. What'll you have? It's on me."

Lauren Musso eyed the latte the counterman had just set on the glass. "One of those. Only make it decaf. If I have caffeine, I'll be bouncing off the walls all night."

It looked as though she didn't need caffeine for that. I nodded at the counterman, and he set to work concocting another iced latte.

"I can drink the stuff all day long," I said. "Doesn't bother me a bit." I handed her the decaf with my left hand and kept my right gripped around the high test. "Let's go outside."

We walked out toward the fountain. Rows of white metal tables, each with four matching chairs, all bolted to the pebbly surface, ranged along one side of Embarcadero Four, facing the cascading water in the Vaillancourt Fountain. Most of the tables and chairs were unoccupied at this late afternoon hour. I saw a man and a woman seated nearby, drinking coffee as they perused a map of San Francisco. Beyond them, a homeless man with uncombed hair and a bristly gray beard probed one of the trash cans. He was looking for something to eat, I guessed. All around us the pigeons were doing the same, pecking at crumbs and morsels left by the lunchtime crowd.

Out on the plaza near the fountain, three adolescents with baggy jeans and skateboards were practicing their acrobatics. Two women sat on the low stone rim of the fountain, talking. One trailed her hand in the water. I turned to the left and led the way to a table at the end of the row, where we were less likely to be overheard.

"Cassie Taylor told me you needed some information on Bates," Lauren said, after we sat down. She eyed me warily. But, I reasoned, she had agreed to meet me, so she must be willing to talk. "So what do you want to know?"

"Did Cassie tell you anything about me, or my reason for asking?"

She sipped her latte. "Not really. She told me you're a private investigator and you're looking into Rob Lawter's death. I didn't know he was dead. I was shocked when Cassie told me. Rob was such a nice guy."

"You don't have any contact with your former coworkers, then?"

Was there a chance, I wondered, that someone at Bates might find out I was working undercover at the company? If Lauren was on the phone to Gladys or Nancy, or one of the Bates attorneys on a regular basis, that was a risk. But if no one had bothered to let her know about Rob, maybe the risk was negligible.

Lauren smiled, somewhat ruefully. "Occasionally. I still have some friends in the company. Not in the legal department, though. Unless you count Martha Bronson, who used to be my secretary. She just bailed out for a better job. You see, after the way I was treated, I'm not particularly keen on talking with any of the legal staff."

I recalled what Gladys had told me about why Lauren Musso no longer worked at the company. I wanted to get Lauren's take on the situation. "What happened? Were you fired?"

"Fired?" The word triggered a flare of heat in her dark eyes, one she almost immediately masked. "No, I wasn't fired. Not in so many words."

"Laid off, then."

"The British have a term for it. Made redundant." Lauren's smile turned chilly. "That's accurate. They wanted to give my job to someone else, so I was redundant. Superfluous. Excess baggage."

As she spoke, the bitterness in her voice grew stronger. She gave me a sidelong glance from her dark eyes. "Oh, I know I sound like a disgruntled ex-employee. I suppose I am. It took me over eight months to find a job after Bates let me go. That's a damned long time. The severance money had run out, and I was borrowing from my folks so I wouldn't lose my condo. That's a hard pill to swallow, at my age. Especially since I'm a good lawyer, a hard worker. I didn't like being told I wasn't doing my job. Because I was. It's just that the rules changed."

"How had they changed?" I asked, sipping the iced latte.

She wrapped her hands around her own cup and leaned forward over the painted white surface of the table. "Let me give you some background here. I worked for Bates six years before the leveraged buyout. I left a good job to go there." She rattled off the name of the law firm. I recognized it as one of the largest in the city.

"I was an associate on the partnership track," she continued. "I'd been at the firm since I got out of law school and passed the bar. They never had any complaints about my job performance. In fact, I took a salary cut to go to Bates. Alex Campbell needed a corporate lawyer, so he wined and dined me, really put on the hard sell to get me to come to work for him. So I did. And I did a damned fine job of it, too. But after the LBO, it was a different story. I couldn't do anything right."

"Because the rules changed," I said, repeating her words.

She nodded. "I should have seen it coming. But I was focused on doing my job, being a good soldier, showing the company they could count on me. I worked overtime all during the hostile takeover bid and the LBO. I thought being a team player would help me keep my job. No one in the legal department got laid off, of course. They needed us to mop up the blood."

Her mouth twisted, then she continued. "Then, two months after the LBO, I was out of a job. And damned mad at Alex Campbell. I thought he had a stronger backbone than that. But he was just like the rest of the executives, scrambling around trying to save their own jobs and letting their underlings be the sacrificial lambs. Those jerks at Rattlesnake and Viper wanted their own lawyer in that corporate slot, and Alex said, sure why not. We'll get rid of Lauren, and bring in someone from Berkshire and Gentry."

"A yes-man?" I thought of the seemingly affable Hank Irvin, who now occupied Lauren's position over at Bates.

"That's an oversimplification." She paused, and the fingers of her right hand beat a rhythmic tattoo on the table surface. "They wanted someone who would more readily see the world according to what is best for R&W rather than what is best for Bates."

"Someone," I speculated, "who, when Bates goes public again, will write the annual report so cleverly that the shareholders don't know exactly how many stock options the executives are getting."

She snorted with laughter. "Oh, hell, they all do that. The Securities and Exchange Commission should give out awards for best snow job of the year. Of course, most people see all those lines of type in an annual report or a prospectus, and their eyes just glaze over. They never read it. If they did, they might get angry. I think the people who write that stuff do it on purpose, so no one will read it. Y'know what gets me?"

I looked at her expectantly over the rim of my cup. I was sure she'd tell me. Lauren Musso was on a roll, and I was just as happy to sit back and listen.

"These corporate types   of which I am one, I admit   are always talking about giving good value to the shareholders." Her tone gave the words emphasis. "That's the excuse these days for all the downsizing and reorganizing that's going on. Gotta cut those health benefits and lay off a bunch of people, make the company lean and mean and profitable, so we can give good value to the shareholders."

She laughed again, although what she was describing wasn't funny.

"Of course, they're not talking about Mrs. Jones who decided to take a flyer on fifty shares of Amalgamated Whatsis. Or the low-level employee who funnels twenty bucks a payday into the employee stock option plan so he can feel like he's got a stake in the company." She shook her head. "Oh, no. *They're* the shareholders, all those executives with their big fancy offices on the top floors of every company in America." She waved her hand at the skyscrapers of San Francisco's Financial District.

"They're the ones who are heaping stock options on themselves, while they hold rank-and-file employees to salary freezes, or minuscule wage increases that barely keep up with inflation. Something is really skewed when executives make so much more than the people they employ. I mean, how much is enough?"

She glared at me, in proxy, but I didn't have an answer. In fact, I agreed with what she was saying.

"The whole system is obscene," she continued. "I finally get a job, at this manufacturing company here in San Francisco, and they start having layoffs, too. I'm starting to feel like Typhoid Mary. 'Layoff' used to mean you'd get recalled to work, eventually. Now it just means you're shitcanned, out the door, never to return. You know what the latest euphemism for firing people is? 'Disappearing.' Sounds like those people who were 'disappeared' by death squads down in Latin America, doesn't it?"

Disconcertingly so, I thought. For a moment I was quite grateful to be self-employed, even if there were times over the past few years when I wondered if J. Howard Investigations was going to make it.

"What have you heard about this plan to take Bates public again?"

Lauren looked spent, as though venting her anger had taken a lot out of her. She shrugged. "I've heard they're working on an S-1. That's a registration statement that they'll file with the SEC prior to the IPO, the initial public offering. But I don't know what percentage of the company they plan to sell, or what the common share price will be. Or when they're going to file the S-1. My source tells me the IPO will happen before the end of the year, though."

"Who is your source?"

She flashed a smile. "Sorry, I can't tell you that." She stopped and took a sip from her iced latte.

"As for that IPO," she said, "you can bet a lot of the Bates execs have cut themselves in for a big piece of the action. Stock options that will let them pick up shares at a lower price. What they don't realize is that their jobs aren't safe, either. R&W doesn't give a damn about Bates. It's just another cash cow to them. And once the cow runs dry, R&W will just toss the company aside."

"How would they do that?" I asked. "Sell it?"

"Here's an example of what's going on these days. I've only been employed for a couple of months, and now it looks like I could be out of a job again. This company I'm working for now is planning to move a lot of its operations to the border. Rumor has it they'll shut down the office here and open one in San Diego. As for the factories, I'm guessing they want to take advantage of NAFTA. Don't have to pay those people in the *maquiladoras* in Tijuana a living wage, like you do here in California. Just take those jobs over the border."

It was true that many companies were moving out of both the Bay Area and California. In the former case, I'd heard that housing costs and traffic congestion were factors. As for leaving the state, those two items also applied as negatives. So did the pluses of states with lower taxes, lower wage bases, and less regulation.

I thought about Hank's trip to El Paso, and Project Rio. Was it company expansion, or something else entirely?

I glanced across the table at Lauren, who was gazing moodily at the remains of her iced latte. "Well, there I go running off at the mouth, and I haven't answered any of your questions. My checkered tenure at Bates certainly doesn't have anything to do with Rob falling out a window."

"It might," I said. "It looks as though Rob didn't fall."

Lauren paled. "Murder?"

"Before he died, Rob was concerned about something that was going on at work. He said he was about to blow the whistle. But I don't know exactly what he was going to expose. I thought maybe if you could just give me some background information about some of the people who work at Bates. Maybe that would give me a lead."

"Well . . ." She shrugged. "If you think it will help."

She gave me her take on the people who worked in the Bates legal department, starting with Nancy Fong and Gladys Olivette, whom she liked. It was downhill from there. It was evident from the tone of her voice, and her earlier words, that she'd lost all respect for Alex Campbell, the general counsel. Evidently Patricia Mayhew had been a difficult person to work with as long as she'd been at Bates.

"I'm sure Patricia wants to be the next general counsel," Lauren added, "when R&W cans Alex. But it was clear the minute Hank Irvin walked in the door that he's the designated replacement. And he's made sure ever since to stay on the good side of both Rittlestone and Weper. If either of those guys has a good side."

"What do you know about David Vanitzky?" I asked, curious about the whiff of danger emanating from Bates's chief financial officer.

"The pirate. Oho!" She grinned. Her description matched the one Gladys had given me. "He has an eye for the ladies, but I think he likes the horses better."

Cards, too.

"Vanitzky's one of R&W's men," Lauren said. "They booted the old chief financial officer, Len Turley, out the door, just like they did me. Gave him a better severance package than I got, I'll bet."

"Is Vanitzky qualified for the job?"

"Oh, I'm sure he's just a whiz with figures." She laughed. "He must be to spend that much time at the rail at Bay Meadows or Golden Gate Fields and still come out even. Or maybe it's female figures. He's been divorced twice, probably because he has such a roving eye. I heard a rumor before I left that he was dallying with a woman in marketing. Let's just say David Vanitzky's best qualification to be chief financial officer of Bates is that he is a loyal foot soldier of Rattlesnake and Viper. Which is probably why the hottest rumor over at Bates is that Jeff Bates's tenure as CEO is limited."

So Bette Bates Palmer had been correct when she told me it was only a matter of time before Rittlestone and Weper removed her brother as head of the company and replaced him with their own man.

"And David Vanitzky is the man in line for that job?"

"Of course. That's the only reason he's got an office down the hall from Jeff Bates."

"Just what does the chief financial officer do?" I asked.

"He's supposed to look after the financial health of the company," Lauren said. "He oversees accounting, audit, pension funds, although Ed Decker in human resources has plenty of responsibility for the retirement investments."

I wondered again about the conversation I'd overheard between Hank Irvin and David Vanitzky, concerning a million bucks and figurative blood all over the floor.

"Tell me about Ed Decker."

"I wouldn't trust him as far as I could throw him," Lauren said. "Oh, I don't mean I think he'd abscond with the pension fund. But Ed's a knife-in-the-back kind of guy, always looking out for number one, and too bad if you get in his way. I think he hoped being made senior vice president of human resources would lead to something bigger, like a spot on the board. But it hasn't. I wouldn't be surprised if he was put out to pasture, and soon."

Her prediction seemed accurate, given that severance agreement I'd revised, the one with Decker's name on it.

"There are several other former R&W people in positions over at Bates," I said. "Nolan Ward in production, for one. Laverne Carson is being replaced as human resources director by someone named Tonya Russell from R&W's Chicago office."

"They're never 'former' R&W people." Lauren sneered. "Believe me, their first loyalty is to Rittlestone and Weper, not Bates. Vanitzky was Frank Weper's right-hand man for years, even before Rittlestone hooked up with Weper. And Nolan Ward served the same function for Rittlestone, chief spear carrier and toady. Nolan has no experience for that production job. Neither does Tonya Russell have any human resources experience. She's a lawyer. She was in my class at Penn. I'll bet they get rid of Ed and make Tonya the senior VP in charge of HR." She looked at her watch. "I've got to go. I hope what I've told you helps."

"May I call you if I have additional questions?"

"Sure." She took a business card from her purse and scribbled her home phone number on the back. "Anytime."

We both stood, and I walked to a nearby trash can to dump the containers that had held our drinks. Somewhere above me I heard a woman's voice, and I looked up, catching sight of a dark-haired woman standing near the railing on the mezzanine level of Embarcadero Four. She radiated intensity as she gestured. It seemed as if she was doing all the talking. Her back was to me as she talked with a man whose face I couldn't see. Then they moved. I saw their faces clearly enough to recognize both of them.

"Well, well," Lauren said, her voice snide as she joined me at the trash can. "Looks like our old friend Patricia Mayhew is consorting with the enemy. That's Yale 'the Rattlesnake' Rittlestone, in the all-too-scaly flesh."

CHAPTER *22*

W HY WAS PATRICIA MAYHEW MEETING YALE RITTLE-
stone at Embarcadero Four at six-thirty Monday evening?

I thought about the possibilities as I boarded the 7:10 P.M. ferry
for the return voyage to Oakland. True, their meeting could have
been business related. Rittlestone and Weper had an office at Embarcadero Four. The firm owned a majority share of Bates Inc. Patricia was a Bates lawyer. She may have needed to consult with
Rittlestone on a corporate matter.

She certainly hadn't mentioned any off-site appointments during
the legal department staff meeting earlier today. In fact, the only
meeting she had mentioned was her one o'clock with Nolan Ward in
production. She'd gone downstairs, and as far as I knew when I left
the office at four-thirty, she hadn't returned. I'd take a look at her
calendar tomorrow.

Besides, Patricia didn't deal with corporate matters. Hank Irvin did.

I recalled the sight of Patricia and Rittlestone standing on the
walkway at Embarcadero Four. Had there been something furtive
about their manner? Or was that just my imagination? I'd been so
steeped in corporate intrigue over the past few days, it was possible I
was reading too much into their tête-à-tête. Lauren Musso had said
Hank made sure to stay on Rittlestone's good side. Perhaps Patricia
was trying the same tactic.

Patricia wasn't in her office the next morning when I delivered the
first batch of mail. Before picking up the contents of her out box, I
glanced at the weekly calendar, which lay open on the credenza be-

hind her desk. The only meetings noted for yesterday were the ones I already knew about, the legal department get-together and Patricia's date with Nolan Ward. His big empire in production included the buyers who purchased fruits, vegetables, and other commodities that went into Bates Best products, as well as the plants that produced them and the merchandisers and marketers who sold them to grocery stores all over California.

There was nothing to indicate that Patricia had gone over to R&W's office in San Francisco. She may have done just what I'd done, headed for the city after work. If that was the case, it made her rendezvous with Rittlestone look less like business and more like a personal encounter.

Behind me I heard the doorknob rattle. By the time Patricia came through the door, I was standing by her out box, scooping its contents into my arms.

"Good morning," I said cheerily.

Patricia echoed my greeting, with somewhat less cheer. In fact, her voice was lukewarm as she muttered the words. Blue mood, I thought, to go with the navy blue suit she wore. Her mouth looked tight, and there were dark circles under her eyes, as though she was under a strain. She set her briefcase on the surface of her desk, opened it, and handed me a dictation tape. "I need this by noon," she said.

I gave her a can-do smile, but inwardly I groaned. I already had a number of projects, including one left by Hank Irvin on his way to the airport yesterday. Since he'd found out I knew how to use the database program on Bates's computer system, he wanted to input information on the company's trademarks. I told him I'd come up with some suggestions and samples during his absence. If that weren't enough, Nancy had enlisted both Gladys and me to help put together Alex Campbell's company-wide survey on compliance with the Americans with Disabilities Act.

It was going to be a busy week.

I returned to Cube City. Gladys sat at her cluttered desk, sipping coffee as she opened her stack of morning mail. I didn't see Nancy.

"And here I thought things would slow down, with Hank out of town."

"Dream on." She made a face. "Alex wants this ADA stuff out by the end of the week."

"Patricia just handed me something else," I said, fingering the dictation tape she'd given me. "She must have dictated it at home. I guess she left early last night, but she didn't say anything to me."

"She should let you and me know about things like that," Gladys declared as she stood and picked up the mail she was about to deliver. "She always lets Nancy know. Nancy keeps track of where everyone is."

That was a useful piece of information, I thought, watching Gladys's back as she left the room. Since Nancy was conveniently away from her desk, I took a chance and stepped around the partition, into her cubicle. There was a standing file near her telephone, crammed with neatly labeled folders. One of them read "Vacation." That might be a place to start, but just prowling around Nancy's desk was risky. My hand moved toward it, then the phone rang, startling me.

I glanced down, and saw Nancy's calendar. On it she'd made notes in a tiny cramped hand, detailing absences from the office as well as meetings, not just for herself but for everyone in the legal department.

I read the first note for tomorrow, Wednesday. "AC, benefits, 9, AC, DV, ED, TR, MU." I processed this alphabet soup in a matter of seconds. Presumably that meant Alex Campbell had a meeting tomorrow morning at nine, the subject employee benefits. The initials must be the meeting attendees. In addition to Campbell, they included David Vanitzky, Ed Decker, Tonya Russell, and Morris Upton. On the square for today, Tuesday, I saw "AC, SetCon, 10." So Alex was due to attend a settlement conference this morning. "TX" was written next to "HI" on Monday, Tuesday, and Wednesday, signifying Hank's trip to Texas.

I scanned Monday, looking for Patricia's initials. There it was, a notation for "PM," for Monday afternoon, accompanied by the words, "dentist, 4."

The phone stopped ringing. I stepped away from the desk, just as Nancy stepped from the corridor into the room. She seemed surprised to see me near her cubicle. Her dark eyes inquired why.

"Your phone was ringing," I said. "But I didn't catch it in time." I hoped my explanation sounded halfway plausible.

"Don't worry about that." She frowned slightly, and her gaze seemed to penetrate me. "You don't need to answer my phone. It rolls over to voice mail." As if to confirm her words, the message light on the phone began blinking.

I wasn't sure she believed me. I moved back to my desk and put Patricia's dictation tape into the transcriber. From the corner of my eye I watched Nancy, still standing, glance quickly around her cubicle, as though to gauge whether anything had been disturbed. Then she picked up the phone and punched in the required numbers to retrieve the voice mail message.

Working at Bates as a temp was something of a double-edged sword. It got me in the door, at least. There was no way I could have obtained such access without the subterfuge.

But my disguise had its limits. Being too inquisitive would arouse suspicion. The temp had no business snooping around Nancy Fong's desk. And I had a feeling Nancy was suspicious. Nor did I have any official reason to search Rob's vacant office. But I intended to do it at the first opportunity. Trouble was, if I drew too much attention to myself, someone might take a closer look at Jeri Howard the temp and find J. Howard Investigations, down on Franklin Street.

I hit the rewind button and fitted the soft rubber earpieces of the transcriber into my ears. Not that they fit all that well. I knew from experience that by the time I finished the tape, my ears would be hurting.

Patricia's reason for leaving early yesterday afternoon had been a dental appointment. Maybe she had, in fact, gone in for her semiannual checkup and teeth cleaning. Maybe her dentist was in San Francisco. But somehow I wasn't buying it.

The tape finished rewinding with an earsplitting electronic beep. I winced as I turned down the volume. Then I depressed the foot pedal and began listening as Patricia dictated yet another memo on the FDA's food-safety proposal, detailing her discussion with Nolan Ward.

Patricia wasn't a mumbler, but she had a tendency to dictate a word or a phrase, then change her mind about what she wanted to say, which meant a lot of deleting and retyping for me. Periodically she also stopped talking for long periods of time, as she collected her thoughts or framed what she was going to say next. So I was treated to interludes of music and the sound of traffic outside the room where she'd dictated the tape. Her home, I guessed. The music was jazz, heavy on the saxophone. At one point I heard the distinctive clang of a cable car bell. So Patricia lived in San Francisco.

Toward the end of the tape, I heard a man's voice in the background, tantalizing, the words muffled and inaudible, to me anyway. At that point the tape clicked, as though Patricia had hit the stop button. When the tape started again, she dictated a revision of the long paragraph I'd just typed. Had Patricia simply revised what she'd said earlier? Or had the man I'd heard had a hand in the revision? I played the tape again and again, experimenting with the volume, tone, and speed controls on the transcriber. But I still couldn't make out what the man was saying.

Finally I gave up. But I moved the now-discarded paragraph to a new document, planning to compare it with the final document.

I finished transcribing Patricia's tape before noon. The resulting document was ten pages long. I cleaned up the punctuation and formatting, ran the spell checker, and printed out a copy. I left the pages in the center of Patricia's desk. Then I went back to Cube City and compared the original paragraph with the revision. It appeared that Patricia had softened the language on her recommendation concerning inspection of produce by Bates buyers. Why? Because the man in the background told her to do so? I wondered if the indistinct voice belonged to Nolan Ward. Patricia had said she was working closely with him on the food-safety project.

Gladys interrupted my reverie. "Let's go get something to eat. I'm starved."

On the way over to the deli where we'd eaten last week, she informed me that Hank had called to say that he might be delayed in getting back to Oakland. Evidently, he had to make a side trip. I waited until our sandwiches had been delivered to our outside table, then I cast a preliminary fishing line.

"Did Hank say where he was going?"

"Something about New Mexico," Gladys said, wrapping both hands around a turkey on whole wheat.

"Albuquerque? Santa Fe?"

"No." She thought for a moment. "Carlsbad, that was it."

I was eating falafel in a pita, with hummus on the side. "It's in the southeastern part of the state. My parents and my brother and I went to Carlsbad Caverns one summer, back when I was in high school. The caverns are spectacular. We saw the bats fly out at night, too. That was impressive."

"Bats?" Gladys grimaced. "You mean, like vampire bats?"

"Mexican fruit bats," I assured her. "Perfectly harmless. They eat lots of insects."

Gladys was still making a face, as though she didn't believe in benign bats. "No, thanks, honey, I'll pass on the bats. I'm a city girl, born and bred. Anyway, he was complaining about the heat when he phoned. Said this trip to Carlsbad meant he won't be coming back till Thursday."

"Project Rio must be an important deal."

"Like I told you," she said, "it's probably a new plant."

Whatever it was, I wanted more clues about Project Rio. They came in the middle of the afternoon, in a fax. Both Nancy and Gladys were away from their desks when the fax machine buzzed and whirred. It began spitting out pages. I picked up the cover sheet. It was from Hank to Alex Campbell, with a copy to David Vanitzky. It was marked "Confidential," and the subject was "Project Rio."

I quickly read the one-page letter that followed. It sounded as though a hitch had developed regarding the purchase of ten acres of land in El Paso. Hank and Walton, the El Paso attorney, had gone to Carlsbad to meet with the owner, someone named C. J. Mullin.

I made a copy of the fax for Vanitzky and another for myself. When I left the copy room, I returned to Cube City and hid the extra in the company directory. I delivered the original to Alex, then walked to the west hallway, where Vanitzky and his secretary had offices opposite conference room one. The door to Vanitzky's inner office was closed, so I handed the fax to Esther Roades. I'd heard her described as a battle-ax and a dragon lady. But the tall, capable-looking white-haired woman reminded me of a math teacher I'd had in the eighth grade.

Back in Cube City, I sat in my workstation and surreptitiously pored over the fax. The parcel of land in El Paso was on Executive

Center Boulevard. Ten acres sounded like a lot of land, but I didn't know how much land was required for a plant. C. J. Mullin, the owner, had an address on North Shore, in Carlsbad, and an attorney named Pete Sanchez, who had an office on Canal Street in the same city.

Should I make a quick trip to Texas and New Mexico? Or could I get the information I needed long distance, and by snooping around Hank's files? Now that I was working this temp job, it wasn't merely a matter of clearing my calendar and getting on a plane. If I had to go anywhere, it would mean calling in sick, or some other subterfuge.

At the end of the day I headed for my Franklin Street office. Shortly after I arrived, Ruby Woods opened the door and poked her head in the gap. "I need your time card. If you want to get paid for this job. Which, I might add, is necessary if you want it to look legitimate."

I reached in my purse for the Woods Temporaries time card. "I'd have forgotten if Nancy Fong hadn't reminded me that she needed to sign it." I handed the card to Ruby, and she pulled off one carbon and returned the slip of paper to me.

"How's it going?" she asked.

"I've turned up a couple of things that look interesting. But I need more time."

When Ruby had gone, I checked my messages. Cassie had called, so I went down the hall to her law firm. She'd obtained a copy of the class action wrongful termination lawsuit that had been filed against Bates after the first round of layoffs that followed the leveraged buy-out. I sat down in the chair opposite her desk and read through it quickly as Cassie told me she'd talked with one of the attorneys on the case, someone she knew from law school at Hastings. The nine named plaintiffs, six women and three men, alleged age or sex discrimination as the reason they were terminated.

"Some of them sued individually at first," Cassie said. "Then they were combined into a class. My law school buddy says the plaintiffs have a better than even chance of prevailing, given the current climate in California courts regarding age and sex discrimination claims. He also said discovery is showing a pervasive pattern of preference toward young white men, so it looks like Bates is facing serious damages."

"Trouble on all fronts," I said, standing up and glancing at my watch. "I'll have to plow through this later in the evening. I'm meeting Eva and the inspector over at my new house in twenty minutes."

"Hope everything's in good repair," Cassie said. "I'll talk with you later."

Everything at the Chabot Road house was in fairly good shape, Eva and I learned later, including the stove and refrigerator. That was good news. I didn't want the expense of replacing them. As it was, I'd been shopping around for a washing machine and dryer, since the house had the necessary hookups. The plumbing was old but adequate, and the electrical wiring was up to code. It appeared the only necessary changes would be cosmetic. I was having both the exterior and interior of the house painted and the hardwood floors sanded and polished, an unexpectedly generous housewarming gift from my mother, who owned a restaurant in Monterey.

After the inspector left, I stepped out onto the balcony overlooking the backyard, hoping to see another hummingbird, as I had before, among the colorful blooms of the abutilon. I didn't, but there were lots of other birds. And I didn't know what they were.

"Surveying your estate?" Eva said, her voice teasing as she came out on the balcony.

"Contemplating the fact that I don't know a chickadee from a sparrow. Look at all those birds in that pine tree. I'll have to get myself a bird book." I heard a squawk overhead that didn't sound anything like the birdsong emanating from the tree. Raising my eyes, I saw a flash of green. I laughed. "It's a parrot. See it, on the telephone wires."

"Must have escaped," Eva said, following the direction I was pointing. "There's a whole colony of them over on Telegraph Hill in San Francisco."

"There's a parrot in Alameda, too. It hangs out with some pigeons near the hospital." I'd seen that parrot many times, flying around with a flock of pigeons. It made me think of myself, I thought with an inward smile, the exotic private eye who found herself in amongst all the office pigeons.

"Termite inspection next," Eva said as we headed for the front door. "Then the appraisal. Your loan's already in the works. Looks like we could close by the middle of October."

"How soon can I get the keys? Since Mom's paying for the paint and polish, I'd like to make the arrangements."

Eva said she'd find out, and we parted company. I wanted to go home, but I hadn't done any work in my own office. I headed back to Franklin Street and powered up my computer while I listened to the messages on the answering machine.

The background check I'd started on Charlie Kellerman had borne fruit. The last place he'd held a job was the same place I was working undercover.

CHAPTER 23

WHEN I WALKED INTO CUBE CITY WEDNESDAY MORN-
ing, Nancy Fong wasn't at her desk. I soon learned the reason why.

"Nancy called in sick," Gladys told me as she tackled a pile of
mail with a letter opener. "We'll have to cover for her. As though we
didn't already have enough to do."

"What's wrong? Or did she say?"

I sat down in the swivel office chair, set my latte on the desk, and
looked at the paper that had accumulated overnight. Letters to be
answered, documents to revise, and more of both to file.

"She didn't have to." Gladys pulled a memo from an interoffice
envelope and whacked the sheet with a date stamp. "She gets these
killer migraines that lay her low for a day or so. When she gets one,
she says she can't function at all. I hope she'll be back tomorrow. In
the meantime, you and I will have to pick up the slack."

She thumped the date stamp emphatically on another document,
wielding it with obvious irritation at the prospect of doing someone else's work when she already had more than enough of her own.
But as far as I was concerned, Nancy's absence from the office gave
me the opportunity to do some sleuthing without feeling as though
Nancy's eyes were on my back. Rob's office was the first place I
wanted to go.

But I had to wait until Alex went into that meeting at nine o'clock.
I got busy sorting the papers that had piled up on my desk. Gladys
had already opened Alex's mail and placed it on his desk. I needed an

excuse to get into his office, and Patricia provided me with one. In her out basket was a newspaper article clipped from the San Francisco *Chronicle* and taped onto a plain sheet of paper. I quickly scanned the article. It was about a product recall involving one of Bates's competitors. A yellow Post-it directed me to make a copy for Alex, so I headed for the copy machine, then to the general counsel's office.

Alex wasn't at his desk. I glanced at my watch as I slipped the article into his in basket. Five minutes to nine, time enough for a quick look around. Evidently Nancy had made all the preparations for the meeting the day before. Five manila folders were arranged on the surface of Alex's conference table. I read the names on the labels—Alex, Ed Decker, Tonya Russell, Morris Upton of public affairs, and chief financial officer David Vanitzky.

What were they going to talk about? I reached for the nearest folder, hoping for a peek at the meeting's agenda or something else that might tell me. There wasn't an agenda, but I did see two photocopies. One was several pages long, an article from the *Chronicle*, on California laws concerning exempt and nonexempt employees. The other appeared to be from a magazine, and the subject was payroll fraud.

I heard a voice from the hall, so I stepped away from the conference table. I was standing near Alex's out basket, picking up the few files that he'd placed there, when the general counsel walked in. He didn't look surprised to see me there. That's one thing I've discovered about secretaries. They can be invisible.

"Good morning, Jeri," Alex said. His voice was pleasant enough, but he looked preoccupied. He held out several sheets of paper. "I need five copies of this for the meeting."

"Will do." I headed for the copy machine. Someone else was using it. While I waited my turn, I grabbed the staple remover someone had left on top of the bookcase that held the copy paper. I yanked out all the staples, reading through the document, trying to get a sense of the contents.

It was a three-page letter from the manager of a mutual fund, with a two-page chart attached. On my second read through I realized it had something to do with the Bates Inc. retirement plan. Bates had money invested in this fund, lots of numbers behind the dollar signs.

The fund was losing money. In fact, it was hemorrhaging. And the fund manager was scrambling to explain the blood loss.

Blood . . . Suddenly I remembered the scrap of conversation I'd overheard between Hank and Vanitzky last week, when I'd started working at Bates, my second day of listening at keyholes and peering through cracks in the door, like a voyeur or a Peeping Tom.

"There's blood all over the floor," Vanitzky had told Hank. "Mopping it up ain't gonna be pretty. In fact, you and I are gonna get bloodstains all over our hands."

What had sounded then like a cryptic remark now made some sense. Vanitzky knew about the problem with the mutual fund. He was warning Hank that solving the problem would be messy. Hank had said something like "the first I've heard of it." Was he unaware of the situation until Vanitzky clued him in?

I read through the letter again, focusing on words like "shortfall" and "discrepancy." What the fund manager was saying between the lines was far more interesting than the words he'd used. It sounded as though he'd come quite close to accusing someone at Bates of dishonesty and mismanagement. He hadn't named any names, though.

I looked at the dollar signs on the chart and all the numbers after them. That was a lot of money. Other people's money, the employees who had a stake in the retirement plan. And someone in authority was playing with it as though it were Monopoly money. Who had the clout and access? Ed Decker did. And so did David Vanitzky.

My turn came at the copy machine. I punched in the user code and department code and made six copies of the letter and its attachment, rather than five. I put the original and the five copies on top of the papers I'd taken from Alex's out basket and concealed the extra copy in the pages of another document. Then I walked back to the general counsel's office.

Four members of the committee had already assembled. As I set the papers on the desk, I saw Alex talking with Tonya Russell, the new human resources director. This was the first time I'd had a close look at her. She was a large, well-proportioned woman with pale blond hair and a complexion to match. She favored pastel suits, and today's number was blue. Her band-box appearance contrasted with that of Ed Decker, the senior vice president who headed human resources, at least for now. He was red-faced, bulky through the torso in his gray suit, and his hairline had receded halfway up his shiny dome of a head. His head was inclined slightly as he stood listening to another man I'd never seen before. He was frowning, then I saw him scowl, as though furious at what he was hearing. He started to interrupt the other man, who raised a placating hand and kept on talking.

I knew who the other meeting attendees were, so this must be Morris Upton of public affairs, the man responsible for damage control at Bates. He was short, with a wiry frame. He also wore a blue suit, this one with a red power tie glaring against the background provided by his white shirt. He had a full head of dark hair shot with gray and a round face with a mouth that was at the moment mobile. I had no trouble at all picturing him in front of a TV camera giving a statement to a reporter.

As he talked with Decker, Upton toyed with the corner of one of the file folders, as though the folder's placement on the table didn't suit his sense of order. He sensed my eyes on him and looked up. His own dark eyes held only a modicum of curiosity as they flicked over me. Then, his curiosity satisfied as he identified me as office help, he dismissed me. He looked pointedly at his watch, with an air of impatience.

As I turned to go, I glanced at the brass carriage clock on the corner of Alex's desk. It was six minutes past nine o'clock, past time for the meeting to start, and David Vanitzky hadn't yet arrived. Late, or he knew how to make an entrance.

As the temp who'd delivered the copies, I was now even more superfluous than usual. I made my exit to the corridor. A few steps beyond Alex's office, I once again came face-to-face with Bates's chief financial officer, who had just come through the fire door that led to the stairwell near the elevator.

Vanitzky looked dapper, but then he had every time I'd seen him. The dark gray pinstripes looked as though they'd been cut specifically for him, and perhaps they had. His tie was dark gray silk. No doubt the small red stone that glittered from his tiepin was a ruby. It looked for all the world like a drop of blood.

He glanced at me and smiled. It was a friendly smile, far more intimate than I would have expected for an encounter between a secretary and the company's second in command. Then his gray eyes moved past me, toward the closed door leading to the general counsel's office. The smile changed. Now Vanitzky looked like a shark, ready to consume its prey. Hand on the knob, he opened the door. He didn't say anything. He just stood there, stood surveying the other men who'd assembled for the meeting.

I was right. Vanitzky knew how to make an entrance.

"I see we're all here," he said, his voice taking on a chill. "Let's get started."

Vanitzky closed the door. I had an irrational desire to listen at the keyhole. A picture flashed in my mind. Jeri on her knees with her ear to the door. Now wouldn't that attract a lot of attention.

Besides, this was my chance to get into Rob's office. As I walked down the east hallway, past the door to Cube City, I looked to make sure no one saw me, then I pushed open the door of Rob's office. Since it was on an interior wall, I had to turn on the light in order to see clearly. That was unfortunate, since it might tip someone to my presence. But that couldn't be helped. I had to be able to see what I was doing.

The office looked different than it had when I'd first glimpsed it, last Thursday. The tall stacks of folders representing work in progress were now mostly gone. They had covered the surface of Rob's desk and the tops of the filing cabinets. Now only one stack remained on the desk, and the tops of the cabinets were clear, with lines of dust outlining where the folders had rested. Four white cardboard file boxes sat on the carpet, in a semicircle to the left of the desk, all of them about half-full of folders.

I knew what had happened. Both the police and corporate security chief Buck Tarcher had examined the office. Now Nancy Fong was sorting through the folders, filing them into the boxes, probably by subject matter.

I searched the desk first, feeling as though the trail was already far too cold. But perhaps something in this office would tell me what Rob had been so concerned about at the time of his death. I'd take any clue I could find, however small and insignificant.

The desk was a typical secretary's desk with a typing return on the right-hand side, giving the whole affair an L shape. Since the advent of computers, typewriters were few and far between, so the return

now held Rob's monitor and keyboard. The computer itself was a
tower model, tucked into the kneehole under the surface. The desk
drawers yielded little beyond the usual things that clutter a desk—
pens, pencils, paper clips, notepads, rubber bands, and a lot of dust.
I even looked under the plastic divider trays that held all of these
things, to see if Rob had hidden something there. Maybe I was too
late. But maybe not. If Tarcher had found anything during his internal investigation, surely he would have told Sid. And Sid hadn't said
anything to me about new leads in the case. Or maybe he was holding out on me.

I turned on Rob's computer, not expecting to get far. The temporary password I'd been given when I started work at Bates got me
into the network, but it wouldn't enable me to get into Rob's files.

I switched off the computer, frustrated, and turned my attention
to the files in the cardboard boxes, and those that remained on top of
his desk. The labels on the folders at least told me the scope of Rob's
job. Since Rob's position as a paralegal meant he worked for all the
attorneys, his work had covered the whole spectrum of cases handled by the legal department. He'd done research, looking up
statutes and case law for the employment law matters that were
Alex's specialty, as well as the regulatory law that was the focus of
Patricia's work for the company. For Hank, Rob had done most of
the paperwork on trademarks, filing applications, renewals, and use
affidavits.

The brown plastic wastebasket under Rob's desk had long since
been emptied by the cleaning crew. However, in the corner of the
back wall, I saw another wastebasket, this one red plastic with white
letters that read "RECYCLE—WHITE PAPER ONLY." It was half-full of
discarded sheets of paper, most, but not all, white. I pulled the contents from the recycling bin and placed them on the surface of the
desk, in a rough stack, and started skimming through them, one by
one. I found a memo to all employees about corporate giving and
how the company was cutting back on its donations this year. I
already knew this from my weekend visit with Joe Franklin, but I
hadn't expected the company to cry poor mouth and announce it.

Farther down the stack I found a photocopied page streaked with
black toner from the copy machine, no doubt tossed into the recycling bin because words here and there were unreadable. It was a

copy of a memo from Alex to Jeff Bates and David Vanitzky, on the subject of the union's multiemployer pension fund.

I quickly read through the memo. Like many employers, Bates contributed to a pension fund for its union employees who worked in the food processing plants and drove the trucks. The fund got contributions from more than one employer. It sounded as if Bates wanted to pull out of that fund and set up its own pension plan for union employees. As the company's labor and employment lawyer, Alex was giving the CEO and CFO his take on the possible consequences of that action. Alex couched his words in a lot of legalese, but his meaning was clear. The unions would go on strike.

I found nothing else of interest in the recycling bin, so I turned my attention to the filing cabinets. I moved quickly from drawer to drawer, but nothing caught my eye. The bookcases held a variety of publications one might usually find in a corporate legal department, the subject matter ranging from intellectual property to hazardous waste to antitrust.

I was about to give up my search when I saw a piece of paper stuck between volumes of the state's Food, Drug, and Cosmetic Act and the *California Regulatory Law Reporter*. I tugged on the sheet with thumb and forefinger, gently working it from its hiding place.

It was a photocopy of an article dealing with foodborne pathogens, in this case Escherichia coli 0157:H7, commonly known as E. coli. Had it been placed here inadvertently? Or on purpose?

Whatever it meant, I'd have to figure it out later. I folded the single sheet several times, until it was a small square, then stuck it into the pocket of the skirt I wore, glancing at my watch at the same time. In my zeal to search Rob's office, I'd lost track of time. How long had I been here? Twenty minutes, half an hour, or more? Long enough, I feared, for someone to notice I wasn't where I was supposed to be.

I flicked off the light, opened the door, and stepped into the corridor, colliding with a large moving body. I stepped back, muttering, "Excuse me."

Then I focused on the face that was glaring at me suspiciously, the eyes whose interest in my surreptitious activities signaled trouble.

It was Buck Tarcher, the corporate security chief.

"WHAT ARE YOU DOING IN THERE?" TARCHER DE-manded.

"I beg your pardon?" I said politely, wide-eyed with innocence and stalling for time.

Tarcher had no intention of letting me pass without an explanation. "I asked you what you were doing in that office."

"Looking for a file."

It was the truth, in a way. I gave him a baffled look that asked what else a secretary would be doing in an office. Of course, I was no ordinary secretary. And the office in question was that of someone who'd been murdered.

At that moment the cavalry arrived. Gladys rounded the corner from the south hallway, looking monumentally pissed off. If I'd had to make a guess as to why, I'd say she was irked because I'd disappeared for awhile.

"There you are," she snapped, putting hands on her hips and a lot of emphasis on the first word. "I've been looking everywhere for you. I need you to do something, right now."

"I'm on my way." I sidestepped Tarcher and headed toward Gladys, hoping my smile put a better spin on the situation. Tarcher's glare didn't reassure me. And Gladys was feeling overworked, underappreciated, and ready to bitch at the first target, namely me.

"Where did you disappear to?" she grumbled when we entered Cube City.

"I was looking for something. I thought it might be in that paralegal's office."

"Well, leave it for now. Patricia just dumped a load of stuff in the rush box. With Nancy out of the office today, it's hard enough keeping up with all this work. I'm up to my ears in dictation tapes, and I can't be expected to do them all."

I apologized for my absence, grabbed the first of several dictation tapes that had to be transcribed yesterday, and put my nose to the proverbial grindstone, trying to get back in Gladys's good graces. I liked her. Besides, I didn't want to lose someone who'd proved to be a good source of information. Her verbal explosion seemed to have taken care of her injured feelings, though. As I made a dent in the work that had piled up, her good humor returned.

My run-in with Tarcher, however, left me with that eyes-on-my-back feeling the rest of the morning. I didn't think the corporate security chief had been mollified by my explanation for having been in Rob's office.

That was only part of the reason for the feeling. The other part was Vanitzky, who I encountered in the hallway as I returned from a trip to the copy machine. The chief financial officer was just exiting the general counsel's office. I guessed the meeting was over, though I saw no sign of the other attendees. Perhaps he'd stayed to talk further with Alex.

When Vanitzky saw me, he smiled again. What was it about the sly upturn of his mouth that made me feel as though he knew more about me than I wanted him to?

I pushed away my disquiet and detoured into Alex's office to empty his out box. If I was lucky, he'd have written or dictated some notes on the meeting. I was more than a little curious to know what had gone on. But I had no such luck. The dictation tape I spent the next half hour transcribing contained a number of letters and memos, none of which had anything to do with the items I'd glimpsed in the meeting folders.

One of the letters Alex had dictated was to go to an attorney in Washington, D.C. On the tape the general counsel said the address was in Nancy's Rolodex. I stopped transcribing, got up, and walked over to Nancy's cubicle, flipping through the cards to find the one for the attorney, whose last name started with an M. The Rolodex fell open to Patricia Mayhew's home address. Montclair, in the Oakland hills. I thought of the cable car I'd heard on the tape she'd dictated, and my assumption she lived in San Francisco. Where had she been when she'd recorded those words? Nolan Ward's place? I flipped Nancy's Rolodex to the Ws. He lived in San Francisco, all right, on Nob Hill near the route of the Powell Street cable car.

At twelve-thirty I told Gladys I was going to lunch and headed downstairs. My Franklin Street office, the one where I was Jeri Howard, private investigator, was a brisk fifteen-minute walk from the corporate headquarters of Bates Inc. I'd probably have expended the same amount of time if I drove and parked my car in the lot where I rented a space, so I walked, telling myself the exercise would do me good after being cooped up in an office all morning. That left me with half an hour to bolt down a sandwich from the corner deli and check the mail and messages. Not much time to accomplish what needed to be done, which was why I'd be back after five and early tomorrow morning.

I'd been working as a temp at Bates for only a week, but that eight-to-four-thirty schedule was taking a toll on my own business. I'd been at my own office at seven this morning, and yesterday morning, before I went to the temp job, but there were things a private investigator needed to do during the business hours when the temp was typing letters, such as the asset search an Oakland attorney had requested. Not being available was disrupting my investigative business.

I missed the flexibility of being self-employed. Working for myself meant I didn't have to check in with anyone else concerning the pattern and structure of my day. I could take two hours for lunch if I wanted to, or I could close my office early and head home if things were slow.

And they would be slow, if I spent too much time being Jeri the office temp instead of J. Howard Investigations. But Rob Lawter had hired me, and paid me, and I owed it to him to find out who killed him, and why.

I unfolded a letter from the building management and digested the unwelcome news that my office rent was being raised. Great timing, now that buying a house was going to increase my monthly expenses. I thought about that studio apartment above the garage of the new house. It was a good-sized space. As my real estate agent suggested, I could turn it into an office.

But this downtown Oakland location was far more accessible for my clients. There was also the issue of my privacy. Did I really want some of the people I'd encountered in my years as an investigator knowing where I lived? Last spring I'd weathered a scary incident involving a stalker, one who'd shown up at my apartment and left a calling card. I didn't want a repeat episode.

I'd just finished returning a phone call when my office door opened and Ruby Woods walked in. She held out the envelope she carried in her left hand. "I was gonna stick this under your door, then I heard your voice."

"What's that?"

"Your paycheck. Courtesy of Bates Inc., by way of Woods Temporaries. Next week make sure I don't have to come looking for your time card."

I laughed. "It almost seems as though I shouldn't take it. Since I'm on an assignment." She made a move to take the envelope away, and I grabbed it. "On the other hand, the building management just upped my rent."

"Mine, too," she said, shaking her head.

I opened the envelope and took out the check that represented the two days I'd worked at Bates last week. It was pitifully small. "Damn, by the time the feds and the state take their bites, there's hardly anything left. Why should I be surprised, though, with the self-employment tax I have to pay every year."

"Don't I know it," Ruby said. "You should lower your withholding, especially now that you're buying a house. When is the housewarming, by the way?"

"Sometime after I move in and unpack. And since I haven't even given 'em the down payment yet, I think we're getting ahead of ourselves." I looked at my office clock. I needed to leave in just a few minutes in order to make it back to Bates by one-thirty. "I hope I'm not going to be doing this Bates gig for much longer." And I wasn't sure how long, especially after this morning, I could keep up the pretense of being the temp. "Do you suppose your friend Laverne could do us a favor?"

"Depends on what it is," Ruby said. "She doesn't know about you."

"And I don't want her to know about me. I need some information on a couple of Bates employees. One of them is current, Leon Gomes. The other is a man named Charlie Kellerman. He doesn't work there any longer, and I think he was fired for misconduct."

Ruby thought for a moment, frowning. "With Kellerman, I could say a friend of mine was thinking about giving him a job, and could Laverne tell me anything about him. On Gomes, since he still works there, I don't know whether she'll be able to tell me anything."

"Don't push it. I don't want to put you at risk."

She nodded. "I appreciate the thought. But in for a penny, in for a pound. Leave it to me. I'll see what I can do."

I got back to the legal department a minute or so after one-thirty and set to work again. The next three and a half hours went quickly, and at five I was out the door again. Before I went back to my Franklin Street office, however, there was something I wanted to do.

Seeing all those birds, and the parrot, in the backyard of my new house had given me an urge to identify them. There was a large chain bookstore over at Jack London Square. Surely they'd have some sort of bird book I could use as a reference. So instead of retrieving my car from the Bates parking lot, I set out on foot toward the bookstore.

As I reached the Embarcadero, I suddenly felt a prickle on my neck. There was that eyes-on-my-back feeling again. I was being watched. Before I crossed the wide street, I looked to my left, as though looking at traffic. I didn't see anyone following me from the Bates building.

On the other side of the Embarcadero I walked the block from Webster to Franklin, then around to the front of the bookstore, which faced the buildings along the estuary. It was a big barn of a place, and I wasn't familiar with the layout, so I wandered the aisles for a moment, searching for books about birds. A field guide, or some such thing, that would help me tell the difference between a sparrow and a finch. Maybe I should figure out what kind of parrot I'd seen flying around with the pigeons while I was at it.

I found the section with books on nature and animals and examined the titles. There it was again, that prickly feeling. I was definitely being watched. I pulled one of the books from the shelf and flipped open the pages as though I were examining it. Then I turned to my left, head down, using my peripheral vision to sweep the interior of the bookstore. Nothing there. I placed the book back on the shelf and chose another volume. I turned to my right, pretending to read the pages of the book.

Now I saw David Vanitzky's head and the shoulders of his dark gray pinstriped suit. He was in a nearby alcove full of magazines and newspapers, about ten feet away, sauntering casually along a rack of business publications. He carried a couple of paperbacks in his left hand. Was he buying them, or was it camouflage?

I turned back toward the shelves and replaced the book. Then, right in front of me, I saw what I'd been looking for: *Birds of San Francisco and the Bay Area.* I pulled it from the shelf and leafed through it. Then I heard a voice next to me.

"Are you into bird-watching, Ms. Howard?"

I glanced to my right. Vanitzky had loosened the knot in his dark gray silk tie, and the bloodred ruby tiepin glowed in its gold setting. He looked elegant, as relaxed as a well-fed cat.

"Reference material, Mr. Vanitzky. What about you?" I glanced at the books he held. From the names on the covers I identified them as mysteries.

His eyes met mine and held them with his gaze. "Oh, I like a good detective story now and then."

Damn. Was he on to me? I looked at his sharp-featured face, searching for any indication that his reference to the books was an oblique reference to me. The chilly gray eyes gave nothing away.

I smiled noncommittally. With the bird book in my hand, I walked toward the cash registers arrayed at the front of the store. He fell into step beside me.

"You don't seem the bird-watching type," he commented, his voice friendlier than his eyes had been.

"You don't know me," I told him, with a sidelong glance. I stopped at one of the cash registers, waiting for the clerk to finish with the customer in front of me.

"No, I don't." He turned to face me. His eyes had warmed up a bit. "Let's remedy that. Care to join me for a little after-work libation?" He jerked his pointed chin in the direction of Jack's Bistro on the other side of Broadway.

I hesitated a second. Then I nodded and moved to the counter, where the clerk rang up my purchase. Vanitzky stayed behind me, close enough for me to get a whiff of the predator. Just who was stalking whom? I wanted information. Having a drink with him seemed like a good opportunity to get it.

But I was betting he wanted something from me. He must have had a reason for following me here. No way did I think this was a chance encounter. I recalled what everyone had told me about Vanitzky's reputation with women. Was the elegant shark in the gray suit putting the moves on the office temp? Possibly. The pheromones were definitely in play. Maybe that's what was in the wind. But there was something else going on besides a male-female attraction.

With our book purchases in hand, we walked from the bookstore, across the plaza at the foot of Broadway. Jack's Bistro was located just this side of the Waterfront Plaza Hotel. The hotel was more up-scale in its present incarnation, but it used to be a more utilitarian place called the Boatel. One night about eighteen months ago I'd had a confrontation not far from here, with a killer who had a gun. Both of us had wound up in the dark cold water of the estuary.

I pushed away the thought of that night as David Vanitzky held the door for me. Inside, the decor was striving for the look of an Italian trattoria. The restaurant windows opened on the estuary. In the bar I saw glass-topped tables and wrought-iron chairs with padded seats. Neither Vanitzky nor I was there for the view, however. We took a table near the bar. He ordered Scotch. I opted for a glass of chardonnay.

"Are there any specific birds you'd like to watch?" he asked, picking up the book I'd just bought.

"Not really." I gazed at him steadily. "I just like to know what I'm looking at."

"Do you?" He smiled as the cocktail waitress delivered our drinks. When she headed back toward the bar, his eyes followed her, as though he couldn't resist assessing the sleekness of her figure.

"Thanks for the wine, Mr. Vanitzky." I picked up the glass and took a sip. Just what the hell was he up to? I felt as though I'd joined the ballet and I was tippy-toeing around the stage of the Paramount, trying to get a grip on my partner.

Now the gray eyes slewed back toward me, twinkling with amusement as he reached for his Scotch. "Oh, call me David. And I'll call you Jeri."

"Are you in the habit of having drinks with secretaries?"

"Depends on the secretary." He knocked back about half his drink and set the glass down on the surface of the table. "You're an attractive woman. Do I need another reason?"

"Depends on the reason." I took another sip of wine. "I've heard stories about you."

"Already? You've only been working at Bates a week. Stories about my business acumen? Or my success with women?"

"Stories about your ego, maybe."

"Ouch. A well-placed shot." He saluted me with his glass. Then he swallowed the rest and signaled the cocktail waitress for another. "I won't ask you where the stories came from."

"Just what is it you want to ask me?"

"How long do you plan to work at Bates?"

I shrugged. "I understand they're shorthanded in the legal department. So I guess I'll stay as long as they need a temp."

"Temp doesn't pay all that well. Interested in earning more money?"

His voice lowered as he spoke, and he leaned forward. Now he looked like a predator again, with his lean face and his hawk's beak, with his gray eyes like a raptor's looking for prey. I found myself leaning back, involuntarily, as though I wasn't sure what he'd do with me if he caught me.

"Just what sort of proposition are you making . . . David?" I picked up my glass and fortified myself with wine. I wondered if his secretary was about to retire. On the other hand, the intimate tone in his voice made it sound as though he had something carnal in mind, such as getting me into the sack. I wouldn't put it past him.

I chose my words carefully. "You're right, temping is a short-term option. If you're talking about a more permanent job, I might be interested. Is there a position available in executive territory? Perhaps in the office of the chief financial officer?"

"I'd rather you stayed right where you are." His voice turned soft and deadly, and there was a wicked gleam in his eyes. "In the legal department, working with Hank Irvin. As long as you report back to me."

"YOU WANT ME TO SPY ON HANK IRVIN."

I stared at him, considering the implications of what I'd just heard. From the way he'd led up to it, I wouldn't have been at all surprised if Vanitzky had asked me for a date. I was almost disappointed that he hadn't. I'd been enjoying the dance so far. But the relationship he'd just proposed offered some intriguing possibilities.

Vanitzky wasn't one to beat around the bush, now that his cards were on the table. He leaned back, fingers tracing a pattern on the side of his glass. The seductive intimacy evident in his voice a few minutes earlier gave way to the clipped tones of the corporate shark. He seemed quite confident that I'd do what he asked.

"That's precisely what I want you to do." He raised the glass to his lips and swallowed some more Scotch. "I'll make the compensation worth the risk, of course."

"Why?" Go ahead, I thought. Drop the information in my lap. He didn't say anything, so I gave him some encouragement. "Does this have something to do with the possibility that Hank Irvin will be the next general counsel?"

"You know about that." He didn't frame the words as a question. In fact, he wasn't even surprised that I knew.

"I heard it on the grapevine," I said, with a deprecating shrug. "Secretaries hear lots of things." And the Bates grapevine was working overtime these days.

David laughed. "Exactly my point. Secretaries run the whole damn outfit. Corporate America would collapse without them."

"If that's the case, why aren't they paid better?" I couldn't resist the barb, especially after that tiny paycheck I'd received earlier today.

"I'm prepared to remedy that inequity. Handsomely." His voice insinuated intimacy. After all, we were about to become partners in crime. "As a secretary, you're perfectly positioned to gather information."

"Oh, yes. Secretaries are invisible, almost like office furniture." I sipped wine, watching his face over the rim of my glass. I was beginning to understand how he'd risen so high in the cutthroat corporate world. This guy didn't miss a chance to slip the knife into the back of the guy on the next rung up the ladder. "As a temporary employee, of course, I have no loyalties to any particular person, or department."

David's eyes twinkled. "I see we understand each other. I knew you were sharp the minute I laid eyes on you."

I set the glass down and ran my finger around the rim. "How much money are we talking about?" He named a figure that was more than tempting. I tilted my head to one side, as though I were considering asking for more. "Just what do I have to do to earn that? Is there something Hank's done that piques your interest? It seems to me I need to know what's going on, so I'll know what to look for."

He looked at me as though he was assessing just how far he could trust me. "You know Hank used to work for a law firm in the city, Berkshire and Gentry."

I nodded. "I've heard of them. Quite large. Lots of important clients. Including Rittlestone and Weper."

"And I used to work for Rittlestone and Weper."

"Still do, don't you? You, Nolan Ward in production, Tonya Russell in human resources, and all those other Rittlestone and Weper graduates who moved to Bates after the LBO."

He studied me. "You have learned a lot in your week in the legal department."

"Isn't that why you're interested in me?" I challenged him with a stare.

He smiled. "I work for Bates now. Of course, Rittlestone and Weper own a controlling share of Bates. So I suppose in a roundabout way I do work for R&W."

Of course he did, even if the chain of command wasn't as direct as it had been before. David was Frank Weper's former assistant, a high-level player over at Rittlestone and Weper. He probably still reported to Weper.

Or maybe David Vanitzky didn't have any loyalty to anyone but himself.

I drank some more chardonnay, wondering why David didn't trust Hank. From what I'd heard on the company rumor mill, Hank made the move from his partnership in that big law firm, at R&W's behest, for the express purpose of taking over as general counsel from Alex, who might not be ready to retire. But if R&W wanted Alex out, they'd make it happen.

And if R&W got rid of Jeff Bates, the current chief executive officer, I was now looking at the man who was going to succeed him. Unless whoever was behind David on the corporate ladder slipped a shiv between his ribs.

Did David suspect Hank of being the man with the knife? It sounded as though Rittlestone and Weper's point man didn't trust Berkshire and Gentry's point man. Could this presage a bloody power struggle was going on behind the scenes at Bates?

"Do you think Hank is interested in something other than Alex Campbell's job?" I asked.

Now it was David's turn to shrug. "Finding out what Hank's career plans are is your job."

"Suppose someone finds out I'm collecting information for you. I'd lose my job. What about you? Aren't you worried someone might retaliate?"

"Retaliate?" He laughed, but his smile didn't extend to his cold eyes. "Anything's possible. But you see, Jeri, I know where the bodies are buried. Too damn many of them."

From the look on his face, I was certain he'd buried a few of them himself. And his knowledge of where the bodies were buried might just be the reason someone wanted to bury David Vanitzky.

"What makes you think Hank wants to climb higher up the corporate ladder?"

David narrowed his eyes. "I'm an ambitious man. I recognize the symptoms when I see them."

"If Hank is making a move, he must have someone in his corner who'll back his play," I said. "Who do you think that might be?"

"Let's not mention any names right now."

"I see. Playing your cards close to the chest."

David smiled. "Always a good idea," he said, "in a high-stakes game."

"Just how high are the stakes?"

He didn't answer. Instead he gulped down the rest of his Scotch and stared at the glass as though he was debating the wisdom of having another.

"Suppose I find out Hank's career plans are more ambitious than you think they should be. What happens then?"

His hand tightened on the glass as he growled, "I'll get out my shovel."

My enlightening after-work libation with David Vanitzky was very much on my mind as I unlocked my office door that evening, wearily contemplating another hour or so of catch-up work. The red light on my answering machine was blinking rapidly, so the first thing I did was take down the messages. Most of them related to other on-going investigations, but two were about the Lawter case.

The first was from Sally Morgan, the neighbor who'd heard noises in Rob's apartment the night he went out the window. The second was from Rob's niece Robin Hartzell. She told me it wasn't a good idea to call her. She'd try to reach me again later, she said, either here at the office or at my apartment. I looked at my watch. Six-thirty. She probably had to get away from the house in order to get in touch with me.

I picked up the phone and called Sally Morgan. After I'd identified myself, she said, "I thought you should know there was a woman here today, asking questions about Rob."

"Really? When did you see her?" I leaned forward in my office chair and picked up a pencil, moving my lined yellow pad into position.

"I took the day off because I had a doctor's appointment and some errands to run. I got home about two o'clock and saw her in the hall, trying to talk with Charlie Kellerman. Then she started asking me questions. Like what happened the night he died, and whether anyone else besides the police was asking about it. I didn't tell her about you."

"Thanks. What did she look like?"

"She was Asian," Sally Morgan said. "Chin-length black hair with lots of gray streaks, brown eyes. Round face with a little mole just to the left of her mouth. Mid-forties, I'd guess, about five foot three."

I dropped the pencil onto the pad. I didn't need to write down the particulars. The woman Sally Morgan had just described had to be Nancy Fong, who was supposedly home sick with one of her migraines.

What was she doing over at Rob's apartment? And what was she after?

CHAPTER *26*

IT WAS NEARING EIGHT O'CLOCK WHEN I DECIDED TO CALL it a day. A long one, considering the time I'd spent at Bates and here at my own office.

My stomach rumbled and growled as I turned off the computer. What did I have in the refrigerator, I wondered, that didn't require much more than a can opener or a quick pass through the microwave? Or maybe I should stop at the Chinese restaurant down the street and grab some take-out before going home.

The phone rang, and I sighed wearily. Should I pick it up, or let the machine take it? I opted for the latter. But when I heard Robin Hartzell's voice, I quickly snatched up the receiver.

"I'm here," I told her.

"Mom and Leon went out to dinner," she said without preamble. "They just left, and they won't be back for an hour or so. Doug's over at a friend's house, supposedly studying. Now's your chance to look through Rob's stuff."

"I'll be there in twenty minutes."

I pushed aside my hunger pangs and all thoughts of dinner, heading for my car and the Nimitz Freeway. Fortunately the evening rush hour was over, and I made good time as I headed south. I took the Davis Street exit and headed east toward downtown San Leandro. I parked the Toyota around the corner on Parrott Street and walked quickly to the Hartzells' house on Clarke. Robin had the front door open as I came up the walk.

"It's all in the garage," she said, her voice conspiratorially low.

She led the way through the living room and kitchen to a side door. The double garage was dim, even after Robin switched on the overhead light. Immediately to my left, I saw a washer and dryer against the back wall, with a red plastic basket full of sheets and towels resting on the concrete floor in front of the washer. Next to these appliances, another door led to the backyard. Two tall metal shelves stood against the opposite wall, crowded with tools and equipment, boxes of Christmas decorations, and several suitcases.

Rob's possessions took up about half the space in the garage. The furniture was stacked in the far corner, next to the metal shelves. Boxes were piled in the middle of the oil-stained floor. I walked toward them, wondering where to start. The carton on top of the nearest stack had "KITCHEN" written on the side in black letters. Beyond that I saw several more, labeled "BEDROOM" and "LIVING ROOM."

"I don't know where anything is," Robin told me. "Since Leon and his buddies packed all of it. Looks like they went room by room; at least they labeled the boxes."

"The things from his apartment can wait, for now. What I'd really like to look at is the box that came from his office at work. One of the secretaries, Nancy Fong, brought it to your mother last week."

"Oh, that one." Robin crossed to the shelves. "Mom didn't even look through it. Said she couldn't deal with it right now. So she stuck it up here with the Christmas stuff."

She pulled down a medium-sized cardboard box that had once held reams of copy paper, set it on the floor, and pulled off the lid. I peered inside, then reached for a spiral-bound Sierra Club calendar, about five by seven inches. In addition to keeping track of appointments, people frequently jot down important information on their calendars. In more than one case, notes have led me in the right direction.

"May I keep this for awhile?" I asked Robin.

"Sure. Take anything, if you think it will help."

I tucked the calendar into my purse, then knelt to examine the other contents of the box. There were a couple of books, one a dictionary of legal terms and the other a paralegal handbook. Beneath these was a neatly folded cardigan sweater, tan with leather patches at the elbows and pockets at the front. I checked the pockets, finding only lint and a receipt from the same deli where I'd had lunch with Gladys.

Next I saw a knit muffler, black wool with white diamonds, and a pair of brown leather gloves. I stuck my hands into the gloves. My fingers encountered something in the index finger of the left glove. I pulled out a rolled-up bit of lined yellow paper. Since it wasn't the sort of thing Rob would have left in a glove accidentally, I assumed he'd hidden it there. When I unrolled it, I saw some scribbled notes. There didn't seem to be any rhyme or reason to them, but I saw the date "1985" and the word "listeria." I'd have to figure that one out when I had more time, so I tucked the paper into my purse next to Rob's calendar.

Several small items rattled inside a letter-sized envelope with a Bates Inc. return address. Inside I found a gold Cross pen-and-pencil set with Rob's initials engraved on each piece and a silver bookmark with a red ribbon tassel. The other items in the box included a small square Sony clock radio, a blue ceramic coffee mug, a small tin box with a geometric pattern that contained several bags of herbal tea, and a glass paperweight with seashells embedded inside.

At the bottom of the box were a manila file folder and three family photographs, all five by seven inches. The picture frames were inexpensive, plain wood and glass. I picked up each one and examined the photographs. The first was a formal shot of Rob's sister, looking as though it had been taken in a studio several years ago. In this shot, Carol Hartzell seemed to be less beaten down by life than the woman I'd met on my first visit to this house. The second photo was more relaxed, a current Christmas picture showing Carol with both her children, seated on a sofa I recognized as the one in the living room.

The third photo had been taken outdoors in a place where there were windswept golden dunes and blue waves crashing against the shore. It showed Robin and her brother Doug, both smiling and relaxed, their hair blowing in the breeze.

"This was taken at Point Reyes," Robin said, her voice wistful as she fingered the edge of the frame. "Last spring."

I glanced at the photo, then picked up the file folder. I opened it and leafed through the contents. Here were some Bates Inc. forms concerning Rob's medical and dental benefits, and a photocopy of his W-4, several statements from the Bates 401(k) plan, and an out-dated flyer about an earthquake preparedness meeting. At the bottom of the stack I found three photocopies, all appearing to be work related.

The first was a printout from the Food and Drug Administration's "Bad Bug Book" Web site. It concerned foodborne pathogens on produce from countries outside the United States, including hepatitis A on strawberries from Mexico and cyclospora on raspberries from Guatemala. The second printout, from the same source, dealt with the rise in salmonella cases in the United States. The third item was a long article from a medical journal. In addition to hepatitis A and cyclospora, it mentioned E. coli, as well as salmonella, botulism, campylobacter, cryptosporidium, and listeria. The latter was the same word written on the bit of yellow paper. I was skimming through the first paragraph of the article when the sound of an engine vibrated through the closed garage door, signaling that a vehicle had turned into the driveway.

"They're home." Robin's whisper was urgent. "You gotta get out of here." She waved toward the door that led out to the backyard. "Through there, then around the garage. There's a gate by the trash cans, but it's unlocked."

I folded the copies and tucked them into my purse, moving toward the door. Robin followed, then realized she was still holding the photograph. She turned to put it back into the box, but it slipped from her fingers and fell to the floor. I heard the tinkle of glass breaking on the concrete.

"Damn," she said again, her voice sounding loud as the vehicle in the driveway cut its engine. I heard voices, Carol's and Leon's, and the hard metallic slam of a door.

Robin squatted on her haunches to retrieve the frame, her hands carefully picking through the broken glass. Then I spotted something white that had slipped from behind the photo.

"Wait a minute." I quickly tugged the corner and removed a rectangle that turned out to be three sheets of letter-sized paper, folded together in quarters.

"Take it and go," Robin ordered. We'd both heard voices again, this time coming from the house.

Instead I reached for the two other photos and quickly turned them over, pulling down the backing. Sure enough, there were similar folded sheets of paper behind the backing of each one. I pulled them out and stuck them in my purse as I flew out the back door, into the darkened yard, then rounded the corner and flattened myself against the side of the house. I heard the door connecting the garage and the house open.

"What are you doing out here?" Leon's voice was loud and suspicious.

"I'm missing a sock," she told him, her tone sullen. "Thought it might be in the dryer." I heard a sound as she opened the appliance's door, then slammed it shut.

In the dim space between this house and the next one I saw a couple of recycling containers, a trash can, and a gate made of the same chain link as the fence. I opened it as quietly as possible, then headed around the corner to the relative safety of my car.

Once inside the Toyota, I snapped on the overhead dome light, looking through my booty. The white sheets of paper, eleven in all, were all photocopies, and they were all similar. At the top of each one was the legend "Call Sheet," but the dates were different, ranging from late July to late August. They appeared to be customer complaint forms, showing the caller's name and phone number, the date and time of the call, and, in what I recognized as Rob's handwriting, some notes about the subject of the call. The car's dome light was dim, so I had to squint to make out the words. At the bottom of the one with the most recent date, I saw a word that looked like "listeria," with a question mark behind it. I unrolled the yellow paper and examined it again.

"Listeria" and "1985," I read, and to one side, what looked like several initials. What did it mean?

I heard voices and looked up. A couple of teenage boys were walking toward my car, talking loudly and laughing. As they stepped into the light from the streetlamp on the corner, I recognized one of them as Doug Hartzell. I switched off the dome light, set the papers aside, and started my car, pulling away from the curb just as Doug and his friend came abreast of my parking space.

I headed for Oakland, thinking about what I'd just found. Listeria was some kind of bacteria. I sifted through my memory, trying to recall where I'd heard about it. Something about contaminated cheese, down in Southern California, I thought. The reference to listeria fit right in with the copies I'd found in the file folder. And earlier today, I'd found another article on foodborne illnesses when I'd searched Rob's old office at Bates. Had Rob been interested in these subjects because they were part of the regulatory aspect of a food industry job? Or was there another reason?

On the drive home, I wondered just what potentially hazardous bacteria might lurk in the Bates Best products in my kitchen. I even hauled a can of beans from the cupboard and a carton of yogurt from the refrigerator when I got home, ignoring the plaintive cries of Abigail and Black Bart, who had followed me to the kitchen in anticipation of food.

The label on the can of California pinquitos, little pink beans, proclaimed its contents as prepared pinquito beans, water, salt, sugar, red chili peppers, dehydrated onion, cumin, and dehydrated garlic. Nothing about the specter of botulism, which according to the article I'd found in Rob's things, was an obligate anaerobe associated with canned food. The carton of raspberry yogurt made me think about the possibility of cyclospora, the pathogen mentioned in the Web site printout. But the small print on the white plastic carton labeled Bates Best listed only active yogurt cultures, including acidophilus, as well as pasteurized nonfat milk, raspberries, modified cornstarch, fructose, kosher gelatin, citric acid, tricalcium phosphate, and red dye number 40.

I read labels all the time, but usually I was looking at calories, or fat and sodium content. Now, as I stuck the can into the cupboard, the carton into the refrigerator, and turned my attention to the cat food, I wondered how susceptible the food I ate was to the microbes detailed in the "Bad Bug Book."

I spread the items I'd found in the garage on my oak dining table. First I examined the rolled-up bit of yellow lined paper that had been tucked into Rob's glove. Was it my imagination, or were two of those initials "LG"? Leon Gomes? What might he have to do with something that happened in 1985 involving listeria?

I sifted through the call sheets. In each case, someone had phoned Bates to complain about a product, and Rob had fielded the calls. The first sheet was dated July 29 and the last, August 26. Judging from the area codes, the calls came from all over the Bay Area. I picked up the pad I kept next to the phone and made a list. Of the eleven callers, seven had consumed ice cream in four different flavors. Three had eaten ice cream novelties such as bars or sandwiches, and one wasn't sure whether what made him sick was yogurt or ice cream. Eight of the call sheets also contained a six-digit number, but not all of these numbers matched. Was this a batch number? I got up and examined the contents of my refrigerator again. Sure enough, the yogurt carton contained a sell-by date and a six-digit batch number.

I made myself a cup of tea, then glanced at Rob's engagement calendar. He'd noted each of the eleven calls there, as well as the six-digit numbers. There were four different batch numbers, none of them in succession. Stuck between the pages for the month of December, I found two short newspaper articles. One was about a Fremont dairy that had been cited on July 10 of this year for fecal contamination of milk. The other concerned a 1994 salmonella outbreak that sickened nearly a quarter of a million people in several states. It had resulted from ice cream being hauled in tanker trucks that had previously transported contaminated liquid eggs.

I sat back in my chair, thinking. There was no indication that anyone had taken any action on these calls. Surely Bates had some standard follow-up procedure to deal with customer complaints.

I picked up the phone and called Kaz Pelligrino, the doctor I've been dating since the beginning of the year. I wasn't sure I'd find him at home, but he answered on the second ring.

"Tell me about foodborne illnesses," I said, fingering the yellow slip of paper on which Rob had written "listeria" and "1985."

"Not even a 'Hi, Kaz, how are you?'" He chuckled, but he knew how I was when a case was worrying me. "This isn't my specialty, but I'll tell you what I know. I have some personal experience. There are two kinds of food poisoning. One happens when something is at the wrong temperature and bacteria gets into the food. The classic case is potato salad with mayonnaise left out in the sun at a picnic. You eat it, you get sick in a matter of hours, and it's over. The other kind is basically an infection. You ingest live organisms, and they start growing inside you. It takes longer for you to get sick, and it's worse. Getting over it takes time and antibiotics. Now, can you be more specific? Which bacteria interests you?"

"Let's start with listeria," I said, "then move on to salmonella and whatever else crops up in dairy products."

"Listeria is a group of bacteria. The disease listeriosis is caused by one species called Listeria monocytogenes. It's present in the environment, soil, dust, water. It usually gets into the food chain through fecal contamination."

"There was an outbreak down in the Los Angeles area, right? Involving cheese, as I recall."

"Mid-eighties," Kaz confirmed. "I was working down there at the time. There were over a hundred and forty cases, and forty-six people died. It was traced to soft, Mexican-style cheese manufactured with contaminated milk. There was another outbreak two years later in Philadelphia. Healthy people usually don't contract listeriosis, but people with weakened immune systems are vulnerable, like my HIV and AIDS patients, and also elderly people, newborns, and pregnant women. Most of the deaths occur in these groups."

"Is the food involved usually dairy based?"

"No. There was an outbreak in Canada that was traced to the cabbage in some coleslaw. And a recall of contaminated hummus, just recently."

"Okay," I said. "Salmonella next."

"Salmonella and campylobacter are the most common," Kaz said. "In fact, salmonella cases have doubled in the past twenty years. Both of them are reportable illnesses, which means if a doctor treats a case he's supposed to report it to the local health department. If they get reports from several doctors, they'll start investigating, to see if they can trace the source."

"How long does that take?"

"Sometimes weeks or months. Now, you were asking about dairy products. Salmonella also shows up in produce. Also in eggs. Contamination when they're laid, through cracks, for example, like contamination from the cow's udder when it's milked. There's also one species of salmonella that can infect the chicken and contaminate the eggs before the shells are formed. As for campylobacter, that's the personal experience I was talking about."

"You had it? What was it like?"

He chuckled again. "Thought I was gonna die. There's a rule of thumb—the worse the disease, the longer the incubation period.

With salmonella, the onset is anywhere from six hours to four days. Campylobacter crops up in two to five days. Mine hit three days after I ate a casserole made with chicken and cheese. That was back in the days before I became a vegetarian. In fact, the experience had a lot to do with my becoming a vegetarian. I was one sick fella— diarrhea, vomiting, cramps, and a fever of a hundred and three degrees."

"Fruits and veggies aren't all that safe, either," I pointed out, leafing through the papers I'd found in Rob's things. "You said salmonella shows up on produce. I'm looking at an article that says E. coli has shown up on lettuce. And don't forget that company here in the Bay Area that had to recall its products made with unpasteurized apple juice."

"Pasteurization is the key," Kaz said. "The food is brought to a certain temperature and held at that temperature for a period of time. There's a reason our great-grandmothers cooked everything until the meat was well done and the vegetables were mushy. Back in the days before adequate refrigeration, they assumed the food supply was contaminated. They knew that heating food to a high temperature for a long time was the only way to get rid of the bugs. But today people eat sushi and rare meat. Consumers want a fresh, year-round supply of produce, which sometimes comes from countries where farming methods are different."

"And you get cyclospora on raspberries and hepatitis A on strawberries," I finished. "So food poisoning has moved away from that spoiled potato salad you were talking about."

"It's no longer limited to botulism in Aunt Sadie's improperly canned green beans," Kaz said. "Something like that occurs in someone's kitchen and affects only a few people. Food processing happens on a massive scale, and it affects millions of people. It's out of the kitchen and into big companies with multiple facilities and wide distribution. That's why something like an E. coli outbreak spreads so rapidly."

Multiple facilities, I thought. Bates had them all over the East Bay, like the dairy plant Leon Gomes managed.

CHAPTER 27

SINCE PATRICIA WAS THE BATES ATTORNEY WHO HANDLED food law, I wanted to take a closer look at her files. She even provided me with the opportunity for some sleuthing on Thursday morning. As I stepped out of the elevator on the fourth floor, she got aboard, carrying a thick accordion folder under one arm.

"I'm going to a meeting in Nolan Ward's office," she said, dispensing with good morning. "I should be back by ten. I left a tape in the rush box. I'd appreciate it if you'd do it first thing."

The elevator doors closed, blocking her from view. Patricia was certainly spending a lot of time with the head of production. She didn't say what the meeting was about, so I guessed it was the FDA food-safety proposals she'd mentioned in the legal department staff meeting earlier this week. Given what I'd found out last night, I had a heightened interest in food safety. Patricia's absence, if only for an hour or so, would give me an opportunity to examine her files.

At the door of Cube City, I met Gladys, who held a stack of filing in her arms and breezily informed me that she was going back to the file room to catch up on the ever-present, unstemmed flow of filing. Nancy was back, she added as she headed down the corridor past Rob's old office.

I shot Gladys an inquiring look. She shrugged. "I guess she's over her migraine, but she seems a little grumpy. Of course, she's always a little grumpy, if you ask me."

When I entered Cube City, Nancy stood at her workstation sorting through the pile of papers that had accumulated yesterday. "Good morning," I said, and she returned my greeting.

I settled in at my cubicle. A moment later, I glanced up and saw Nancy looking at me. Her phone rang. She dropped her eyes and reached for the receiver. As Gladys had said, Nancy seemed to have recovered from the migraine that had put her out of commission yesterday. But I was picking up on an undercurrent that hadn't been present when I'd last seen her, Tuesday afternoon. Did it have something to do with the fact that she'd been asking questions at Rob's apartment building Wednesday afternoon? Was the migraine in fact a ruse?

I picked up the dictation tape Patricia had left in the rush box, then plugged it into the machine. I began transcribing a series of memos, to Alex, Nolan Ward, and the manager of the canned goods plant in Oakland. It had something to do with a discharge of water from the plant and an objection filed by the local water quality board.

When I'd completed the tape, I removed the memos from the printer and headed for Patricia's office, hoping I wouldn't be interrupted. As I stepped into the east hallway, Hank Irvin rounded the corner, carrying his briefcase and a garment bag. He must have come to the office straight from the airport, and he looked preoccupied.

"I thought you were due back from Texas yesterday," I said.

He glanced at me and smiled. "Got delayed. I'm glad to be back. It was hot down there."

"Really? What part of Texas were you in?"

"El Paso," he said, pushing open his office door. "Is Alex here?"

"As far as I know. Though I haven't seen him."

Hank disappeared into his office. He hadn't mentioned his side trip to Carlsbad, New Mexico, but there was no reason why he should share that information. I turned and opened the door of Patricia's office, wondering what Hank would say if he knew David Vanitzky had asked me to spy on him.

I set the completed memos in Patricia's in box, then turned my attention to the documents and file folders neatly arrayed across the wide surface of her desk. I saw one file on weights and measures, and another labeled "Environmental Protection Agency." I didn't see the file on the Food and Drug Administration's food-safety proposals. Presumably that was the folder that had been stuck under Patricia's arm when she went downstairs for her meeting.

I was leafing through Patricia's calendar when I heard the door open. Quickly I moved to the out basket, scooping up the papers there as Nancy Fong entered the office.

"Hello," I said, and walked toward the door. "Hope your head is better."

"I'm fine." She shrugged, as though the migraine meant nothing, and folded her arms over her chest, wrinkling the front of the blue linen dress she wore. "Buck Tarcher called me this morning. He says you were in Rob Lawter's office yesterday."

I gave an offhand shrug as I reached for the doorknob. "I was looking for a file."

"Did you find what you were looking for?" Nancy said, her face solemn.

"No." I smiled as though it didn't matter. "Turns out the file was here in Patricia's office all along."

"I'd rather you didn't go in that office. I've told Gladys that, as well."

"Why?" What I really wanted to ask her was what she had been doing at Rob's apartment yesterday.

Nancy didn't say anything right away, as though she had secrets to keep. "Orders from Tarcher," she said finally, a classic cop-out. "You don't need to know."

"No, I suppose I don't." I shifted the papers I held from my right arm to the left and stepped out into the hallway. "Guess I'd better get back to work."

For the rest of the morning, I felt as though eyes were on my back each time I stepped away from the cubicle. One pair of eyes belonged to Buck Tarcher, the head of corporate security. I didn't think the office help usually had much interaction with Tarcher, unless they were suspected of wrongdoing. At eleven o'clock, I saw him in the corridor outside Alex's office. Call me paranoid, but I felt as though I were the suspect and Tarcher was bearing down on me.

But it could have had something to do with the trouble surrounding the retirement plan. That was where David Vanitzky and his knowing gray eyes came in. He was taking part in whatever was going on behind the closed door in Alex's office. When I passed David in the hall as he left, he glanced my way. I knew he was expecting some payback on my implied agreement to spy on Hank.

The third pair of eyes were Nancy's. Every time I looked up, it seemed as though she was looking away. Maybe it was beginning to dawn that I might not be an ordinary temp legal secretary. Maybe I was being paranoid. Maybe not.

But I remembered a poster I'd seen once. It said, just because you're paranoid doesn't mean they're not out to get you.

I didn't think Gladys had noticed Nancy's interest in me. We were all too busy. Now that Hank Irvin had returned from his mysterious trip, he was playing catch-up, trying to clear away the projects that had stacked up in his absence. He was in and out of Cube City constantly, piling dictation tapes in the rush box. Some of them were agreements, but one was a memo to Alex. The subject line was "Sheffield," and it indicated that an acquisition was proceeding according to plan, with no anticipated problems. I hadn't seen Sheffield mentioned before, in any of the papers I'd filed or typed.

Nancy left for lunch at a quarter to twelve, without saying where she was going. At noon, Gladys and I walked over to the deli for sandwiches. I needed some more information, and I was hoping my office mate could give it to me.

"What happens when someone calls in a complaint about Bates products?" I asked while we waited our turn at the counter.

She gave me a sidelong glance. "Why? Did you get a bad box of crackers?"

I extemporized. "No. A friend of mine is going through a hassle with a grocery store about some spoiled meat. It got me to wondering what the process was like at Bates."

Gladys didn't answer until after the man behind the deli counter took our orders. "Usually the switchboard forwards those calls to public affairs. But sometimes they come to the legal department. On any kind of call like that, we're supposed to fill out a call sheet. We make copies, one for the appropriate attorney, one for public affairs, and one for the department that should be handling the situation. If it's a complaint about a Bates product, the call sheet goes downstairs to production. We used to have a food-safety guy named Al Dominici who handled those things. But he retired in March, and they never hired anyone to replace him. Guess they thought it was more important to eliminate one more position. So now I don't know what production does with call sheets after they get them."

"Sounds like you've gotten a few complaint calls."

Gladys rolled her eyes as she popped the tab on her root beer. "Yeah. I hate them. Some people have legitimate complaints, of course. For the most part, they're reasonable on the phone. It's the nut calls I hate. That's what I call 'em, whether the people are crazy or not. They scream, make threats, call me names. Those are the ones I hang up on."

So Rob had received eleven calls in a month, I thought. Presumably he'd followed policy and forwarded them to production. Why then had he kept copies of the call sheets, concealed behind the photographs on his desk?

After lunch I found an excuse to visit production on the second floor when I returned from a trip to the mail room. I made my way through the hallways, lined with office doors like those on the fourth floor. I'd checked the company directory, and Sue Ann Fisk was listed as Nolan Ward's secretary.

Ward's office was located in the corner where the north and west hallways met. His door was closed, but a woman with curly gray hair sat behind a desk in a nearby cubicle, talking into a telephone receiver. On her desk I saw a plastic photo cube showing snapshots of two young children, a couple in their twenties, and a much older man I guessed was her husband. A glass vase held a drooping collection of pink carnations, and she had a mug at her elbow, with what looked like an herbal tea bag floating in the water.

"Sue Ann Fisk?" I asked, when she'd hung up the phone.

She smiled, showing off lots of laugh lines and some uneven front teeth. "That's me. Can I help you?"

"Jeri Howard. I'm working up in legal. I wanted to follow up on some call sheets that were sent down here."

"D'you have dates? And the names of the callers?" She turned to her keyboard, exited her word processing program, and entered a database program.

I'd noted the information on a notepad. Now I took the sheet of paper from my skirt pocket and handed it to her.

"Eleven? That's a lot." Sue Ann played with her database for a few moments, then turned and looked up at me. "I'm sorry, I'm not finding any of these names, or these dates, either."

I frowned. "You're sure?"

"I'm afraid so. Maybe you'd better double-check on the names and dates."

"I will. Do you suppose the sheets could have gotten lost in the interoffice mail?"

She took a sip of herbal tea. "I could see losing one or two. But eleven? I don't think so. Besides, I log the sheets as soon as I get them."

"So you open the mail," I prompted. "And log them right away."

Sue Ann shook her head. "Well, not exactly. I open the mail and take it in to Nolan. We used to have a man who worked in this department named Al Dominici. He was our food-safety manager. Anyway, he followed up on calls. But Al retired a couple of months after Nolan became department head. Now Nolan handles the situation, or directs it to one of the plants. After he's signed off on the sheets, he sends 'em back out to me, and then I log them."

So it would be easy enough, I speculated as I looked at Ward's closed door, for the head of production to intercept a sheet if he didn't want it logged.

Sue Ann noted the direction of my eyes and smiled, ever helpful. "I can ask Nolan about it as soon as he's finished with his meeting."

"Let me look into it on my end," I told her. "Maybe I don't have the correct names or dates."

"You know," she said. "Someone asked me for a printout of all the calls we'd logged concerning dairy products. It's been about a month ago. Now who was it?" She thought for a moment, then shook her head. "Can't put a name to it. If I think of it, I'll call you. What's your extension?"

I gave her the number. Then, as I turned to leave, I heard voices, then Ward's door opened. I saw a fortyish man about my height, maybe shorter. He'd removed his suit coat and loosened his tie, as many of the men here did when they were working in their offices.

He glanced out at Sue Ann and me, looking tense and distracted, then back into his office as though he were waiting for someone to leave. I guessed this was Ward. He looked familiar, as though I'd seen him in the hallways.

The man who walked past Ward a few seconds later was more than familiar. Leon Gomes strode through the outer office, dressed in his work clothes with the Bates logo on the breast pocket of his shirt. He looked like a thundercloud just itching to rain on someone, and I didn't want to be in his path.

CHAPTER *28*

I DUCKED MY HEAD AND DROPPED THE PAPER I WAS HOLDING onto the carpet. As I knelt to retrieve it, I hoped Leon wouldn't see me. Or if he did, that he wouldn't recognize me as the woman who'd visited Carol almost two weeks ago, to pay my respects on the death of her brother.

But he was scowling too hard and walking too fast to pay any attention. He barreled past me and into the hallway. I got to my feet, stuck the paper into my pocket, and smiled politely at Sue Ann. She didn't see me either, since she was handing Ward a couple of phone messages. He spoke to Sue Ann, asking her when one of the callers had phoned, and his voice was high-pitched, clipped. It didn't sound like the voice I'd heard on that tape Patricia had dictated.

I went back upstairs, thinking about what I had, or hadn't, discovered in production. I was sure that Rob would have followed policy, as outlined to me by Gladys, and sent the call sheets downstairs. But what happened to them after that? Had he, too, decided to check and see if anyone was following up on the complaints? Had he found out that there was no record of the call sheets being logged by Sue Ann, and decided to do some investigating on his own? He may have kept copies of the call sheets for his own files, or dug out the copies Patricia should have received. The next step would be to find out if Patricia had them.

Nancy favored me with another speculative look when I got back to Cube City, as though wondering where I'd been. I ignored her as best I could and picked up another dictation tape Hank had put in the rush box. It was a long one, judging from the amount of time it took to rewind. I plugged the earphones into my ears and started transcribing what seemed to be an asset purchase agreement regarding the Sheffield properties. But it didn't tell me where those properties were located. On the tape, Hank instructed me to leave a blank space in lieu of addresses.

At three, Gladys stood up and announced, "I'm taking a break. I'm gonna walk over to the coffee place and get a mocha. You ladies want anything?"

"Nothing for me, thanks." Nancy picked up an armful of papers and headed across the hall to Alex's office.

"Sure. I'll take a latte." I would have liked to go with her, but I was in the middle of the tape, and Hank had indicated that he wanted the document on his desk before the end of the day. I dug into my wallet for some bills and handed them to Gladys.

"Did you and Nancy have words?" she asked. "She's been glaring at you all day."

I'd noticed. But now I shrugged, as though it didn't matter. "She got upset because I was in that paralegal's office yesterday, looking for a file. You know, when you came looking for me."

"Tarcher was there." Gladys frowned. "Was he hassling you, because you were in there?"

"He seemed upset, too. I don't understand it. Have I stepped into someone's turf? I mean, I'm just the temp. I don't know anything about office politics."

That wasn't entirely true. I was soaking up as much information about Bates office politics as I could.

"I don't understand it, either." Gladys took the money I handed to her and tucked it in her change purse. "What is the big deal with that office? Rob's dead. We need to get those files out of there. But Nancy acts like there's a seal on the door. And I've seen Tarcher lurking around in there a couple of times over the past week. Doesn't make any sense. Anyway, I hope Nancy and her moods don't get under your skin. You're the best temp we've had. I'd like to keep you around for awhile."

"Thanks," I said, smiling at this compliment. Nice to know my skills as a legal secretary were still in demand.

Hank bustled into our shared office and pulled some pages from the printer. He turned to Gladys. "I want this faxed right away. And I want you to pull that O'Brien file and—"

"I'm taking a break," she told him, her face hardening. "California law says I'm entitled to a ten-minute break, morning and afternoon. I didn't take one this morning, and I'm taking it now."

She swept past him and down the hall toward the elevator. Hank stared after her with astonishment. "What did I do?" he said helplessly.

He really didn't have a clue. I reached for the papers he held. "I'll take care of this," I said, moving toward the fax machine. He nodded, mumbled his thanks, and disappeared, leaving me alone with his fax.

I sat down at my desk and glanced at the pages. The first was a cover sheet from Hank to Art Walton, the attorney in El Paso that he'd received a fax from earlier in the week. The cover sheet was marked "Confidential," and the subject line read "Project Rio." The document to be faxed was a brief paragraph from Hank indicating that things were moving along as expected and there were "no problems re Sheffield." Was the Sheffield purchase part of Project Rio? That meant the addresses left out of the agreement I was typing were in El Paso.

Nancy returned from Alex's office and picked up her phone. I stepped over to the fax machine, punching in the required numbers before placing the sheets facedown in the feeder. By the time the pages had fed through the fax machine, Gladys had come back from her jaunt to the espresso place, her mood evidently improved by a caffeine fix from the mocha she held in one hand. She surrendered my latte.

"I sent Hank's fax," I told her, taking a restorative sip of my coffee.

"Thanks." She sighed. "I get so irked with these attorneys. They all act like they're the only ones who need work done, and they all want it done right now. I just had to get some fresh air." She tapped the sign she'd stuck up on the wall of her cubicle, the one that read LACK OF PLANNING ON YOUR PART DOESN'T JUSTIFY A CRISIS ON MINE. She grinned. "I should make a copy of this for all of them. They probably wouldn't get it, though. I guess I'd better go look for that file."

She headed down the hall again, this time toward the filing room. I moved back to my cubicle. Nancy was still on the phone, and I strained my ears to pick up her end of the conversation, especially when I heard her ask to speak to Mr. Rittlestone's secretary.

She was quiet for a moment, probably because whoever had answered the phone on the other end had put her on hold. Then she straightened and she spoke again.

"This is Nancy Fong, Mr. Campbell's secretary. Please tell Mr. Rittlestone that Mr. Campbell has rescheduled his appointment. He will be available at five-thirty." She paused, listening. "No, Mr. Bates is out of the office today. The meeting will be in conference room one, here on the fourth floor."

Nancy disconnected the call and punched in another number. I heard enough of this second conversation to realize that she was canceling whatever Alex had on his calendar for this afternoon at five-thirty.

This meeting must be important, especially if Rittlestone was coming to Oakland for it. Since Rittlestone and Weper owned a controlling interest of Bates, I would have expected him to exercise his power and summon the company's executives to the R&W office in San Francisco. But I knew Rittlestone came to the Oakland office. He'd been here Tuesday, standing on the steps of the building with David, right before he'd turned and nearly knocked me down.

It seemed this afternoon's meeting would be held in the absence of chief executive officer Jeff Bates, and after most of the rank-and-file employees had vacated the building. I wanted to know what went on in that conference room. Unless I was a fly on the wall, there was no way for me to find out, short of listening at keyholes. That was a slim option, but still a possibility.

I finished the tape I was transcribing for Hank and printed out two copies, one for him and one for myself. Then I tackled a tape Patricia had left in the rush box. It was a four-page memo, and when I'd completed that, I headed across the hall to deliver the original. When I walked into her office, she sat in her chair with the telephone receiver in her right hand, looking at it with a peculiar expression on her face. I guessed that she'd just received a call, or perhaps she'd been checking her voice mail. Whatever the case, from the look on her face, one of the messages had contained bad news.

Slowly she set the receiver back in its cradle. She looked at me as though she'd never seen me before, then shook herself slightly, to dispel a mood. She took the memo from me. "Give me a few minutes to review this. I'm sure I'll be making some changes."

I was sure of it, too. I detoured to the restroom. When I picked up the memo, Patricia had made more than a few changes. All four pages were now covered with scribbles in red ink, and she'd added several paragraphs on the back of the last page.

I finished the revisions and took the memo back across the hall. Patricia was standing on the other side of her desk, pulling papers from the thick accordion file she'd been carrying earlier. It was the one containing all the files on the FDA food-safety proposals, and I wanted to look through it. But it always seemed to be in her custody.

The phone rang as I set the memo on her desk. She made no move to answer it. Instead she stared at it as though it might bite her.

Ordinarily I would have let the call roll over into her voice mail, but Patricia's earlier behavior, coupled with the look on her face now, made me more than a little curious. I picked up the receiver on the third ring.

"Patricia Mayhew's office," I said.

"She there?"

The voice was male. I'd heard it before. But where?

I glanced at Patricia, whose mouth had tightened. She shook her head, indicating that she didn't want to take the call.

"I'm sorry," I lied glibly. "She's not available. May I take a message?"

"You just put her on." The voice was low and brusque. "I'm tired of leaving messages."

My eyebrows went up. The voice didn't belong to the man I'd heard on the dictation tape. It was rougher, not at all businesslike.

A personal call? I remembered what Gladys had said about Patricia going through a messy divorce. Was the man on the other end of the phone her estranged husband? But why did the voice sound familiar? I'd talked with this person before, and as far as I knew, I'd never encountered Patricia's ex, either on the phone or in person.

The caller said he'd been leaving messages. Messages Patricia didn't want to hear. Which was why, presumably, she'd made no move to answer the phone.

I covered the receiver with my palm. "He won't take no for an answer."

Patricia just stood there, not moving. She frowned, as though her downturned mouth would make the caller hang up.

The man was talking again. I raised the receiver to my ear again. "Put her on, damn it," he growled, words slurring. "She either talks to me now, or I keep calling."

Recognition bloomed, like a flame igniting dry tinder. I opened my mouth in another attempt to put the caller off, then movement caught my eye. Patricia had walked around to this side of the desk, and now she reached for the phone.

"Patricia Mayhew." Her voice was as sharp as jagged glass. She waved at me in dismissal, indicating she didn't want anyone overhearing her end of the conversation. As I edged toward the door I heard her say, "I told you not to call me here."

I'll just bet she had. I opened the door and walked out into the hallway.

I could think of several reasons why Charlie Kellerman would call Patricia at work, none of them good.

CHAPTER 29

FOUR-THIRTY ROLLED AROUND, NOT SOON ENOUGH FOR Gladys. As soon as the number came up on the clock, she switched off her computer and stood up. "I'm out of here. See you all tomorrow."

After Gladys walked out of Cube City, I stretched my arms, flexing my shoulders, then I exited the word processing program and turned off my own machine. I took my time gathering my belongings. Finally I said good night to Nancy, who was still in her cubicle. She glanced up at me and murmured a response.

I walked out into the east hallway and quickly past Rob's old office to the north hall, where the restrooms were located. Coming toward me was Ann Twomey. She was Jeff Bates's secretary, a tall middle-aged woman who favored conservative suits. She smiled at me as she entered the doorway leading to the copy room. I pushed open the door to the women's restroom. Two women were there, changing from work clothes into jeans. I entered one of the stalls and used the toilet. By the time I came out and washed my hands, they'd departed, carrying dresses on hangers. I went back into the stall and waited.

In the week or so I'd worked at Bates, I'd noticed that the building cleared out quickly at quitting time. Those employees who were paid hourly were the ones most likely to leave at four-thirty. Bates, like many companies, wasn't interested in paying overtime unless it was absolutely necessary. Executives, like the attorneys, stayed longer. It was expected of them, in return for their larger salaries.

I was sure Hank would be working late that afternoon, to make up for lost time after three days away on business. It made sense for him to linger in his office, taking advantage of the next hour or so when he wasn't likely to be interrupted by the phone or other people. For all I knew, he was scheduled to attend that five-thirty meeting with Yale Rittlestone and Alex.

As for Patricia, after the phone call she'd received from Charlie Kellerman, I wondered if she'd bail out of the office early, or stay to work. With any luck, it would be the former.

Nancy Fong was paid hourly, but would she stay at her post longer, because of the five-thirty meeting? I was hoping she wouldn't. The fewer people there were hanging around the hallways at Bates this afternoon would mean fewer people to wonder why Jeri Howard was there. That is, if I got caught. I wasn't planning on getting caught, but anything could happen.

I hid out in the restroom as long as I dared, then I exited at ten minutes after five. I moved quietly as I walked along the east hallway toward Cube City. It looked as though there was still a light on in Patricia's office. That meant she was working late. I heard her talking, but couldn't make out any words. Hers was the only voice I heard, so that meant she was speaking into the phone.

I peered in the doorway of Cube City. Nancy was still at her desk, her back to me. I retraced my steps to the north hallway, which was fortunately empty. I glanced back the way I'd come, just in time to see David enter Hank's office.

I retreated past the copy room to the freight elevator, then dodged into the legal department file room. I waited there, hoping no one would need to retrieve a file from one of the cabinets. I left the door ajar, just a crack, and saw Tonya Russell walk into the copy room. The high-tech photocopier hummed and whirred, then Tonya went back to her office.

It was now twenty minutes past five. I left the file room and went back to where the north hallway turned the corner into the east hallway. The door to Cube City was open, and it looked as though the light was on. I'd been hoping that Nancy would be gone now, but evidently she wasn't. Then I saw her step out of Cube City, carrying her jacket and a canvas tote bag. She shut the door and headed in the direction of the elevator.

I heard voices, then the door of Hank's office opened. He and

David walked out, then Hank opened Alex's door. A moment later, the general counsel joined them. All three men walked out of sight into the south hallway. I went in that direction. As I passed Patricia's door, I heard her voice, still talking on the phone, I guessed. As I approached the door of Cube City, I figured if anyone surprised me in the hallway, I could dodge inside and spin a story about how I'd forgotten something and had to come back.

I looked around the corner into the south hallway. Just then the elevator bell pinged and the doors opened.

"Hello, Yale," David said.

It was about twenty feet from where I stood to the area in front of the elevator. I wished I could get a closer look, but I'd have to settle for examining them from my point of concealment.

The four men assembled in front of the elevator were shaking hands as they greeted one another, and for a moment my view was impeded by Hank's back.

Alex looked worried. Was it a bad sign that Rittlestone had left his San Francisco office and journeyed to this side of the bay?

This was the third time I'd seen Rittlestone. The first was just a glimpse, at Embarcadero Four, with Patricia. I'd gotten a closer look Tuesday when he was standing on the steps outside the Bates building with David. Now I saw him more clearly, noting that he was not as tall as David. That put him at six feet, I thought, possibly a shade over. He had a slim, wiry build, athletic and tanned, and he wore a black suit that contrasted with his straight blond hair. His expression was bland in its smoothness. His manner was cool as he traded greetings with the others, and I got the impression he was enjoying Alex's discomfort. I had a feeling his eyes were cold.

My guess was confirmed when Rittlestone turned and I saw his face. In that moment, he surveyed the others as though he were in a fish market and they were stretched out on the ice, bellies shining and eyes and mouths gaping open. Which of them would get eaten first?

"Let's get on with it," he said coldly.

They walked past Jeff Bates's corner office and disappeared into the west hallway, headed toward conference room one. I followed, hoping I wouldn't get spotted by some secretary working late. I had to know what was going on at the meeting. I'd heard plenty of rumors about Hank being anointed to replace Alex as general counsel. Was this it? Was Alex being handed his walking papers and his golden parachute?

The west hallway was clear. Both Jeff Bates's and David's offices were dark. I moved toward the conference room door, hoping that I could eavesdrop on something, anything.

I could hear voices, all right. But they were all talking at once. I tilted my head toward the door and concentrated on who was saying what. I picked out Alex's voice, cautioning restraint, then Hank saying something I couldn't quite make out.

Then I heard David, clear as a bell and with a tone that made him sound more unconcerned than his words would indicate. "If word gets out about this, we're fucked."

Rittlestone's voice was icy and unmistakable. His words were flavored with irritation. "It's your job to keep us from getting fucked, David. Nobody's going to find out. Is that clear?" He paused. I pictured him looking at each man in the conference room, as though waiting for their acknowledgment.

Were they talking about the retirement money after all? Or maybe the subject of the meeting was the big secret known as Project Rio. What else was going on at Bates that was so hot it had to be kept under wraps?

"Have there been any inquiries?" Hank said. Alex answered him, but I couldn't hear the words. Then several voices spoke at once.

Rittlestone silenced them when he began talking again. With a start, I realized where I'd heard his voice before. It was on the tape Patricia had dictated earlier in the week.

I edged closer to the conference room door, then froze as I heard the faint ping of the elevator. The doors opened and closed. I moved farther down the west hallway, away from the conference room. I dodged around a corner to the north corridor, then peered back the way I'd come.

Rounding the corner from the south to the west hallway was the man I had hoped to avoid. Buck Tarcher. He paused for a moment at the door to the conference room, as though he was listening to what was going on inside.

I headed for the place I'd hidden earlier, the restrooms. I pushed open the door marked "Women" and quickly hid in the stall on the far end.

According to Gladys, the corporate security chief patrolled the Bates building each evening before leaving. He moved at random, she said, picking one or two floors, skipping one section of offices while thoroughly searching another. Just my luck that he'd picked this floor tonight. However, since the executive offices, legal department, and human resources were on this floor, no doubt he kept a close eye on it at all times.

I hoped Tarcher's inspection tour didn't include checking the johns. I waited, hearing him whistle something as he made his way along the hall. Damned if he didn't go into the men's room. But his visit turned out to be a call of nature rather than a stall-by-stall search. I heard water rush through the pipes as he flushed.

He passed on the ladies. Hallelujah, I thought, straining my ears as the tuneless whistle receded. I waited a few minutes more, then I emerged from my hiding place. I retraced my steps from the north hall to the west, peering around the corner first, to make sure no one was there. The coast was clear so far. But I couldn't hear any voices coming from the conference room. Was the meeting over? Then the door opened and Hank came out. He walked to the south hallway, as though heading for his office.

I circled around the long way, past the restrooms and to the east hall. Patricia's office was dark. She must have gone home. I waited, then saw Hank come out of his office and head back toward the conference room.

Then my luck ran out. When I turned the corner into the south hallway, Patricia opened the door of Alex's office and walked out, looking upset. I was at the doorway of Cube City, and as she glanced my way, I put my hand on the doorknob, as though I'd just left the place. It was the best I could do at short notice.

"You're here awfully late," she said conversationally, glancing at her watch.

I shrugged and fiddled with the zipper that closed my shoulder bag. "I'd already driven out of the parking lot, then realized that I'd left something in my desk. Had to come back."

I didn't elaborate further, and Patricia didn't ask. Did she believe me? I couldn't tell. She didn't look as though she was interested in my reasons for being here after hours. She looked worried, as she had since she'd gotten that phone call from Charlie Kellerman.

I wanted to ask her what she'd been doing in Alex's office. Instead, I walked toward the stairwell and got the hell out of there before the corporate security chief made another stroll in my direction. Patricia might be too preoccupied to wonder about me, but Tarcher was already viewing me with suspicion.

Between Tarcher, Nancy Fong, and David Vanitzky, the pincers were moving closer. My tenure as a temp at Bates was short-lived.

CHAPTER 30

HEADED FOR MY FRANKLIN STREET OFFICE, INTENDING TO put in an hour or so on my investigative chores before going home to my cats. I was unlocking my office door when Ruby Woods appeared, coming through the door that led to Woods Temporaries.

"I thought that might be you," she said, her face serious. "We need to talk."

"What about?" I held the door for her, then flicked on the overhead light. My answering machine blinked red at me in rapid succession. Ruby sat down in the chair in front of my desk, and I took my own chair, leaning back. "What happened? Did Laverne come through with information on Charlie Kellerman and Leon Gomes?"

"Yeah, she did. But first, I got a call this afternoon from someone at Bates, asking for information on your background."

I leaned forward, elbows on my desk. "Who called you?"

"A woman named Nancy Fong."

I'd been expecting to hear Tarcher's name. But I wasn't surprised to learn that it was Nancy. I wondered if she'd caught a glimpse of me at Rob's funeral service, despite the hat that I'd hidden behind.

"What did she ask?"

"The usual things," Ruby said. "She wanted to know where you worked before, and whether you had any references. I gave her the story we agreed on. But, Jeri, I'm concerned. Tomorrow is Laverne's last day, so I won't have any contacts over there. Granted, Bates is discontinuing its business relationship with my firm at the end of the month. But if things get sticky, I could wind up with a black eye. What will we do? Or do we need to do anything?"

"I don't know," I told her, and at that moment, I didn't. "Let me mull it over while you tell me what Laverne found out. By the way, see if she can get a home phone number for a man named Al Dominici. He retired from Bates in March."

"Okay. As for Charles Kellerman, I've got the details right here." Ruby pulled a piece of paper from her jacket pocket and unfolded it. "He used to work in the Bates production department."

"Nolan Ward's department," I added. And Dominici's. Somehow it all fit, but not as tightly as it should have. Had Rob known Charlie from work? It was probable, but I couldn't ask either of them. Rob was dead, and Charlie wasn't talking. "What did Charlie do in production?"

"Procurement. Something to do with buying fruits and vegetables for the Bates Best label. But Kellerman's an alcoholic, big time. He was fired in April, five months ago. Laverne said he'd been given three warnings over a period of about eighteen months. The booze was affecting his job performance so much that the company finally offered to put him into an alcohol rehab program, which was covered by his health insurance. But Kellerman refused. So they terminated him. Not much else they could do."

"I suppose not. No severance package, I suppose."

Ruby shook her head. "Not when he was fired under those circumstances."

"So how does a guy like Kellerman pay his rent?"

"According to Laverne, he's living off whatever savings he had, plus some support from a brother. But that's it."

Unless Charlie was augmenting his income with a little blackmail.

That was as good a reason as any for Charlie's reticence about what he'd seen and heard the night Rob went headfirst out his apartment window. That was why Charlie had the kind of money to buy the expensive booze instead of the rotgut he usually drank. And I had a pretty good idea who he was putting the touch on.

Alex was the Bates attorney who handled employment matters. No doubt he'd been consulted on a regular basis regarding the separation of Charlie Kellerman from his job. But Patricia was constantly in meetings with Ward, usually in his office in production. So

Charlie must know who she is. Surely he'd seen her, time and again, on the second floor of the Bates building.

That was why he'd called her this afternoon, leaving her in a state of panic and worry. He'd seen her again, quite recently, and he'd recognized her. I was left with only one conclusion as to where he'd seen her. Patricia had been at Rob's apartment the night he died.

I left off speculating why Patricia had been there, and turned my attention to the other person I had doubts about. "What did Laverne say about Leon Gomes?"

"He's worked for Bates eleven years," Ruby said. "Started out in the plant that makes crackers and cookies, then moved to the dairy plant in Oakland. Good track record, evidently. He was recently promoted to plant manager."

"How recently?"

Ruby consulted the paper. "Since May. A little over four months."

"So Leon works for production, too. And Ward signed off on his promotion. Where did Leon work before he came to Bates?"

"A small company in the Los Angeles area." Ruby handed the paper to me. "Here's the name. That's all Laverne was able to get from his employee file."

I could do some trolling on the Internet to find out more about the company. In the meantime, I had other things to worry about. If Patricia told Nancy about catching me in the hall tonight, the jig was most definitely up. I wasn't sure I wanted to face either of them Friday morning. I needed more time to continue my undercover stint as a temp at Bates. There must be a way to forestall any confrontation over my cover story.

Suddenly I thought of all those articles I'd been finding in Rob's files, about foodborne illnesses. I leaned back in my chair and grinned at Ruby.

"I'm going to get food poisoning tonight. Something I'll eat for dinner won't agree with me. I'll be so sick, I'll wind up in the Kaiser emergency room."

"You're not going to work tomorrow," she said slowly. "I'm supposed to call Bates and tell them you're sick."

I nodded. "Call sometime around nine o'clock, after the workday has started and the people in legal are wondering why I haven't shown up. I need a day to follow up on a lead. This is the first thing that comes to mind, and I think it will work. If I'm lucky, I'll still have that temp job come Monday morning. And if I'm even luckier, I'll have figured out what's going on over at Bates."

"If you're not lucky, we'll both be out of business. I'm beginning to think this wasn't a good idea after all." Ruby got to her feet and headed for her own office.

I grabbed the phone directory from the shelf behind my desk. It was too late to call my travel agent, but I could buy my ticket direct from the airline. I punched in the appropriate number and was surprised when I got a real person instead of a recording.

"When's the first available flight to El Paso?" I asked.

THE FIRST AVAILABLE FLIGHT TO EL PASO ON FRIDAY WENT through Phoenix. The departure time left me wincing. Six-thirty in the morning, which meant I needed to be at the Oakland airport by five-thirty. Ouch.

I called Cassie and asked her to feed Abigail and Black Bart during my absence. That done, I played back the messages on my answering machine, returned phone calls, rescheduled a couple of appointments. I logged onto my computer and queried one of the databases I used about the firm where Leon Gomes used to work. Then I headed home to pack.

Some twelve hours later, I was on a jet heading southeast, for the city known to the Spanish conquistadors as *El Paso del Norte*, the pass leading to the north. As I picked my way, less than enthusiastically, through an airline breakfast, I contemplated my next move. The first order of business was a look at that property in El Paso that Bates had been negotiating to buy.

According to that fax I'd read about Project Rio, the parcel was located on Executive Center Boulevard. I'd guessed, because of the project's name, that the land was also located somewhere near the Rio Grande, the mighty river that rose in the Colorado Rockies and flowed south through New Mexico, finally forming the border between Texas and Mexico.

When the flight attendant picked up the tray containing the remains of my breakfast, I leaned over and pulled my purse from under the seat in front of me. I'd brought my copy of the Sheffield agreement I'd typed yesterday. Now I read through it again. It looked as though Bates was buying processing plants, more than one, and I was sure they were located in El Paso. I'd also brought some maps from the stash I kept in my office. I sifted past Texas and New Mexico, and found the one for El Paso, then unfolded it and looked at the street key.

Executive Center Boulevard began just east of the Rio Grande at U.S. 85, which hugged the riverbank where Texas, New Mexico, and the Mexican state of Chihuahua came together. The street then ran east across Interstate 10, at a spot that appeared to be several miles north of the campus of the University of Texas at El Paso, better known as UTEP.

I changed planes in Phoenix. The jet touched down in El Paso International at a quarter to twelve, Mountain time. I grabbed my gray nylon travel bag from the overhead compartment and headed for the rental car counter. After producing my credit card and a current California driver's license, I was awarded the keys to a Geo Prizm, which proved to be a jarring shade of purple. I stashed my overnight bag in the trunk, then opened the driver's side door and made sure everything, from the lights to the windshield wipers to the air conditioner, was working properly.

It was hot in El Paso, a lot hotter than it had been when I left Oakland early this morning. Before I was even out of the airport's environs, I'd switched on the air conditioner. I drove along Montana Avenue, driving west until I reached the freeway.

Traffic in El Paso was light by Bay Area standards. Interstate 10 threaded its way through the westernmost city in Texas, running roughly east to west before turning north toward Las Cruces, New Mexico. I passed the downtown high-rises that loomed to the south, between the freeway and the river. Over the border, Ciudad Juárez was blurred by the haze. The freeway curved to the north, and I sped past the exit for UTEP. I changed lanes and started looking for the sign indicating an exit for Executive Center Boulevard. When it came into view, I reached for the turn indicator and slowed as I moved along the off-ramp.

I wasn't sure whether the address I sought was on the east or west side of the interstate, so I turned right, heading east. After a few blocks, it was clear I needed to go in the other direction. I made a

U-turn at the next intersection, and headed west instead. On the other side of the freeway, closer to U.S. 85, I found what I was looking for, and something I wasn't.

I knew from reading the fax Hank had sent to Alex that the land in question was ten acres. I'd guessed, and so had Gladys, that Bates was going to build another food processing plant. They certainly could do that, if all that open field went with this parcel of land. But I wasn't expecting the office building.

The building was on the north side of the street, all on its lonesome in the middle of an empty asphalt parking lot, with open land beyond. The structure appeared to be of recent vintage, five stories high, its walls gray and the windows filled with darkened glass. A tall chain-link fence separated the parking lot from the street. I continued slowly along the boulevard, in the right-hand lane. Ahead I saw a turnout into the parking lot, but there was a gate across the entrance. On the gate was a large real estate sign advising me that the building, and presumably the land all around it, was for sale.

I pulled into the turnout and shifted the Geo into park. An office building, I thought. What did Bates Inc., headquartered in Oakland, California, need with an office building in El Paso, Texas?

I had a possible answer, but it would require some digging. I quickly made a note of the name and phone number of the real estate agent, then pulled back onto the road. I drove farther west. I was nearly to the point where Executive Center Boulevard intersected U.S. 85 when I saw a large industrial building on the north side of the road. It had a shut-up look and a gate spread across the driveway. There was another For Sale sign here, same company as the office building, but a different agent. The name above the main entrance of the building read "Sheffield Foods."

I made a U-turn and drove back toward Interstate 10, heading downtown to delve into the El Paso County records relating to real estate transactions and property taxes. When I emerged from the City-County Building, I ignored my hunger pangs and asked for directions to the public library.

The office building I'd seen was seven years old. It had been vacated earlier this year by a manufacturing firm that had moved to bigger quarters. It now stood empty, and that, evidently, had prompted the owner to put it on the market. The taxes on the building, and the land on which it sat, were paid by C. J. Mullin of Carlsbad, New Mexico, the same Mullin that Hank had gone to see earlier in the week.

Further digging revealed that Sheffield Foods was a longtime family-owned food processing business, much like Bates Inc. But it no longer existed. It had gone belly-up two years ago, after being taken over by TZI, Inc., the same firm that had mounted a hostile takeover of Bates. Bates had fought off TZI by making a deal with Rittlestone and Weper. Sheffield had, from what I read in the El Paso papers, been run into the ground by TZI. There were Sheffield processing plants all over El Paso, and now Bates was going to buy them.

I went outside into the late afternoon sunlight, hungry enough to eat the sidewalk where I stood. I found a taqueria and ate my fill of Tex-Mex, contemplating what I'd learned.

TZI was headquartered in Houston. It had been in the takeover racket for about ten years, and it didn't have a good reputation. I could see why Jeff Bates and his board hadn't wanted to succumb to TZI's advances. It had a reputation for taking over a company, firing all the executives and managers, and bringing in a TZI team to run the place. If that didn't work, TZI cut its losses and disposed of the assets and the employees. That was evidently what had happened to Sheffield Foods.

I wiped my hands on a napkin, took a final swallow of my root beer, and pulled my cellular phone from my bag. I didn't have a phone number for C. J. Mullin, just an address, on North Shore in Carlsbad. When I called directory assistance for Carlsbad, New Mexico, I was told the number was unlisted. Damn.

Next I called the real estate company whose number I'd seen on the For Sale signs in front of the office building and the Sheffield plant. I got passed to three people before I found the agent who was handling Mullin's property. I told him I wanted to get in touch with the owner of the building on Executive Park Boulevard.

"I'm afraid you're out of luck," he said. "That sale's pending."

"Suppose I make a better offer?"

"Well . . ." He paused, dollar signs no doubt dancing before his eyes. "You can name your figure, but this deal's almost done."

"I'd sure like to talk to the owner," I cajoled, "before I go any further. I have a few questions."

"The owner doesn't want to be disturbed," he said. "I'm sure I can answer any questions you might have."

"Let me talk to my partner, and I'll get back to you."

I disconnected the call before he could ask for my name and a phone number. It looked as though the only way I'd get a chance to talk to C. J. Mullin was to go to Carlsbad.

I retrieved the rental car from the parking lot where I'd left it, then drove back the way I'd come, past El Paso International. Montana Avenue was also U.S. 62 and 180, which headed east and north toward New Mexico. Before I left the city limits, I stopped at a grocery store and bought several bottles of chilled water, as well as some soda.

It was about a hundred and fifty miles to Carlsbad, a good three hours of driving on a two-lane ribbon of highway that cut across the unforgiving desert terrain. Most of the way I was driving due east, with the setting sun at my back, rotating the dial on the radio to pick up whatever stations I could. When I passed the Salt Flats, the highway turned northeast, curving along the perimeter of Guadalupe Mountains National Park. The road twisted up Guadalupe Pass, under a looming chunk of mountain called El Capitan, then leveled off again.

Twilight had almost given way to darkness when I stopped at the park visitor center, to stretch my legs and use the restroom. I got back on the road. Once I crossed the state line from Texas to New Mexico, the condition of the road worsened. Farther to the north I passed the billboards and motels of Whites City, clustered at the entrance to Carlsbad Caverns National Park. It was past nine when I headed into the southern outskirts of Carlsbad.

I knew little about the place, other than its proximity to the Caverns. It had a small airport that I'd passed on my way into town. The buildings I'd seen looked as dry and dusty as the hills to the west of town. The highway turned into Canal Street, lined with motels, restaurants, and businesses.

I stopped at a Best Western motel with a restaurant, checked in, and asked for a room at the back, away from the highway noise. I purchased a city map from the clerk before settling into my room. Then I sat on the bed, unfolded the map, and studied it. Most of Carlsbad was south and east of the Pecos River that meandered through town. C. J. Mullin's address was, as its name implied, on the north shore of the river.

I set the map aside and took a hot shower. Then I put on the oversized T-shirt I slept in and pulled down the covers of the bed. I flipped through the cable channels until I found a movie I'd never gotten around to seeing when it was in Bay Area theaters. After watching half of it, I was glad I'd saved the ticket price. I switched off the bedside lamp and went to sleep.

Mullin lived in one of Carlsbad's wealthier residential areas, I discovered Saturday morning. After eating pancakes for breakfast at the motel restaurant, I climbed back into the rental car and headed north on Canal, crossing the river and turning left on Orchard Lane. I took a left on Alpha and then a right on North Shore, cruising slowly, peering at house numbers in the growing twilight. Big houses sprawled across tree-shaded lots, and their well-kept backyards sloped right down to the river. Cottonwoods and pecan trees predominated, with the latter shedding their fruit liberally on the lawns and the streets.

The Mullin house looked as though it had been built in the 1950s, a buff brick one-story ranch style with a paved circular drive, and a garage on the right. There was a dusty red pickup truck parked in front of the garage. I pulled into the drive and parked.

I rang the bell and kicked at a stray pecan. I thought I heard voices in the house, but I wasn't sure. They could have been coming from one of the neighboring homes. Then the door opened, and I found myself looking into the face of a leathery-skinned woman somewhere between fifty and seventy. She wore cowboy boots, faded blue jeans, and a loose-fitting western-cut shirt in a red and yellow check.

"I'm looking for C. J. Mullin," I said.

She gazed at me with a pair of pale blue eyes, then the edges of her thin mouth quirked upward in a smile. When she spoke, her voice was flavored with a Southwestern twang. "You found her."

CHAPTER 32

"YOU'RE C. J. MULLIN?"

So much for preconceived notions, I thought.

"That's right," she said with a nod. She stood with one hand on the door and the other on her hip. Her smile was friendly and her eyes curious at finding a stranger on her doorstep. From inside the house I heard children's voices striving to be heard over the noise of a television set.

"Do you own ten acres of land on Executive Center Boulevard in El Paso?"

Her smile dimmed as her eyes narrowed. "I think you'd better tell me what this is about."

I reached for one of my business cards and handed it to her. "My name's Jeri Howard. I'm a private investigator from Oakland, California. I'd like to ask you some questions."

C. J. Mullin's eyes flicked over the printed words on the card, then back at me. Her face was wary now. "I'd like to ask a few questions myself. Why is a private investigator from Oakland here in Carlsbad, asking questions about some land in El Paso?"

"I'd have called," I told her. "But your phone number isn't listed. And I couldn't get it out of your real estate agent. Besides, I'd rather talk with you in person."

That was the truth. Frequently, face-to-face contact was better than getting information over the phone. It gave me the chance to read faces and body language. At the moment, however, neither C. J. Mullin's face nor body was providing me with much information.

"Not sure I would have told you anything over the phone anyway," she said slowly. "Not sure I'll tell you anything now. Why should I answer your questions?"

"Can't think of any reason why you should," I said frankly. "Except curiosity. You satisfy mine, and I'll satisfy yours."

C. J. Mullin's face changed again. She relaxed, and her eyes twinkled with amusement. I heard the thud of footsteps, then a boy of about six or seven appeared behind her. He was towheaded, his fair skin tanned, with freckles dusting his nose. Barefoot, he wore a pair of green shorts and a yellow T-shirt decorated with a damp stain and some crumbs. He paid no attention to me, focusing instead on the older woman at the door.

"Grammaw," he said, "Jimmy let Beau out the back door, and he won't come back."

"Beau'll be fine, Tommy," she told him. "He'll come in when he feels like it. Go on back to the kitchen and finish your breakfast." She gave him an affectionate pat on the shoulder. The boy turned and disappeared. C. J. Mullin glanced at me with a hint of a smile, and explained. "Got my grandkids this weekend."

"Three boys?" I asked.

"Two. Beau's a dog. He's not used to the boys being around, so I figure he got out the back door on his own." She looked over my shoulder. "In fact, there he is now."

I glanced in the direction of her gaze. A big golden retriever with dust on his paws and wisps of dried grass in his coat ambled into view around the corner of the house, moseying toward us across the green lawn. When he brushed up against C. J. Mullin, she reached down and scratched him behind the ears.

"What's the matter, fella? All this company getting to you?"

The dog wagged his tail and snuffled at her fingers. Then he turned his attention to me, with a thorough inspection of my hand, my shoes, and the legs of my blue slacks. Then he sat down on my foot and leaned into my right leg, adding a liberal overlay of red-gold fur to the cat hair that was already visible on the navy cotton. I massaged the spot between his ears, and he groaned with pleasure.

"Are we going to satisfy each other's curiosity?" I asked, wondering if I'd piqued C. J. Mullin's interest sufficiently for her to let me in.

Maybe the fact that her dog seemed to like me made her open the door wider. "Well . . . shove Beau off your foot and come on in."

Beau and I followed her into the house. She wore her gray-blond hair long, pulled back into a single braid that fell all the way to her waist. The heels of her cowboy boots clicked on the umber tile that covered the floor of the long central hallway, the sound echoed by the fainter click of Beau's toenails. On my left was a wall punctuated here and there with paintings and photographs, mostly landscapes reminiscent of the mountains and high desert of this part of the country. On the right, an open doorway led to a big kitchen with white appliances, knotty pine cabinets, and more red-brown tile.

A portable television set sat on one end of a counter, its sound turned too loud. The program was one of those Saturday morning cartoon shows, and the two boys at the round table weren't paying much attention to it. Tommy, the one I'd seen, and an older boy I guessed was Jimmy were spooning cereal from bowls. Their grand-mother crossed the room and turned down the sound. Then she sur-veyed the spilled milk and cereal on the table's surface.

"You boys have made a mess for sure. Make sure you clean it up when you're finished. And if you want to go with me to the sale, you better get yourselves cleaned up and put on some shoes." Tommy and Jimmy murmured their assurances that they would do both of these. Then C. J. Mullin turned to me. "You want some coffee?"

"I would like that very much. I take it black."

There was an automatic drip coffeemaker nearby on one of the counters. She poured the strong black brew into two mugs as Beau detoured into the kitchen and drank noisily from a big stainless-steel bowl, splashing water onto the tile. My hostess handed me one of the mugs, then led the way past the counter that separated the kitchen from a formal dining room with a long rectangular table.

The living room was at the rear of the house, with windows and a wide sliding glass door looking out at the Pecos River. The glass was open, and there was a slight breeze coming through the fine mesh screen door that hadn't been closed all the way since the dog had es-caped earlier. On this autumn morning several paddleboats loaded with people were making slow progress against the river's current. I could hear their faint laughter as the boats went by.

I glanced around me, at the room's comfortable furnishings. The big red and gray Navajo rug in the center of the room was probably the real thing, since it looked old and timeworn. A collection of Indian pottery my father would have envied was arrayed on the glass-fronted shelves of the barristers bookcases on either side of the stone fireplace. I leaned closer to examine a large black-on-black pot on the mantel.

"Is that a Maria Martinez?" I asked, mentioning the famed potter from San Ildefonso Pueblo.

"Sure is," Mullin told me. "My grandpa bought it from Maria herself. Have a seat." She waved at the worn brown leather sofa. I sat down on one end and watched as, with a pleasurable sigh, Beau sprawled on his side on the tile in front of the fireplace.

C. J. Mullin sat down in an overstuffed armchair and rested her booted feet on top of the matching ottoman. The blue eyes in her tanned face pierced me as before.

"Do you represent Bates?" She took a swallow of coffee, then set her mug down on a nearby table piled with magazines.

"No. I can't tell you who my client is, but it's not Bates." I didn't add that my client was dead.

"Anybody from Bates know you're here?"

"I hope not."

"Then what's your interest? Does your client want to buy the property?"

I shook my head. "I want to know what Bates intends to do with that ten acres of land you own, and the office building sitting on it."

"I guess that must be why you hope nobody from Bates knows you're nosing around this deal." She smiled. "Sounds like industrial espionage, or some such thing."

"Believe me, it's not."

"Well, I don't know exactly what Bates plans to do with that parcel," C. J. Mullin said. "Nobody's come right out and said what they plan to do with it, least of all that tight-mouthed young lawyer that come out here earlier in the week. Mostly it's been lawyers talking to lawyers, you understand, and none of them saying anything more than necessary."

She sipped her coffee before she spoke again. "I would guess Bates wants to put people in that office building. No point in buying it if you're gonna leave it empty. As for the rest of the ten acres, I figure they'll build a plant on it. That would be the logical thing to do."

"I do understand," I said, not believing that she was as uninformed as she claimed. "But perhaps you've heard something."

"This transaction hasn't exactly been on the top of my list of priorities. I got a ranch to run. In fact," she added, looking at the watch on her left wrist, "I got to be at a livestock sale at eleven o'clock. I'm leaving as soon as I corral those two yahoos."

She glanced to her right as her grandsons, who had evidently finished breakfast, ran through the dining room into the living room. Beau, in front of the fireplace, growled low in his throat as though he'd been pestered quite enough since they'd arrived and he didn't want any more of it. Mullin intercepted the boys and sent them off down the hallway in the direction of the bathroom, with instructions to wash their faces and put on their shoes.

"That El Paso property is just one of my investments," she told me. "Haven't been able to put a tenant in that building since the last tenant moved out. So I put it on the market. I want to sell, Bates offered a good price, and looks like we're about to sign on the old dotted line."

It looked like the three-hour drive to Carlsbad, and the overnight stay, had been wasted time. I swallowed my disappointment with some coffee and tried a different tack. "Bates is a food processing company. I noticed, just down the road from your property, that the old Sheffield Foods plant is up for sale. It would make sense for Bates to buy that, too, if they're going to expand their operations into the southwest."

Surprise passed over C. J. Mullin's face. "Expand isn't what I heard."

"So you do know more about the deal than you've said."

"I didn't say I knew." There was a touch of irritation in her voice. "Hearing rumors isn't the same as knowing."

"I'm just as interested in rumors as I am in facts. What have you heard?"

"Those Sheffield plants have been on the market since the company folded, about two years ago. There's six of 'em, one near my building and the rest spread out all over El Paso. I guess they'd need some modernizing to go back into production. But I figure that's what's going to happen. I heard it from a very good source. One of my old college roommates lives in El Paso, and her husband works for the city. According to her, he's mighty happy that an outfit like Bates is buying up all the old Sheffield plants and moving its operations to El Paso."

I'd suspected as much. "The whole damn company?"

"The whole damn company," C. J. Mullin repeated, reaching for her coffee. "Corporate headquarters, production, distribution, the whole works. Means tax revenue for the city, and lots of jobs for the locals."

And what did it mean for the people who already had those jobs in California? No wonder Hank was being so secretive about Project Rio. He and the other powers behind this proposed move didn't want word getting out until the signatures were on the dotted lines, the money had changed hands, and the deal was done. No doubt corporate taxes in El Paso would be a lot less than in Oakland. Maybe environmental laws in Texas were less restrictive than those in California. I'd bet salaries were lower, too.

Moving Bates to the banks of the Rio Grande might make sense from a strictly business standpoint. But it meant empty plants in Oakland instead of El Paso, and betrayal for people like Gladys and Nancy. They'd be out of work.

Something of what I was thinking must have showed on my face. C. J. Mullin frowned. "Is there something underhanded about this deal with Bates?"

"Depends on how you look at it," I said, raising my coffee mug to my lips.

CHAPTER *33*

AFTER TALKING WITH C. J. MULLIN, I RETURNED TO THE Carlsbad motel and called the airline. If I pushed it, I could get back to El Paso in time to catch a late afternoon flight that would get me to Oakland late Saturday evening. I made the reservation, checked out, and gassed up the rental car before heading out of town. I kept the speedometer hovering just over the limit and my eyes on the seemingly endless strip of two-lane blacktop until I hit the outskirts of El Paso. I turned in the rental car and had just enough time for a snack before I boarded the plane.

It was good to get home. In my absence, Cassie had stopped by my apartment to feed Abigail and Black Bart. Nevertheless, both cats met me at the door with loud protestations of neglect and imminent starvation. I dropped my travel bag near the sofa and walked back to the kitchen to check their bowls, which, as I suspected, had food in them.

"Nice try, guys, but no dice."

I knelt to give each cat scratches behind the ears. I knew they missed me when I was gone. Black Bart, the more standoffish of the two, butted my hand gently and rumbled with a steady purr as he allowed me to stroke his head. Abigail's behavior was positively shameless. She purred like a well-tuned Harley as she rolled onto her back and presented her fat belly. I tickled her, and she grabbed my hand with her forepaws, nipping my fingers in what I preferred to call love bites.

When I straightened, I filled the teakettle and set it on the burner.

I was still wired from my trip and what I'd discovered about Bates's plans to purchase the office building and the existing Sheffield Foods plants and move the entire company to El Paso. A cup of tea would settle me as I unpacked.

When I walked out of the kitchen I saw that Cassie had left some mail and Saturday morning's Oakland *Tribune* on my dining room table. I sifted through the envelopes. There was a note from my mother in Monterey, a couple of bills, and some junk mail, which I tossed into the kitchen recycling bin.

The teakettle whistled, and I lifted it from the burner, then poured hot water into a mug and set an herbal tea bag afloat. I carried the mug and my overnight bag to the bedroom and unpacked. That chore done, I walked back to the dining room and sat down at the round oak table to open the mail. Then I unfolded the newspaper, skimming through the headlines and stories on the front page before turning to the inside pages.

The headline on a small story at the bottom of page three caught my eye. "OAKLAND MAN KILLED IN HIT AND RUN." I read a little farther, then I spilled hot tea on the table as I set the mug down, hard.

The Oakland man the story referred to was Charlie Kellerman.

I read quickly through the story, which was shy on details, probably because the incident had occurred late enough Friday evening so that it barely made the Saturday edition of the *Tribune*. Kellerman had been crossing Lakeside Drive near Seventeenth, a scant three blocks from his Alice Street apartment. According to the brief article, he'd been struck by a car traveling at what witnesses described as a high rate of speed. The impact had thrown Kellerman about thirty feet. He'd landed near the curb, mortally injured, and he was dead by the time the paramedics got to the scene. The vehicle kept going. It was described as a sedan, but the witnesses couldn't agree on color or model.

I picked up the phone and punched in Sid's number at home. "It's Jeri," I said when he answered. "I want to know about that hit and run that killed Charlie Kellerman."

"I was wondering when you'd call."

"I've been out of town since Friday morning. Just got back. What have you got that's not in the paper?"

"Kellerman's not my case. Besides, why should I tell you?"

"Come on, Sid. Rob Lawter goes out a window, and now his next-door neighbor is the victim of a hit and run. Surely you don't think this is random."

"Just between you and me and the lamppost," he said candidly, "no, I don't. Particularly since a couple of witnesses told the detectives that it looked like the car accelerated right before it hit Kellerman. I've told the guys handling the case that I think it's connected with the Lawter case. Suppose you give me your best guess as to a motive. Why would anyone want to kill a poor old drunk like Kellerman?"

"He saw whoever Sally Morgan heard in Rob's apartment that night. And he was collecting some cash to keep his mouth shut."

"Good guess. Any candidates?"

"He called Patricia Mayhew Thursday afternoon. She's one of the attorneys who works for Bates. And she didn't look any too thrilled to be hearing from him. By the way, Charlie used to work for Bates. He got canned six months ago, after three warnings and refusing to get treatment."

"That much I knew. Wayne and I figured Kellerman was holding back," Sid added, mentioning his longtime partner. "So we got some background on him, courtesy of Buck Tarcher, the security guy over at Bates. Have you got any information that suggests Mayhew killed Lawter? Or Kellerman?"

"Not yet. But I'm working on it. Are you going to give me anything on the hit and run?"

"According to the lab, there were small paint chips on Kellerman's clothes. There usually are after impact. Green, with a little rust mixed in. Seen a car like that lately?"

"Yes, I have," I said slowly. "That Buick sedan parked in the driveway at Carol Hartzell's place."

Sid chuckled. "Bingo. And it was reported stolen last night. The Hartzell kids discovered it was gone when they got home from school yesterday afternoon. They thought Leon Gomes or their mother had it. They didn't realize it had been stolen until Carol Hartzell got home from work. The San Leandro police took the report about an hour before Kellerman got hit."

I turned this information over in my mind. Once again it was looking as though Leon Gomes had something to do with Rob's death, and quite possibly that of Charlie Kellerman. I voiced my suspicions to Sid.

"Gomes and Hartzell were playing cards with friends the night Lawter died," he reminded me. "They got home before he went out the window."

"They say. Robin said they got home after midnight."

"I told you before I wasn't convinced the girl was right about the time. So yes, I'm discounting it for now. As for last night, they went to a movie after they reported the car stolen."

"Is there any way to check that out?"

"I doubt it, unless someone at the movie theater remembers them. And that's unlikely. Now, I gotta go, Jeri. You get any more information, you call me."

I disconnected the call. Motive and opportunity, I thought. Leon had opportunity, but I wasn't sure about his motive.

It seemed likely that whoever killed Charlie Kellerman was the person he'd been blackmailing. And I didn't think Charlie had called Patricia Thursday afternoon just to pass the time of day. She was somehow involved in this messy business. But how, and why?

Where did Leon fit in? I remembered the thundercloud look on his face as he left the Bates production department office Thursday afternoon. What was the connection between Leon and Patricia? And was Carol part of the puzzle? Would she want to kill her brother? I couldn't come up with an answer to that one.

I called my office. When I got my answering machine there, I punched in the code that would let me access the messages that had been received. There were four messages. Sally Morgan, who lived on the other side of Rob's apartment, had called sounding agitated and telling me it was urgent. I figured she was calling to tell me about Charlie's death.

The second call was from Bette Bates Palmer. She didn't say why she was calling, but she wanted to talk with me as soon as possible. The third message was from Darcy, saying she really had to talk with me and suggesting lunch on Monday. The fourth caller was Ruby, who recited the home phone number of Al Dominici, the former Bates food-safety manager.

I debated about calling any of them, due to the lateness of the hour. But Sally had sounded upset enough that I decided to go ahead. When she answered the phone, I said, "It's Jeri Howard, returning your call. Sorry for the delay, but I've been out of town. I heard about Charlie Kellerman, though."

"Oh, my God," she said, her voice ragged. "It was awful."

"You saw it happen?" Neither the article nor Sid had given the names of any witnesses.

"Yes. I'll never forget it." She took a deep breath. "I'd had dinner with a friend who lives over on Lakeside Drive. I was walking home. People cross the street there at Seventeenth and Lakeside all the time. There's a crosswalk, but no stoplight. Lakeside's pretty heavily traveled and people drive so damn fast."

I knew the intersection she was talking about well. Oak Street became Lakeside after it crossed Fourteenth, and it was four lanes of one-way traffic as it went around Lake Merritt, with the park and the lake on the right side and buildings on the left. Lakeside curved to the left just after Seventeenth, and people had a tendency to speed up as they headed into that curve.

"So what happened, Sally? Did you see Charlie crossing the street?"

"I saw someone crossing the street. I didn't know it was Charlie until he landed in the gutter, practically at my feet." Her voice choked. "He was covered in blood . . ."

"I know you're going to see that picture for a long time." I thought about some of the images that had been engraved on my consciousness over the years, images that were difficult to overcome. "But try to push it aside for a moment and tell me what else you saw or heard."

"The car that hit him sped up," Sally declared. "I heard it. I remember thinking, that idiot better slow down."

"Did you see the car?"

"Not well enough to describe it, or to see who was driving. It was dusk, not quite dark, but dark enough. Someone else who saw it told me he thought the car was one of those American sedans, blue or green." Her voice took on a tentative note. "The thing is, I saw a car . . . I told the police officer this, so I'll tell you. I'm not sure if it was the same car, though."

"Just tell me what you saw," I prompted.

"When I left my friend's building, I saw this car on the opposite side of Lakeside, double-parked with its lights on, as though it was waiting for someone to pull out of a parking place. I think it was green, but I'm not sure, because it was just out of the light from a streetlamp. I turned left and walked up Lakeside toward Seventeenth, and when I was about twenty or thirty feet from the corner, I saw the man in the middle of the street. Then I heard a car rev up and—" She stopped. "It was so awful. It happened so fast."

"Thanks, Sally. If you remember anything else, be sure to call the investigating officer. And let me know."

As I hung up the phone I played the scenario in my mind, as Sally had described it. It appeared that someone had been waiting for Charlie to cross the street. That meant a meeting had been arranged, perhaps to get Charlie out into the open. I was sure Charlie Kellerman's death was no mere accident. It was stone-cold murder, committed with a vehicle as a high-speed and very effective weapon.

My tea had gone cold. I got up to put the teakettle on the burner again. With an eye on the clock, I punched in Bette's number. "Sorry to be calling so late," I told her after I'd identified myself. "I've been out of town, and I just got back."

"Can you meet me at my brother's house tomorrow morning?" she asked. "We'll have plenty to talk about. The rattlesnake struck, and heads rolled."

"What do you mean?" I had a sudden, disconcerting image of a snake coiled around a severed head.

"My brother and Alex Campbell got handed their walking papers Friday afternoon," Bette said, with an I-told-you-so note in her voice. "Hank Irvin's the new general counsel. We expected that. But Yale Rittlestone's taken over the whole damn company. He's made himself chief executive officer."

CHAPTER *34*

J EFF BATES LIVED IN A SPANISH-STYLE STUCCO HOUSE ON
Balfour Avenue in Oakland's Trestle Glen neighborhood. Sunday
morning I parked at the curb and went up the wide concrete steps to
the red-tiled front porch that went with the red-tiled roof. To the right
of the white-painted double doors was a bell, and I rang this. A moment later the door opened. I found myself looking at a solidly built
gray-haired woman wearing blue slacks and a white T-shirt. She had
friendly brown eyes with a lot of laugh lines around them.

"I'm Rita Bates," she said after I'd introduced myself. "Jeff and
Bette are back in his study."

She led the way past the formal living room and dining room and
the staircase that led to the second story. The study was a square
room at the back of the house. It was furnished with a big roll-
top desk, a recliner that had seen better days, and a low, com-
fortable-looking tweed sofa. There were bookcases on two walls,
filled mostly with books, but decorated here and there with memen-
tos and family pictures. One shelf held a small television set, while
another contained a portable CD/radio and a collection of compact
discs. A large window looked out into a yard with a flagstone patio
and lots of yellow and bronze chrysanthemums in round redwood
planters.

I'd seen Jeff Bates a couple of times during my stint as a temp in
the legal department. He was clad in loose-fitting khaki slacks and a
plaid short-sleeved shirt, in contrast to the business suits he'd worn to
the office. Tall and rangy, like his sister Bette, he looked equally fit

and tanned as she did. His hair was completely gray, however, and his face held more lines. Bette had told me he was three years older than she was, which made him sixty-two. Today he looked older, as though Friday's events had taken more from him than his job and his company.

Bette, too, was casually attired, in comfortable, well-worn blue jeans and a shirt. She introduced me to her brother, as Rita went across the hall to the kitchen. She returned a moment later with a tray loaded with coffee mugs and a plate of pastries. I took one of each, and we all sat down for a talk.

"My sister tells me you're a private investigator." Jeff looked me over. "And that you've been working at my company for the past week and a half."

I nodded. "I've been trying to get some leads on another matter, concerning one of your employees."

"Rob, the paralegal, the young man who was engaged to my niece Diana." He frowned, his fingers tightening on the handle of his coffee mug. "I'm not sure what that has to do with the coup Yale Rittlestone pulled off on Friday."

"It may have nothing to do with it," I said. "But I never know until I get some information. Tell me what happened, in as much detail as possible."

"Well . . ." It was obvious that Jeff wasn't convinced that there was any reason at all for me to be here. It was Bette who had insisted on my meeting him here this morning. Now she motioned at him with one hand, as though nudging him forward.

"All right," he relented. "I'd gone down to Los Angeles early Thursday morning, to attend a food industry meeting. Ordinarily I would have flown back that night, but I have an old friend down there that I hadn't seen in awhile. I spent the night with him and his wife in Bel Air and flew out of LAX the next morning. I got to Oakland about one o'clock Friday afternoon. I had no indication that anything was wrong until Yale Rittlestone showed up at two, with that assistant of his, Eric Nybaken."

He paused and took a sip of coffee, as though fortifying himself for the rest of the story. "I wasn't expecting Yale. He walked into my office unannounced. Then he proceeded to tell me he was closing all of our operations in Oakland and the East Bay—headquarters, the plants, everything. He plans to lay off every single employee and move what's left of Bates to El Paso."

He shook his head. "I was flabbergasted, appalled to the point of being speechless. When I found my voice, I objected, strenuously. I told Yale I simply would not agree to any plan to take Bates out of Oakland, let alone out of state. My father built this company from the ground up, and he had feelings of loyalty to the city. He always resisted any suggestion that we move headquarters from Oakland to the suburbs. A lot of good my objections did me. At that point, Yale informed me that Rittlestone and Weper had decided my services as chief executive officer were no longer needed, and that he himself was replacing me, effective immediately."

"You had no idea about the El Paso move?" I had trouble believing that Jeff Bates had been kept that far out of the loop. On the other hand, I knew that many executives were content to let their underlings handle the day-to-day business routine. But I'd pictured the CEO of Bates Inc. as being a hands-on boss. Evidently he hadn't been hands-on enough. Or Rittlestone and his team, both inside Bates and out, had been very good at keeping Jeff in the dark.

His expression was a mixture of exasperation and defensiveness. "None whatsoever. I realize what you must be thinking, but I really didn't. Looking back, I can see little things that should have tipped me off. Yale and I had been talking about expanding the company, going outside Northern California to the western United States. El Paso was mentioned, because it's close to the produce-growing areas of the Rio Grande Valley. The plan, at least as it was presented to me, was to purchase some existing food processing plants that belonged to a company called Sheffield Foods. Expansion of the company, that's what we talked about. Not this wholesale abandonment of Oakland."

He paused, squaring his jaw. "I assure you, Ms. Howard, until Friday afternoon, I thought that's what Bates was planning to do."

"Project Rio," I said. "I suspected what was going on when I saw an office building on that land Bates is buying. Then I did some research at the El Paso courthouse and public library. And I talked with the woman who owns that land and the building. She'd heard rumors from a friend in El Paso about Bates buying the Sheffield plants and putting them into production again. Did you know

Sheffield Foods had been taken over by TZI, the same company that mounted a hostile takeover of Bates?"

Jeff Bates nodded. "Yes. And Sheffield went out of business two years after that. That's why the old Bates board and I wanted to avoid TZI's hostile takeover. I thought turning to Rittlestone and Weper would solve the problem."

His rationale for turning to Rittlestone and Weper as his "white knights" no doubt made sense at the time, from a business standpoint and from what I'd learned about TZI's track record.

But sometimes the business standpoint wasn't the only one to be considered. There were plenty of other factors that got ignored when they didn't come under the heading of "good business." The irony was that the demise of Bates could very well happen anyway under the Rittlestone and Weper regime.

"Presumably Hank knew the truth about the move," I said, "since he's been negotiating the sale. What about Alex?"

"Alex was as surprised as I was," Jeff said. "Evidently Hank has been in Yale's pocket all along. That's why Alex is out and Hank is the new general counsel."

"So when you objected to moving the company, Rittlestone canned you."

Jeff looked pained at my choice of words. "He was perfectly within his rights as a majority shareholder to vote me into early retirement."

"He was not," Rita Bates interrupted. "You had an agreement with Rittlestone and Weper, from the start of this whole damn buyout business, that they wouldn't replace you without cause. As far as I'm concerned, they don't have cause and they've fired you illegally. They're absolutely contemptible, both of them."

Bette seconded Rita's comment with a growl of her own. As for me, I wasn't sure that what I'd heard was the action of Rittlestone and Weper together. It sounded as though Frank Weper was missing from this latest move. What if replacing Jeff Bates had been Rittlestone's decision alone?

"We've been over this a dozen times, Rita," Jeff said. "I knew that losing the chief executive officer position was a possibility when I went into that leveraged buyout. As for cause, let's be realistic. In the real corporate world, disagreeing with the majority shareholders is cause enough. The simple fact is that Rittlestone and Weper have more shares than I do. But I'd hoped that the company's performance in the year since the buyout had convinced Yale that it was wise to leave the current management structure in place."

Bette snorted. "He had no intention of leaving you, or any of the others, in place."

"I never discount the company rumor mill," I said, "and it's been working overtime, based on what I've heard in the short time I've worked at Bates. There have been rumors for months that Alex was out and Hank would replace him. And that you were going to be replaced by David Vanitzky."

Who must be feeling furious at the moment, I told myself, if he'd been expecting to move into Jeff's corner office Friday afternoon. Something told me David's status at Bates was more precarious than he'd thought, whether he knew where the bodies were buried or not.

"Where does Frank Weper fit in to all of this?" I asked.

"I assume he concurs with Yale's actions," Jeff said. "They're partners, even if Frank prefers to remain out of the picture in Chicago."

"But you're not sure. He seems to be an unknown factor. Why did Rittlestone wait until Friday afternoon to spring his surprise?"

Now Jeff smiled. "It's an old trick in corporate public relations. Announce the bad news Friday afternoon. Most newspapers have smaller editions on Saturdays, and much of what goes into the Sunday edition has already gone to press. From what I understand, the same is true of TV. By the time anyone in the media realizes that there might be a story, it's Monday and that corporate press release has been buried under whatever hot news happened over the weekend."

"Thanks for enlightening me," I said.

"As for enlightenment," Jeff countered, "you still haven't told us what all of this could have to do with Rob's death. I thought that was an accident."

"No, it wasn't. I'm afraid he was murdered. I don't know why—yet. But I believe it has something to do with his plans to blow the whistle, as he put it. He intended to expose something that's going on at Bates."

"Something illegal?" Jeff was taken aback, as though the thought that Bates Inc. ever did anything bad was beyond his understanding.

"I assume so. Whatever it is, it's unpleasant enough that someone is willing to go all the way to murder to keep it quiet."

"But what could it possibly be?" Rita asked.

"There are any number of ways a company like Bates can run afoul of the law. Name an agency—FDA, IRS, SEC, EPA. Whatever it is, I have a feeling I'm getting close to the truth."

Was I? My eyes moved from face to face, gauging their reaction. Or were my words merely spoken to convince my audience?

"Tell us what we can do to help," Bette said. She was a woman after my own heart, one who liked to get involved. But at the moment I didn't want the Bates family put in any kind of danger.

"Thanks for the offer," I told them, "but Rob was warned off, and now he's dead. And his next-door neighbor, who may have seen whoever killed Rob, was killed this weekend." Now Bette, Jeff, and Rita looked alarmed, as though they'd never encountered the kind of death I had, the up-close, ugly, violent kind. "The best thing you can do right now, all three of you, is say nothing about this to anyone."

CHAPTER 35

WALKING INTO THE BATES BUILDING MONDAY MORNING felt a lot like walking into an intensive care unit, one where the prognosis for the patient's recovery was precarious.

Word was out on the Sheffield acquisition and the move to El Paso, as well as the Friday afternoon massacre that had tossed Jeff Bates and Alex Campbell overboard. In fact, there were two memos addressed to all Bates employees taped on one of the elevator walls.

I perused both of these as the car rose to the fourth floor. Neither offered much information. The first merely announced the personnel changes, without giving the slightest hint as to what this meant for Bates and the people who worked there.

The second was sparse on details. Amid all the corporate puffery about how the El Paso move would make Bates more competitive in today's business climate and deliver more value to the company's shareholders was the singular nugget that the move was supposed to take place next summer.

My fellow passengers crowding the elevator, the ones whose jobs were going south, looked understandably worried as they glanced at the memos with lowered eyes and gloomy expressions. They talked in low discontented mutters, comparing notes and wondering about their job prospects.

The whole building seemed to be reeling from the double whammy. The boat was rocking still on the fourth floor. According to a conversation I'd overheard in the lobby while waiting for the elevator, the former general counsel seemed resigned to his fate and almost eager to be gone. Alex had cleared his belongings out of his office over the weekend, and Hank was moving in this morning.

As for Jeff Bates, he'd done nothing of the kind, or so he'd informed me yesterday. It seemed to indicate some vain hope on his part that his abrupt dismissal from his position as CEO of the company his father founded wasn't really happening. However, when I stepped off the elevator I glanced to my right at the corner office that belonged to the CEO. In the small outer office I saw Ann Twomey, Jeff's secretary. Now she worked for Yale Rittlestone. If that bothered her, it didn't show on her face. Between her desk and the closed door leading to the inner sanctum there was a stack of cartons. Evidently Ann was doing Jeff's packing for him.

Here's your hat, what's your hurry? I thought, dredging up the old saying.

I wondered whether Yale Rittlestone was already ensconced in Jeff's office, eager to take up the hands-on running of Bates. Somehow I didn't think so. Yale didn't strike me as an early-to-work kind of guy. Besides, he was probably waiting until Ann cleared away all traces of his predecessor.

When I arrived in Cube City, Nancy was at her desk, looking upset in her own quiet way. No wonder. She'd worked for Alex for years. I said good morning. Nancy murmured a reply, but she appeared to be too distracted even to ask me about my phony illness excuse for not coming to work on Friday.

As for Gladys, she was ignoring the filing and the dictation tapes that awaited us in the rush box. Instead, she had the classified section of Sunday's edition of the Oakland *Tribune* open on the surface of her desk, sipping a cup of coffee as she studied the listings in the Help Wanted section.

"Looking for a job?" I surveyed her over the top of the divider.

"Are you shitting me?" She shot me a disgusted look. "The damn company's moving to El Paso next year. They're gonna fire us all. Those sons of bitches."

"Are you going to quit right away?" I asked.

"Hell, no," Gladys declared. "Unless I should see some fabulous job in these classifieds, I can wait until they lay me off. That way I'll draw unemployment and get the severance package. But I'm going to polish up my résumé and interviewing skills, all the same."

"What kind of severance are they offering?"

"No details yet, but it's usually one week's pay for every year you've worked, and some health care continuation. That amount of money won't last me long, with the cost of living in the Bay Area."

"When is the company going to move? I heard next summer, but do they have a specific date?"

Summer was a fairly elastic goal, with plenty of wiggle room. The office building was there, I'd seen it. Presumably the administrative side of the company could move right in and start conducting business. But if Rittlestone and Weper planned to process food under the Bates Best label, they had to bring the long-dormant Sheffield plants up to speed.

"Not that I'm aware of," Nancy said, her voice subdued, from the other side of my cubicle. "Just next summer."

"A lot can happen between now and then," I said.

And the show must go on, I thought, as Patricia stalked into Cube City. To say she didn't look happy was an understatement. She didn't bother to say good morning. Instead she flung a dictation tape into the rush box as though she was tossing a Molotov cocktail through a window. She departed in the same ill humor. I took the lid off the latte I'd bought before coming to work and speculated about the source of her nasty mood. Not that she'd been Little Miss Sunshine most of the past two weeks, but this latest behavior seemed downright ugly.

Was she irked about Hank's elevation to general counsel? Lauren Musso had hinted that Patricia herself wanted the job. Patricia had been at Bates longer than Hank. Of course, he'd been brought into the company from the Berkshire and Gentry law firm for the express purpose of stepping into Alex's job. Had Patricia been cozying up to Yale Rittlestone in hopes of gaining that position? Or did her attitude have something to do with the phone call she'd received from Charlie Kellerman Thursday, the day before he was run down by a car and killed?

"I guess you're short an attorney," I told Nancy, "now that Hank has moved into Alex's office."

"No, that was this morning's bombshell." Nancy's mouth quirked into something that might have been a smile, if she'd been able to put her heart into it. "Tonya Russell has been moved into that slot."

I recalled what Lauren Musso had told me about Tonya. She was an attorney, and Lauren had wondered why Rittlestone and Weper had moved her from their Chicago office into the position of Bates's human resources director. Perhaps they'd been planning this vacancy in the legal department, and the HR job, of barely two weeks' duration, was merely a means to an end to get her in place at Bates. If that was the case, it meant R&W had played a particularly cruel form of job roulette by forcing Laverne Carson to retire.

"Who's filling her job?" I asked. "Another Rittlestone and Weper clone?"

Gladys laughed. "Clone? I like that. You've picked up the Bates lingo. Next thing, you'll be calling 'em Rattlesnake and Viper, like the rest of us."

"I don't know." Nancy shot me another look like those she'd been sending my way on Thursday, as though she somehow knew that I wasn't the run-of-the-mill ordinary office temp. I asked too many questions. "I'll let the people in human resources worry about that. I've got enough on my plate right here in legal."

I wasn't in the mood to transcribe Patricia's tape, so I caught up on filing for the next hour. I was exiting the file room when I saw David Vanitzky in the north hallway, coming out of the human resources department. I could tell from the look on his face when he spotted me that he wanted to talk, but now wasn't the best time. I'd hoped to dodge him and his corporate intrigue awhile longer. He stopped, looked around to make sure no one observed us, and said, "Lunch," in a low tone that sounded more like an order than an invitation.

"Can't," I told him, just as economically. "Got a date." It was the truth. I was meeting Darcy at noon, so I could find out what she wanted to discuss.

Before David had a chance to respond, Tonya Russell bustled out of human resources. "Oh, David, glad I caught you. We need to talk about . . ." He shot me a narrow-eyed look as he turned and headed for his office, with Tonya at his side.

I walked back to Cube City. A blinking light on my phone told me I had voice mail, so I picked up the receiver and punched the necessary buttons to retrieve a message from Sue Ann Fisk, Nolan Ward's secretary down in production. After I listened to it, I told Nancy I had to go down to the mail room and headed for the stairwell. Down on the second floor, I found Sue Ann behind her desk, sticking labels on envelopes.

"You didn't have to come down, you could've just called me back," she said with a friendly smile.

"I had to go to the mail room anyway. What was it you wanted?"

She set aside the sheet of labels, glanced at Ward's closed door, and leaned forward. "Those eleven call sheets you were asking about. It really bothered me that I didn't have those logged. Like I said, that's too many to simply get misplaced. I've been checking around, and I can't find any record of having received them. Struck me as really strange. I mean, you were sure about the dates and all. I even asked Nolan." She glanced at the door again, as though she were afraid that the mention of her boss's name would bring him storming out.

"Did he remember them?"

"No." She paused, and in the ensuing silence, I was about to thank her for her extra effort in trying to locate the call sheets, when she frowned, looking perturbed. She said, almost as an afterthought, "It was the oddest thing."

That piqued my interest, as did the expression on her normally cheery face. "What was, Sue Ann?"

"Why, he acted peculiar." She pointed her thumb at Ward's door. "Like he was nervous about something. Something he didn't want me to know anything about. He asked me why I wanted to know. I said someone from legal had been down here asking about them. And then I remembered. That young man that worked in your department, the one who died recently. Rob, that was his name. He was down here in August. He was asking about the same call sheets you are. And he was the one who requested a printout of the calls about dairy products."

I'd thought so, all along. I peered past Sue Ann, at the door, wishing I could see through it for a good look at Ward. "What was Nolan's reaction when you told him someone from legal was asking about those call sheets?"

"He, well . . ." She said it with body language rather than words, giving a pretty good imitation of someone being taken aback at my snooping. "Then he called in one of the plant managers. He's in there with Nolan now."

"Was it the same manager who was there Thursday?"

Sue Ann looked surprised. "Leon Gomes? Why, yes, how did you know?"

"Just a guess."

It was more than a guess, though. After leaving the Bates house yesterday, I'd gone to the Oakland library, to continue my background investigation on Leon. I'd also made some phone calls of my own, one of them to Al Dominici, the former food-safety manager who'd retired and whose job hadn't been filled. I also called several of the people whose names and phone numbers were on those call sheets Rob had hidden. Both the library and the phone calls answered some questions and left me with others. I was planning to spring those questions on Leon at a time of my own choosing.

Which wasn't now. Judging from the perplexed look on Sue Ann's face, I had to tone down my interest in what was going on behind that closed door. That didn't mean, of course, that I was going to stop pumping her for information.

"That guy," I continued, "Leon, you said his name was? When he came storming out of Nolan's office the other day, I figured something terrible had happened. You mentioned one of the plant managers, so I wondered if he was back for a return engagement. Any idea what's going on?"

"I don't know," she said. She glanced down at her phone console. "Nolan's on the phone, his line's lit up. I don't have any idea who he's talking with. Now, Leon Gomes runs the dairy plant. He was promoted to that manager slot late last spring, and as far as I know, he's done a good job. Nolan's real pleased with his work."

"Do Nolan and Leon talk frequently? I mean, that might be a sign something's wrong at the plant."

"Yes, they're on the phone quite a bit," Sue Ann said. "And Leon comes up here for meetings, and such. But I'm not aware of any problems down at the dairy plant." She sighed. "It's been one of those days, Jeri, and it's not even noon yet. Of course, we're all on edge, what with this business about Mr. Bates and Mr. Campbell."

"And moving to El Paso," I added.

"I don't think any of us will be moving to El Paso." She shook her head slowly, and her face turned bleak. "From what I hear, only the executives are going. Everyone else, the hourly people like me, will be out of a job. They can hire people in Texas for less salary." She smiled again, but this time it seemed to be with an effort.

"My husband's on permanent disability. He can't work, so I have to. He gets some disability pay, but it's not enough. I'm past fifty. I know it's illegal to discriminate against people my age, but employers do it all the time. I don't know what I'm going to do."

CHAPTER 36

WHEN I'D CALLED DARCY SUNDAY NIGHT TO FIND OUT why she wanted to get together for lunch on Monday, she'd insisted she couldn't discuss it over the phone. In fact, she'd been rather cryptic about the whole thing. But that was Darcy. She had a highly developed sense of drama. I figured her need to talk had something to do with her living situation, and the fact that she wasn't getting along with her mother.

We'd arranged to meet at noon, on the corner of Webster and Second. But Darcy was waiting, if you could call it that, right outside the Bates building.

I could hardly miss her. She was wearing black slacks and an over-sized T-shirt so yellow it was a toss-up as to whether she looked like a big lemon or a large bumblebee. I spotted her when I approached the glass double doors in the reception area. I paused and surveyed the scene that awaited me at the bottom of the steps. When I pushed open one of the doors and left the building, Darcy didn't see me right away. She was too busy staring at Yale Rittlestone.

The new CEO of Bates had just exited the passenger seat of the shiny gold Mercedes I'd seen him get into last week. He stepped right into camera range. The camera and microphone were wielded by a crew from nearby Channel Two, the Oakland independent. Rittlestone was flashing a smile as he spoke to the reporter, a small woman who kept peppering him with questions. At Rittlestone's elbow was Morris Upton, the head of public affairs, in his ubiquitous navy blue suit and red power tie. He had pasted on a grin that looked forced. No doubt he was trying to put a favorable spin on the media attention.

It seemed the local news media had decided not to give that Friday afternoon press release from Bates short shrift, as Morris no doubt had wished. Instead, the changes at Bates wound up on the front page of this morning's Oakland *Tribune*, along with an extensive sidebar on the history of the company, from its founding by Clyde Bates back in the thirties. It could have come straight from Diana Palmer's corporate history of her grandfather's company, and when I read it, I wondered if it had. The *Trib* had also done a shorter sidebar about Rittlestone and Weper, using smiling head shots of both men.

There was an additional story in the business section of today's San Francisco *Chronicle*, which had reprinted the *Forbes* magazine cover showing the smiling golden boy, Yale Rittlestone, and his partner Frank Weper, who definitely looked like the gray, stodgy partner. The *Chron* article had speculated about what this meant for Bates, now that the founder's son was no longer the CEO.

I knew what was on the agenda, as did the employees—the El Paso move. But I doubted the local newspaper and television reporters knew. If they'd found out that yet another Bay Area business was leaving the region, there would have been more headlines.

I toyed with the almost irresistible prospect of making an anonymous phone call to several reporters. Might be fun to step back and watch the shit hit the fan. However, I fought down the impulse. I gave it about twenty-four hours before one of the employees who was going to be without a job made that call.

A corporate drone, male variety, also in a blue suit, had the car's trunk open. I guessed he was Rittlestone's personal assistant, Eric Nybaken. I saw several banker's boxes, but the guy in the suit was leaving the heavy lifting to one of the mail room workers, who hefted boxes onto a hand truck.

Darcy loitered on the sidewalk, practically leaning on the bumper of the Mercedes. It was as though she wanted to get into Rittlestone's lap.

What was she up to? With Darcy, I never knew. She couldn't be all that interested in Rittlestone, even if she had thought him attractive when she'd first seen him last week. Come to think of it, she'd been even more interested when she realized my interest in the man, moving quickly to the obvious conclusion that it had something to do with the case I was investigating.

I caught Darcy's eye as I walked down the steps and edged past the media people, heading for the corner of Webster and Second. By the time I'd reached the Embarcadero, she'd caught up with me, casually, as though she hadn't intended to run into me on the street.

"What was that all about?" I asked. "I told you he was too old for you."

"I've changed my mind. He's not as good-looking as I thought. Something about the eyes. They're awfully cold, don't you think?"

"Yes, I do. So why were you ogling him?"

"Had to make sure it was him. It was, all right. The guy I saw, I mean." She stepped off the curb and headed blithely into the street, without even looking to see if there was any oncoming traffic. Fortunately there wasn't.

"I thought it was him, when I saw his picture in the papers this morning. But I had to be certain. So I took a chance he might be around that Bates building today and came over for a look. I lucked out. Not five minutes after I got there, he arrived in his coach with his entourage."

"What are you talking about?" Now it was my turn to catch up with her.

"Your Mr. Yale Rittlestone." She grinned at me as we reached the other side of the Embarcadero and headed across the parking lot toward Jack London Village.

"He's not my Mr. Yale Rittlestone. I wouldn't have him on a platter. Do you mean you've seen him since last week, when we were together?"

"I certainly have." She twirled around to face me, laughing. She was playing with me, and enjoying it.

"Come on, Darcy, this is serious. Tell me when and where you saw him."

"Is this just corporate intrigue?" she asked. "I mean, Dad's in the computer business, and you should hear what those people do to each other."

"It's more than that."

"You mean, there's a murder involved?" I didn't answer right away, and a shadow passed over her face. I knew she was thinking of the events that brought us together last summer. "I thought so. I thought it must be something big for you to be working undercover at that place. Is Mr. Rittlestone a suspect?"

"I'm not sure," I told her. "Let's just say I think there's more underneath that glittery smiling facade that bears looking at. Tell me when you saw him."

"Friday afternoon, about three, maybe a little after."

That was indeed interesting. According to Jeff Bates, Rittlestone and his assistant showed up at the company around two o'clock to conduct the Friday afternoon massacre. I'd assumed that Rittlestone stayed after Jeff departed. But evidently he'd fired his predecessor and then left the building. But that didn't necessarily mean anything.

"Did you see him here in the neighborhood?"

"He was at the Lake Merritt BART station," Darcy said, mentioning the nearest stop, located about seven or eight blocks from the Produce District. "What was he doing there? Guys like that don't do mass transit. They get driven around in fancy cars like the one we just saw." She jerked her head back toward the Bates building.

She had a point, but I could think of some instances where Yale Rittlestone would get on a bus or a train. "He might ride BART from San Francisco to Oakland, and back again. Aside from the ferry, that's actually the easiest way to get from this part of town to the city. What good is a Mercedes if it's stuck in traffic on the Bay Bridge?"

"But he wasn't getting on a San Francisco train," Darcy argued, playing her trump card. "He got on a Fremont train. I was heading that way myself, so when I recognized him as the man I saw a few days earlier, I got onto the same car. He got off in San Leandro."

"Did he indeed?" I said, more to myself than to her. All I could think about was the short walk from the San Leandro station to Clarke Street.

"Sure did. Why would a big-deal corporate raider go to San Leandro? The article I read in the newspaper says Bates has some plants there, but do you really think a guy like that goes down to the plant to watch 'em can tomatoes?"

"No, I don't."

An idea was taking shape in my head, and I wanted to process it for awhile. Besides, we'd reached the deli, and I thought it wise to delay any further discussion until we were alone again. For the sake of variety I ordered tuna salad on whole wheat and a cream soda. Darcy chose a pasta salad and a bottle of flavored water. We carried our lunches down to a bench that faces the estuary, and I asked her about her living situation.

"I really have to find a place of my own." She twisted the cap off her bottle of water and took a swallow. "Mom's trying." She grinned. "In both senses of the word. Well, she's making the effort. I give her credit for that."

"That's the most grown-up thing I've heard you say this week," I said, only half joking. I unwrapped my sandwich and took a bite.

She pulled the lid off the container of salad and poked at its contents with a plastic fork. "You told me once you didn't get along with your mother, either."

"We've had our problems. It's gotten better over the past year." But we'd had a very unpleasant fight the last time I'd gone down to Monterey to visit her. It was only in the aftermath of those harsh words that we'd flung at each other that relations had slowly started to improve. "What does your father say?"

"He doesn't want me living by myself," Darcy told me. "He says if I got a roommate, it would be okay. But I looked into that, and I don't think it would work. I can just see me living with someone like Heather, my friend from high school. We always egged each other on. We'd be three times as much trouble as we are individually."

"What about renting a room in someone's house?"

Darcy washed down a mouthful of salad with some water. "I've investigated that, too. In fact, that's why I was on BART Friday afternoon. This woman I work with lives down in Castro Valley and rents out rooms in her house. I went down there to look at the place, but I decided it wasn't for me. Too far out. I think I'd like to narrow it down to Alameda, Oakland, or Berkeley. You live over by Lake Merritt, don't you? How is that neighborhood?"

"I won't be living there much longer. I'm buying a house."

I started telling Darcy about the house on Chabot Road in Rockridge, and how wonderful it was going to be when I closed the deal and moved in. When I told her about the studio apartment above the garage, her eyes lit up.

"Jeri, that would be perfect."

Omigod, I thought. I can't believe I mentioned the studio. Now I'm in trouble. I could even be a landlord.

"You said it's just off College Avenue. Walking distance to the Rockridge BART station, right? I could look after your cats and everything when you're out of town," she crowed. "And you could look after me."

"You take a lot of looking after." I looked at the hopeful glow on Darcy's face and asked myself just what I was planning to do with that studio apartment anyway. But did I want a precocious eighteen-year-old living over my garage?

"I'm not as high maintenance as I used to be," she said with a grin. Then she dug an elbow into my side. "Besides, didn't I just give you an important clue?"

"Just what I need, a sidekick." I heaved a sigh. "I'm not promising anything. I suppose we could at least discuss it with your parents. But I'm telling you right now, no wild parties."

CHAPTER 37

WHEN I GOT BACK TO THE BATES BUILDING, YALE RIT-
tlestone, his entourage, and the media had long since departed. I stepped into the empty elevator and pressed the button for
the fourth floor. The doors began to close. Then a gray-clad arm
snaked in between them, and the doors opened again. The arm was
followed by a lanky body in a well-cut gray suit as David Vanitzky
stepped in beside me. He didn't say a word, just gave me a once-over
with his chilly eyes. When the car started its ascent, he looked up, as
all elevator passengers do, at the indicator that marked the passage
of each floor.

"Where were you Friday?" he asked abruptly.

"Out sick," I told him.

He looked at me as though he didn't quite believe me. "Meet me
after work. At the bookstore. I'll be in the biography section."

I favored him with an enigmatic smile, but didn't say anything. Let
him wonder whether I'd show up or not. The elevator doors opened
onto the fourth floor. He gestured with his right hand, polite to a
fault, and waited while I stepped out and walked toward Cube City.

Just as I rounded the corner, Hank stepped out of the office that
had been his and was now, presumably, going to be occupied by
Tonya Russell. "Jeri," he said, "I've got a project for you." His words
sounded more like an order than a request, and his smile was a little
less ingratiating than it had been when he was just one of the attorneys instead of the new Bates general counsel.

"Sure thing. What is it?" I pasted on my best eager-to-please expression and waited for him to elaborate further.

"I need you to move my files." He gestured toward the corner office. "Get some boxes from the mail room guys and load the files in them. Make sure to keep them in order. Then have the guys move them to that office. Don't want you to hurt your back or anything," he added, twinkling his blue eyes at me. "Then you can put them in the cabinets in there. Shouldn't take you more than a couple of hours."

"I'll get right on it," I told him.

Nancy and Gladys were at their workstations in Cube City. I told them where I'd be for the next few hours as I stashed my purse in the bottom drawer. Nancy didn't say anything, but a curious look passed over her face. Gladys glanced at me as she picked another tape out of the rush box.

"Better you than me," she said, with a hint of venom. "Mr. Irvin's been full of himself all day. I might be tempted to tell him just what I think of this whole damn El Paso move, since I heard on the grapevine he's been in on the thing up to his big blue eyes."

Gladys had a point. Why had I been blessed with moving Hank's files? Didn't Hank trust either of the secretaries who'd been working in the legal department for a long time? He had reason not to, in Nancy's case. She'd been Alex's right arm for over fifteen years, and it was obvious she mourned his loss. As for Gladys, she might just damn the torpedoes and give him an earful he didn't want to hear.

Whatever the reason, he was handing this private investigator the opportunity I'd sought for more than a week. I was going to get a crack at that Project Rio file.

I went downstairs and got a half-dozen flattened storage boxes, similar to those I'd seen earlier in Ann Twomey's office, from the mail room. Back on the fourth floor, in Hank's old office, I put them together and pulled open the top drawer of the filing cabinet that had previously been locked. Quickly, I rifled through the file folders, looking for the Project Rio label. It wasn't there. Nor was it in the other file drawers. It looked as though the folder I sought was already on Hank's new desk. If that was the case, maybe I could get a look at it when I unloaded the boxes.

But first, I had to fill them. I set to work, taking care to keep the folders in alphabetical order. I had just finished emptying the second drawer of the lateral filing cabinet when the door opened. I looked up, expecting to see Nancy or Gladys. Instead, it was Tonya Russell's round fair face, wearing a perturbed expression as she surveyed the office that was going to be hers.

"Well," she said. "He's not wasting any time, is he?"

I shrugged. "I'm not sure what you mean."

"Moving into the corner office." She walked into the room, the skirt of her green suit swishing around her legs. Her fingers drummed a little tattoo on Hank's desk as she glanced at the papers arrayed on it.

I stuck the lid on the box I'd just filled, then picked up another empty. "Why shouldn't he move into the corner office? He's the general counsel now, isn't he? I guess that's what they call a done deal."

Tonya's only comment on this was a frown and what sounded like a low and speculative hum. I got the feeling Tonya wanted to look at Hank's files as much as I did. I maintained my noncommittal expression until she'd departed. If Tonya seemed surprised, or even somewhat resentful, of the fact that Hank had been made general counsel, something wasn't exactly right. She was an R&W import, just like Hank. Was it possible that the right hand at Rittlestone and Weper didn't know what the left hand was up to?

I quickly finished packing up all of Hank's files, as well as the contents of his desk, which included some personal belongings. Then I called the guys in the mail room. Two of them rode up to the fourth floor in the freight elevator, bringing with them a hand truck. They loaded the boxes, and I led the way to the corner office.

"Quick work, Jeri," Hank said, as the mail room guys trundled in their handcart and stopped, looking around.

You bet, I thought. Now leave, so I can search the place. But he gave no indication that he had any intention of leaving. He was seated at the desk that faced the door, reading through the documents in a file folder.

"Just tell me where you want these."

"That first filing cabinet," he said, indicating the one closest to the desk. The two mail clerks unloaded the boxes in front of that cabinet and left.

I positioned myself so that I could watch Hank from the corner of my eye, and pulled the lid off the first box, checking my watch as I did so. It was a quarter after three. If I had to complete my chore while Hank was there, putting file folders into drawers was all I'd be able to do. And I wasn't sure I could risk hanging around after work on the chance of getting in here. These file drawers had locks, too, and besides, I was supposed to meet David after work.

I started pulling folders from the boxes and placing them in the filing cabinet. A few moments later, I heard an electronic buzz to my left and glanced up to see Hank feeding several sheets into a shredder. Destroying the evidence? I thought. Of what? I was itching to get my hands on the materials he was reading. Somewhere on that desk, I was sure I'd find the Project Rio file. I hoped it wasn't the file he was purging.

Like an answer to prayer, the phone rang. Hank hit the button on the speakerphone and barked an impatient, "Hank Irvin."

It was David Vanitzky's voice I heard through the speaker. "Yale wants you and me in his office, right now."

"Be right there," Hank said, then he disconnected the call. I saw him gather up the papers he'd been reading and stick them into an accordion folder. He leaned down and opened a desk drawer, one with a small metal key sticking from a keyhole. He dropped the folder inside, shut the drawer, and turned the key. Then he stuck the key in his pants pocket and stood up. He left the office without a word to me.

Well, why not? Secretaries are part of the furniture.

I quickly lifted the box I'd been unloading onto the surface of the desk, so that it would obscure the view from the office door and look as though I'd set it there to empty it. I grabbed a stray paper clip from one of the documents in the nearest file, and squatted on my haunches, unbending the clip.

I'd picked my share of locks, large and small. This one was no challenge. It took me all of five seconds to open the drawer. There were several items inside, but the folder I'd been looking for was on top. I picked it up and looked at the label. It was indeed the Project Rio file.

Now if Hank would just stay closeted with Yale and David. I left the drawer open, in case it might lock if I closed it. Then I straightened, set the file inside the half-empty box I'd been unloading, and pulled out the inch-thick stack of papers on the El Paso move. What was it about this deal that Hank Irvin didn't want anyone to see? Had he already shredded all the incriminating stuff?

I skimmed through the papers. Mostly they were copies of letters and memos, at least in the first half of the stack. In the back of the file I found some drawings and specifications of the planned remodel of the six Sheffield Foods plants in El Paso. Then I came upon a few pages of notes, written on yellow lined papers, in what I recognized as Hank's handwriting.

Before I had a chance to read the notes, I sensed danger. Maybe it was the shadow of someone near the opaque glass of the door, or the rattle of the knob as someone's hand touched it. I shoved the notes into the file and the Project Rio folder back in the drawer. By the time the door swung open, I was back at work, at the more mundane task I was supposed to be doing.

I looked up. Buck Tarcher stared at me with a pair of suspicious eyes. "What are you doing in here?"

I shrugged as though the answer to his question was quite obvious. "What does it look like?" I waved a hand at the boxes and the open file drawers. "Mr. Irvin asked me to move his files into these cabinets."

"Where is he?" Tarcher demanded.

"In a meeting with Mr. Rittlestone."

I gazed at Tarcher, waiting for him to speak, but he didn't say anything. Instead he turned on his heel and stalked out of the office. I waited for a count of fifty, barely breathing, wondering if Tarcher would come back, accompanied by Hank, to accuse me of spying.

But he didn't. Then I knelt again and stuck my hand into the still-open drawer. There were some other files underneath the Project Rio folder, and I wanted a look at those, too. The pages I glanced through were a grab bag of information, and I couldn't determine whether any of it was relevant. The one exception was a handwritten note I found in a folder containing information on Hank's employee benefits. The note was on letterhead that looked familiar. In fact, I'd seen it when I was filing some employee benefits correspondence. I folded it and stuck it into my pocket.

I glanced at my watch again. Ten minutes to four. I'd been pushing my luck so hard it was a wonder I hadn't been caught. I shut the drawer and went back to putting files in drawers, working as quickly as I could. My timing was impeccable. Hank returned from his meeting not long after I'd finished examining the contents of the drawer.

"Still at it?" he asked, as though he'd expected me to be finished and gone.

"I've been taking my time," I told him. "I want to make sure I get all these files back in order. But I'm almost done."

He seemed impatient for me to leave, so I finished quickly, gathering the boxes and carrying them to the entrance of the freight elevator. That done, I detoured to the restroom.

"Oh, there you are, Jeri," Nancy said when I returned to Cube City. I'd seen Gladys just before I walked through the door, entering Patricia's office. So Nancy and I were alone. "I checked with Hank, but he said you'd finished a little while ago."

"I was in the restroom," I told her. "What's up?"

"Mr. Tarcher wants to see you in his office. As soon as possible, he said."

"Really?" I hoped my face didn't show what I was feeling. Busted, I was sure of it.

I sat down at my workstation and took my purse from the drawer where I'd stashed it. Unzipping the handbag, I removed a small tube of hand lotion, which I uncapped. I squeezed out some of the cream and rubbed it into my skin.

"Did he say what it was about?" I asked as I put the cap back on the tube and stuffed it into my purse. I kept the purse on my lap.

"No, he didn't." Nancy looked at me as though she knew perfectly well what it was about. "You'd better go down there now. His office is on the first floor, past office services and the mail room."

"I'll find it," I said, standing up and smoothing my skirt.

I left the computer on, as though I planned to return. After all, it was only a few minutes after four, and I was supposed to work until four-thirty. I moved toward the door, keeping the strap of my purse close to my body, holding it on the side away from Nancy.

Once out of Cube City, I rounded the corner just as Gladys came out of Patricia's office. She gave no indication of having seen me. I headed for the stairwell. No way was I going to get caught in an elevator. And no way was I going to let Buck Tarcher get a crack at me.

I hurried down the stairs, my feet tapping a frantic rhythm on the linoleum-covered risers. On the first floor I pushed through the door and quickly scanned the reception area. No sign of Tarcher. I was afraid he might be waiting for me, that Nancy might have called to let him know I was on my way down.

By the time I got out the front door of the Bates building, I felt as though I'd been holding my breath all during my exodus from the fourth floor, all the way down the stairs. I released it in a sigh, and took in another lungful as I started walking.

The jig was up, in more ways than one.

CHAPTER *38*

I T WAS TOO EARLY FOR DAVID VANITZKY TO MEET ME AT
the bookstore where we'd had our initial encounter last week.
When I got to the store, I went upstairs to the café and nursed a latte
and a piece of cheesecake while I waited, examining the note I'd
smuggled out of Hank's office. The letterhead was that of one of the
pension plan fund managers, which made the implications of the
words I read plain.

I used my cell phone to call my office and retrieve my messages.
One of them was from Al Dominici. When I'd talked with him Sunday afternoon, he'd sounded too sprightly to be a retiree. But he'd
told me he'd gotten fed up with the changes at Bates since the leveraged buyout.

"Those guys from Rittlestone and Weper may know how to put
together a deal that'll make 'em rich, but they don't know diddly-
squat about running a food business," he said. "The bottom line's
more important to them than safety. When Nolan Ward ignored my
recommendations about some problems we were having in one of
the plants, I decided it was time to get out of there."

I'd laughed, then explained why I was calling and asked for his
help. Maybe he'd gotten the information I was after. I punched in his
number.

"I did what you asked," he said, sounding as energetic as he had
the day before. "I checked with a couple of my buddies in the
Alameda and Contra Costa County health departments. They both
got reports of salmonella cases in August, from doctors who treated

eight of the people on that list of names you gave me. One case was pretty serious, a kid who wound up being hospitalized in Walnut Creek. Eight out of eleven means it's probably just the tip of the iceberg."

"So they've started investigations," I said.

"Yeah, but like I told you yesterday, it takes time. I don't think anyone's contacted the company yet. The next step is to talk with the doctors, to determine which species of salmonella they're dealing with. Then they'll interview the people who got sick. Most of the time the investigators don't have any idea what caused an outbreak until they trace it back. Now that I've mentioned the possibility that it's ice cream, my friends are going to call health departments in some other counties, to see if they've got reported cases. Then the investigators will go to the stores, buy some of the products with those batch numbers, and do some testing."

"What would Nolan Ward and Patricia Mayhew do if someone suggested recalling the products," I asked, "without any hard evidence of salmonella?"

"They'd have a meeting," Al said. "To talk about the pucker factor."

"Pucker factor? What the hell is that?"

"Risk analysis. That's where you sit down and balance the cost of keeping the stuff on the shelves as opposed to the cost of pulling it. If the expense of a voluntary recall is high and the risk of liability is low, they'd probably keep it on the shelves. But salmonella? That puts the risk through the ceiling. I can't believe they'd ignore it."

"I don't know that they did," I told him. "I need more information."

"I know one thing for sure," he declared. "If I was still working in production, we wouldn't be having this conversation. I'd have gone straight upstairs to Jeff Bates and had that product pulled by the end of the day."

I disconnected the call, wondering how much bad news it took to make Patricia and Nolan pucker. Then I looked up and saw David stride through the front door to mingle with the rest of the after-work shoppers. By the time I got downstairs, he was at the biography shelves, leafing impatiently through a thick trade paperback about Winston Churchill. I stopped beside him, eyeing a recent book about Humphrey Bogart that I wanted to read. Then I glanced up and down the aisle where we stood, looking for eavesdroppers and observers. I spotted a secretary who worked in human resources, heading this way.

"We can't talk here," I told David in a low voice. "Let's walk."

I turned and headed out of the bookstore. I waited near the flagpole at the foot of Broadway. David showed up a few minutes later. I set off again, with David following about ten feet behind me as I strolled along the walkway at the water's edge. I kept walking until I reached the ferry terminal and the Franklin Delano Roosevelt Pier at the foot of Clay Street.

The next ferry wasn't due to leave for San Francisco until five minutes to six, but there were a dozen or so people on the pier. No doubt some were waiting for the ferry, but others were exploring the pier and the rest of the waterfront. I quickly scanned them and didn't see anyone I recognized from Bates. I walked along one side of the pier, then stopped and leaned forward against the wooden railing, looking down at the City of Oakland fireboat and the water lapping against the pilings.

David stepped up beside me, his back to the railing. I moved away from him, toward a nearby bench, then turned to face him. He'd loosened his tie, and now he unbuttoned the top of his crisp white shirt, showing a few gray hairs sprouting from the neck of the T-shirt underneath.

"I think you'd better tell me the other reason you wanted me to spy on Hank Irvin."

He ran a hand through his unruly gray curls and tried to intimidate me with his predator's eyes. "Never mind that. I don't think you had any intention of doing it anyway."

"After Friday afternoon's events, spying on Hank is a little like locking the barn door after the horse is long gone. I'll bet the walls of that barn are feeling a little shaky right now. Do you still know where all the bodies are buried?"

He narrowed his eyes and stared at me. "What are you getting at?"

"Answers to questions such as *why* are very important to me. Also who, what, where, when, and how."

I reached into my shoulder bag and pulled out one of my business cards. I handed it to him. He squinted in the afternoon sunshine as he read it, then he raised his eyes and stared at me.

"J. Howard Investigations? What the hell does this mean?"

"It means I'm a private investigator."

He looked at me incredulously. Then he leaned against the railing, threw his head back, and laughed, loud enough to garner some looks from the other people on the pier.

"Son of a bitch," he said finally, shaking his head. "I must really be losing my edge. Time was, I'd have spotted you right away."

Suddenly his bony face changed, like quicksilver. Humor vanished and he was deadly serious now. His hand snaked out and clamped around my wrist. "Who hired you?"

Two could play the physical game, and I wasn't afraid of a scrap. I moved my arm, bending his far enough back to cause discomfort. He released me. When he spoke again, his tone was calmer, but not by much.

"Who hired you? Was it Yale Rittlestone? Or maybe Hank?"

"A dead man."

He glared at me, not getting it. Why did he think the two men he'd named had set an investigator on him? It looked as though David had more to worry about than the rest of the sharks swimming in the corporate waters over at Bates.

Wheels turned in David's head, then light dawned in the gray eyes. "For God's sake, you're talking about that paralegal who fell out a window a couple of weeks ago."

"His name was Rob Lawter. He didn't fall. He was pushed. And someone beat him up badly before he went out that window."

"Murder," he said. "And you think somebody at Bates . . . Well, why should I be surprised at murder?"

"Seen a lot, haven't you, up to and just short of murder?"

He didn't answer my question, or his own. Instead, he circled around me as though he wanted to examine every angle. "So, you're working for a dead man. That doesn't sound like a growth industry."

"I'm not interested in growth. I'm interested in justice. And finding some answers. I've still got a few bucks left on the dead man's retainer check. I intend to keep looking until I find out who killed him. And why."

He assessed me with his gray eyes. "I'd hate to have you birddogging my tail."

"You'll find me doing just that, if I don't get some answers."

Now he raised his eyebrows, half-amused, half-serious. "You think I killed him?"

"If I did, you'd be in jail. I have friends down at the Oakland Police Department."

"How does this affect our business relationship?" A sly smile crept over his face.

"We don't have one."

He chuckled. "Oh, yes, we do, Jeri. Especially if you want to continue your little charade as a secretary in the legal department."

"My little charade seems to have reached the end of its usefulness. Buck Tarcher's had his gimlet eyes on me since last week. He wanted to see me in his office this afternoon. I ducked out without dropping by to see what he wanted."

"I'll handle Tarcher," he said, with a dismissive wave of his hand. "I'll tell him I hired you. Which I thought I had."

"You're very sure of yourself, aren't you. I could have sworn your perch at the top of the corporate ladder was a little shaky after Friday afternoon."

"It could be." His face closed up, and I sensed the quiet hush of receding bravado.

"Come on, David, level with me. Why did you want me to keep an eye on Hank? Why did you ask if he or Yale Rittlestone hired me? Why didn't you ask about Frank Weper?"

"Because I've worked with Frank Weper for fifteen years. I know him pretty well."

"You're sure?"

He glowered. "Yes, damn it, I'm sure."

"Then where is he in this picture? He seems to be missing."

"That's because he's been kept out of the picture. By Yale." I must have looked skeptical, because David elaborated. "I had a feeling Hank was in Yale's pocket, ever since they brought Hank on board from Berkshire and Gentry. But I didn't expect what happened Friday afternoon. Yale's not following the script."

"So there was a script."

"There always is," David said. "Frank and I have been doing these buyouts for years. We usually follow the same pattern."

"One that had you stepping into the CEO job at Bates."

He shook his head. "Only as a fallback position. If that were the case, I'd be running every company we'd bought. The deal was that if Jeff Bates and the company performed the way we hoped, we'd leave Jeff in place as CEO. The last time I talked with Frank, that's what he wanted to do."

"You're telling me Weper knew nothing about the Friday after-noon massacre?"

"Hell, no." David struck the pier railing with his hand. "Frank's been in Florida since last week. His daughter got married Saturday, and he only got back to the office in Chicago this morning. I assure you, he was not happy to hear about this." David glanced at the fancy Rolex on his wrist, then put his hands on his hips. "Right now he's on his way out here. I'm picking him up at SFO in about three hours."

"What about this El Paso move? Is that part of the script, too?"

He shrugged. "There was some talk about moving the company out of the Bay Area, even out of state, to cut costs. El Paso wasn't specifically mentioned. It makes good business sense, though. Those Sheffield plants are newer, and the laws in Texas less restrictive."

"Tell that to the people you're going to throw out of work," I snapped. "Jeff Bates says there was some talk of expanding opera-tions into the western United States. Is that true, or was it just a story he was fed?"

"I think it was something Jeff wanted to do. Maybe Yale encour-aged him in that line of thinking. I don't know."

"So it wasn't part of the script. What about the money that seems to be missing from the Bates pension fund?"

David widened his eyes. "How the hell do you know about that?"

I smiled as I quoted his own words to Hank Irvin. " 'There's blood all over the floor. Mopping it up ain't gonna be pretty. In fact, you and I are gonna get blood all over our hands.' "

"Did you have your ear to the door?" he asked, a challenging note in his voice. "How much do you know?"

"Enough. It sounds as though someone is playing with the retire-ment plan money. To the tune of more than a million dollars. And if the feds find out, you're all going to be fucked. I believe those are your words, as well. I had my ear to that door, too. Who is it?"

"The evidence points to Ed Decker," David said. "But I'm not sure. He's the senior vice president in charge of human resources, so he's got the clout to play footsie with the fund managers. That's why I brought Tonya Russell in from Chicago, to keep an eye on him."

"Which cost a very nice lady named Laverne Carson her job," I said. David just looked at me, as though he didn't see how one related to the other. "You really don't get it, do you? People aren't just pawns to be moved around a chessboard."

"Okay, I'm a coldhearted, corporate son of a bitch," he said. "I admit it. But what does that make you?"

"Someone who peeks through keyholes and steals pieces of paper, I guess."

I pulled out the piece of paper I'd found in the locked drawer of Hank's desk. I held it up so David could see it. "Can you think of any reason why Hank should receive a personal note from the manager of the fund that's losing money? Particularly with a date in August."

David took the note and looked at it closely, shaking his head. "No, I can't."

"When I overheard you talking with Hank last week, it sounded as though he didn't know anything about the situation, until you took him into your confidence. Am I right?"

"You are," David said slowly. "He acted as though that was the first he'd heard of it."

"But it wasn't, according to this." I fingered the edge of the note. "I think Hank knows more about that million-plus dollars than he's letting on. Why else would he be communicating with the fund manager? He had me type a separation agreement for Ed Decker. Were you aware of any plans to fire Decker?"

He shook his head again. "Only if we found out he engineered the pension fund losses."

"Looks like Decker's being engineered as the fall guy," I said. "Hank's covering his tracks and shifting blame to Decker. He drafted that agreement before you told him about the pension fund. And Eric Nybaken signed off on it. So whose idea was it to get rid of Decker?"

I'd been wondering whether Yale Rittlestone's fingerprints might be found on what David referred to as the pension fund losses. From the look on his face, he was now entertaining thoughts along the same lines.

"Whose idea was it to move Tonya from human resources into legal?" I asked.

"Hank's. I argued against it."

"Then she must have been getting close to finding out the truth. So Hank and Yale had to get her out of human resources. It's a theory, but that's my best guess as to how it lays out. As for proving it, well, that could be a little tougher."

"How does this help you find out who killed that paralegal? Rob? . . ."

"Lawter. Let's put it this way," I told him. "I know a little bit about a lot of things. Several of them have the potential to put Bates and its top executives, including you, in one hell of a lot of trouble. Capital T trouble with various governmental agencies, as well as the people who work for the company and the people who buy Bates Best products. Rob knew too much about one of these scenarios, and it got him killed. It's a question of determining which one. The pension situation is one possibility. But I have another scenario that's looking better. I just need more time."

"What you need is my help," he said. "Such as keeping Tarcher off your tail. So you're still working for me."

"Not bloody likely," I said, prepared to argue. Then I looked past his shoulder and drew in a breath. "It's Patricia Mayhew. She's coming to catch the ferry."

"She must be going over to Yale's place in the city," David said. "You know she's sleeping with him."

"Yes, I had figured that out. If she sees us together . . ."

"She'll think I'm living up to my reputation as a roué and a ladies man," he finished, "skating as always on the sharp edge of a sexual harassment charge. Might as well take advantage of it."

He moved toward me. One of his arms went around my waist. Like a pair of lovers, we strolled away from the railing into the shelter of the stairs, where we couldn't be seen from the ferry dock. From the corner of my eye I saw Patricia join the others waiting for the ferry, which had just docked. I lost sight of her as several passengers got off the boat. Then I saw her again as she and the others walked up the gangway and onto the boat.

"She's aboard," I said.

But David didn't release me. Instead he turned toward me and pulled me against the length of his body. His mouth came down on mine.

He had a soft mouth for such a hard case. I kissed him back, feeling a surge of guilty pleasure. I hated to admit it, but David Vanitzky was bad-boy sexy. The lure of the guy with the dangerous smile was, for me, somehow more attractive than the safe guy next door.

I put both hands firmly on David's shoulders and pushed him away. "Take advantage is right." I stepped away from him. "You enjoyed that way too much."

He grinned at me, unrepentant, like a cat who'd had too much cream and figured he deserved it. "So did you, though probably not as much as I did. And you'll never admit it. Well, back to business, shall we? I keep Tarcher away from you, and you continue your investigation."

"Why is it that when you speak I catch a whiff of brimstone?" The ferry blew its horn, and the gangplank rattled as the crew took it up. "Negotiating with you is like striking a bargain with the devil."

He moved closer, leaning so that his lips moved against my ear in a knowing whisper. "At the moment, you need the devil. Horns and all."

CHAPTER 39

WHEN I ARRIVED AT MY FRANKLIN STREET OFFICE, I took a chance on calling Robin Hartzell at home. It was after six, dinnertime, and it was likely the whole family, including Leon Gomes, would be there. I figured I could hang up if someone other than Robin answered the phone. Fortunately, it was she who picked up the receiver. I could hear voices in the background, Carol and Leon both, and the blare of the TV set.

"I've got to take another crack at Rob's things," I told her.

"The history assignment?" she said, for the benefit of the others, who might be listening. "Let me go back in my room. I'll tell you what pages we're supposed to read."

A moment later the din on the other end of the phone receded, and I heard a door close. "I thought you weren't gonna call me at home," she said, keeping her voice down.

"Had to. When can I get into that garage?"

Robin sighed. "I think your best bet is to do it during the day. That way Mom will be at work and so will Leon. Before I go to school, I'll leave that door from the garage to the backyard unlocked. All you'll have to do is come in that gate at the side of the house."

It was risky, given the fact that Leon seemed to come home from the Bates dairy plant at odd hours. But at the moment it was the only option I had. It also meant I'd have to feed Nancy some story about why I had to be away from Bates tomorrow morning. That is, I added, if David followed through on his promise to get Tarcher off my back. I had visions of arriving for work and getting apprehended before I got to the elevator.

"I'll be there," I told her. "As early as I can. Before you hang up, I need to know about that green car. The one I saw in the driveway the first night I was there."

"Mom's car? It got ripped off."

Robin dropped her voice even lower as she told me essentially the same story Sid had related to me this past weekend. Robin and Doug had noticed the car missing when they got home from school, but neither of them gave it much thought. Their mother wasn't due home from work until five-thirty or six. Leon had keys to Carol's car, so they thought he'd taken it somewhere. It wasn't until Carol and Leon got home, she on BART from San Francisco, he in his silver van, that anyone realized the car had been stolen.

"Your mother works at Rittlestone and Weper over in the city," I said. "Is it possible someone there could have lifted her keys? Maybe had a copy made?"

"I guess so," Robin said. "I was there once. She's the receptionist, and she works behind this thing that looks like a combination of a counter and a desk. It's right out in the open, and she keeps her purse in one of the desk drawers. I don't think she locks it up or any-thing. Anyone could get into it. But who the hell would want to steal a rusty old Buick?"

Someone who wanted to commit murder, I thought. Before I could ask any further questions, I heard a click on the line, as though someone in the Hartzell-Gomes household had picked up another extension.

I raised my voice an octave and said, "Yeah, well, I'll see ya in class tomorrow." Then I hung up the phone.

Buck Tarcher wasn't waiting for me at the elevator of the Bates building on Tuesday morning. I assumed that David had held up his end of our pact. When I walked into Cube City, about five minutes after eight, Nancy Fong looked at me with a mixture of surprise and alarm. I was late, but judging from the expression on her face, she really hadn't expected to see me.

"I'd like to take an early lunch," I told her, making it up as the words left my mouth. "I have a . . . job interview. For a permanent position. I shouldn't be gone more than an hour or so."

She sat at her workstation, sorting through the morning mail, her brow furrowed. "I guess I don't see any problem with that," she said finally. She picked up her letter opener and began slitting envelopes. "What time do you need to leave?"

"Ten-fifteen." Since I'd played the early lunch card, I didn't think she'd buy off on my leaving any earlier.

"All right. So you'll be back by eleven-fifteen."

"Or eleven-thirty at the latest," I assured her. It was a promise I might have trouble keeping. If Robin had been able to leave the door unlocked and I had an uninterrupted opportunity to search Rob's belongings, I'd be there as long as it took to find some more pieces of the puzzle. And I wouldn't care how Nancy felt about it.

Nancy finished opening the envelopes and began removing their contents, marking the first page of each with her date stamp and putting the items into separate piles for the attorneys. When she finished, she gathered the mail and left Cube City to deliver it.

"She's in a mood this morning," I commented.

Gladys, standing at the printer waiting for it to print out a document, looked over her shoulder and shrugged. "She's always in a mood. When you weren't here at eight, I asked if you'd called, and she acted as though you weren't coming in at all."

Which indicated to me that Nancy knew very well why Buck Tarcher had wanted to see me in his office last night. David may have handled Tarcher, but Nancy was still a wild card that could mess up the game.

"I noticed that Hank's old office is dark," I continued.

"Yeah," Gladys said, picking up pages from the printer, "Tonya Russell hasn't moved in yet. I hear she's not too thrilled about getting shoved into the legal department."

She didn't know the half of it, I thought. "Is Patricia here?"

Gladys laughed, but without humor. "Oh, yes, Miss Charm and Personality has poked her head out of her cave and growled a few times." She waved the pages at me. "This just had to get done right away. Don't they all?"

Business as usual at Bates, I thought. The employees' shock and dismay at word of the loss of Jeff Bates and Alex Campbell was starting to wear off, and resignation about the El Paso move was already deadening the blow. No doubt most of the people who worked here would do as Gladys planned, bide their time, look for other jobs, and wait until they were let go, so they could get the severance pay. Some, who were older, would take early retirement. Most of the Bates workforce were people with families and obligations, both of which required money.

I had obligations as well, to my own business as a private investigator, and the sooner I resolved the Lawter case, the sooner I could get back to my own life. I was starting to feel the way I did when things began to fall into place. Having made an excuse to get out of Bates that morning, it seemed the next two hours dragged. I transcribed tapes, filed, answered the phone, and as soon as the readout on my digital watch hit ten-fifteen I grabbed my purse and hurried out of Cube City.

Twenty minutes later I parked on Parrott Street in San Leandro and walked around the corner to Clarke. The neighborhood had that middle-of-the-day look streets get when most people who live in the houses were at work or at school. I didn't see any delivery trucks, or mailmen, or neighbors watching from the windows. I walked quickly up the driveway of the Hartzell house, then along the sidewalk between it and the house next door. The gate was unlocked, as it had been on my previous visit. I opened it and stepped inside, moving past the garbage cans and recycling bins.

In daylight, the backyard looked bare and uninviting, with patchy brown grass and a concrete square of a patio furnished with cheap plastic chairs. I reached for the knob on the door leading to the garage, and it turned. Robin had kept her end of the bargain.

Once inside I turned on the overhead light for some illumination. I looked at the boxes piled in the middle of the garage. It looked as though they'd been moved since the last time I'd been here. In fact, several of them had been opened, and some of the contents were sticking up from the loose flaps.

Had someone started unpacking the boxes, preparing to sort through Rob's things, deciding what to keep and what to discard? Or was someone looking for something, as I was?

Where to start? I approached the boxes. Where would Rob have hidden something important? I recalled the three call sheets that he'd secreted behind photographs of his family he'd kept at work. What if he used the same hiding place at home? Somewhere in all this mess must be other photographs, posters, artwork he'd hung on the walls of his apartment.

I had a lot of work to do and not much time to do it. The boxes from the kitchen were among those that had been opened. A quick and cursory glance through those revealed nothing more than pots, pans, flatware, and dishes. The other boxes, labeled "BEDROOM" and "LIVING ROOM," were more likely, so I concentrated on those.

In no time, the suit I wore, one I'd borrowed from Ruby, was covered with dust and grime. I'd broken a fingernail and bruised my knee. And my back hurt from moving boxes around. I found more framed photographs, as well as a couple of photo albums, but nothing was hidden behind the pictures. Nor was there anything stashed in the larger pieces that had been wrapped in the newspaper and leaned against the wall.

Eleven-fifteen came and went, and so did eleven-thirty. As noon approached I had to face the possibility that Leon Gomes would come home for lunch. Don't think about that, I told myself. Just keep looking.

The box in front of me held two oversized self-sealing plastic bags, the kind I use to store things in the freezer. Inside them were eight-by-ten color photographs, matted but unframed. The first was a shot of the Point Reyes lighthouse, and the second showed a group of elephant seals snoozing on the sand down at Año Nuevo State Reserve.

I opened the Point Reyes bag and slipped a finger between the picture and the matte, and felt something that I was sure didn't belong there. After I pulled it out and had a good look at it, I reached eagerly for the elephant seals.

By the time Leon Gomes came home for lunch, at twenty minutes past twelve, I was ready for him. I straightened, stretching and working the kinks out of my back and thighs, as I heard him kill the engine of his van and unlock the front door. He moved into the kitchen, whistling as he opened cupboards.

I walked across the concrete floor to the door leading to the kitchen. Leon Gomes whirled around as I entered the kitchen, nearly dropping the jar of mayonnaise he held. On the counter in front of him were two slices of bread and a package of deli cold cuts.

"Who're you?" he demanded. "What the fuck are you doing in my garage?"

I smiled. "We need to talk, Leon."

CHAPTER 40

"I SWEAR TO GOD, I DIDN'T HAVE ANYTHING TO DO WITH IT."
Leon Gomes was sweating, and his voice was shrill with
panic. He was wearing his work clothes, dark brown pants, light
brown shirt with the embroidered Bates Best logo in blue on the left
breast pocket. Right now damp half circles stained the armpits of
his shirt, and moisture beaded on his upper lip.

He'd started to sweat when he saw the three sheets of paper I was
holding. He knew what they were. No doubt he'd been looking
for them when he and his buddies packed up Rob's things and
moved them out of the apartment. Judging from the way those
boxes out in the garage had been disturbed between my last visit and
this one, he was still looking for them. But I'd found them first.

His hand shook as he set the jar of mayo on the counter. Now he
was backed up against the cabinets, all thought of lunch forgotten.
The only thing on Leon's mind at the moment was saving his ass.

"Rob didn't kill himself." I leaned forward. "He didn't take a con-
venient fall from that window, either. He was murdered, and you
know it. You're into this up to your eyeballs."

"I had nothing to do with it," he insisted. "It was Nolan."

"And you were only following orders. Passing the buck up the
chain of command. Now that's an innovative defense. Dates all the
way back to World War Two. So you're telling me Nolan Ward killed
Rob?"

"Hell, I don't know who killed Rob. I just know it wasn't me."

"Just how far up the ladder of responsibility does it go?"

"I don't know."

"Yes, you do." I fingered the papers, all three photocopies, all three smoking guns. "First we have an invoice and a newspaper article." I held up the paper, onto which Rob had copied both items. The article was the same one I'd found tucked into Rob's calendar. "The article says this dairy in Fremont was cited for fecal contamination of milk, a leading cause of salmonella. The invoice says you bought raw milk from that dairy on July twenty-first, after it was cited. Is this dairy one of your regular suppliers?"

He shook his head. "No, no. But Nolan was always after me to cut costs. The guy who runs the dairy, I know him from way back. He lost some business after he got that citation, and he was trying to get back on his feet. He cut me a deal on several tankers of raw milk. And Nolan okayed it."

"Which brings us to item number two," I said. "A memo from you to Nolan, dated July twenty-fourth. Seems you had a little problem the day before with some equipment at the plant. As I understand the pasteurization process, you're supposed to bring raw milk to a high temperature and hold it at that temperature for a period of time. That kills bacteria like salmonella. But if something goes wrong in that process and the milk doesn't get pasteurized . . ." I glanced at the memo, then back at Leon. "Suppose you tell me just what went wrong that day with the diversion valve."

Leon took a deep, shaky breath. "The heat exchanger's got yards and yards of pipe, with thermometers at either end. We pump the raw milk through, so many feet per second, and by the time it gets through all the pipe, it's supposed to be pasteurized. The diversion valve is at the end. If the thermometer shows the temperature of the milk has dropped below the correct levels, the valve's supposed to send the milk back through the heat exchanger."

"But the valve malfunctioned."

"Yeah. The alarm went off. We fixed the valve right away. But some of that unpasteurized milk must have gotten into the ice cream mix. Hell, we produce thousands of units a day. I didn't know anything was wrong."

"Until Rob came to you in late August, and told you about those eleven calls he'd received. All of them from people who complained they'd gotten sick after eating ice cream products from your plant."

Leon's voice took on a defensive whine. "So? It's not like anybody died."

"Not yet, anyway. Certainly not like that listeriosis outbreak down in LA in 1985. Forty-six people died." I watched Leon's face turn gray and sag. "Oh, yes, I've done a background check on you. You used to work for a company that made cheese, the same company that the listeriosis outbreak was traced to. Seems to me you've made a habit of cutting corners as well as costs."

He didn't say anything, so I continued. "I spoke to some of those people who got sick. One of the worst cases was a six-year-old girl who wound up in the hospital. But that's not your problem, right? Rob thought it was. He made copies of those call sheets before he sent them down to production. Maybe he figured that no one would do anything about them. That seems to be the case, ever since Al Dominici retired. Nolan has a tendency to ignore anything that might increase costs or slow down production."

"I don't know anything about that," Leon muttered.

"Yeah, you just make product and move it through on schedule. Salmonella in the ice cream? No big deal. Who cares if people get sick? Not you."

I heard a gasp of indrawn breath and looked up to see Robin Hartzell. I hadn't heard her come through the front door. She was glaring at Leon as though he were some disgusting lower life-form. "What're you doing here?"

"I cut class," she told me. "To see if you needed any help."

"What did you hear?"

"Enough." She advanced on Leon. "You son of a bitch, if you killed him—"

"I didn't." He raised his arms as if to ward off a blow. Robin looked angry enough to hit him.

"Let me finish this," I said, putting a restraining hand on her arm. I turned to Leon. "So Rob checked up on you. He discovered your link to that listeriosis outbreak. Since you manage the dairy plant, which makes Bates Best ice cream, he thought that pointed to you. I don't know when he found this memo about the diversion valve, but a few weeks ago he confronted you about the situation. He threatened to tell the authorities."

"Yeah, yeah, he said we should recall all the ice cream we made that day." Leon shrugged, as though it were no big deal. "Hell, I thought he was overreacting. The stuff had been out on the market for a month, and this was the first I heard of anyone getting sick. Besides, I don't have the authority to order a recall. Only people who can do that are those high muckety-mucks at corporate. Nolan would have to approve it, and he wouldn't make a move without getting a go-ahead from that lawyer up in legal."

"Patricia Mayhew. Who else would Nolan check in with?"

"Him and that Rittlestone guy are joined at the hip," Leon said. "He's the one put Nolan in charge of production in the first place. Hell, Nolan wouldn't take a piss unless Rittlestone told him it was okay."

It looked as though the rungs of the ladder were getting higher every time Leon opened his mouth. "So Rob was down in production sometime in late August, asking about those call sheets, and he discovered that Sue Ann Fisk had no record of them." She still didn't, as I'd discovered on Monday.

"Which meant someone intercepted them," I continued. "Probably Nolan. For all I know, Sue Ann did log those sheets, and Nolan deleted them from the record. Which brings us to item number three."

The third photocopy was marked "Confidential" and dated Wednesday of the week that Rob died. The same day he'd come to my office, when he told me he didn't have all his facts lined up yet, but expected to have them soon. The paper I held in my hand was the confirmation he'd been anticipating. He must have found it in Patricia's files that afternoon, or the next day.

It was a note from Patricia to Nolan describing a conversation she'd had with Yale Rittlestone that day, on the subject of a voluntary recall of the ice cream that was probably contaminated with salmonella.

"I've discussed it with Yale," she'd written. "We've already sold all the units produced that day. This is the first we've heard of any alleged problems. There doesn't appear to be much risk. Besides, with the upcoming initial public offering, Yale says we don't need the black eye a recall would bring. Let's ignore this and see if it goes away. I'm sure we can neutralize Lawter."

"He showed you this, didn't he? When?"

Leon glanced at the incriminating photocopy. "Yeah. Wednesday night, the day before . . ." He stopped, swallowed, then spoke again. "He even gave me a copy. Said he wasn't gonna be neutralized. He said if we didn't recall the ice cream voluntarily by Friday, he'd blow the whistle, with the health department, the press, everyone."

"What did you do then?"

"I talked to Nolan," he said. "Thursday morning. I told him he'd better talk with Mayhew and Rittlestone. Nolan said he'd take care of it."

"What happened then?"

"I don't know. I swear I don't. Nolan told me to go back to the plant and keep my mouth shut. He'd handle it. So I went back to the plant. I didn't hear a thing. Until the cops come to the door Friday afternoon, to tell Carol that Rob's dead."

"And you didn't ask yourself why he was dead," I said, "other than to decide he'd conveniently killed himself." Leon didn't answer. He avoided my eyes, and Robin's furious glare. "No, I guess you didn't. It was easier that way. Like telling yourself you had nothing to do with Rob's murder."

I LEFT LEON TO THE NOT-SO-TENDER MERCIES OF ROBIN, and headed back to Bates. It was nearly two when I walked into Cube City. Gladys looked startled at my begrimed condition. Nancy Fong was just plain mad. Given her quiet and almost passive manner during the past two weeks, the angry woman who propelled herself at me was a jarring sight, one that left Gladys openmouthed with astonishment.

"You've been gone for nearly four hours." Her voice was just this side of shouting, certainly loud enough to be heard out in the hall-way. I shut the door of Cube City, then turned to face her. "I know you're not a temp," Nancy snarled. "I don't know who the hell you are, but you'd better tell me before I pick up that phone and call Buck Tarcher down in security."

It looked as though she wasn't even going to wait that long. Her hand was reaching for the phone as I pulled my license from my purse and held it in front of her.

"I'm a private investigator," I told her.

Nancy's hand froze on the phone. She turned and examined my license. Gladys abandoned whatever she was doing and left her cubi-cle for a better look.

"Well, I will be damned," Gladys said. "Who you working for?"

"Rob Lawter."

The phones started shrilling in all three cubicles. We ignored them, and the calls rolled over to voice mail.

"Then he was murdered," Nancy said finally. "The police told

Alex that Rob got a threatening note. And that it looked like someone had been in his apartment that night. But I had a feeling, when I
first heard the news. Something just didn't fit."

"So you did a little poking around his apartment building that day
you were supposed to be home with a migraine." I smiled at her. After a moment, her mouth moved into what might have been a smile.

"Not that it did me any good. Neither of his neighbors was very
informative."

"What made you think Rob's death wasn't an accident?" I asked.

"Rob was preoccupied, that last week," Nancy said. "As though
something was bothering him. After he died I looked through his
files, but I couldn't find anything. I didn't know what to look for."

"Well, I do," I said. "At least now. Where are Patricia and Hank?"

"Hank's in a meeting with Yale Rittlestone. Patricia's in her office.
At least, she was fifteen minutes ago." Nancy narrowed her brown
eyes, and her dislike of the current Bates regime was plain. "Are they
involved in this?"

"We're about to find out. Gladys, call Sue Ann Fisk. Don't tell her
anything, just find out where Nolan Ward is." Gladys was on the
phone before the words were out of my mouth.

I turned to Nancy. "Who else is in that meeting with Rittlestone?
And where are they?"

"Frank Weper and David Vanitzky," she said. "They're in Rittlestone's office. I overheard Rittlestone telling Ann Twomey that they
weren't to be disturbed. So it must be important."

If what David had told me about Weper's reaction to Rittlestone's
coup was true, I was willing to bet the two partners were having
it out.

Gladys hung up the phone in her cubicle. "Sue Ann says Nolan
just left. He's on his way up here to see Patricia."

Which meant Leon had called Nolan after I left the house. Had
Nolan warned Rittlestone or made the attempt? I was hoping Rittlestone's secretary was taking his do-not-disturb words to heart.

"Gladys, go down the hall and keep an eye on Rittlestone's office.
I need to know if that meeting breaks up. Right now I've got to talk
with Patricia. Before Ward gets to her."

Gladys gave me a mock salute and opened the door. "I guess I can think of a reason to chat up Ann Twomey," she said as she headed for the south hallway and her assignment.

"I'm going with you to Patricia's office," Nancy told me, mouth twisting. "I wouldn't miss this for all the tea in China."

When Nancy and I pushed through the door, Patricia gave no indication that Nolan had preceded his trip upstairs with a warning phone call. She had several file folders open and spread out on the surface of the desk in front of her, and she glanced up as we entered. The strain of the past two weeks had left her looking haggard. She pushed back her dark curly hair and mustered up some of her imperial mien, directing a single word to Nancy. "Yes?"

"Have at it," Nancy told me. She stood with her arms folded and her back against the door, so that anyone who tried to open it would have to knock her down.

Now Patricia's face moved from tense to alarmed. It wouldn't take much to send her over the edge. Now she pushed back her chair, half rising from its padded seat and back. "What is this?"

"An inquiry into the murder of Rob Lawter. You should be able to answer my questions, since you were there the night it happened."

She froze. Then she dropped back into the chair, gripping its arms. "I don't know what you're talking about."

"I'm talking about a salmonella outbreak that will probably be traced to Bates Best ice cream. One you chose to ignore."

Her mouth tightened, but her expression remained impassive as I laid it out for her, the information I'd uncovered myself as well as what I'd bullied out of Leon Gomes. "Rob obtained a copy of your memo to Nolan. Yale Rittlestone was more concerned about the IPO than he was about people getting sick. Rob was about to blow the whistle and give Bates a bigger black eye than you ever thought possible."

I moved toward her, placing my hands on the desk and battering her with my words. "It would have been so much simpler to pull the damn ice cream." I shook my head. "There would have been some publicity, but that's why companies like Bates pay spin doctors like Morris Upton. So it cost the company some bucks and some bad press. You'd have been better off in the long run for handling the situation as soon as possible."

Now she wouldn't meet my eyes. I favored her with a grim smile and continued my rundown of the facts as I saw them.

"But you didn't handle the situation. You and Yale and Nolan ignored the problem and hoped it would go away. You knowingly let that contaminated ice cream stay on the shelves. And you tried to 'neutralize' Rob with a threatening note. But when he found your memo—"

The door rattled as someone tried to open it. I glanced over my shoulder. Nancy stood her ground. Whoever was outside, probably Nolan, knocked. This was confirmed when I heard his high-pitched voice. "Patricia? Are you there?" There was another knock.

"We're in a meeting," Nancy said in a low voice.

"I need to talk with Patricia," the man insisted.

"We'll just be a minute," Nancy said, gripping the doorknob.

Patricia rose from her chair again, as though she wanted to make a break for the door. I pinioned her with my eyes and said, "Sit down. You're not going anywhere until I get some answers. And you'd better starting talking. You've got more to worry about than losing your license to practice law. The way I see it, you're looking at a murder charge."

The possibility of jail time finally sank in. Her face crumpled. "I didn't kill him. It was—"

"Don't tell me it was an accident," I said harshly. "I'm not in the market for swampland in Florida. Rob didn't fall out that window, any more than Charlie Kellerman happened to be crossing the wrong street at the wrong time." Now her face went white around the mouth.

I nodded. "Oh, yes, I know about that, too. Charlie saw you that night, and he recognized you. He was putting the bite on you for money. When the bite got too big, you arranged a meeting with Charlie. When he walked across the street, your good friend and bed partner Yale Rittlestone ran him down with a stolen car. Now which one of you killed Rob?"

Patricia started to shake, as though she had palsy and she couldn't control the shudders. When she finally spoke, the quaver extended to her voice. "It wasn't supposed to be like that. We were only going to talk with him, try to make him see reason."

"Your version of reason is damned skewed," I told her.

"Yale offered him money. Rob was insulted. He started shouting. He said people like Yale think they can buy off the whole world. Well, not this time, he said. Not this time." She gasped in some air. "Yale lost his temper. He has a temper. He hates being thwarted. He was shouting back. And he hit Rob."

More than once, I thought, remembering the autopsy report.

"It happened so fast," Patricia said. "I don't know if Rob stumbled, or if Yale pushed . . . the window was open . . ." She stopped and buried her face in her hands.

"I'll bet Yale was going to pay off Charlie, too. No temper there. Just cold-blooded premeditated murder."

I gazed down at her. Then I glanced sideways at Nancy, who had moved away from the door, an expression of utter contempt on her face as she stared at Patricia. "Call the Oakland Police Department, Homicide Section. Ask for Sergeant Vernon or Sergeant Hobart. If they're not in, anyone will do. Just get the police here fast."

"Where will you be?" Nancy asked.

I smiled. "It's time I had a talk with Yale Rittlestone. But he's not going to like what I have to say."

CHAPTER *42*

NOLAN WARD HAD BEATEN ME TO YALE RITTLESTONE'S office, or at least the exterior chamber that was staffed by Ann Twomey. At the moment, the CEO's secretary was taking her role as gatekeeper quite seriously.

"He said he wasn't to be disturbed," she said stubbornly, standing between Nolan and the closed door that led to the inner sanctum. "No matter what."

"That's telling him, Ann," Gladys chimed in. Arms folded over her chest, she was perched on the front of Ann's desk, a modern oak piece that faced the door leading to the hallway. The surface of the desk was neat and orderly, an appointment book open near the phone console. Next to this was a box of tissues and a flowered china mug resting on one of those plug-in coasters that kept the contents, in this case tea, warm.

"But this is urgent," Nolan insisted.

"That's what they all say." Ann had obviously heard that one before. Dressed in a camel-colored coatdress and heels, she was taller than Nolan by a few inches and certainly more imposing. Now she loomed over him, giving no indication that she planned to back down. I appreciated her success in keeping him out of the CEO's office, but now I wanted in and both Ann and Nolan were barring my way.

I looked at the closed door, feeling the emanations from behind it. I could hear voices, too, raised in anger and passion, all talking at once.

I traded looks with Gladys, who straightened in anticipation. "They're all in there. Jeff Bates, too. Is the shit about to hit the fan?"

I nodded and moved toward the door. "Is it ever."

"Oh, great. Can I watch?"

"Just as soon as I get in there."

It was getting crowded in front of that door. Without a word Gladys picked up the mug of tea that had been sitting on Ann's desk. Then she slid off the desk, walked the few steps toward the door, and dumped the tea all over the front of Nolan's suit. Some of it splashed on Ann's coatdress. Both of them jumped back, gasping with astonishment. Nolan scrabbled in his pockets for a handkerchief, spluttering an expletive as he mopped at his tie.

"Good grief," Gladys said, setting the mug on a nearby filing cabinet. "I'm so sorry. I tripped over my own feet. How clumsy of me."

I stepped between Ann and Nolan and reached for the doorknob. Nolan grabbed my arm, but I twisted away and sent him reeling into the wall.

"What in the blue blazes is going on around here?" Ann demanded. She didn't wait for any explanations. Instead she picked up the phone and punched in a number. "Security? Mr. Tarcher, come up to Mr. Rittlestone's office right away."

When I walked into the CEO's office, Yale Rittlestone was on my left, standing behind the desk positioned midway on one of the exterior walls, between two windows. He was in the middle of a heated argument with David Vanitzky. Now he stopped in midrant and glared at me, furious at being interrupted.

"We're in a meeting, damn it. I don't want to be disturbed." Then he realized I wasn't Ann. "Who the hell are you?"

I let him stew for a moment as I surveyed the room. Hank Irvin was standing to Yale's left. He looked startled as he recognized me as the office temp. Or perhaps he was beginning to realize I was something more.

The man just beyond Hank, seated in a chintz-covered wing chair, was much older, with a deceptively mild face and eyes hidden behind spectacles. Frank Weper, in the flesh, and a black suit that made him look like an undertaker. His eyes flicked over me and then dismissed me, just as quickly.

Jeff Bates, former occupant of the CEO's desk, was in the far corner of the other exterior wall. He'd been looking out the window. When he turned and saw me, his mouth opened as though he were going to speak. I shook my head.

David stood in the middle of the room, between Yale's desk and a round conference table. He looked surprised, and then his face turned cagey, as he waited for me to make my next move. I walked toward David, then turned and gazed at the man behind the desk. From the corner of my eye I saw Gladys standing in the doorway, blocking Ann and Nolan from entering.

"Get out," Rittlestone shouted as he moved around the desk, heading toward me. "We're trying to conduct business in here."

I didn't budge. That irritated him even more. I could see it in the way his jaw clenched and his fingers curled toward his palms to form fists. He was used to being obeyed, and he didn't like it much when people didn't snap to as ordered.

"I have no intention of leaving," I told him, keeping my voice level. "As for your business, it's over and done with. I'm a private investigator working for a man named Rob Lawter. You killed him, and another man named Charlie Kellerman. And you're going down for murder."

On hearing my words, Hank Irvin looked as though I'd hit him in the stomach. Then his face changed quickly. I could see the wheels turning as he considered ways to disassociate himself from Rittlestone.

"Murder." Frank Weper spoke from the wing chair, using the calm tone of someone who considered murder a means of leverage rather than a crime. "Well, this does throw a different light on things, doesn't it?"

"This woman's crazy. I don't know what she's talking about." Yale waved his arm toward the door. I glanced in that direction and saw Buck Tarcher muscling his way past Gladys. "Get her out of here, Tarcher."

David stepped behind me and moved toward the door, as though to intercept Tarcher. I kept talking.

"I'm talking about salmonella. The very word is enough to scare most food processors. But not you. You, Ward, and Mayhew conspired to keep contaminated product on the shelves. Rob Lawter was threatening to blow the whistle. When he wouldn't back off, you and

Mayhew went to his apartment and argued with him. You hit him and pushed him out a fifth-story window. Kellerman saw both of you that night, recognized Mayhew, and started blackmailing her. You had her arrange a meeting in Oakland. After she paid him, he crossed the street. Before he got to the other side, you gunned the car you'd stolen and ran him down."

I let the impact of the words hit the listeners, then I continued. "You stole that car from one of your R&W employees, Carol Hartzell. She's Rob's sister, by the way. But you knew that, just like you knew she lived with Leon Gomes, the dairy plant manager. You also knew she had a car, a green Buick. You swiped her keys, had a duplicate made, then went to San Leandro on BART last Friday afternoon to steal that car. Better to implicate Leon, because he bought the contaminated milk and he knew too much."

"This is utter nonsense," he said, appealing to his listeners. From the looks on their faces, he wasn't making a sale.

"You were seen," I told him.

I didn't elaborate on the identity of my witness or what exactly that witness had seen. My words were enough to send Rittlestone careening toward me, fists raised. I grabbed one of the oak letter trays on his desk, heaved the contents away, and blocked the blow with the tray. Rittlestone came at me again.

The corporate security chief, who'd been standing in the doorway taking all of this in, moved forward. But I wasn't sure who he was planning to help. Neither was anyone else. I heard Jeff Bates shout, "Buck, no."

David blocked Tarcher with his own body. I sidestepped Rittlestone, then used his momentum to spin him around. I dropped the letter tray, delivered a right to his solar plexus, and finished him off with a left hook.

We'd been attracting a crowd. Now I saw Sid, Wayne Hobart, and some uniformed officers cutting through the employees who milled in their path.

I reached down and grabbed Rittlestone's arm, hauling him to his feet. He shook away my grip, panting slightly as he looked at the new arrivals.

"Sergeant Vernon, Oakland Police Department," Sid said, hauling out his shield.

"Officer, arrest this woman," Yale demanded. "She burst in here, making a bunch of wild accusations. Then she assaulted me."

Sid gazed at Rittlestone, then at me. "I got a call from Nancy Fong, who said Jeri Howard wanted us at this location, ASAP. Ms. Howard I know. You I don't. Suppose you explain it to me."

"Sergeant Vernon and Sergeant Hobart are from Homicide," I told Yale. "They're the officers investigating the murder of Rob Lawter. This is Yale Rittlestone. He killed Rob Lawter, and Charlie Kellerman."

"I assume you can prove these allegations," Wayne said, moving past me to take up a position on Rittlestone's left.

"I've got a couple of witnesses ready to roll all over him. I'd be happy to lay it out for you in great detail. We can do it here, or downtown."

"Suits me either way." Sid stepped in front of Yale. "Mr. Rittlestone, I'd like to ask you a few questions."

Yale threw off Wayne Hobart's hand, which was hovering near his arm. "You can't do this to me," he snarled at Sid.

Sid's eyes took on an expression I knew well, one that said, oh, yes, I can.

"I don't have to talk to you," Yale continued. He turned and snapped his fingers at Hank. "You're the general counsel. Do something."

Hank kept his mouth shut. He was looking at the floor, the furniture, anything and anyone but Yale Rittlestone.

"Perhaps we'd better do this downtown," Sid said in a deceptively pleasant voice. "Will you come with us, please?"

"I'll do nothing of the kind," Yale said as he attempted to shove his way past Sid. A couple of uniformed officers grabbed him before he got to the door.

"I guess we'll do it the hard way," Sid told Rittlestone as he and Wayne flanked their suspect. "Let's go."

CHAPTER *43*

"F UNNY," I TOLD MY FATHER, PUTTING AN ARM AROUND his waist. "This day seemed to take forever getting here. But it's only been six weeks since I looked at the house."

He put his arm around my shoulders and squeezed. We stood on the sidewalk in front of my new house on Chabot Road, on a warm Saturday in October.

"Time is fluid," he said. "When we're anticipating something, it slows down, like that molasses in January we're always hearing about. And when we look back, as we do at Christmas or New Year's Eve, we wonder where the year went."

Sid stepped out the front door, clad in blue jeans and a paint-stained gray sweatshirt with the sleeves cut off. He scowled at me. "We're gonna have a hell of a time getting your bedroom furniture down those stairs."

I put my hands on my hips and scowled right back at him. "Grouse, grouse, grouse."

Kaz, my doctor friend, appeared behind Sid. His curly black hair was caught back, as usual, in a ponytail. He wore black pants and a black T-shirt, and he was nodding as he agreed with Sid. "The stairs are kind of narrow, Jeri."

"Well, what if we carry it through the side gate and into the house from the lower level?" I waved my hand toward the gravel drive that led to the garage.

"That might work," Sid said. "If the slope's not too steep. Anyway, the gate's wider than those stairs." He turned to Kaz. "Let's go take a look."

They headed around the house. I turned to Dad, then jumped out of the way as my kid brother Brian zoomed toward me with three large cardboard cartons strapped onto a dolly.

"Hey!" Brian said. "Don't just stand there. We gotta get this stuff unloaded. I'd like to get back to Sonoma sometime before midnight."

Dad and I walked toward the big truck I'd rented. I'd invited about fifteen people to help me move. As my Grandma Jerusha used to say, "Many hands make light work." My helpers and I had spent most of the morning carting my possessions out of my old apartment and into the truck. Now it was time to reverse the process at the other end. Cassie was in the back, handing boxes down to Vicki Vernon, Sid's daughter from his first marriage, and several of her roommates, all of them University of California students who shared a house in Berkeley.

Joe Franklin was issuing orders to Eric, Cassie's husband, as they maneuvered my sofa down the metal ramp to the pavement. Joe did love to boss the job. But since he was a retired Navy admiral, it went with the territory.

The big oak sideboard that had belonged to my grandmother sat on the front lawn, along with some smaller pieces of furniture. I tucked a dining room chair under each arm and marched across the lawn toward the front door, stopping as Dad and Wayne Hobart, who had stacked boxes on another dolly, hauled it into the house. I followed them inside. All my plants were arrayed on the deck, out of the way, and Lenore Franklin, Joe's wife, and her daughter Ruth and granddaughter Wendy were in the kitchen, opening boxes.

"You don't have to unpack," I told her.

She laughed. "Believe me, Jeri, I'm a veteran of many moves. It feels so much better if you know where the silverware is. This place will be lovely when you get it all put together. Have you thought about what you're going to plant? Bulbs would look terrific in the front."

"When I'm ready, I'll use you as my gardening consultant."

"For now," Ruth said, "we're kitchen consultants. Where do you want us to put the plates?"

I told them, then headed back outside, in time to see a smaller rental truck pull up to the curb. My tenant had arrived, accompanied by her father and younger brother. Dan Stefano slid from behind the wheel, as Darcy and Darren piled out of the truck. Darcy gave me a hug. At that moment, Sid came around the house, followed by Kaz. I made the introductions.

"That's your ex?" Darcy said, eyes twinkling as both men walked toward the larger truck. "He's a hunk."

"He's too old for you. Old enough to be your father."

Darcy just smiled. She and her brother unlocked the back of the smaller truck and started unloading her possessions. I'd been teasing her about being a computer nerd like her father, but she had more to put inside the studio apartment than just a mattress and a computer.

Darcy's father looked at me as though he expected me to back out on this landlord-tenant arrangement. "Are you sure you want to do this?" Dan said. "I mean, she can be a handful. As we both know."

"I guess I'm committed." I grinned at him. "She did give me a lead on this last case. And, in a way, you helped finance the down payment on this place. We'll be fine."

"Well, in that case, I guess I might as well make myself useful." Dan wiped his hands on his khaki pants and went to help Sid, Kaz, and Wayne as they carried my bedroom furniture down toward the gate.

Time, I thought, reaching for the second pair of dining room chairs. As I looked back at the events of the past few weeks, I saw that they had, as my father said, moved in rapid succession.

The district attorney had charged Yale Rittlestone with the murders of Rob Lawter and Charlie Kellerman. Patricia Mayhew was an accessory to both killings, but in the interests of cutting her own losses, it looked as though she would testify against her lover. Besides, her prints, and those of Rittlestone, were all over Rob's apartment.

Carol Hartzell's green Buick was found abandoned in the long-term parking lot at Oakland International Airport. The physical evidence from the car and from the victim's body proved it was the vehicle that ran down Kellerman. Sid told me Yale's fingerprints were nowhere to be found on the car. He'd probably worn gloves from the time he took it until he left it in the lot. No doubt he'd discarded the gloves along with the key, then taken a bus from the airport to the Coliseum BART station for his return trip to San Francisco.

The evidence against Yale for the Kellerman killing was circumstantial, without Patricia's testimony. But a clerk at a downtown San Francisco hardware store recognized Yale as the man who'd had a car key duplicated there. The clerk came forward with his statement after the whole mess hit the news.

The media had parked on the steps of the Bates building for days. As Al Dominici had predicted, the eleven calls Rob had received were the tip of a much larger iceberg. Investigators in ten counties were following up on over fifty reported cases of salmonella resulting from Bates Best ice cream products, and the numbers were expected to rise. With that, and the pension fund losses, the first wave of lawsuits had already been filed.

"We'll be answering class action complaints till the statute runs," Gladys predicted when we met at the Jack London Village deli for lunch, two weeks after that last confrontation in the CEO's office. "If it's not the damn salmonella in the ice cream, it's the pension scam. Things are in a hellacious mess. I wonder if we'll ever get it sorted out."

She gave me a gossipy gleeful rundown of the unsettled state of affairs at Bates. As I'd suspected, Hank was involved in diverting retirement money from one of the mutual funds in which it had been invested. He'd cooked up the scheme with the fund manager and tried to make it look as though Ed Decker was responsible. Tonya Russell had found the beginnings of a paper trail in the two weeks she'd served as human resources director. As Gladys had pointed out, the two scandals left investigators from several federal, state, and local agencies swarming all over the Bates building as well as the company's plants.

And Leon had moved out of Carol's house, Robin Hartzell had told me. Her mother took a dim view of his involvement in her brother's death.

"I hear Frank Weper is over in San Francisco," I said, "trying to salvage whatever's left of Rittlestone and Weper."

"Yeah, looks like the El Paso thing is totally off. Hallelujah," she added, raising her bottle of root beer. "I've still got a job—if the company comes out of this okay."

"You and Nancy must be run ragged, with only one attorney."

"Well, Tonya Russell did move into Hank's office, and they called in Laverne Carson and several other retirees to help mop up the blood, including Al Dominici and the guy who used to head up production before Ward. Thank God Alex is general counsel again. I don't know when he'll get around to interviewing attorneys and paralegals for Bates, but in the meantime we've got two lawyers and a paralegal from Berkshire and Gentry camped out in conference room one. I heard Alex even asked Lauren Musso if she wanted her old job back, but she turned him down flat."

Jeff Bates was also back as chief executive officer, and his sister Bette had told me he'd insisted on her being named to the Bates board. I knew she was looking forward to doing battle for the family company again.

It would be a hard fight, though. In addition to the lawsuits and the penalties imposed by governmental agencies, the buying public was weighing judgment on Bates Inc. Consumer confidence, and sales of Bates Best products, had dropped precipitously with news of the salmonella outbreak and the product recall. The jury was still out as to whether the company could be salvaged.

"What about David Vanitzky?" I asked. Was he still chief financial officer, playing the part of the right-hand man no matter who occupied the CEO's office?

Gladys laughed. "Oh, yes. That man would land on his feet if they dropped him from the Transamerica Pyramid."

"He's a survivor if I ever saw one." I smiled.

After all, as David had told me, so cocky and self-assured, he was the man with the shovel, the one who knew where the bodies were buried.

Elaine Stefano and her mother, Adele Gregory, showed up a couple of hours later, after we'd carried most of my belongings and Darcy's into their respective dwellings. Everyone but me was taking a break in the backyard, sprawled out on the grass around the big cooler I'd stocked with beer and soft drinks. I was in the front yard with one last box of odds and ends when I saw a dark blue car pull up to the curb. Adele was at the wheel. She and Elaine got out, and Adele walked over to greet me, carrying a shopping bag from Macy's.

Elaine stood behind her mother, not saying anything at first. She was a real estate agent, and I saw her appraising my new house. "Not bad," she said finally. "It looks like you got a bargain."

"I think so. What brings you here?"

"We've brought housewarming gifts," Adele said. "Where is everyone?"

"Out in the backyard."

I set the box I'd been holding down in the foyer, shut the front door, and motioned them to follow me, wondering if Elaine had come on her own, or if this visit was prompted by Adele. I led the way past the garage and the studio apartment upstairs that was now occupied by Darcy.

As we went through the back gate, I heard laughter. Darcy was entertaining the assembled helpers with one of her stories. She stopped when she saw her mother and grandmother. "What're you doing here?"

"I brought you a present." Elaine reached into the shopping bag Adele carried, and took out a large gift box with a ribbon tied around the middle. She handed it to Darcy, who stared at the box for a moment, then slowly untied the ribbon and pulled off the lid. "Towels. I figured you could use some towels."

Adele placed a box in my hands. It was small but heavy. I thanked her and opened the gift, a silver trivet that would look great on my sideboard.

There was an awkward silence as Darcy examined the towels, thick and pale blue. Then she looked up and smiled. "Thanks, Mom. I do need them." She waved in the direction of the garage apartment. "Come on, I'll show you my new place."

"Hey, Jeri," Sid called. He and his daughter were seated side by side, cross-legged, taking sips from the same can of beer. "You promised me pizza to go with this beer. Where is it? I was hungry an hour ago."

"Pizza! Pizza!" The rest of my movers took up the chant, demanding that I feed them after all their hard labor. I stepped through the French doors into my newly arranged bedroom, located the directory, and started flipping through the yellow pages as I reached for the phone on the bedside table. "How many should I order?"

"Lots!" came the chorus.

JANET DAWSON'S first novel, *Kindred Crimes*, won the Private Eye Writers of America Best First Private Eye Novel Contest and was nominated for Anthony and Shamus awards as well. She is a member of the Mystery Writers of America and Sisters in Crime and has written six other Jeri Howard mysteries: *Till the Old Men Die, Take a Number, Don't Turn Your Back on the Ocean, Nobody's Child, A Credible Threat*, and *Witness to Evil*. Dawson worked as an enlisted journalist in the navy before moving to Alameda, California.